HOMEWORLD LOST

J.N. CHANEY
SCOTT MOON

VARIANT
PUBLICATIONS

LAS VEGAS, NV • GARDEN CITY, KS

CONNECT WITH J.N. CHANEY

Don't miss out on these exclusive perks:

- Instant access to free short stories from series like *The Messenger, Starcaster,* and more.
- Receive email updates for new releases and other news.
- Get notified when we run special deals on books and audiobooks.

So, what are you waiting for? Enter your email address at the link below to stay in the loop.

https://www.jnchaney.com/homeworld-lost-subscribe

CONNECT WITH SCOTT MOON

Want to know when the next story or book is published? Sign up for my newsletter:
https://www.subscribepage.com/Fromthemoon

Thanks,
Scott Moon

facebook.com/groups/ScottMoonGroup
twitter.com/scottmoonwriter
instagram.com/scottmoonwriter

JOIN THE CONVERSATION

Join the conversation and get updates on new and upcoming releases in the awesomely active **Facebook group**, "JN Chaney's Renegade Readers."

This is a hotspot where readers come together and share their lives and interests, discuss the series, and speak directly to J.N. Chaney and his co-authors.

facebook.com/groups/jnchaneyreaders

CONTENTS

1

Five minutes passed in slow motion. Every atom of my body felt energized, like I could do the impossible. Crossing the walkway to my ship felt like it had happened years ago, though it was all I could think about now that I was strapping in. No one without the highest security clearance would see my cinematic-worthy hero walk.

How uncool was that? Freaking top-secret protocols.

This was the most advanced ship of United Earth, one of two that had been built in secret. The first had exploded eight hundred million kilometers from home. Experimental backup ships were always more reliable than the primary, right? That's what I'd heard. No worries.

This was my moment to shine.

For authorized eyes only.

With complete government and corporate deniability.

My brain flicked to the two hundred page non-disclosure agreement I'd signed. I pushed the thought away and focused on systems checks. Flipping switches felt more satisfying than tapping touch screens, though I did plenty of that as well. Numbers scrolled up the right panel, then turned green one after another.

After a successful test and return to the Sol system, my parents, and my aging grandfather, who always wanted someone in the family to be an astronaut, would know the Gantz family showed up and showed out. *Represent, Pops. We're in the history books now.*

One way or another.

My heart pounded. Cascading physical energy that had felt good before worried me now. What was this, a cage fight? Hell no. This was fucking science. There were rules.

My annoying brain pulled up the clause about covert disposal of my remains if this went bad.

Well, that's fantastic.

I'd watched the first attempt at faster-than-light travel. No more partial light-speed attempts. This was the real deal. We were going there, even if the truth had just a little more to do with quantum physics than I understood.

Lieutenant Colonel Tate Collins had become the fastest human in history by about a hundred orders of magnitude, then vanished in an explosion that had appeared only on top secret video feeds. The public would never glimpse evidence of the incident. There weren't even remains to covertly bury.

Laughing hysterically might have been okay because there

was no one here but me, and I had complete control of my helmet mic. I tempered my mirth for the sake of personal dignity. Pops, the most notorious prankster in the Gantz clan, had taught me how to laugh at myself without being the joke. *It's all about dignity, Noah. Never pass up a chance to laugh, but don't be a clown by accident.*

Was it wrong that I loved that old hard-ass more than anyone in the world? Freaking hero to me.

My focus returned like a laser beam. The energized feeling came back but was under control now. This was happening, and everything was going to be fine.

"Nice hero walk, Major Noah Gantz," Major Kenneth Britz said through the radio.

"Glad someone saw it." We'd been using our full rank and name since the promotion ceremony last year. It was one of those private jokes no one else got. Absolutely hilarious.

He chuckled. "There are over a hundred people in this room, including three presidents, a prime minister, and the King of Belgium. And they're all impressed."

"Belgium has a king?" I studied power readings that I'd already checked three times. At what point did attention to detail become diagnosable? I pulled back my hands and exhaled.

"I'm subscribing you to Audible when you get back. Maybe you can listen to a book since you can't be bothered to read one."

"Hey, I'm a veritable bookworm. See there, that was a big word. Get off my back, Britz."

"Ouch. We're doing last names only again. Harsh. What was the last book you read?"

"*A Connecticut Yankee in King Arthur's Court.*"

"That was an assigned book in high school. You're hopeless."

Reading lists weren't high on my priorities. I was probably going to die in an explosion millions of kilometers from Earth. My friend's efforts were appreciated. No one else from mission control seemed to care. The ship—hell, a piece of this ship—was worth more to them than I was.

"Listen," Britz said. "This is about all the time we have to shoot the shit. So I'll wrap up. You're going to rock this mission, buddy. I personally went over everything that could have gone wrong with the Collins fiasco. Our team has improved fifty percent of the components on your version of this ship. No problem was too small to get a complete overhaul. This thing is like new."

"You mean never been tested."

"Well, yeah. If you want to be negative." He paused. "Big shots are lining up at the comms station and main view screen. Stop picking your nose or whatever. This will work. Just like Collins."

"What?" My heart sped up.

"That came out wrong. Relax. You shouldn't be worried at all. Trust me. My security clearance is higher than yours."

"That means what?" I asked, really not feeling this turn of the conversation. We should have stuck to jokes and ribbing. "He's not actually dead but living in some decadent resort community for intergalactic test pilots? Come on. You can't say

4

crap like that. Now I'll have nightmares about it." I'd seen the video. Lieutenant Colonel Tate Collins was definitely dead. Last time I checked, ships exploding did that to people.

"Don't worry about it. I know you're going to be okay. Take my word for it, brother."

"Fine." He had to evoke the bond between pilots. There was no way to argue now. And he was right. This ship, and my training, cost trillions of dollars. Everything that could be done to make it safe had been done.

"Major Gantz, are you there?" The program director's voice was as deep and smooth as ever.

"I'm here, sir. Is it too late to hit the head? Three cups of coffee is one too many, apparently."

He chuckled without really seeming to feel it. "The suit can handle that, Major. Stand by for final checks and the countdown. Our launch window is closing. It's game time."

"Yes, sir." I listened to flight control and did my job. One switch at a time, the second-best experimental FTL ship in human history fired up its engines.

I was launching from the surface of the desert for one reason. The amount of energy required to create a warp bubble was almost unimaginable. My ship's fusion plant was unequaled. This one-person vehicle could power a small nation for two months, which was why it was bigger and uglier than anything we'd created before this program. In theory, it could create the field needed for FTL by itself, but this was a government project, and they didn't want a public failure at any cost. So they stacked the deck with terrestrial based fusion complexes. Success if it kills us, that was their mantra.

That left the ship with enough juice-generating capacity to come back twice. Because that made sense to someone above my pay grade. I wasn't complaining. Who had two thumbs and didn't want to be lost in space?

This guy.

"Control is ready."

"Gantz is ready," I replied. Every part of me was cool, almost disassociated from the process now. By the numbers, that's how we did this.

"Prepare for countdown. Countdown underway. Ten, nine, eight..."

"... ONE."

My ship shook like a landslide as it climbed into the air, then forced its way free of both gravity and atmosphere. Two screens displayed my acceleration. Others showed structural integrity, weather, worldwide air traffic, and the position of every satellite in orbit.

All of that was behind me now. There was no chance of collision. A hundred miles around the launch pad had been cleared of observers. Exactly eleven months prior, the first FTL attempt had the same security in place around the exclusion zone around the platform. The importance of this mission was finally sinking in.

I saw Earth falling away with impossible rapidity. That view wasn't supposed to be there. All the psych advisors warned against it, but I'd convinced Britz to include a shot of home. The guy was solid. Always willing to help a brother out.

Call me sentimental. Gazing on the brilliant blue sphere was the most fulfilling experience of my life. No matter what happened, I always had that.

"This is for you, Pops." I held the controls. Every part of my body was locked into the seat, all the way up to my wrists. This wasn't a test of strength. Nothing had been left to chance. Yet I couldn't let go if I wanted to. Not now.

Because I just exceeded point one light speed. Only three other humans had done that. Two of them had occupied positions of honor on my teenage poster wall.

Both acceleration monitors displayed dots from left to right, then all the way down in a continuous flood of nonsense. "Hey, what's up with my readings?"

No one answered. No one *could* answer. I knew that. Talking was a reflex, a human need not to be alone when the shit was hitting the fan. Something wasn't right.

Collins. Why didn't you warn me?

I shook away the irrational complaint. We'd never known each other, not really. And how would a ghost get clearance with the United Earth Deep Space Program—unless he knew the King of Belgium.

"Initiating sensor reboot. Systems check in progress." I went through emergency procedures with calm efficiency. Years as one of the UE's most prolific test pilots had taught me how to handle

7

a crisis. Today was a bit outside the norm. My thoughts had been wandering. Now was the time to take charge of my emotions and just do the work.

The results came back blank. I tried another subroutine, then unfastened my arms to allow greater mobility. A touch of a button removed protective gear from my upper body that was not supposed to come off. No one expected me to do this much work after launch. I should have been a glorified passenger. Instead, I had to be pilot, copilot, navigator, and engineer at the same time.

So basically, this was just another day as a test pilot—stressful, but still better than combat. The only life on the line now was my own, and I had volunteered.

Pops seemed to be watching. It was an illusion. I allowed it. He both calmed me and inspired me to be the best version of myself. A tear ran from one eye as I realized with the white-hot intensity of a true epiphany how much I wanted to make him proud.

A tremor I hadn't initially noticed decreased. For several seconds, the ship raced across the void of space with no apparent resistance. That seemed fair since there wasn't atmosphere, only radiation and widely dispersed space dust. At this speed, even a speck could end the mission. I hoped the shield and armor held.

Was this what light felt like as it flashed across the galaxy?

I laughed and didn't care who heard me, now or later when the flight recorder was reviewed. I was moving fast enough to pierce a warp bubble!

Was I?

Vision distorted. I couldn't feel my body. Thinking was impossible. My laughter probably sounded like the shrieks of the damned now.

Didn't matter.

Nothing mattered.

Sensation returned, though it seemed like I was in someone else's form, getting shaken apart. A tiny voice in my head said I was going *around* light speed, not exceeding it.

Terror like I'd never imagine seized me. Existential mind trip or not, this was real, and I didn't want to die.

My vision returned in time to see a flash of light. Heat burned my soul. My warp-field-distorted senses thought my flesh was melting off my body.

And maybe it was.

Pain didn't mean what it used to. My mind went anywhere but here. I would really need to give Britz shit for blowing smoke up my ass. That wasn't what hurt. He'd meant well. My real pain came from the total failure this moment proclaimed. *I'm sorry, Pops. My best wasn't good enough today.*

2

A LIGHT APPEARED in the darkness. There was no way to move toward it. "My star drive was busted, Pops. Can't get the trillion-dollar hunk of junk to go."

I murmured this and other nonsense, and suspected I wasn't where I thought I was. The safety restraints of United Earth FTL 2 were gone. I'd been pulled from my escape capsule seconds before it was too late. How I understood this with my eyes closed was a bit fuzzy. Saying I was not at my best was a serious understatement. I didn't want to think about what kind of creature had dragged me free of the billion-dollar debris cloud that had been my ship.

"Can whoever keeps turning my body inside out please stop?"

Shut up, Noah. You must be drunk. Or dead.

May I save your life?" asked a woman's voice in my mind.

"I'm sorry, what?" My words slurred. I struggled to move and couldn't. More importantly, I endeavored to think and was disappointed. My brain lacked access to real information and was just filling in the gaps with imagination. Why wouldn't I want the disembodied voice to save my life? What a stupid question. "Who are you?"

"I am Kayan, a living starship. Young by the standards of my people, but old enough to know the value of survival."

"Oh. Well. I'm definitely not out of my mind." Pain proved I was still alive, and just to be certain I got the message, it was everywhere—bones, skin, muscles... my freaking brain.

"You lost a considerable amount of blood," the voice continued. "Your ship disintegrated when it entered this galaxy. The escape pod ejected, but improperly. The crude device was little more than a space coffin with no inertial dampeners. Your body has gone into shock. Trauma and exposure would have killed you had I not felt the anomaly and responded to investigate. Having explained far more than there is time for, may I save your life, please?"

Nice. Adding the word "please" was never wrong. Medical personnel should always strive to be polite when scooping up your melted limbs and blocking the pain that was *everywhere*. I thought of Britz. What I wouldn't give to be reading a book now. Wouldn't that be glorious? Pops lingered in my head. He wasn't saying much. Maybe he was still trying to figure out how I'd screwed this up when all the best minds of United Earth had been my support team.

I wanted to shrug this off with a joke, but waves of panic

surged just below conscious awareness. Nothing made sense. I'd probably died and hadn't adequately prepared for the afterlife or whatever this was.

Brain trauma had blinded me. No bueno, señor. Blacking out was a huge relief.

Until I awoke seconds later in more pain than before. Forcing my eyes open took serious willpower. I laughed when I wanted to cry and observed a ceiling pulsing in time with my vision. The colors transitioned to hot, angry reds when I tensed up, then slid across a cooler spectrum of blues and sea greens when I relaxed and breathed. A transom beam near a portal—not a door, a portal—caught my attention. For some reason, I really felt it was important to know if it was made from metal or something else I didn't recognize.

Nothing was familiar here. Pain was rampaging through my imagination, kicking over apple carts and making shit up from too many video games played in college.

"I was in my ship… What the actual hell is happening?" My words sounded almost human. "Collins, are you listening, damn you?"

He was dead. Lost in space with the particles of his destroyed ship. I was the idiot who tried again, just to prove the FTL warp bubble was possible and should continue to be funded. My pride caused this. I'd assumed that after a successful test there would be a public announcement and I could go home a hero. Give Pops a big hug and a fist bump, then go fishing and sip a beer.

The second test had been doomed from the start. Fucking government cover-ups were bullshit. I should have listened to the

Flat Earthers. There was a group with some sense. Deny everything, including evidence. That was the way to stay out of situations like these.

"I'm sorry, Pops."

"Can I save your life? This is the thirty-ninth time I have asked this question in nearly as many variations. Am I mishandling your language?"

"Fine! Just do it and stop asking."

"Good. Now there are changes that must be made. Sacrifices and obligations. I suppose you can't read or sign anything. Verbal acknowledgment must suffice."

This chick was killing me. I tried to rub my temples and couldn't raise my hands a millimeter. There shouldn't be room for a headache, not with my body so jacked up.

I forced myself to relax and think despite the pulsing agony that was my life now. Moving was impossible. All I could see was a room with far too much of its own vitality, like it was alive. Steel and carbon fiber wasn't supposed to have a heartbeat. There had to be a more rational explanation. Maybe I'd been shrunken down and injected into the veins of a real astronaut. For, I don't know, reasons.

The voice had been a woman like none other. What did that even mean?

It means something, Gantz. Stop calling her a chick, or Pops will kick your ass. An officer and a gentleman, that's what you're supposed to be. Grow up, put on your big boy pants, and figure this shit out.

What was with that question? Can I save your life? Seriously.

My thoughts drifted to words and definitions, specifically, sacrifice and obligation. What was I getting myself into.

Sleep felt like the only reward that mattered. Darkness, my old friend, thank you for never letting me down. My inner self laughed. Maybe he was drunk. Perhaps the voice had given me some really good drugs because I was feeling a tiny bit better.

"I said my name is Montow."

"You don't have to shout. I'm not deaf, or an idiot." My right eye opened first, which allowed me to squint at the owner of a new voice.

Yeah, someone had given me some serious drugs. The guy standing over me was maybe five feet ten inches tall, and stout. Saying his face was flat was an understatement.

And his head was shaped like a soup can. Someone had forgotten to give him a neck. Or teach him to blink. The transparent layer protecting his eyeballs fascinated me. I wanted to poke one with a finger to see if it quivered like a jellyfish.

"Good," he practically yelled. Each word came slow, like he thought I was both mentally challenged and new to the English language. "The translator is working. And you hear me. My name is Montow. I'm the Engineer-captain."

I frowned. That last word felt like a mistranslation. Like I would know since I had no idea what he meant by *translator*. "Call me Noah."

"Is that your complete name? I do not wish to offend."

"Major Noah Gantz, United Earth Deep Space Exploration Corps. Call me Noah."

"Ah, yes. I will refer to you by the moniker you select."

Montow's word choice was like someone learning English from a dictionary. I huffed inwardly. That was ungenerous. Whatever this imaginary stranger was using to bridge the language gap was far more sophisticated. Why did I get the sense he didn't understand the process much better than I did?

"Thank you for granting permission to maintain your life," said the woman's voice in my head—not Montow's rather gruff old tone.

"Don't mention it." I started to pass out. A heavy blanket of exhaustion cocooned me in relief.

"Why would you do that, Kayan? I was just starting to talk to him." Montow sounded frustrated, but not angry. He'd get over it, and so would I, right after I slept for about three days.

A hundred variations of my launch ran through my head. I watched myself from all possible angles until I was bored with the reruns. A presence was with me, and it never grew tired of gathering this information. Knowing what caused my injuries mattered to this benevolent force saving my life. How was she spying on my memory? The same way I could see its thoughts of the past.

I turned away from scenes too strange to imagine. Nothing could survive in space, no matter how big you were or how much you enjoyed choking down space fungi. A vibrant red nebula covered the background of this panorama. I watched it like this was a field trip to the cosmosphere, interesting but also so chill it made me want to nap right there with the rest of my eighth grade class.

"May I continue with these changes?"

"What happens if I say no?" The question just popped out, though my lips hadn't moved.

"You will live but little else."

"Well that sucks. I want to be a badass. This isn't *All's Quiet on the Western Front.*"

A pause followed. "An interesting book. Though I would know more of it if you hadn't skimmed, then relied on *CliffsNotes* to get a passing grade."

"Busted," I muttered, unable to raise my hands in the traditional gesture of surrender that went with the remark. My head ached, but so did my bones if I was being honest. Life sucked.

The voice was strong, soothing, and neutral. "May I turn you into a badass, by your own definition, or do you wish me to stop?"

"Sure. Bring it on." My muscles immediately relaxed. Pain ebbed. My brain started to work.

"Much of your body must be reshaped at the molecular level. I will touch your mental abilities as little as possible in order to preserve your memories and sense of self. We are going to share biomass when this is over. I hope you are truly okay with this transformation."

"One hundred percent." Did she catch my sarcasm? Was it sarcasm? I had no choice. Piercing the warp bubble like I did should have killed me. "How did you find me, Kayan?"

She wasn't wasting time. Apparently, the voice didn't know about waiting rooms or the remorseless bureaucracy involved with receiving any kind of medical treatment on United Earth. Old gripes weren't where I needed to spend my energy.

The test flight was what mattered. How did I get here?

Could I remember details? Absolutely. Pops never allowed me to say "I can't." Mom and dad hadn't been a fan of giving up early either. Second by second, images of my United-Earth-built cockpit clarified. Sorting through pain-scrambled memories wasn't easy.

Nothing worthwhile ever was.

I wasn't alone. Kayan was in my head, spectating with a fraction of her mental ability as she scanned my ruined body molecule by molecule. Some physical elements she left untouched. Others she replaced with her own biomass—which glowed like something miraculous under a microscope when I tried to look at what she was doing.

Does my presence bother you, Noah? We share cognition, though I have built what you would call firewalls to safeguard your sanity.

The feel of her was reassuring. *I'm good with it, I think. Can I ask you to give me space if I need it?*

Of course. Please continue your review of the flight data. I find it interesting. In many ways, your people are unique. Creativity is a rare thing, Noah Gantz. While the warp bubble is a flawed theorem for anyone wanting to survive the process, it gives me much to think about.

Glad to help out. With the assistance of my new living starship friend, I was able to watch the last few seconds of my time in the Milky Way. Welcome to my final moments.

Noah Gantz, you survived, the ship crooned. *Don't live in the past. The future holds great potential.*

Easy for you to say. I stared at my energetic attempts to salvage the mission.

The old version of myself fought panic as he ran calculations and made adjustments to the flight plan. That was definitely against mission protocol, but the alternative had been to melt. Call me crazy, but the prospect of watching my flesh slide off my bones hadn't been all that appealing. The test ship was traveling at a much higher percentage of light speed than UE Deep Space Exploration scientists had anticipated. Neither the ship, nor a certain Noah Gantz, could withstand much more acceleration.

Becoming energy hadn't been part of the plan.

Numbers blurred together. My hands phased in and out of view. I knew it was my perception that had been the problem at that point. Otherwise, I wouldn't have a memory of the incident.

Right before the ship exploded, I reversed thrust in a last-ditch attempt to slow down. That the engines could do that, I knew, but the technique was expressly forbidden. We'd covered the ship's abilities hundreds of times. There were many problems with slamming on the breaks, the simplest of which was that it would leave me stranded far beyond the UE Space Program's ability to recover me.

And there was the stress it would place on the vehicle and its dumbass pilot.

Was this what Collins had done, or had he rolled the dice and punched it?

From what I knew about the guy, he was a cautious

perfectionist. He would have slowed and used his remaining time fixing the calculations. Pops would tell me to just haul ass. Speed fixed everything in his book, no matter how often he tried to be a responsible role model.

Doubt had followed fear, and for the first time, I surrendered. One second of hesitation followed my decision, then I typed commands: reverse thrust in three, two, one. Reverse.

Oh, no, Kayan thought. *That was not the right decision. The other one kept going, I think.*

What other one? I needed to know. Was Tate Collins out here? Could we team up and get home, or at least stay alive?

Silence could feel menacing when the voice had been in your head and left abruptly. I didn't like it. Right when I was about to shout for her to come back, she spoke in my thoughts again.

Forgive me, Noah. I was attempting to account for your measurement of time. Months, perhaps years prior to me finding you, there was a similar disturbance in this sector. None of my people were near enough to investigate. I was wrong to make assumptions.

"Okay," I said aloud. "That's your story, and you're sticking to it."

"Noah," she said, her voice grave. "My brothers and sisters told me not to save you because they feared you would be like the other one. You must not be distressed. You must rest and recover. Can you do that?"

I answered by losing consciousness. This time, there wasn't even a dream to prove I was still alive.

THE 1981 CHEVROLET SILVERADO C10, burnt orange over white paint, climbed the mountain switchback leading to Breckenridge, Colorado. Pops slugged my thirteen-year-old self in the shoulder, then pointed at the opening to the Eisenhower tunnel. "There'll be snow coming down in sheets on the other side."

"That's the best part, Pops." All of it was good when I was with my grandfather, even if he wouldn't tell me stories of dogfights and surviving behind enemy lines. He was the biggest, toughest man in the world to me no matter how tall or short he stood next to other men. And who cared if he had age spots on his bald head.

The forty-year-old pickup raced past electric cars charged from the Denver Area Fusion Reactor—a facility no one had known existed at the time. I liked the way the restored V-8 motor sounded in the mile-and-a-half tunnel.

"I miss Mom and Dad."

"Me too, kid."

"It's not fair."

"Life will never be fair, Noah. Don't surrender the second most important advantage God gives us after a loving family."

I tuned out the monkey brain spaz fest in my head. Anger wasn't a problem, not when I was in the C10 with Pops. It was time to listen. This wasn't a lecture from a schoolteacher or a screaming coach. This was the only family I had left. "What's that, Pops?"

"Friends."

"My friends are idiots just like me."

He laughed long and deep. "Oh, you're smarter than I thought. Am I on that list of morons you hang with?"

"You're the gang leader. Always causing trouble."

He flipped on a loud, archaic blinker, then passed the next three battery cars like they were standing still. "I shouldn't teach you the need for speed, kid, but damn it, I think it's in the Gantz blood."

"Dad already gave me the bug."

We both knew I was telling the truth. My parents had been taking me skiing in Breckenridge since I was five. Our favorite slope had been Mach 1, a double black diamond where pride was left between the moguls.

"Just remember, kid. Take care of those who take care of you, and when nothing else works, haul ass."

3

Pops would understand. He certainly wouldn't blame me for what I'd become. Note to self: be careful about agreeing to medical interventions when under the influence of certain death. I pulled back the sleeve of the jumpsuit and marveled, not for the first time, at the absolutely amazing fabric. It felt as rugged as denim and as soft as silk.

Laughing felt good. Had I really been stuck on my wardrobe when my body underneath it was cybernetic?

That wasn't right. There were no machine parts in me, not really. The ship was alive. What did that make me now, a bio-borg? I locked that idea down and threw away the key.

Three weeks. I still couldn't believe this was another galaxy. Piercing the warp bubble hadn't gone as our scientists expected, but here I was—farther away from Earth than any of them imagined possible. How much additional time would it take for me to be physically and mentally recovered? Kayan had rescued me, but not my ship.

I should be thankful to have rebuilt body parts and clothing like nothing United Earth had ever seen.

The fit could be adjusted with a tap or three. I caught myself smacking my index finger on different sections to watch it relax and contract. Once, I double tapped my chest and felt the shirt harden like body armor. It remained extremely thin, but I thought it would deflect a blade or flying shrapnel.

My body had some serious weirdness I needed it to conceal. Recovering was taking time, though less than expected. What was three weeks or a month in the galactic scheme of things? I didn't even know where I was or how far away the test flight had sent me. Was this a new galaxy, or hell?

Maybe it didn't matter.

Organic sheeting—that was the only thing it could be called—covered everything from the backs of my hands to my shoulders. A section of my back had it too, but I wasn't looking that hard for mirrors or cameras that could show me that part of my changed physique. Better to just keep it out of sight, out of mind. The muscles underneath these new layers reminded me of my early days in the military, back when all my free time was spent in the gym or on the track.

During my enlisted days as a Security Forces noncommissioned officer, we hadn't been training for open water swims like SEALS or mountaineering missions like Green Berets, but my team took guarding top secret air bases seriously, and we were as jacked as the gym could make us. Later, as a pilot, I focused more on managing my blood pressure during high G maneuvers.

The tops of my feet and sides of my legs were very similar to my arms, though the protective layers were tougher. Light pulsed lethargically through veins below the surface. This didn't happen all the time, and it wasn't bright, but it definitely was not human.

Overwhelmed with the strangeness of it all, I found a wall and leaned back until I bumped my head softly. One, two, three impacts helped me face how screwed I was.

What would happen if I was in another accident?

Sheeting expanded from my legs, arms, and back. The sensation wasn't unpleasant but sure as hell got my attention. I watched a clear layer spread over my entire body in less than a second.

"Hey, hey, hey! What's that doing?" I could breathe fine, contrary to my instinctive fear the sight of it inspired. Movement was easy. This wasn't a restraint device or an attack.

No one answered, and I was already encased from head to toe. I paced the passageway, looking for someone or something to explain the alien prosthetic's reaction.

I'd been stressing about the FTL bubble crash I barely remembered. My last thought before the clear layer encapsulated me was about getting in another accident.

The prosthetic reacted with powerful protective qualities. It didn't look like armor, but my breathing and body temperature remained ideal. I'd just been covered with a temporary environmental suit.

Relax, Noah. Think. Ask questions. Get answers. Figure this out.

Where was I?

What was I? A stranger in a strange land with strange-o-ramic body parts. And there was a very nice and considerate voice in my head named Kayan, who was the ship, apparently. Montow had explained that so many times I wanted to punch him in his soup-can head.

He'd grown buzz-cut hair and an equally tight beard to look more like me—before I shaved everything to meet United Earth military standards. All those years I'd wanted a beard were history. Now I *needed* to be Noah Gantz. Everything I could do to remember who I had been was precious. That said, I encouraged Montow to keep the hair. "You look sharp. Very mountain man."

He had asked what that was and then wandered away as though pondering the examples I provided. Hopefully he didn't think he *had* to have a grizzly bear for a sidekick now.

I pulled down the sleeve to cover most of my hand. I needed Kayan to make me gloves. For now, I took a special pair of sunglasses and went in search of Montow. It was about time to give those freaky, non-blinking eyes a vacation.

"Kayan, where is Soup Can?"

"Montow is on the bridge reviewing navigational charts. You don't have to say my name before speaking to me. In fact, you can just think it."

"Right. But can we just do it my way for now?"

"Whatever trips your boat," *it* said.

"Uh, yeah. Boat tripping is the way to go."

"Please don't confuse the language translator further. Mine is very powerful but has limits."

Lights glowed at the perfect brightness ahead and behind me as I walked the passageways in search of the Engineer-captain. "Kayan, we're speaking English. It confuses everyone, even native speakers."

"Ah, yes."

"Do you have a gender?" I asked, not sure why it mattered. The ship was alive, but that didn't make it human. My brain was still grappling with the basic concept of Kayan.

A moment passed. "Not in the sense of your species. My kind reproduce much differently."

I held up one hand to signal a stop. We'd worked out basic nonverbal cues during the first few days of our association. "I don't want the gory details."

"It is pretty gory, now that you mention it."

"Hey! Stop means stop."

"Right." Images that had been coalescing in my brain evaporated. "Why do you ask?"

"It's not polite to call someone 'it'. I was just wondering. No biggie."

"Which gender would you like to call me?"

I thought about it. "You sound like a famous actress I can't quite remember, and ships are referred to as feminine by tradition."

"Could this be because of the very strange custom of only

allowing men on the early oceanic adventures of your people?" Kayan asked.

"Probably, but be careful about making assumptions based on my knowledge of history. I never finished my minor in that field."

"Understood," Kayan said. "You redirected your major and minor studies to beer and girls for most of your sophomore and junior years at Colorado State University. Had you finished, you would have possessed a bachelor's degree before applying for Officer Candidate School."

"Ouch. Now you made it ugly."

"Did I?"

"No. Those were good times. The parts I remember."

"The things you did for twenty bucks…"

"Hey! Don't go there."

"Of course. Was that not an excellent joke?"

"It was okay. Let's focus, all right?" I wasn't totally cool with Kayan rummaging through my memories, but so far the ship had remained respectful of privacy boundaries.

"Of course, Noah. If you don't mind, I have systems checks that need attention. Being a living starship takes work, just so you know."

I gave a thumbs-up and sauntered onward, feeling relaxed. Was my situation as crazy as it was screwed up? Yeah. Did that mean I had to mope around a living alien starship pining for home? Not all the time. One of the benefits of my link with Kayan was that she didn't feel fatigue, pain, sickness, or low energy. At least she hadn't yet.

She, it, he…whatever… assured me that would not always be the case, but over three weeks of health and vitality was setting a tone I liked. I was still human but didn't see why this couldn't be a little vacation before everything went to hell again. What was wrong with getting a boost of badassery from my new extra-galactic friend?

The portal to the bridge was open. I walked through without hesitation and found every workstation vacant. The chairs were more like oval phone booths that could lock a person in an "emergency pod." Kayan and Montow both explained, in their own very different ways, that these were for system jumping. The part that made me uneasy was the way they seemed to never be in exactly the same place.

Why wouldn't a ship that could travel through space have the ability to move the furniture around? The explanation didn't satisfy my need for order. Pilot training had merged things like checklists with my natural ability to handle ambiguous situations. That was a Gantz thing, for sure.

The science team back on United Earth would call what Kayan did "using a warp bubble." Less informed science fiction novelists referred to the process as space folding or hyperspace. The details of how it worked were both complicated and simple, depending on whether you were a test pilot like me or a living ship who traveled the galaxy in search of space fungi to consume. At the end of the day, it didn't matter what name I gave it so long as I didn't get blown up again.

I cupped my hands to my mouth. "Captain Montow! Are you here?"

He wasn't, but that didn't mean I could just walk out with any degree of certainty. The bridge didn't have a clear starting and stopping point. Nothing did on this ship. The borders of the room were unclear and ruled by shadows. Dozens, maybe hundreds, of the emergency pods dotted the landscape in seemingly random patterns.

Where I walked, light glowed. I tried to explain to Kayan this wasn't necessary, that I could adjust it myself or use a flashlight. The ship had pretended ignorance that it was even happening and only asked me if I was having trouble seeing. When I said no, the conversation moved to other subjects. Having a mind link with Kayan was both convenient and difficult to manage at times. I needed to practice totally new communication methods.

Life here took a lot of adjusting. The bridge and other rooms changed slightly after I complained. While there were still a lot of pods and maze-like corners of the command center, the number had decreased. The ship was learning my language and my history while simultaneously adjusting the environment around me.

That raised so many questions.

I left to wander the decks in search of Montow. Maybe he would have answers. Each passage sloped upward or downward, sometimes slightly and other times at a steep grade that should have been problematic.

It wasn't, of course. Kayan had thoroughly adapted me to the vessel, or vice versa in some cases. My cabin, for example, was way too similar to my academy dorm room, complete with three other bunks for roommates I didn't have. I also noticed that the floor seemed to be more level each time I revisited an area. The ship was pliable, apparently.

Light glowed from one of the *engine* rooms. Inside, I found Montow scraping green slime from organic conduits. Calling them veins wasn't accurate. There were tubes inside of tubes, and often cables that might or might not function like tendons. As a reluctant science major who really only wanted to be an astronaut, I hadn't taken more than the minimum requirements in biology. And when I was in the class, my interest had been in Jenny McCraw.

"What a mess," I said as I put one hand on Montow's thick shoulder.

He looked old when he turned his head. The black buzz cut had streaks of gray now, and so did the impossibly dense beard that covered everything to his collar bone—not from hanging down, but from where it grew. "Nuclear chains are never easy to manipulate."

"Say again?"

"Which part don't you understand?"

"The part where a living organism has nuclear components."

He stared at me with tired, unblinking eyes. Crow's feet extended in all directions from the translucent coverings over the not quite human, oversized, pupils. "How else would a ship generate enough power to travel the stars? Admittedly most of the real gusto comes from the fusion pods under her belly, but we're not allowed to go there—ever."

"Shouldn't you and I be dead from radiation?"

"That stays within the conduits. What kind of half-assed technology do your people use on Orth?"

"Earth."

"Ugh."

I wasn't sure if he was expressing consternation or was again mispronouncing the name of my planet. My hands weren't oozing tumors, and I hadn't developed superpowers, so I took his word for it. Like I did most things on Kayan.

"These are for you, buddy."

Montow stopped what he was doing and examined the oversized, custom-shaped sunglasses Kayan had made at my request. He didn't reach for them. It was like he was sniffing the gift with his nearly nonexistent nose. Slowly, like they might be more dangerous than the nuclear time bombs in the room, he took them with both hands. Every movement was careful.

"What are they for?"

I pulled out my own version and placed them on my face.

He smiled and imitated me. Large, cube-shaped teeth showed in that grin, and it was about as threatening as a bowl of Tic Tacs. For all his size and muscle mass, and for all his gruff demeanor, he wasn't a fighter. That wouldn't be a problem. Not a single threat had occurred since my arrival, and the vessel had no weapons. It wasn't a warship. Montow had explained that dozens of times as well, though Kayan seemed confused by the question or was just refusing to answer when I asked for confirmation. It seemed her kind were prohibited from creating or using weapons. Or maybe it was a natural aversion, like my horror of cabbage.

"Can you see? I wasn't sure about the tint," I said.

"Yes. It is quite nice. Much of the glare is gone. Kayan never gets the lighting right. I'm not sure how you can stand it. Thank you, friend."

"Anytime. That's what I'm here for."

He gave me one of his puzzled looks. Kayan's language translators weren't perfect. Unbothered by the ambiguity of my words, he went back to work. I watched for a while and tried to decide what part of my statement had confused him. It didn't matter. Alien cultures were hard to fathom, even with the help of a living starship.

"Noah, can you come to the bridge?" Kayan asked.

I recognized the tone the ship used that went to everyone in the room. Calling it a radio channel wasn't quite right, but it was essentially a public address mechanism when it sounded like this. "What about Montow?"

"He may come if he so desires. There is a Gavant ship in this system."

Montow jerked upright and smashed his head against a ridge of the engine pod. Lights went out at its border. He rubbed his head, caught my worried look, and waved at where he'd been working. "That is no problem. There are currently one hundred and sixty-eight pods functioning, not including the fusion plant we discussed. Regaining optimal functionality can wait a bit longer."

"Ah. Good to know. Let's get to the bridge. Kayan, we're on the way."

I ran through the passageways because I felt good. Why not

stretch my legs? Montow pounded after me. A sprinter, he was not. His feet were nearly as thick as his legs. Running took most of his concentration. Pops had been a champion cross-country runner back in the day, or so went the family legend. He'd never lost the habit. The best days of my life were training for the Air Force Academy and putting in the miles with my best and oldest friend.

"Why… are we… in such a hurry?" Montow asked.

I slowed to be polite. "Gavants are who we're running from, right?"

"Yes. But Kayan did not say that we were under attack or even discovered. Nor was there a description of this ship. It may not be a vessel of war or any type of hunter."

His argument felt off. Our conversation over the last few weeks had often dwelt on the expansionist nature of the Gavant Reach and their proclivity to building warships. Like most new topics, I didn't know how much was lost or altered in translation. Gavant, in French, meant something about gluttony. Sarah Boucher had explained it once, right before she politely explained that she only wanted to be friends, then went back to Paris at the end of the semester. My decision to enter the Air Force as a means to becoming an astronaut hadn't thrilled her, or that's what I'd told myself back then. It could have also been that I wound up enlisting, due to some slacking off in college. I'd reasoned I could let the Air Force pay for the rest of my degree, but she was already out the door.

She was very French. Who knew what she'd been thinking about her undisciplined American boyfriend?

Reach was just what it sounded like: an empire, though I wasn't sure of the exact origin. Empire of Gluttons, or maybe the Glutton's Reach, was what I came away with. Neither Montow nor Kayan told me that was wrong. These guys conquered every star system they could find and generally pushed everyone around. Kayan and her passengers were looking for a safe refuge from their influence.

"I just felt like running," I said. "You tell me when to worry, okay?"

"This sounds like a good plan." He caught his breath. "Your people are mentally unbalanced to enjoy running when walking is an option."

"No argument there, though some like it more than others."

"I never want to visit your world if there are going to be people darting here and there for no reason."

We strode onto the bridge. I counted the emergency pods and came up with the same number as the last three times.

"What are you doing?" Montow asked.

"Nothing." I planted my feet in the base of the standing pod-chair Kayan liked me to use. "Fill us in. Who is flying this Gavant ship, and what do they want?"

"Is it built for war or stealth?" Montow asked.

"The *Kon* is a Gavant warship—heavy cruiser class in human terms."

Montow swiped his thick fingers over a screen Kayan provided. He read the text quickly, his mouth moving as he seemed to scan the words. With the dark glasses covering his eyes, I lost the ability to see exactly what he was looking at. His head moved slightly as he read top to bottom, then at an angle.

I focused on my own viewer. At my joking request, Kayan had made it holographic. The *Kon* resembled a space crab with banks of giant engines at the rear and center. The texture and paint scheme wasn't familiar, but the weapons were obvious. This thing had a lot of guns. "Do all of those do the same thing? And do you know their range and cycle rate?"

Kayan answered. "They have three types. For simplicity, I will designate them long, medium, and short range. Those in the last category are for defensive use."

I nodded along. Aliens they might be, but some things about warships appeared to be universal. Of course, that was when a cable a hundred thousand kilometers long spooled out behind the ship. "What the hell is that?"

Montow grumbled something I didn't catch, then spoke more clearly. "It is a compressed net. This ship knows Kayan, or one of her species, is here. They intend to capture us."

Kayan made a keening sound that hurt my head, especially since it seemed to come from inside mine. I steadied my breathing and crossed my arms over my chest as she had instructed. This was the preferred posture if something she did made me uncomfortable and she was unable to immediately assist.

Montow curled into a ball on the floor and quivered like he'd been hit with a stunner.

"Kayan, please stop making that noise."

The soul-killing wail dwindled to nothing and was replaced

with an elevator music rendition from my favorite 90's rock anthem.

Montow rolled to his knees. I helped him up and was proud of how much my recovery had restored my strength. With the exception of being quadrillions of miles from home and partially encased in alien body parts, I would definitely recommend this as physical therapy. Maybe I would start working out again to see what I could do.

"You okay, Soup?" I asked before I caught myself.

"Why do you call me that?"

"It's a huge compliment where I'm from."

"Then I thank you. Should I return the gesture in a similar way?" he asked, his minimal chin raised so he could peek out from beneath the heavy sunglasses.

"Not necessary. We're even, I think."

He made one of his undefinable noises deep in his throat, then shook his head. This almost looked like the top of his neck was twisted back and forth because his skull was about the same width and thickness. Only the bone structure marked it as anything close to human. Sort of. The hair and beard helped him appear less strange. I needed to thank him for that when I figured out how to word it.

"More of your confusing metaphors. Perhaps we should focus on the Gavant threat."

"Yeah. Let's do that. Kayan, tell us the rest."

The ship spoke in the public address tone, which I realized was a matter of ideal frequencies. Montow, like all of his race, the Hellenger, heard much lower sound waves than I did, and probably saw in a different visual spectrum. Having alien friends was cool.

"I have alerted the rest of the crew as well," Kayan began.

I shot a look at Montow but said nothing. He hadn't told me there were other people aboard.

"The *Kon* has a history with my kind," Kayan continued. "It appears she has recently delivered one of my origin to a confinement system and is greedily looking for another capture. Her efforts do not seem to be strenuous, however. I suspect her captain is just hoping to get lucky while they enjoy their recent success. I am using the human tradition of referring to non-living ships as female, for your information."

"Ah." Montow exhaled. "That makes sense. Thank you for the clarification. I thought the translator was malfunctioning or that these eye-protecting devices had side effects."

"Are they to your satisfaction?" Kayan asked.

"Yes. Very much. The human made a considerate gift, though I originally suspected he did not want to look at my unblinking eyes anymore. Much as I am disturbed by his constantly opening and closing *lids*. So gross."

"What do we do?" I asked, hoping to change the subject.

"Very little." Kayan turned from the distant Gavant vessel. "I am near the edge of this system and will now leave. It will cause hunger, as it was unscheduled and I was not able to clean this system of the Oort."

I rubbed the back of my neck. Sometimes my head hurt when the ship's words didn't make sense. "Oort?"

"Oort is the primary fungus Kayan's kind feed upon. There

are no other good uses for the stuff, and most races barely give the fields notice, or map their locations," Montow said. "It is damn hard to find."

"Good to know." I stepped out of my pod chair and stretched. "How about you introduce me to the rest of the crew?"

"Not all will be glad to see you. Grum is conciliatory. Start with him. I have work to do." With that, Montow marched back toward an engine room.

"Grum is a Walen," Kayan said.

"Never met one."

"You soon will. He is working on a circuit board in the viewing lounge."

I wrestled with the words and fixed on a better translation. "You mean the observation deck?"

"Yes. But you should be careful. Not all my passengers enjoy the experience."

"Show me the way."

Images floated in the air ahead of me. The hologram screen was rocking it today, or maybe this was a ship induced hallucination. It was hard to know the difference. I saw a tendril trailing away from what looked like a ventral fin on a killer whale. Only then did I realize I wasn't sure exactly what Kayan looked like from outside. At the end of the lazy tendril was a perfect sphere. Details were hard to see without magnification. I guessed that the observation deck would provide a 360-degree view of space.

That would definitely freak some people out, but I had

excelled at space walks. Few of us had avoided disorientation and sickness during the tryouts. Only Collins had been more solid in the void.

And look where that got him.

I focused on the present and went in search of Grum. Kayan refused to elaborate on the biology or behavioral norms of Walens. This was going to be a first-contact scenario. Hopefully, I didn't screw it up.

4

THE ENTRANCE WAS ANOTHER PORTAL, though this one was closed. I examined the seals and thought it was more than just airtight. A complicated discussion with Kayan over engineering terms eventually confirmed my suspicions. This door was as strong as the rest of her exterior and was, among other things, impervious to solar radiation.

That meant the observation deck and the umbilical walkway connecting it were designed to be discarded. My enthusiasm for this adventure diminished.

"Are you well?" Kayan asked.

"What happens if you're forced to discard this part of the ship?"

"I will not unless there is significant damage or doing so becomes necessary to save the rest of my form. Losing the lounge is painful." Seconds passed. "You will receive ample warning before such an event. There are no asteroids in the area, and we are not under attack. Do not worry."

"Okay then." I approached the portal, and it opened. The light adjusted ahead of and behind me as usual. "I'm safe as a babe in arms."

"You are."

The joke went right over Kayan's head, or bow, I thought. Mistakes were made daily, but all in all, it was amazing how normal my life seemed here. Home really was where you made it. That thought sparked intense sadness and a longing for my Earth family.

Earth family. Seriously? You're way out there, Gantz.

"Are you well, Noah?" Kayan asked. "What is this change to your hormones?"

"I'm fine."

"My interpretation of your thoughts and dreams are imperfect, but it seems this is what people say when they are not fine."

"This time it is what it is."

"Thanks for the not very helpful assurance. We must take care of each other, Noah. Please allow me to help when I can."

I let the conversation drop and entered the twisting, zero gravity interior of the umbilical connection. From here I saw several others, though most were fastened to hull areas beneath protrusions that looked like, but probably weren't, short wings. In theory, there could be a dozen *observation* pods trailing behind the ship simultaneously. I wondered what actual purpose they served, or if other passengers had designed them.

I thought about what the ship had told me. Kayan said things like that, but I had little comprehension of how I could return the favor. My ship had exploded, or melted, or come apart. The details were still a mystery and not something pleasant to think about. Kayan had saved my life—literally put me back together and sheathed my most damaged parts in protective layers.

What exactly could I ever do to repay that miracle? So far, this was a one-way relationship. I screwed up. Kayan saved my ass. Now I was a long way from home.

Making my way through the tube felt natural and easy. I zero-gravity-crawled the last section like one of the early astronauts in those space station videos. The image made me smile, and I hoped Kayan didn't comment on my improved mood. A little privacy was never a bad thing. Lack of it was the hardest adjustment I'd had to make thus far. Even when I was alone, I wasn't.

The portal on this end was translucent. Through it I saw a humanoid figure standing with his, or her, back to me. It never occurred to ask if Grum was a man or a woman. I guess I would find out.

The barrier opened at my approach. I got to my feet and stepped through into decent gravity. My stomach protested but quickly adjusted to the change as Grum faced me.

I learned right then what a Walen looked like. Nearly as tall as I was at six one, some of Grum's height could be attributed to his neck. It wasn't a grotesque or even weird length, but I did notice the attribute. He lacked hair and had open, honest eyes.

When he blinked, I realized I'd been holding my breath in anticipation of another Hellenger-like trait. Grum's eyes closed from all sides, like a camera lens. It was fascinating rather than disturbing, but I thought I would get used to it. Honestly, his blink was at least as fast as the human version, so it didn't draw much attention.

His hands held a circuit board covered with twisting wires and data chips—or that was what they seemed like at first glance. I noticed each hand possessed two thumbs and four fingers. The thumbs were on opposite sides of his palm. I thought the arrangement seemed mechanically efficient, but I would need to wait and see.

"Are you Grum?"

His eyes went wide as he lowered the device he'd been working on. "You know my name?" He hurried forward, deftly stowing his project in a jumpsuit pocket as he moved. "Kayan told me you are very unique, and she seems to have a high regard for your worth. I am honored to meet you. Can we be friends? I would like one. Montow is not fond of me. Maybe. It is hard to know with the captain."

"Slow down, kid."

He frowned, then puzzled out the translation Kayan provided. "I am young. Please tell me that isn't an insult like it would be to a Hellenger or a Tyton."

"I meant it in the best possible way."

"Oh. Good. Does your race have sarcasm? We do. And what you just said seems a bit… disingenuous."

I moved closer and spread my hands. "Humans tease people

they like. Let's start over." I offered my hand. "Noah Gantz, from Earth."

He stared, then wrapped his fingers and thumbs around mine, staring at what he was doing the entire time. "This is an interesting custom. I am sorry about your missing thumbs. I am Grum, son of Gramm, of Walen."

"Good to meet you. Nice place. Look at all the stars," I said.

"The view is spectacular. Montow doesn't like coming here, but I do. Neither does Wozim."

"Why is that?"

"Wozim doesn't like the crawlway. Says it is undignified. He's a Tyton. To be honest, he scares me even though I wish he would teach me to fight. Maybe you can do that?"

"Sure. Why not? What about Montow? He seems like the mentor type."

"He says it's not right to waste time gazing at beautiful things or learning to fight when there is no need. Hellengers are practical and hardworking. Montow takes this to a new level. He has no sense for adventure," Grum said. "I don't think he would be an effective combat instructor, even if my petition was accepted."

I toured the room and took my time gazing at the star field. My breathing and heart rate slowed. This was what monks must feel like on the mountain top. What I saw was a fraction of the universe, but it seemed like everything in existence. Kayan was larger than I had imagined. Translucent colors drifted over a metal exterior, or what looked a lot like metal. There was something off-balance with the ship. It seemed Kayan had swallowed something enormous, which was pushing other sections of the ship into weird configurations.

"What do you do for fun, Grum?" I left the observation alone. Later, when I had more information, I could ask better questions.

"Fix things," he said. "And read. Do your people use a written language? I love adventure stories."

"Really? I wouldn't have guessed."

He struggled with my answer. "About which part? Both things were true. I'm no exaggerator."

Again the translation was slightly off, but insightful. "Would you mind showing me around? I've only seen a fraction of the ship."

He nodded vigorously. I made a note to catalog nonverbal responses and check them against what I knew. Hopefully, some elements of communication were universal. "We can come back here anytime, though you should know Kayan rotates the bubbles without explaining why. Kind of like the crash pods, and your cabin for that matter. Don't leave anything you will miss. I had to wait a standard month to get one of my favorite books back. That is also how I realized she rotates these things."

"Good to know." I waited for him to gather odds and ends into a backpack he pulled tight and slung into place by shoulder straps.

"Ready." He waited until I waved toward the exit, then led the way.

I followed, wondering how much easier my introduction

would have been to Kayan's passageways with this *kid* as a guide. He was enthusiastic and free with information.

"What do you do for a living?" I asked as we worked through the twisting tube.

"Maintenance, mostly. My people receive a broad education before leaving our birth communes. So I have all the skills, including basic combat. When I left Walen Prime, I felt ready to handle the galaxy. Why wouldn't I have? My family and teachers taught me every imaginable skill. Opportunities seemed to stretch outward in every direction."

"Good question, and you're probably going to tell me the answer."

"Ah, sarcasm. Your people must be a lot like mine." He opened the portal aperture, moved across the threshold, and waited for me with his hands tucked through the straps of his light pack. "I walked about five microns before I realized other races specialized in certain fields and achieved unbelievable levels of ability. Maybe someday I can convince my people their generalist mindset isn't the only way to study."

"Microns?"

"Figure of speech. I learned immediately."

I nodded. "I've seen the engine rooms a lot since Montow seems obsessed with cleaning and repairing them. Organic power plants are amazing."

"Show me your quarters, then I can orient your knowledge of the ship from there. Keep you from getting lost, because it's easy."

I went along with his plan without informing him that Kayan

didn't allow me to be lost. We moved through a passageway barely taller than I was and narrow enough to drag my fingers along opposite walls.

"Don't let Montow see you doing that," Grum said. "He says it bothers Kayan."

"Does it?"

Not at all, Kayan answered me privately.

Grum shrugged. "Hell if I know."

"What can you tell me about the Gavant?" I asked.

"Never seen their ships."

"We just did, a heavy cruiser called the *Kon*. Montow explained it had probably just delivered one of Kayan's kind to a slave colony or something."

He went pale. "A detention system. Specially made for living starships. They never come out. Some people say they are forced to eat each other or get tortured for Gavant weapons development."

There were no words for how I felt. A bottomless dread grew in my gut. Kayan said nothing. I got the impression this was one of the times she wasn't paying attention. Maybe the topic was too painful.

Grum led me to a cavernous room with lights running up the walls in converging angles. I thought of ancient cathedrals if someone had decorated them with fading glow sticks. There were only two entrances, one at each end. The far one was closed with lights running across its surface, almost like an out-of-order warning.

"What is this place?"

"The music room. Come. Stand in the center."

I joined him in the middle of an intricately decorated circle on the floor, then stared upward. The lights only seemed more fascinating from here. "Should I hear something?"

"Wait for it."

It wasn't long before swells of sound filled the place. "That's like an orchestra warming up."

"Don't know those terms." Grum leaned his head back and allowed his arms to hang at his sides. He closed his eyes, then opened them to reveal lights reflecting in his vision.

Nothing had ever felt more relaxing. I could practically feel my body healing, which forced me to remember the changes Kayan made to save me were far from complete. A United Earth doctor would have me on bed rest for weeks just to be sure, then twice as long in physical therapy. Here I was walking around an alien starship with my new friend, and for the most part, in better shape than I had ever been in my twenties. This led me to wonder what else was going on inside of me.

"Did Kayan save your life too?"

The young Walen stared at me with a strange expression. "I stowed away, just like the rest of the passengers. That is the only method of securing passage. Is that not how you joined us?"

Kayan spoke in my head, and for the first time, I couldn't understand the words, though the words felt like a warning.

I also doubted anyone could sneak onto the ship. "Something like that, I guess."

"Oh. Well, we all have our own destiny, I suppose."

The entrance whooshed open behind us to admit Montow.

"What are you doing? This isn't work. Get out of here and help me find the source of the power fluctuation. Kayan needs us, Grum. Or have you forgotten?"

"Relax, Montow. The ship would let us know if there was a crisis," I said.

"Maybe. Your relationship with our host is special. Don't try to deny it. But there is a reason I was chosen as the captain." He ran his eyes over the lights, paused, and touched the sunglasses. "Everything looks much different. I see why you enjoy this." A long, deep exhalation escaped his lungs. With his recently developed beard, it was hard to see if his lips were parted. "But that doesn't matter. Both of you must help me find Qurks. They are causing problems with Kayan's systems again."

"We got rid of them after we dumped their hive queen on the moon at Illin 5," Grum complained.

Montow huffed and stormed out, apparently intent on getting back to work.

"I don't know my way around, Grum," I lied. "Let's stick together."

"Of course." He dug something like a notebook out of his pack and flipped through stiff, slightly reflective pages.

I moved away and spoke with Kayan. For the first time, I did this without activating my vocal cords or moving my lips. It felt uncomfortably alien for some reason—like maybe I was going insane. The ship told me I would get used to it, but I couldn't imagine feeling comfortable with this.

What are these Qurks?

An embarrassment, though they shouldn't be, Kayan answered.

Many of my kind suffer with the affliction, and some believe their existence is not only natural, but necessary. Even so, these persistent nests of the creatures are one of the reasons I left my home system. My younger self thought it possible to find a solution to the infestation and return home with no one the wiser. Just when they seem to be gone, they reappear and start breeding. Montow is kind to search for a remedy.

Do they hurt you?

Not at all. Some medical professionals believe that transporting living creatures is necessary to all of my people. In many instances, that means Qurks. They go so far as to say each of us have them, but then deny their existence for outdated social reasons. As I said, it was a foolish vanity of my youth that set me on this path. Many other events have kept me on it.

I understood more than Kayan said but couldn't articulate my thoughts. My theories and concerns remained private. There were limits to what the ship could know and understand of my mind.

Which was a relief. This was a weird situation to establish there were limits between us, but I was definitely grateful for the revelation. Privacy was still on the menu.

Listen, I have an idea.

Kayan waited.

You don't know if they're actually dangerous, but that doesn't mean they aren't. If your doctors are like human doctors, they make mistakes.

I am in complete agreement, Noah.

We could run a test.

Please explain.

The first step is finding these things, then maybe capturing one. I worked on multiple hypotheses at once but shelved most of the ideas for later when they could be acted upon.

Grum is quite good at capturing them. That was how we mitigated the last breeding season and managed to herd them below decks. What do you call this type of hive leader? Alpha? Your thoughts on dangerous predators are jumbled, Kayan shared. *I will explain to Montow and Grum that I wish to capture as many as possible for experimentation. You must promise the testing will not be cruel.*

Are these things like hornets? Because I'm not sure fair treatment should be a consideration if these are hive creatures. And besides, whatever we do can't be worse than dumping them on a moon.

Illin 5 and all its satellites are very nice. You would like it there. Lots of plants and waterfalls.

I'll put it on my list of places to visit.

The rest of my response was drowned out by Montow screaming on the public address comms.

5

Grum rolled up his sleeves to show me his hands and forearms.

"Paper cuts?"

He stared blankly. "I don't understand. Is that a problem in your world?"

"One of the worst." What I saw on his skin were layers of confrontations with a bramble bush or he was super clumsy. According to Kayan, Walens were anything but. "Tell me how you got these."

He shrugged. "I was herding a bunch of them into the shuttle and had to pick several up. This wasn't their fault. Their claws are sharp and they're only animals."

"Only animals. You mean insects. Hive creatures."

"That just means a group of animals," Grum said. "At least that is how Kayan and Montow explained the translation when I was new here."

"On Earth we have names for every group of animals: herd of cows, murder of crows, clowder of cats, flock of seagulls."

"Oh. Well, maybe we should see them and compare notes."

"Good idea." I followed him into a cramped passage. Lights blinked along the ceiling and floor in time with the veins on my hands. I lowered them and tried not to look. It was distracting and reminded me how much this journey had altered me. "Pandemonium of parrots. A crash of rhinos. Skulk of foxes. Pod of dolphins. Pride of lions. Brood of chickens. Colony of ants."

"Your language confuses Kayan," Montow said.

"Nah." I thought I would know. "She loves English."

Not particularly, Noah. I need only to point to the many versions of the word 'there'. Whoever constructed your communication algorithms was drunk, the ship said privately.

I walked bent over. "Are we getting close?"

"Yes," Kayan said. "A significant group of the monsters is in the next temperature regulation exchange. I could easily destroy them, but it seems a harsh solution. And you desire to imprison them for your experiments."

"When you say it like that, it makes me sound like the villain."

"All villains are heroes in their own mind." Kayan's soothing tone almost slipped this jab past my defenses.

"Ouch. Maybe we could table the dark introspection until we deal with this alpha hive or whatever." I reached the lens-style door, but held up one hand to keep it closed. As hand signals went, it wasn't overt or specific, but we'd worked out the nuances of my gestures. Mostly. I hoped. "Listen, Grum. We go in just far enough to see these things. If I say, ah hell no, then we're out of there. Got it?"

He nodded. "They are not terrifying. Just staring at you and slashing their appendages around lazily, like they have all the time in the world to murder you." He held up his arms. "These are battle wounds, remember."

"I'll put you in for a medal."

"Really? That's a great honor, right? Maybe Wozim will respect me."

"Remember sarcasm?"

"Dang, you got me."

I still hadn't met this scary Wozim character. Now wasn't the time to worry about it. If he was such a badass, the guy should be helping with this. I raised one of the flashlights I'd asked Kayan to make for us.

"You won't need that," the ship said. "I will adjust the light for you."

"I like to be prepared."

Kayan didn't comment.

Grum hefted his light appreciatively. "Backup illumination is a great idea. I don't get the VIP treatment like you, Noah. Got stuck down here once when Kayan and the others forgot about me. Took forever for my vision to adjust."

I expected the ship to argue or explain, maybe even apologize. Silence was the only response.

"Let's do this." I approached the door and it spiraled open. Inside, the lights quickly adjusted. The temperature transfer corridor curved gently for a hundred meters. Towers of dull metal spotted the area. The pattern took a moment to recognize. I was still adjusting to the way the ship thought, including how she conceptualized shapes. "Where are the Qurks?"

"They hide when the lights come on."

I rolled my eyes and realized none of my new companions understood the expression. Which was probably for the best. There weren't many hiding places. The towers pulsed in a slow rhythm. While their rough texture would make them easy to climb, anything using them for concealment only had one option —stay on the side opposite us.

"Each of these are designed to expose as much surface area as possible," Kayan explained. "Air, fluid, and various mixtures are used, depending on the workload of my power plants in other parts of the ship. Energy is routed through here. Farther into the passage you will see the problem."

"Follow me." I edged forward, light held ready to club one of these things if necessary. The room curved more sharply near the end. If I was setting up an ambush, that would be the place to do it. These creatures didn't have ranged weapons, so that was just paranoia. I made a note just in case.

Grum stepped on the back of my feet. His breath warmed one side of my neck.

"Not that close."

"Sorry."

Movement caught my attention but I wasn't fast enough to see what it was. I stopped and held up one hand for Grum to do the same.

Several creatures dashed for the end of the passage and made the corner before I got a good look. Startled, I froze instead of giving chase. "What the...?"

Grum nodded energetically. "Never seen that many at once."

"They had fur."

His blank look told me a lot. "So what?"

"Wasps and ants and stuff don't have fur." I thought back and immediately doubted myself, but still believed I had it right. "They didn't move like bugs."

"If you continue to their hiding place, the problem will become evident."

I had seen way too many horror movies to walk into an ambush. Now that they were gone, or some of them were gone, I wasn't in a hurry. Grum followed my lead and managed to not step on my feet. Tower after tower revealed nothing. We reached the abandoned hiding place a short distance before the final curve.

"Stay here until I call you."

"Sure thing, Noah. I will be ready to lay down my life for the cause."

"Cool your jets, champ. This isn't that type of mission." Gripping the flashlight with both hands, I rounded the tower with it raised overhead.

And saw my first Qurk.

"They left one. I think it's hurt." The *hive* creature had six legs, a bushy tail, and golden retriever fur. Its face, however, was far more exotic. The puppy features were there, but it had the pointed ears of a lynx and whiskers sticking out to each side.

Grum leaned around me to see. "That is a young one."

"You people need to work on your adjectives. This isn't a hornet monster or whatever you had me thinking it was." I leaned closer. "Hey buddy, I'm Noah. We're not going to hurt you."

"Noah," it yowled.

I stepped back. "They talk." I could almost hear Pops laughing.

"Not exactly," Grum said. "Montow says they are vocal mimics."

The creature sniffed my hand when I offered it and didn't bite, scratch, or otherwise try to murder me. So far, I couldn't see what was wrong with it, but assumed it had been left by the others. It yawned and I immediately doubted Qurks were damaging Kayan. Unless the den-like nest interfered with the ship's functioning.

There was one thing I didn't like—red and black slugs with circular mouths full of teeth and glowing green slime. Worried for the furry cat-dog creature, I reached to flick them out of the habitat.

"Noah!" The creature bared its teeth in a clear warning to back off.

"Why did it do that?" Grum asked.

Several ideas came together. "The others left food for this one. I think the Qurks are eating the slug things that probably eat Kayan's circuitry. We were hunting the wrong rodents. Didn't you say some of your kind believe the Qurks are natural and necessary?"

"That is correct, Noah." Kayan floated several indistinct images in my awareness.

I struggled to understand what these glowing shapes meant. We'd talked about them. The ship was trying to present images I could see but the resolution wasn't quite there.

"You are my eyes, Noah. While I know much about myself through various sensations, it is impossible for me to see in this manner or with such clarity."

"You can see us," Grum argued.

"Not with human depth and detail. Noah's vision is exceptional. What he has shown me makes this power loss mystery embarrassingly obvious. Qurks may not be blameless, but the real problem is a Fyr infestation. That, I know, can be remedied."

"Oh. Good thing you bonded with him more than the rest of us," Grum said quietly.

I leaned toward the six-legged *puppy-kitten* staring back at me, then held out both arms. On cue, the Qurk crawled up and curled against my chest. It had this adorable club tail that was surprisingly dense.

"You're a lot heavier than you look, mutt." I shifted its weight. "Not really a mutt, though, are you?"

It didn't say my name this time. Falling asleep took all of the creature's attention.

"You captured one," Grum said. "When should we start the experiments?"

"Uh, let me think about that. Scrape up those evil slug things." I bounced the Qurk like a baby and watched the Walen work. He deftly scooped up the disgusting blobs into a bag. Meanwhile, my new friend extended and retracted its claws several times. I clenched my teeth, then stared at blood soaking through my sleeve. "Shit, these things have sharp claws. That went right through the organic sheeting protecting my forearms."

Grum gave me a troubled look. He seemed to notice the backs of my hands for the first time. I got the sense that what Kayan had done to me wasn't natural, and definitely wasn't something she'd *shared* with the other passengers.

"Let's get out of here, unless Kayan needs us to remove these nests."

"No worries, Noah. I'll handle that now that I understand the dynamics of this sub-ecosystem." Kayan again attempted to show me an image, but it was blurry and evaporated the moment I concentrated on it. "Later, I will ask you and the rest of the crew to search for the Fyr slugs."

"Can't wait." I headed into the main passageway, glad to finally stand straight.

Grum emerged behind me, then called out. "Wozim! We caught one."

I stared at a seven-foot-tall, densely muscled monster out of a horror movie. He had horns like a bull, a scorpion tail partially covered in armor, and eyes ready to burn us where we stood. That last part was an exaggeration brought on by surprise, but still. This dude was terrifying. The deep red tone of his rough skin reminded me of a demon, or a devil, despite the sheer ridiculousness of my reaction. His clenched fists were like giant sledgehammers.

He wore a weird kilt with at least five sword and knife sheaths woven into it. The blades seemed to be part of the armor.

Grum hurried toward the brute. "Come look. Don't you want to see our prize."

Wozim glared down on the young Walen, shifted his gaze to me, and grunted. There was no hint of curiosity. He didn't welcome me to the ship, or conversely, warn me to stay out of his turf. The Tyton merely went into a room and closed the door.

Grum's shoulders slumped. I wanted to kick Wozim's giant warrior ass for hurting my friend's feelings. But of course that was a bad idea. Good thing it didn't matter now.

"Come on, Grum. Let's find someplace to put this critter and see what's wrong with it," I said.

6

"Noah," yowled the Qurk.

"That's my name. Don't wear it out."

The six-legged, golden retriever puppy-kitten thing gave me a confused look and sat up without using its rear pair of legs. When I tried to touch them, it nipped at my fingers.

"You care for this creature?" Kayan asked.

"Don't get excited." I placed my hand on the floor of the padded basket Kayan had fabricated and waited. Sure enough, the creature I needed to name rested its chin on my palm and closed its eyes. Moments later, it slept. "What do you think we should do with it?"

"Noah, why must you create these predicaments?" Kayan said. "Life was simple before you arrived in your ruined ship. My passengers kept to themselves. We suffered whatever damage the Qurks and Fyrs caused and did the best we could. Now you have

Grum following you around, Montow coming out of his shell, and have located a mascot."

"No one asked you to save me."

"You gave the correct permissions for my intervention."

"I'm pulling your chain, Kayan. I'm glad to be here."

I wasn't sure the ship's assessment of the pre-Noah days was accurate. As far as I could tell, Montow did nothing but work. He was more talkative than Wozim, but not by much. The Gavant warship sighting had disturbed the captain.

Lights pulsed through the alien veins on the back of my hands. Words died before they reached my lips. The furry friend sleeping on my hand curled into the corner of the basket, allowing my careful retreat. What was wrong with its legs? Nothing looked broken. His littermates had just abandoned him. Qurks were jerks.

Montow and Grum strode in and headed for their pod-chairs and workstations facing a row of holographic screens projected from the ceiling.

The captain stopped. "You still have the rodent."

"Not a rodent."

He raised his sunglasses to give me a skeptical look with his unblinking eyes. "We must consent to not reach a consensus."

"Agree to disagree."

"Yes. That is what I said." He pulled up a holographic screen covered in star maps and columns of numbers. "Passengers are secondary to the journey. You must learn this."

"Whatever you say." Montow was in a mood this morning, and I didn't feel like arguing.

Grum stood back and said nothing. He never took sides. "Tell me about the journey. Where are we headed?"

He scratched at his beard with one hand then pointed at a section of the middle screen. Lines crept from our location to one star system after another. "These are not far apart in galactic terms. Which is good. Kayan hasn't fed often enough, and has never consumed a complete meal since our time on board." He motioned to himself and Grum.

"Why not?" This was the first I'd heard of the problem and I was embarrassed I hadn't asked Kayan sooner.

"The ship will only say there are fewer fungi fields in each star system," Montow said. "I believe the Gavant armadas are destroying these fungus colonies to prevent their captive ships from getting far if they escape. What use is it for them to leave the detention system if they starve before reaching a friendly sector?"

"Seems like a lot of work," I said. There were a lot of pieces missing to this puzzle. Why were the Gavant capturing the living starships? What were they doing with them? Was there something we could do to help?

"It is, but they only pursue space fungus eradication in conjunction with other goals. I do not believe they travel out of their way to destroy Kayan's food source, but when they find collections of it, they burn the fields to atoms or scatter them beyond the heliospheres. The Gavant have many fleets. A directive to all of them has a catastrophic effect."

"My people will lose the ability to exist if this continues,"

Kayan said. "We have worried about the problem for a thousand of your standard years."

Montow magnified a side screen. "This is Ryyth. We should continue our journey to it. If any part of the galaxy is safe from the Gavant, it is this one."

I moved closer as an image of a blue and green world magnified. Ryyth appeared below it and my heart ached with homesickness. The biosphere turned as though we had achieved high orbit.

"These are images from memory. I was young. My early voyages were rushed and impatient, so I didn't stay long. Worlds such as these are not often of interest to my people. This one is different. There are small fields of food. In times past, it wasn't enough to bother stopping for. Now, it may be enough to sustain me until a better solution is found," Kayan explained.

Montow spoke in a low, somber voice. "Before I was cast out, there was talk among my people that the Gavant could not hurt anyone on Ryyth. The reasons were unknown, and that was also in my youth. Forty standard years have passed, but I still believe this is our best way to remain free of the Gavant hunters."

"Why are they after us?"

Montow tipped his soup can head side to side, just enough for the gesture to be noticeable. I thought it was like a shrug, or a thinking motion. "I cannot say they are after you, but it is good form to include yourself in our worries."

"Not like I have a choice."

"And now you have made this unattractive." Montow pulled up other star systems and planets between our location and our destination. "This will not be a short journey, and there are significant dangers along the way. Kayan needs fuel now, and will continue to run short."

"Perhaps you need a dead ship," Kayan suggested. "I would not be offended if you transfer your allegiance to something made of non-living metal and cold fusion power plants. Each of you must do what is needed to survive."

I cringed at the phrase dead ship. For a second, my brain had translated death ship before realizing she meant mechanical vessels lacking sentience. I also balked at the term allegiance. Was Kayan worried about loyalty? Had that been a problem before my arrival?

"Do we vote? Should we get Wozim in here?" I asked.

Montow and Grum stared at me. "He doesn't take orders."

"How about an invitation? A request?"

Montow shrugged. Grum looked uncomfortable.

"Watch the creature." I pointed to the basket as I headed for the door. "We really should get the Tyton's input on our destination. It's time to introduce myself."

"Good luck," Montow said. "You will need it."

I moved through the halls with barely a thought to my route or my destination. As part of the ship, navigating the passages was usually easy. Kayan hadn't explained the times it wasn't, but I assumed it was like any organism with an incomplete knowledge of itself. When I wandered places not normally of concern to my host, we both became lost. Weird, but real as anything about this place.

"Don't overthink it, Noah."

"Are you talking to yourself?" Kayan asked.

"Sort of."

"Why?"

"No idea. Feels good."

"I will remember this fact and not assume you are crazy in the future." Kayan again attempted to share a mental image, but only briefly. The second my mind resisted, she resorted to words. "Montow has found a food source. When you are done being disappointed, I may require your assistance."

"You got it, Kayan. Anything for my host." I knocked on the door and quickly realized the material absorbed vibrations caused by my knuckle strikes. Wozim didn't respond. I made a fist and pounded on the portal.

Nothing.

"Could I open this if I wanted to?"

Kayan made a warning sound. "Not recommended. While I am sure you are an adequate warrior, angering a Tyton in this manner is not conducive to remaining in one piece."

"You're probably right." I waited a while, then knocked again. Persistence could pay dividends, so I stuck with it for ten or fifteen minutes, hammering the portal every minute or two.

A slot above my eye level turned transparent. Wozim's angry eyes stared down.

"Hey, there you are. I'm Major Noah Gantz. We're deciding where to take the ship and I thought you might have an opinion."

The slot closed.

Knocking and waiting soon bored me. "This guy is not winning Mister Congeniality any time soon."

"Agreed," Kayan said. "Humans have many strange competitions."

"No arguments there. Show me this fungus field." I headed for the bridge.

Montow was waiting but Grum was gone with the basket. All five screens showed variations of a cloud halfway across the system. "This is not a substance Kayan or any of her kind has used for sustenance, but the ship agrees it might have some value as fuel."

"If I can choke it down," Kayan said.

Montow explained without being asked. "A Gavant battle group must have come this way and eradicated the edible space fungus. Their methods for doing so are unknown to us, but most likely involve their energy weapons or certain missiles."

"I can consume this waste and filter small amounts of the fuel I need from it."

"So this is well-done fungus? Kind of like barbarians who char their T-bones beyond recognition?"

Montow looked over his huge sunglasses. "Who would do that? Are your people still living in caves?"

I shrugged. "What do you need me for, Kayan? You said you might need my help."

A significant pause followed. I waited and used the time to study Montow. He seemed lost in thought. The inability to read his mind was surprisingly frustrating and I realized how intertwined I was with Kayan. Mind reading was a strong term.

It wasn't like that. There was just always a connection and easy understanding between us.

No connection was perfect, of course. We still required language most of the time.

"I have completed an assessment. Barring some unforeseen malfunction of my intake mechanism, your assistance will not be needed outside," Kayan said.

My eyes went wide and I pointed toward a holographic screen. "You mean, out there? In the void?"

"Yes. You should equip yourself with the gear I have grown for that purpose. Test the fit. Make a list of questions and suggestions. We can work out modifications when there is time."

I smiled and spread my arms wide. Extravehicular activity had been one of my strong points in the advanced space exploration school. Theory was about to become practice.

A map image of the ship appeared in my imagination. For a moment, I was speechless. This was the first time she had successfully shared information through purely visual means.

"Do you see it?" Kayan asked.

"Yeah," I said, then followed the map to the equipping room. Finding my way was different. Was it better? Maybe, maybe not. Following intuition as opposed to an actual map was an easier experience when it worked. I hoped I could integrate both with practice.

None of my fellow passengers accompanied me, and that was fine. For some reason, I was in a mood for relative solitude. Kayan was always with me, of course. Yet, as the days progressed, I understood that we were not one being. A time would come when we would separate.

Like when I found my way back to Earth.

Was that what I longed for? Did I have an obligation to report back to my superiors? Absolutely. Thinking about the impossible journey wrecked my mental health so I tried not to dwell on it. Dreams, nightmares, and sudden obsessions would come on their own. Why make it harder on myself?

The equipment room was another new place. The lighting was different, more of a blue or purple tone depending on which way I focused. My eyes adjusted easily and I wondered if I should find a mirror and look for other changes Kayan had made to my biology.

I raised both hands and studied them front and back. This time, I left the sleeves down. I knew what was there, more of the ship attached to my body.

"The suit is parked against the wall," Kayan said.

I saw the device and hesitated. "It looks like a bigger version of me if I was wearing a helmet with a closed face shield."

"This seemed the best design." The ship tried again to present images around the edges of my vision but failed to bring them into focus. The color aura was too much like an oncoming migraine this time. I winced at the sensation.

"Are you well, Noah?"

How to explain migraine headaches? I let the topic drop. "The images you're trying to send me are making me uneasy."

Kayan's attempt to communicate with images ended. "Always warn me if I am causing you damage."

Again I was at a loss for words.

The suit was taller than I was and larger in other ways. I touched the front and it opened. Acting on intuition, I turned away from it and backed in. Once my arms, legs, and body made contact, the suit closed around me.

Panic overwhelmed me with surprising force. I've never been claustrophobic, and my training had considerably increased my tolerance for small spaces. Astronaut programs increased a person's ability to handle everything. Our trainers had been thorough.

There were three steps to handling a panic attack. Accept it was happening. Regulate breathing and other sensory input. Realistically evaluate the situation and adapt accordingly.

Step two was always the hardest, but I was good at it. A teenage fascination with martial arts had started my training in that arena early. Brazilian jiu-jitsu could be about competition and smashing your opponent, but there were instructors who taught the mental game well. I'd been lucky in that regard. Work smarter, not harder, that was the ticket.

Seconds passed and the suit began to feel like it was part of me. I nearly resisted. What was I becoming? Had I gone too far?

When the helmet sealed, something changed. I looked through the visor and saw everything with perfect clarity. Any flaws in my vision had been corrected.

"I must admit, Noah, your version of vision has been an exciting change," Kayan said.

"You couldn't see anything before?"

"I have always been able to see, but everything is different through your eyes. I value that immensely."

A shiver ran through me. The ship seemed possessive. Plenty of horror movies and books came to mind. My situation could go wrong in so many ways.

I laughed away the stress, and it felt good.

"What are you doing?"

"You heard me laugh before. Humans do that. I think even Walens and Hellengers have a version."

"This has a different tone."

"Call it a stress reliever. My situation amuses me." I strode around the room and raised each arm to test my range of motion. Everything felt great. "This thing is impressive. I may not want to take it off."

"That is an option," Kayan said. "Would you like me to make the necessary modifications to achieve permanence?"

I stopped in my tracks. "Pump the brakes, Kayan. Permanent is forever. This isn't a tattoo."

"I don't understand your hesitance but will respect your wishes."

"I've already changed a lot."

"For the better. You are stronger, faster, and smarter than you were when I salvaged you from your wrecked ship." The lighting changed in a way that made the room seem to revolve around me. I saw everything from new perspectives. The sensation was disorienting because now I was seeing through Kayan's eyes as Kayan saw through mine. "I understand you wish to return to your people. I have the same wants and desires. We have bonded and have many things in common."

"Like neither of us can go home again." Saying the words didn't affect me as strongly as I feared they would. Maybe I was in shock. Or crazy. Pushing the thought away, I focused on the present. "Are you ready to eat?"

"I thought you would never ask," Kayan said. "Please proceed forward. I will place a map icon for my intake mechanism."

I went where Kayan directed, vaguely concerned that the ship had a mouth and was about to chow down on some ruined space fungi.

And then it got weird.

The Kayan suit continued to adjust as I walked. I tried some new moves to expand its repertoire. Just as I expected, it performed more efficiently the more I *trained* it. Skipping forward, I felt like a kid and didn't care. Once I was sure neither Montow nor Grum were watching, I experimented with hopping sideways and even doing a somersault.

I reached the door and signaled it not to open. Dance moves weren't my strong point, but I gave it a try and the suit seemed to be into it.

"What are you doing, Noah?"

"It's called dancing."

A one second pause followed. "None of your memory archives seem to align with this description."

"How rude. You're telling me I can't dance?"

"Sometimes it is necessary to face the truth."

I laughed. "Ouch."

"If you move close to the wall, I will make the material of my hull transparent. Do not feel obligated to watch. From what I understand of your psychology, this could be disturbing."

"Thanks for the warning." I approached with a certain solemnity, wondering what I was about to witness.

The wall disappeared. I stopped dead in my tracks. Kayan could have reassured me but didn't. The sight of space fungi getting chomped on wasn't at all what I had expected.

Sparkling rivers of the stuff were pulled into the side of the ship, probably through some sort of filter. I imagined baleen from a blue whale as an equivalent but would have to go outside to get the proper perspective to confirm my theory.

That wasn't something I was ready for even with my EVA skill. Remaining confident was easier with familiar equipment and a familiar team to support you. Not for the first time, I was reminded how far from home I really was.

Not all of the substance reflected stars and sunlight. Part of the fungi cloud seemed blackened and dead. The actual color was hard to determine, but I assumed the ruined sections lacked reflective surfaces.

I stared in pure wonderment. The celestial beauty of the scene consumed me. There was nothing about the space fungi colony rushing into Kayan's intake ports that bothered me.

A sound grew, and that did upset my equilibrium slightly.

"Is that your stomach rumbling or are you just enjoying the food?" I asked.

"It is a sound I make during consumption of resources. The

volume is greatly decreased due to the low fuel value of this ruined cloud." Kayan seemed sad and worried. "You could watch from the void if you wish to avoid sound."

"Are there other sources in this star system?" I asked.

"There are none. If a Gavant warship has been to the next system before us and done the same thing, I will be in significant distress."

"We'll figure something out." I watched the glorious spectacle of space for nearly an hour before deciding I should do some work. With Kayan's occasional directions, I found the ship's equivalent of an airlock.

The sight of it was alarming but made sense when I considered its function and the way this vessel worked. There were emergency pods on the bridge that I used as a sort of standing chair. If something went wrong, or Kayan had to radically change the environment to manage its biology, I and the other passengers could be quickly and thoroughly protected. I wasn't sure, but I thought the ships could move these things with us inside of them.

The main function of those pods, however, was to sustain us during faster-than-light travel. After the disastrous results of my own experimental ship, this was something I appreciated.

The airlock resembled the pods but was slightly bigger to conform to my current dimensions. The suit gave me extra height and bulk. Basically, I would step into this pod, seal it, and be released outside the ship.

"This seems much faster than the airlocks my people use," I said.

Kayan responded lethargically. "Do you wish for me to review available memories for comparison? I am always improving these types of functions for my passengers."

"Maybe later. Do what you need to do. I'm going to finish my stargazing."

7

WE EMERGED from the space jump without complications. Montow stood before his emergency pod, typing on his version of a split keyboard that hung from his wrists. He held both sections before him as though working on a desk instead of a projected plane of light. Watching his hands work fascinated me. While similar to human hands in many ways, they were completely different in others.

It was hard to articulate how each joint of his Hellenger digits worked. Unlike Grum, he had four fingers and one thumb. Normal. Human. That seemed a sufficient description, until I noticed how each sturdy digit telescoped slightly when typing. It wasn't much, but I saw the difference and couldn't unsee it. A millimeter of extension made all the difference.

I skimmed over the star charts and noted how Montow translated them into something that made more sense to both me and him. I understood what Kayan was presenting, but this version was easier to recall and manipulate. Sometimes, when dealing with the ship's thought process or biology, I was regulated to spectator status. What happened if I found myself separated from Kayan? Would everything I relied on as naturally as breathing abandon me?

Probably.

Just when I thought I knew everything about my host, a new mystery appeared. Kayan hadn't pushed me to don the spacesuit as I feared. The topic hadn't come up again. The system jump went well and being protected in the pod-chairs on the bridge was nice. We hadn't yet detected a Gavant presence. Three space fungi fields existed here, and I thought we would visit all of them before we left on the next leg of our trek across the galaxy. All were at the extreme edge of the system, nearly two thousand AUs by Earth measurement. For comparison, my home world was only one AU from our sun.

Would skirting round the edge be faster than crossing the diameter of the heliosphere? It really depended on where each field was located.

"I'm going for a walk." I headed for the door. "I want to look around and check a few things."

Montow looked at me sternly. "Take the Qurk."

I waited for the creature to come closer. "Come on, buddy. You can do it."

The space puppy-kitten tipped over the basket and floundered forward on its front four legs, dragging the two that remained. His expression was ridiculously happy, so I just squatted down and waited for his arrival.

Montow looked at the furry thing with mild distrust. "You understand it will get bigger."

"Hopefully." I had no idea what I was getting myself into with this thing, but I wasn't about to harm it. Its litter had abandoned the runt. Furry little dude didn't have anyone but Kayan's crew of misfits. Different circumstances but a lot of parallels. I scooped it up and held it in the crook of one arm. What was a good name for this little monster? Hmm.

Rather than be thankful and compliant, the Qurk squirmed and constantly strove to look around. When I wasn't paying attention, he licked my face.

"Oh, that is disgusting," Montow groaned. "Bad enough you touched it, but now it is slapping you with its tongue."

I laughed at his description but let the matter drop. "We'll be back."

I strode away from the bridge, not slowing for doors that opened at my approach. "See that, buddy. I'm hugely important."

It made a sound I didn't recognize but didn't say my name.

"Say my name."

It stared at me. One ear up and one bent sideways.

"You did it once."

"Noah."

"That's it! Now what do I call you?"

The creature made a series of scratchy growls I couldn't

make sense of. Was it answering, or just hacking up a hair ball? There was no way to tell.

I did get an idea, though. "Scratch."

The Qurk puppy-kitten stared at me with zero comprehension.

"You'll get used to it. Scratch it is."

We rounded a corner and spotted an open wall panel. I approached cautiously, one arm covering Scratch protectively as I lowered my stance. "What is going on here?"

I stopped short of the opening and waited for Kayan to chime in with information. Nothing happened. Either this wasn't a problem, or the ship was busy celebrating a system-wide version of a buffet bar.

I squatted.

Scratch made a worried sound, almost like a squeal but more endearing.

"I got you, Scratch buddy." The animal squirmed when I tried to move forward, so I placed him behind me and continued my investigation.

Movement caught my eye. I sharpened my gaze, then tapped my left temple. This zoomed my vision and adjusted filters for better clarity. "Now that's a neat trick." The inspiration to try the technique had come easily.

"Noah," complained Scratch.

I glanced over my shoulder. "It's all right. I'll be careful."

Another flurry of movement drew my attention into the low opening. Scrambling through the low threshold, I saw what I expected. A pack of Qurks darting out of sight. That seemed to be their go-to move. All I caught was fur and six-legged bodies hauling ass.

A loud crack announced a panel opening on the opposite side of the passageway.

"Noah!" Cried Scratch as a trio of strange Qurks darted out and bit onto three of the puppy-kitten's legs. These versions weren't golden furred, but black and red. Their eyes glowed with malevolence, and I saw blood coming from where they latched onto Scratch's legs with pointed teeth.

"Hey!" I lunged the full distance and slapped my palm down as I flopped on my belly. My hand flattened one of the angry creatures, causing it to release its grip and flee into the second opening. The others aggressively dragged Scratch in the short, rough pulls of animals pulling prey off to be slaughtered.

My other hand covered Scratch. I held on but hesitated to engage in a tug-of-war with the small animal as the rope. "Let go, you sons a bitches!"

"Noah! Noah!"

I scrambled onto my knees and soon wrapped both arms around the pup. The dark Qurks refused to let go. Leaning down, I bit one on the back of its neck. My hands were needed where they were to protect Scratch. The thing squealed a sound that could have been a word, and fled. Seconds later, the last attacker followed with all six feet clawing at the hard surface of the deck.

The taste of rank animal fur filled my mouth. Spitting, gagging, and cursing, I regained my feet and stepped away from the danger zone. "Kayan, I need some help here. Send Grum or

Montow, or both. Maybe Wozim if he can be bothered to do something useful."

"Grum is on the way," Kayan said. The ship sounded distracted.

"What's wrong?"

"This first Oort field is giving strange readings. I will tell you when I know more."

"Okay." I moved to the end of the hall and kept an eye on the two holes while I petted Scratch to reassure the trembling creature. Not for the first time, Kayan's translation reminded me there were imperfections and assumptions the ship made with the English language, or more accurately, my vocabulary. I assumed the fungi she'd consumed was called Oort Fungi due to where it was located. In this case, at the absolute farthest edge of a star system.

Grum and Montow arrived out of breath.

The captain sneered. "You are too attached to that thing."

"Don't worry about it."

Grum peeked into the matching holes in the walls, one after the other. "What happened?"

"A bunch of evil Qurks came after Scratch."

Montow snorted. "There is no good or evil with them."

"Well, the fuckers tried to eat our friend."

"Your friend," Montow grumbled.

Grum pulled out the flashlight I'd given him and a wrench. He knelt next to the second hole and looked in. "Whatever did this is gone. Do you want me to go in there?"

"If Montow would hold Scratch, I'd go with you."

Montow extended one large palm. "I'm too big for that passage, so I guess there is no choice." He accepted the animal, then just looked at it crouched on his hand. They stared at each other like the oddest couple on the ship.

"Don't do anything to him," I said, then joined Grum.

"It," Montow said.

I shook my head and took the lead. "I assumed the Fyr were the problem but we might need to rethink that."

Grum crawled after me. "There is a lot about Kayan we can't understand. Especially since the ship won't tell us everything, not even you."

There were no convenient lights in this area. I used the flashlight and was glad I'd kept one on me. Kayan remained distracted, which worried me. Twenty minutes later we had found our way to the first opening, but no dark Qurks.

"Where did they go?" Grum asked.

I reviewed our sojourn between decks. "There were tubes they must have squeezed through. Hunting them this way won't work."

Grum spread his hands and smiled. "We tried."

"Yeah. Gold star for us." I led the way into the main passage. The first thing I saw was Scratch sitting on Montow's wide shoulder, happily licking the side of the captain's face like it was the best treat on the ship.

Montow stared stoically forward and made no move to defend himself. "It won't stop."

I contained my amusement, mostly. "He likes you."

"The way I taste, you mean. This is disgusting."

"Your shoulders are just right for a Qurk perch. Everyone knows it is bad form to come between a man and his Qurk. He's just grooming you. The little guy cares."

He lowered his sunglasses just enough to hit me with the full force of his displeased glare.

I lifted the animal off his shoulders. My friend had limits and they were on display in his expression.

He stormed toward the bridge without another word. I handed the animal off to Grum and went after Montow.

"We have arrived in the first Oort colony," Kayan interrupted. "That is my reason for not responding. There is a problem. Please hurry."

Grum seemed unsure of how to hold Scratch.

"Put him in a pod or something and meet me at Kayan's primary intake ports." I skipped backward a few steps as I spoke, then jogged toward my destination.

"I should have realized this colony was too good to be true. There are Clieg clogging my intakes," Kayan said. "Please don your protective gear."

"My cabin is on the way." I slipped inside a second after the door opened for me and laughed in surprise. The armor had opened like a clamshell at my approach. That wasn't new, but the speed and precision in which it completed the maneuver was. I hopped in and felt it close immediately.

Perfect fit. Nice.

Rolling my shoulders felt natural in the suit. I loved standing taller and stronger than I was without it. Who cared if there was something disturbing about being completely encased in living alien technology? It should be reassuring that the equipment was perfectly tailored to my needs. "What are Clieg?"

"They are a byproduct of the Oort fungi that have grown unchecked. Periodic feeding is important to maintain the balance between our food source and our consumption of it."

"Kayan, where does the food the crew eats come from? Are you processing this stuff for us?" The question was out of my mouth as I thought it.

The ship actually chuckled. "We stock up on supplies at Gavant regulated, or outlaw, outposts. Don't worry, Noah. I wouldn't feed you this highly radioactive material."

"That's a relief. Not a mushroom guy."

"The Oort is only distantly related to what humans might consume. This variation would kill you, but not before driving you insane. The molecular changes needed for life to survive frozen are robust and novel, to put it mildly."

"I'll cross it off my list of culinary experiments."

"If you are ready, please disembark to clear the intake ports. Permanent damage could result if you delay. No one wants that."

In the spirit of thoroughness, I tested my emergency protective layer, that clear extension of my prosthetics that had alarmed me shortly after awakening on Kayan. The sheeting covering my legs, arms, and back shot out under my clothing to encase every inch of skin.

The feeling tickled, forcing me to chuckle privately. Redundant backups were never wrong. When scared shitless, think about the positive. That's what my Uncle Mike always said.

I strode to the airlock pod and backed into it.

Moments later the interior seal sucked shut, and the exterior shield parted. The Kayan suit squeezed me three times.

"What was that?"

"A signal that all systems are functional."

"Great." I crawled away from the pod, then stood to test my contact with the surface. Low gravity pulled me toward the exterior of the hull while my boots also gripped. A few checks revealed this was simple magnetics. Of course the ship was also made of metal alloys. I imagined there were endless resources in the void for a living ship to harvest and metabolize.

"Continue on this course," Kayan advised.

"Can I get a safety line next time?"

Kayan made soothing sounds. "That is possible but unnecessary. You can fly the suit back if separated. I can also recall it from significant distances should you lose consciousness."

"Maybe a line would be like training wheels." I explained the reference to speed the process. Sometimes when the ship explored our shared memories, it came back with unexpected results. We'd also learned that not all memories *shared*.

When would I have the courage to explore the ship's past?

The thought filled me with dread, like I would be ground to pieces by an entity far more powerful and complex than I ever could be. There was something dark in that direction, but also events that had glowed like staring too long into the sun. Could I really handle the memories of a living starship?

Humans weren't meant to filter that much information. For

now, it was enough for Kayan to share its past on a need-to-know basis. This wouldn't last, and I knew it.

"There are the intake ports."

I moved around the curve of the hull and saw what could be the jaws of a great beast. Dozens of times larger than my suit, each of the three screens resembled the mouth of a baleen whale. There were other intake ports, but Kayan had them covered with smooth panels resembling black-and-purple glass.

Chunks of hardened space fungus clogged most of the vents. Each accumulation of non-consumable material grew as I watched.

"Can you stop drawing it in until I'm finished?"

"This takes something you call willpower and is difficult to control. The process is automated for a reason, like your beating heart or rising and falling lungs." Kayan illuminated the surface around the intake vents. "Please begin."

I moved closer.

"Noah, I'm at the primary intake ports," Grum reported. "I put Scratch in a pod and left him some snacks."

"I'm outside now. Is Montow available?"

"He is monitoring from the bridge and working on our future course. I know what to do. This isn't the first time we've had this problem," Grum said. "Kayan eats too much. I didn't think that would be an issue with the shortages of food and fuel everywhere."

"I was also caught unprepared for the richness of this field. The Gavant must have missed the entire system," Kayan said. "Which could be another problem."

"Like?" I unfolded a pry tool from the back of my armor and started breaking free chunks of hardened space fungus. Icons inside my visor promised I was safe from radiation.

"Pirates. System-specific wars. Few civilizations waste time on interplanetary conflict, but it does happen and neither side is ever fun to deal with. Some know about the Gavant and other galactic powers. Others treat us as a first contact scenario."

"What could. Go. Wrong?" I scraped more aggressively and kept my feet away from the vents. "Are any of these warlords human?"

"That is an interesting question. You should know there are seven races of humans. Perhaps you can differentiate between your people and theirs, but they have strikingly similar attributes. Walens, Hellengers, and Tytons are far less like you, just so you know, and are not included in the seven."

I worked for most of an hour, speculating on this new information. Were they from Earth, or had they spontaneously evolved along the same biological and cultural lines? What exactly would that mean? Did it matter?

"What are we going to do about the Fyr and these other Qurks?" I asked.

"Please explain," Kayan said, her voice sounding more even and relaxed as more of the Clieg clusters drifted away into space.

I went through every detail of the dark Qurks and how they had attacked Scratch.

"Interesting. I didn't understand the robust nature of their existence. It is good we found each other. I am learning much about myself."

"Same." I mentally patted myself on the back a few times for not losing my mind or generally freaking out. Better yet, I was actually helpful to an epically powerful life-form.

"We must learn more about the creatures living within my walls and decide which is beneficial and which should be removed. Your friend Scratch gets a pass. I think Montow in particular has developed a fondness for the animal."

"Really? You sure it's not the other way around?"

"Quite certain. Hellenger are intensely private, long-lived, and wise. Montow has much to share with you. From time to time, his good nature supersedes his intense desire to work," Kayan said.

"Good to know." I switched to a smaller tool and continued scraping. "I'll keep that in mind. Still not sure he loves the Qurk."

By the time I was finished and on my way inside, the suit was so comfortable on my body it worried me. Kayan looked like a new ship on the outside and I had a new set of job skills—ship scraper.

The walk didn't take long, and I hardly worried about drifting into the void. What was I doing out here, and how would I ever get home? How many other things would be normal to me by the time this was over?

"Are you almost back, Noah?" Grum asked. "I'm waiting and ready to help you out of your suit."

"Fine." I only realized how the word snapped out after I spoke. "Sorry, Grum. That's not your fault."

"I am not used to receiving apologies," Grum said.

Barely listening, I wanted to stay in the suit. With the durable armor and helmet protecting me, I felt safe. Better yet, the climate control was perfect, and I never got hungry. Cravings were an old memory.

My hands looked different as I turned them over again and again to examine the durable exterior. On impulse, I diverted to pass a closed intake port and gazed into the black-and-purple reflective surface. The Kayan armor and helmet were totally badass.

And I needed to get out of them before I forgot what I looked like. If I was being really honest, I needed some face time with a human before I forgot how to act.

"I would appreciate a hand, if you're still there, Grum."

His happy response warmed me. "Standing by!"

The airlock pod cycled me through. Grum helped me out of the gear. Montow entered and placed Scratch on the deck. The mutt darted forward with all the energy of a puppy-kitten cooped up all day waiting for its master.

And it was running on five of the six legs.

I scooped the critter up and half-heartedly dodged the licking and sniffing. "What did you do, Montow?"

He held a thick forefinger near his blocky thumb. "I massaged the little legs. Put the monster to sleep. Then I just kept doing it until… this."

I held up the animal and tried to see signs of its affliction. "Could it be that simple?"

Montow shrugged. "Your problem now."

"Very little is known about Qurks," Kayan offered. "I am

crawling toward the second section of the Oort field now. The pace is best for fuel conversion."

"Sounds great." I struggled to control Scratch and finally set him on the floor.

"All is not well," Kayan said, though the ship's voice sounded content.

"Alarming." I pulled a glove from my jacket and flung it, hoping Scratch would fetch. All I got was a mildly interested look and a cock of his head. "Can you elaborate?"

"There are still serious problems with the Fyr population on this ship, and possibly some of the Qurks as well."

Montow interrupted. "Could be they're all bad, except for that one." He pointed at Scratch.

"Grum, are you ready for another round of searching?"

"I sure am."

"Then let's get started."

8

"I DON'T SEE how you can wear that suit," Grum said as he crawled behind me. "So tight. And you look like a piece of Kayan came loose. Mine is much better."

I had yet to examine the Walen's space suit, and now wasn't the time. We were deep into Fyr territory, or at least I hoped we were. These narrow passages hadn't been put here for humans or Walens. Kayan either couldn't or refused to confirm our quarry was hiding between decks. The ship was distracted by the proximity of fuel and the constant drain on her energy stores.

I twisted through a gap and saw horizontal and vertical versions of the heat transfer towers where I'd discovered Scratch abandoned by his littermates. Pillars and archways of living ship parts twisted before me in a confusing labyrinth. Most of this section was like steel that had been grown rather than forged. A thin coating protected it. Kayan warned me not to touch those parts even while wearing armored gloves.

A few meters ahead of us, a line of Fyr slugs stretched into the shadows. Most were small, but occasional gluttons had fallen to the floor where they lay motionless. Qurk tracks covered the lower area like they'd been hunting or scavenging this place for a while.

"Bingo."

"Yes, Bingo," Grum said, still unable to see my discovery. "Bingo?"

"I'll explain later. There are a lot of the slugs ahead of us." I gestured for more lights. Kayan complied, though that was all the ship offered at the moment. My flashlight handled the rest. I swept it over the disgusting creatures and tensed in fear that they would suddenly come after us. "I would bet money that these things are causing at least part of the power drain."

"Keep going. Find a place I can see." Grum shined his light, but it did neither of us good from where he was.

"Go back to the last intersection and turn right. See if that tube opens to the same area I'm watching."

Grum and his light backed up. "On it."

He loved the term, though to be fair, he was a pretty big fan of most human words and phrases. Before long, he'd just be one of the guys at work.

Wouldn't that be great, Pops?

My grandfather's smiling face warmed me up. He never did flinch at people who were different. I remember him fixing bikes of any kid in the neighborhood who brought them for work, no matter who they were or what their parents did for a living. Maybe more importantly, neither their race nor gender nor parent's politics meant a thing to him so long as they were polite and respectful.

Light appeared in the labyrinth. I leaned out until I could see which hole it was coming from. "Is that you, Grum?"

"Sure is. In the flesh."

I let out a chuckle. That was definitely a term the Walen kid used haphazardly. "What do you see?"

"A lot. They're coming from the farm and heading to the power plants. That's not allowed. One of the first things Kayan told Montow, who shared it with me."

I wondered why Kayan hadn't broached the subject during my orientation but figured there had been a lot to cover with the ship rebuilding parts of me. "There's a farm?"

"That's the best word for it. Kayan has lots of places we aren't allowed. Things grow on some levels. Better for us to stay away. It's an ecosphere or something like that. My translator is glitchy today."

By translator, he meant Kayan filtering words and making sure we understood each other. I focused on the ship and understood it was in a state of near hibernation for the glide to the next Oort cloud.

"Same." I crawled from the tube, hung by my arms, and carefully lowered my feet to the floor. A wet dampness in the air chilled me. "Why is it so cold in here?"

"Not sure," Grum said as he dropped to the ground farther along the first section of the belowdecks maze.

"Noah," Kayan said. "I can answer that, though my energies are needed elsewhere to keep crucial sections of the ship alive."

I shot a look to Grum whose already expressive eyes were wider than ever.

"This leads to power plants that have not functioned well for years. Long before Montow or the others joined me, something changed within this section that made it too inefficient to operate fully. I suspected the Qurks or Fyrs were the issue and relaxed several seals to the void."

My breath filled the space ahead of me.

"Neither species can be eliminated with cold or restricted atmosphere. A certain amount must exist. Forcing a true purge of this level is not only dangerous, but impossible," Kayan said. "Less than ideal conditions do inhibit their ability to function, however."

"And thus, decreases what they can chew out of your circuits," I said.

"More or less."

Grum chuckled. "Such a cool phrase."

"Yeah. It's the height of human speech." I deadpanned the comment. Neither Grum nor Kayan appreciated my nuanced humor in this case.

Kayan continued. "Can you eliminate them for me? This might be the system I could risk making fully operational. Running at half power has become a useful restriction. There will be a time when we need everything I have to escape the Gavant hunters."

"We're on it," I said. "This seems like the best use of our

time. Would you check on Montow and Wozim? See if they can pitch in."

"Montow is rocking Scratch to sleep and will assist at the entrance to this level when he can. Wozim responded with a comment that is rude in all languages."

"I'm about done with that guy."

Grum moved to my side. "Done? Did you start something? Hanging around with humans is hard. Can't keep up."

"Figure of speech."

"Gotcha. I'll make a note. Not my favorite phrase, in case you're keeping track. What do we do now?"

I followed the trail of Fyr slugs back to its source and had Kayan explain the farm level again. Mostly, she told me not to enter and to keep things from coming out.

"Won't work. You can see where they are chewing through the wall. We block this one, and that will cause new damage somewhere we don't know about."

"Defeat has a sour taste," Grum said.

"Hold on. Maybe these slimy little buggers need a detour." I followed their course until I saw what was necessary. "Kayan, can you change the shape of these walls and heat regulators?"

"In time, but you may do it more quickly," Kayan said. "Be gentle, because it will hurt both of us."

Arms crossed, I studied the traffic patterns for a while and went to each end of their convoy several times. Grum followed loyally but seemed bored. "Are they intelligent?"

"Not at all," Kayan said.

"Okay. Here's what we're going to do."

"WHAT DO THEY CHEW ON?" I asked again. So far, neither of us could determine how the damage was done. The Fyr slugs appeared to be the culprits. Circular mouths full of fangs and a trail of electrical destruction behind them was our proof. Catching them in the act was a time-consuming challenge.

"The circuitry," Grum said. "Montow says it is all grown, all organic." He tipped his head, clearly displaying skepticism in his wide, expressive eyes. "All I see here are melted wires and scorched metal."

"Kayan, can you clarify what we're dealing with? What are we trying to prevent, exactly?"

No answer.

"The ship has a lot to keep track of besides us," Grum said.

Should I tell him I was part of the ship? My thoughts went briefly to the steel-hard compounds protecting the backs of my hands and arms beneath the Kayan armor. The suit I could remove but the rest was permanent. Grum didn't comment. Maybe he hadn't noticed my preoccupation.

We reached the front of a Fyr procession. The first was no larger than the others. I'd expected it to be fat from whatever they were feeding on and dominant, like a slug leader. Instead, the creature squished ever forward, almost to its destination. An unspoiled wall of circuitry waited for plundering. The sheets of slime Kayan grew to slow them wouldn't last long against this many of the things.

My fear of the Fyr was gone. That could be overconfidence.

I hadn't seen them move quickly or change directions. If they knew Grum and I were there, their behavior didn't show it.

"I have never seen this," Grum confessed.

"Be careful." I edged forward but maintained an arm's length from the monster.

When the leader was half a meter from the circuit board, acid sprayed across the distance, instantly melting a hole.

"Fuck!" I jumped back in complete surprise.

Grum stumbled out of sight, also alarmed.

I edged sideways, tripped over the Walen, and fell face-first on the row of Fyr slugs—that I now understood could shoot acid at least a half meter. Several swiveled their faces my way and grew rigid. Each member of the Fyr army squished into a taller stance and clicked their ring mouths of teeth at me.

Retreating was harder than it should have been. Grum was underfoot no matter which direction I shifted. Too freaked out to apologize or worry about his feelings, I shoved him without looking and followed to relative safety.

The single line of Fyr creatures fragmented. Now there were six, with five of them very interested in us.

"They feed on electricity, Noah," Kayan said. "Your body contains such energy, especially in the nervous system, but in all cells as well. Your specific polarity is one of the reasons I was able to do more for you than the others. It seems the Fyr now recognize this fact."

"When were you going to say something!"

Kayan was gone.

"I freaking hate being part of this ship."

Grum looked at me strangely, then shot his gaze to what showed of Kayan's emergency intervention.

I didn't have time for that. "We need weapons."

"Good luck," Grum said. "Kayan isn't a warship. She's forbidden from making tools of destruction. Don't ask me how or why. I think Wozim is the only member of the crew who remains armed."

"He's just a passenger."

Grum didn't catch, or care about, the distinction, but I was fed up with the freeloader. From what I'd seen of the infamous *warrior*, he could rip these slugs apart with his armored tail or something.

Acid shot toward my visor from two of the Fyr leaders.

I hopped back, terrified but also fascinated at how they stayed in their new lines. What kind of brainless freaks were these things?

More importantly, how could I use that?

"Grum, I have an idea, but you need to be adjusting their route the moment they pass."

The Walen hefted his tool bag. "I'll do my best." Wide-eyed and face flushed with an almost bubblegum pink cast, he appeared both scared and eager to please. "Last time I worked directly on the ship it didn't go well."

My attention went to another row of slugs heading our way. Were they moving faster?

"Retreat to the main deck," Kayan said as though from far away. "They won't follow you there."

Grum heard the broadcast as well but was obviously waiting

for me to make a decision.

My plan had been to change the maze and divert these mindless acid spitters into the farm—whatever the hell that deck was all about. Recent events made that plan feel off, wrong, like something that would only get Grum hurt as he tried to alter their superhighway.

Keeping ahead of them as bait would be the easy part. An annoying spark of imagination reminded me I hadn't seen the acid spitting coming. For all I knew, these things were fast as hell or could grow wings.

In their wake, random slags of wires and organic ship material hung ruined. There were a lot of the creatures, and that had diminished the power generation in this area to the point Kayan no longer relied on it, as though it was gone.

Where would that stop?

This might not feel like saving the galaxy, but a sudden conviction assured me it was the first step.

"Well?" Grum asked.

I could tell Kayan was listening and watching now but remaining silent. Was the ship testing me? Could my thought process be so different that I was the only member of the crew who could get rid of these pests?

"Containment comes first," I said. "Then we'll figure out a permanent solution. Stay out of sight, and don't draw their attention. Keep comms working. When I figure this out, you'll be the first to know."

Grum nodded energetically and hurried away from the ridiculous but terrifying advance of the acid-spitting Fyr slugs. I retreated a bit faster and stayed just out of range. Slugs that blasted at me fell to the back of the line, while others moved forward with mouthfuls of burning hate.

I glanced over my shoulder and twice avoided backing into a dead end as the monsters came after me. "This really sucks."

9

TIME DRAGGED. Or maybe that was my hunger growling at me every ten seconds and the fact that I was dying of thirst. This seemed unfair in light of recent upgrades, but whatever. At least I didn't have to piss down here where every twist and corner seemed part of my future and past.

"Kayan, I need to find a way out of here."

"I hear you, Noah. Relax, and you will see the path," the ship said. "This is an area of myself I know only by intuition."

"I'm trying." Around the next corner there was a hatch in the middle of the floor, the fourth or fifth I'd encountered. Kayan was a big vessel with kilometers of passageways, decks, and crawl spaces. It seemed I was going to visit them all.

Solving the Fyr problem now seemed ambitious. Getting back to my room for a shower and something to eat—not necessarily in that order—were my life goals. Grum hadn't answered comms and I wasn't sure if Montow understood how screwed I was.

I climbed down, trudged forward, and saw the first good news yet. Maybe. If the Fyr creatures gathering was a win. My goal was to locate them, right?

This passage was darker than others I'd explored over the last few hours. It was also wider and lower. Touching the ceiling with my hand seemed necessary to prevent me from bonking my head unexpectedly. Five parallel columns of the monsters stretched into the darkness from whence they'd come. A few looked familiar.

"Nope." I turned and ran. Screw these guys. They couldn't be everywhere.

Each turn revealed more of the ship I'd never seen. The walls followed similar lines, and I was out of the tower maze, but nothing looked, or felt, remotely normal. My feet and back hurt, sure signs I'd been at this far too long. Behind me, the passage was empty.

I leaned against a wall and slid to the floor to rest. Thank God none of my crewmates were here to see this spectacle. My plan had failed, my knowledge of the ship was clearly not what I'd expected, and there were no weapons to use against these things. My frustration mounted until I thought Kayan deserved this infestation. What the actual hell? How could I help if the ship wouldn't provide weapons?

The squishy sound of Fyr movement reached my ears. I

knew it as well as the sound of my own breathing at this point. Fear wasn't the problem, or hadn't been. Other than being startled at a few corners, or when a ceiling hatch had dumped a wave of them near me, there was nothing to worry about.

I'd established the range of their acid strikes and was confident about their top speed. Intelligence was harder to measure, but they weren't inventing star travel on their own— let's just say that. Nothing about this was a crisis, other than being completely lost in a ship I should know as well as my host.

"Kayan," I said. "A little help."

This time, the ship answered. "Apologies, Noah. I fell asleep."

"Seriously?"

"Not as you would experience it, of course. The power drain is escalating. Speak quickly."

"I'm belowdecks, far from where I spent all my time since you rescued me. There are a lot of Fyr, and they meet me at every turn."

"You have been identified as a security system. They won't stop until you're gone, no matter where you hide," Kayan said. "Do you recall what I said about your electrical signature?"

"Yes."

"They have marked you as the weakest link to taking me down."

"Wouldn't they want you alive and making as much power as possible?" I climbed to my feet as the persistent as hell slugs came around the corner. "You're their meal ticket, aren't they?"

"The answer is unknown," Kayan said. "Though some speculate these creatures are corpse incubators. Now that I realized they are the problem, and the Qurk who hunt them are merely the symptom, I have recovered information from my archives."

"I need to get back. At least that will give me access to food and allies." I ran to the next intersection, turned down it, and found one of the slug lines already there. Kicking them out of the way would be incredibly satisfying. The getting melted by acid was the part that would suck.

I retreated as Kayan's voice grew weaker, then I tried three more of the small passages before getting clear of this group. They were coming, and I had no doubt more were closing in on this level. This was what it felt like to be herded over a cliff, or into a hole.

"This wall is the farm, right? I've seen the greenish metal on two other levels."

Kayan answered as though coming back from a distant land. "You cannot enter that portion of the ship for any reason."

"Why not?"

"Do not ask, Noah. There isn't time to understand Hoyon."

I thought that meant there would be time later but decided against arguing the point. My course took me around the section, which occupied a large portion of the ship, if its size was a good indicator. What would be more restricted than the bridge and various power plants this vessel used to travel faster than light?

Thirst tortured me. My stomach was driving me insane with

hunger pains. Exhaustion was my only consistent companion, that and loneliness. Kayan had saved me. Montow and Grum had welcomed me—well, the Walen had. But I was still a long way from home and not likely to get any closer.

Not if I couldn't defeat space slugs.

The next alteration in the passage would require me to descend a short flight of stairs. I bent low enough to get a preview and my hopes soared. An area filled with walkways, high ceilings, and thick towers in the distance came into view. Elevators. I was staring at some kind of lift mechanism.

And there were Qurks, at least three different packs hunting with hit-and-run tactics. The larger animals smashed back groups of Fyr while the rest snatched up mouthfuls of the smaller slugs and sprinted away. Not all of these animals were as cute as Scratch. None were, in fact.

They had adapted spines around their faces and membrane sheets that deflected some of the acid attacks. Apparently disposable, these folds of skin and fur were left behind in chunks.

I really hated these acid spitting monsters.

One of the largest, dark-blue-furred Qurks lashed out with his tail, smacking aside a row of slow-moving killers. He turned like an alpha wolf and snapped his teeth to warn his adversaries. Fyr that were more red than black blasted smoking slime up to five meters in his direction.

"Those things are much bigger than I thought." I muttered other things too, like profanity. Lots of creative new swear words combinations. The Qurk could be as tall as I was. Montow had complained that Scratch would get bigger.

What did you feed something like that, besides Fyr?

"Kayan, we need to have a serious talk about the ark you're running." Laughter hurt my side. I held the cramp and bolted through the only uncontested platform in the huge room. On the way across, I stared up and saw a ceiling full of glowing veins like those in my hands.

In that moment, it felt like I was staring at Kayan.

"There is much you don't know," the ship said. "I am expanded."

"What?"

"Hard to explain, Noah. Please get these fire makers out. Work your way forward, then use the elevators." The message faded.

I was nearly there when I looked into the mouth of an opening. It was across the gap and there was no direct access.

Scratch's family might have left the puppy-kitten behind, but I now doubted it had been by choice. Every one of the creatures I now saw could be related to my furry friend. All ages of the pack stared. Sadness exuded from their downcast expressions, drooping ears, and hunched shoulders. The leader snapped at them, and they ran down to a lower level to hunt.

"Thanks for nothing." I ducked into an elevator that worked as expected. There were no guardrails or buttons to push. "Kayan, are you driving this thing?"

"I modified this portion of my organism according to Montow's suggestion. He is useful. My ability to grow metal alloys, for instance, comes from his inspiration." Kayan tried to send an image, but it looked more like a psychedelic drug trip than anything useful. I kept moving.

Twenty meters up, the elevator stopped.

"That's it?" I demanded.

"Keep moving. This level is dangerous. You can climb once you have the suit," Kayan said.

The doors spiraled open. At least that much was familiar. I was never venturing so far from the main deck after this. Exploration was for the birds. Looking down, I saw some of the other levels. Ring after ring of platforms and balconies showed where I'd been. From this angle, the scene really appeared like the inside of something alive.

I could also see where air currents and other elements were pumped through parts of the ship. I didn't want to be there when it happened. Kayan was dehydrated or something. Humans weren't meant to walk around down there, and neither were Qurks or Fyrs. Something needed to be done, something permanent.

Footsteps sounded in the darkness, unrecognizable for several seconds. Then, while my brain was still processing the noise, Wozim appeared in all his massive glory. He wore armor that covered most of his body. The texture was like an exaggerated version of his skin, and it seemed he could pull on gauntlets, close his helmet, and be sealed inside tighter than an astronaut in an extravehicular suit.

He didn't, of course. Wozim the Tyton was far too badass to secure his helmet. The fearsome humanoid swatted rows of Fyr away like gnats as he crossed the walkway. Nice of him to finally help out. A huge bundle balanced on his left shoulder. He stopped, then dumped it unceremoniously at my feet.

"Tools."

I had nothing intelligent to say. "For what?"

He turned his back and walked away. How he had reached this level or whether I was invited to follow remained a mystery. I followed, but quickly lost him in a maze of horizontal and vertical tubes. The grumpy jerk had probably climbed straight up one of them, but the three I tried brought me back to this level—which was doubly annoying because now I was lugging this bag of mystery gear.

Frustrated with the Tyton, and my situation, and everything in general, I focused on something I understood—taking inventory of Wozim's delivery. Two taps on the seal opened the bundle and revealed…more armor.

"Kayan, what is this?"

The ship's voice pushed through static. "This new layer will better protect you from the unique acid chemistry the Fyr are now launching at you. I've included a more robust mapping protocol, what you would call software. Apologies, Noah. Learning what you need is not easy. Helping you help me has not been a perfect or orderly process."

Each feature I examined showed promise. Having these improvements when we started hunting the Fyr would have dramatically shortened the ordeal. Kayan had been silent much of the time but had been analyzing my misadventure. All my screw-ups down here were biofeedback.

I scrambled into the Kayan attachments, then hopped on my

toes several times just to feel the spring in my legs. "This is pretty good. Thanks."

Wozim could have stayed and explained some of this or helped me eradicate the infestation. I brooded on his bad attitude as I adjusted all the new stuff he'd delivered. What was that guy's story?

Distracted, I allowed a Fyr too close. It sprayed acid. I hopped back, then jumped forward to kick it. "Bye!"

The slug sailed into the darkness below. A few more swipes cleared the area. My upgraded armor protected me, but I felt the pain of being burned. Retreating was still a good option.

"Noah for Kayan, how copy?"

"I don't understand," the ship said.

"It's call and response. You answer, good copy if you can hear me."

"Good copy."

The ship didn't have the UE version of comms traffic down pat, but I was ready to move on. Kayan's interior looked different through the visor. The suit was adjusting to my biological needs, and that meant ever-improving vision. I considered jumping and running to test all the metrics but didn't have control of the environment.

So what if I jumped higher in the suit? The gravity fluctuated. I quit noticing it, but I was on a living spaceship on the other side of the galaxy. Everything I thought I understood needed to be relearned.

I studied the high ceiling and walls as I moved away from my tormentors... and saw each surface pulse. The sensation disoriented me for a second. Other signs appeared once I knew what to look for. The currents of life weren't the same here. At times the ship and I were like one thing. This was one such moment, and it revealed the crux of the matter. Kayan's hull had expanded far beyond normal.

The ship was bloated. The strange, rambling nature of these caverns wasn't natural. Did she know what was causing this or would that be like me diagnosing my own medical conditions?

Hard to say without asking, so I did. "Kayan, are you sick?"

"Very much so, but not in the way you probably mean it."

"Clarification would be nice."

A long time passed as I evaded Fyr and made small changes to the environment to slow them. A closed and locked door here, a sealed hole here, and a few chutes I hoped sent them closer to the farm where they would supposedly be less of a problem.

"My kind were never meant for war. Thousands of years interacting with sentient races passed before we even communicated, and longer before we were of service to one another. Transportation has always been our duty to the citizens of the cosmos. One cargo is more prized than all others."

My head buzzed as I climbed spiral stairs barely large enough to allow my passage. In this section, it seemed Kayan had made changes just for me. Why couldn't I find every passage I'd traveled? Because some of them had closed or contracted to their original size.

There were going to be rules on my next trip belowdecks, and I would be keeping maps for later comparison. Kayan wasn't a box with engines and a helm. She was alive and more complex than anything I'd imagined.

"What is in the farm?" I asked when there were no Fyr or Qurks stalking me.

"That is hard to explain."

"That is the largest part of this vessel, and it's stretching your walls. How much of your power hunger is from the Fyr infestation, and how much is from whatever is going on in there?"

The ship didn't answer.

"It isn't an Earth farm. The translation is insufficient." A pause. "You would be, how do I say, digested if you went there. There was Hoyon, the terrestrial version of what I am. It lives but either can't or won't speak. These creatures can be the center of a planetary ecosystem. It needs a home, and when I complete the delivery, it will take most of the creatures in the farm to a planet. The rest will support my metabolism."

I stopped and just processed that information. "How long have you been transporting Hoyon?"

"Five hundred of your standard years."

"Is that a long trip?"

"I can get the Hoyon to a planet, if you will help me. Delivering such a passenger requires changes," Kayan said. "The requirements may be beyond my capacity to endure."

"Is there another option?" I asked.

"Not at the rate my power is degrading. And I must also warn you the Gavant place extra bounties on my people when carrying such a cargo."

"Start making plans. Tell Montow and Grum what we're doing." I jogged toward a twisting ladder leading upward. The main deck was near. Kayan's sense of things was better established here.

"Montow is my captain, as both of your races understand the job," Kayan said. "Perhaps you should ask nicely."

"Diplomacy is my middle name."

10

"THAT'S BECAUSE YOU'RE WRONG!" My voice hurt from shouting. Kayan's power fluctuated twice while Montow droned on about his experience with the ship and questions about why hadn't Kayan said anything before now. Next time I was cast across the galaxy, I would watch out for guys like this.

Difficult. Stubborn. Pain in the ass.

Montow lowered his gaze but left the sunglasses in place. Something about that decision took the wind out of my sails. A rash, angry man would have flung them away and cursed. The captain was listening to my argument, though he didn't agree.

"So what you are saying, essentially, is that Kayan must travel the far reaches of each solar system to feed on the Oort fungi while Hoyon must inhabit a world closer to the sun, in the green zone as you call it?"

I exhaled, closed my eyes, and opened them in a calmer state of mind. "Yes. That's exactly the problem. Kayan has been scavenging for fuel for longer and longer stretches of time as the demands increase. Meanwhile, the passenger has been growing a miniature world in the hull because it is long past time for this thing to leave the nest."

"An interesting metaphor," Montow said.

Grum looked confused. He started to ask questions but pulled them back. Scratch slept on his lap, preventing him from leaving the bridge even if he wanted to.

I shook off my frustration. "What we need to do seems obvious."

Montow nodded, not something that was easy to see. His neck didn't articulate well in that direction. He had picked up the gesture from me, just like I had a few of his mannerisms now. "Kayan could be stranded deep in the system. That would kill us all."

Nothing was as easy as it seemed. "What do you say, Kayan?"

"Montow's calculations are correct, but I believe I can make the transfer and return to more fertile feeding grounds so long as nothing goes wrong and there are no evasive maneuvers required," the ship said to all of us.

Grum shot up one hand to get our attention. "I checked for Gavant patrols in this system and didn't find anything."

"They could arrive after we have committed," Montow argued.

"A city made of cheese could whip through the system playing big band music," I offered, and started pacing aggressively. "We know the risk, and we understand the consequences of inaction. Ultimately, this is up to Kayan."

"I have made poor decisions on this matter," the ship admitted.

"This is now, not the past. We have a chance and I say we take it."

Montow thought in silence. Grum waited. Scratch pedaled his middle two legs to chase something in a dream.

"I must decide," Kayan said. "Thank you for helping me see what was right before me."

I didn't know what to say, and neither did Montow for all his wisdom and experience with the living vessel. Before long, the course changed, and we were on our way to a world time forgot.

THE TRIP WAS QUIET. Montow didn't hold a grudge after my outburst, but he stayed busy with his thoughts and projects. Grum followed me everywhere, constantly asking questions and offering to help. The guy was never in a bad mood.

What kind of jerk got annoyed by that?

Me, apparently.

"Grum. Stop for a second." I removed the leash he'd attached to Scratch, then held one palm before the animal's nose. This caused him to sit on his back two legs. The Walen had been dragging the furry creature up and down the hall after I asked him to train it.

"He can't get up with one still withered," Grum said.

I considered his observation, though the solution came naturally to me. Pops had been especially good with dogs. All of the Gantz were animal people, with a slight preference to the canine variety. Mimi had her cats, and loved them best, but we all grew protective of the expanded clan as we referred to the farm critters.

Holding my palm toward Scratch, I waited several seconds, then moved it closer. This caused the animal to sit deeper on his haunches. It didn't seem to instinctively use the back two, which were powerful on healthy Qurks.

The thick tail seemed more useful for balance than pushing him to his feet. I watched, learned, and tried to remember this was an alien, not a golden retriever with lynx ears and extra legs.

"What now?" Grum asked.

I stepped back and dropped my hand to my side. Scratch immediately pursued. His front four legs were more than strong enough to get the chunky little dude moving. Before long, he was bouncing after me, looking for a treat or a toy or whatever a Qurk wanted most. I repeated the move several times and it continued to work.

"You try it," I said.

Grum stepped forward, a bit nervous, and thrust out his hand like saluting the galaxy's shortest officer. Scratch squealed and retreated, stumbling all over himself and his numerous legs.

"Try again, but go easy. Just put your hand up there and let him take it or leave it," I said.

"Take or leave what?"

"The command to sit."

"That is what you were trying to do? I guess that makes sense."

Grum watched the Qurk pup-kitten sit and then struggle to get up, one of his legs still not responding to his control. "We'll need to do this a lot until he remembers."

"Bingo. Keep at it, and be patient but firm. If it starts getting to be a competition, do something else. Don't make this a contest of wills. Scratch needs to know how to obey simple commands, assuming he isn't smarter than all of us."

"Why would he be?" Grum asked.

I thought about my answer. "Well, I see him as a pet. So that is how I treat him. For all I know, he may be a star lord."

"Unlikely." Grum stared at the animal as it licked himself.

"Some things never change." I headed for the end of the passageway. "I need to check on Montow and Kayan on the bridge. We should be nearly to the drop-off point."

Grum lost himself working with Scratch. He waved at me absently. "Get rid of the Hoyon. Let me know if you need help."

"Will do." I stepped through the door and waited for it to twist close behind me. Lights were low, as were the temperature and gravity. Kayan was conserving power, not a good sign.

"Status?" I asked.

Montow looked at me, maybe to say he was the captain, not me. But he answered. "Arriving now. Kayan will show us the planet and handle the transfer. We can watch but should shield our eyes."

"Deploying an entire ecosystem to a new world will be the easiest thing we've done so far," I joked, and took my standing seat. Each time I used the thing, the urge was to lean the pod a bit farther back and lower it to something resembling a chair. My settings didn't seem to stick. "What does Kayan have against sitting?"

"If you learn the answer, I will pay you," Montow said. "My people are famous sitters."

"Good to know." The screen came to life. Only one because of the reduced power flow. Below us was a world like Earth, though more barren. A stripe around the middle was green. The water was blue and white and wonderful to gaze upon. Part of me wanted to fly down there and build a shelter, start over on this new world and forget where I was from.

Why banish memories of home? Because otherwise it would be too painful to know I would never return.

Better to remain on the starship and keep looking for a way back.

"The transfer will begin soon," Kayan warned.

Grum entered with Scratch, who looked sad. "I think he wants to go down there with his family, though they abandoned him."

"Can we do that, Kayan?" I asked.

"If you hurry. I will locate Scratch's litter and hold them near an entrance to our section of the ship."

I grabbed the animal and ran, careful to follow nonverbal suggestions from the ship. Correct doors opened. Others remained closed. Before long, I was standing in a sort of launch bay with golden Qurks watching me.

"Shit!"

Grum arrived behind me, completely out of breath. "What?"

"That's what they grow up to be?"

The creatures watching us were of all ages. Most were the size and texture of Scratch, but with six functioning legs and the tendency to group together. The older versions, however, were something else.

Each of the adults appeared less like a human dog and more like a wild cat, an oversized lynx to be specific. Their ears were long and nimble. Some were heavy with muscle, others sleek like a jaguar. Yet, they retained a lot of dog or wolf attitudes.

But what caused me to search for the door was the spike on the end of the leader's tail. It looked hard as steel and dangerous as a blade. Two other adults had slightly less prominent versions but kept theirs down. I assumed the one approaching me was the pack leader.

I placed Scratch on the deck, and he smashed himself to the side of my leg.

The hunter stopped less than an arm's reach from my face, then lowered its head to sniff Scratch. The moment drew out before the regal creature stared at me and mewled "Noah."

"That's my name. Can you talk?"

It stared into my eyes for a long time and returned to its kind. All of the golden Qurks followed toward a portal Kayan held open.

"Once they are through, I will seal the deck and begin the drop," the ship warned.

Scratch followed a few steps, nose stretched out to his pride-pack.

I waited, hoping he would hurry.

One, two, three more steps, and my six-legged buddy stopped and looked over his shoulder.

"Go, be with your family."

Scratch gave me a sad look that broke my heart. Telling him to go be with his own kind felt like betrayal, though I knew it was the right thing to do. This ship wasn't a home for a pack animal like that. He needed to be with his own kind—even after they abandoned him.

A few of the younger Qurks watched from the threshold until an older member of the pack hustled them through the door. She stared long and hard at Scratch and I realized she was holding the door open with her presence. The creatures of the farm understood Kayan was trying to help them now and must have some idea how the portals opened and closed.

She gave me a warning look, then focused on my furry friend.

Who sat down and just looked at her.

Several seconds expired before she turned in disgust and darted after the others. The portal twisted shut. With the Hoyon gone, the Kayan's farm wouldn't have anything like Qurks or Fyrs for a long time. Regeneration of the bio took time, and there was no guarantee she would find another Hoyon to transport.

Scratch stared, whined, then stood to sniff the air.

My heart broke a little more. There was nothing to do but wait.

"The drop has begun," Montow said. "You're going to miss it."

Grum shifted from foot to foot, practically dancing with his desire to race back and watch the view screen.

"Go. I'll catch up."

"Okay. See you there." The Walen ran with never-before-seen alacrity.

Scratch met my eyes.

I squatted down and held one palm forward.

He padded toward me on all six feet. His tail painted excited patterns in the air and he jammed his wet nose into my hand when crashing into me. "S'upp," he huffed.

"And that means?" I scooped the animal into my arms and started for the bridge.

The Qurk made no response, like it had never made a noise that sounded like a word, meaningless as it was. We arrived at the very end of the drop. Rainbows of colors cut through the atmosphere as Hoyon and hundreds of organic pods parachuted to fields and valleys.

"Simply the most amazing thing I have ever witnessed," Montow said. "I could die satisfied. There will be a vibrant array of life there in a hundred years."

He wasn't wrong about the miraculous sight. There wasn't much else to say, so I just watched as long as possible and shared the moment with this strange family I was now a part of.

THIS TIME I explored more carefully and found the passages to make sense. Kayan didn't allow me into the more dangerous sections I'd previously trespassed through to search for the Fyr infestation. With Scratch's help, I confirmed entire colonies of the creatures were gone. From the outside, it seemed the farm was now an average-sized room still barred against our entry.

Farm wasn't the right word. Womb or crèche might have been a better label.

"Noah," Scratch barked.

I bent down to search a vent. A single deceased Fyr lay abandoned. I opened the panel, then flicked it to my friend, who gobbled it down in three bites.

"What am I going to feed you now?"

Scratch didn't answer.

"Let's keep going. Kayan, where do you need us to clean?"

"Follow this passage. There will be large open areas in need of attention. I can't say what that should be, but you may decide when you arrive. This is the first time I have completed a crèche transport of a Hoyon."

"Is that normal?"

"For one who is my age, I am only slightly delayed."

I let that go, thinking it didn't mean the same thing in both our languages. If it did, the situation didn't change so why worry about it? "Have Montow or Grum found any Gavant hunters in this system?"

"Not yet. I will be sleeping if you need me, then we will head for the edge of the heliosphere to search for Oort fungi," Kayan said.

I gave the ship a thumbs-up and thought it knew what I meant through one of its numerous senses. A wall screen came to life with perfectly understandable symbols. Knowing this much of Kayan's language felt natural now. Maps of this level and several others made sense. I headed toward the cavern where I'd last been surrounded by Fyr and wished Grum was tagging along. I wouldn't mind his constant, overhelpful presence.

Kayan had presented all manner of conveyances between levels. Now there were only ladder shafts so narrow my shoulders brushed both sides when I descended. Halfway down, there was something like a rubber valve blocking me.

"Can I push through this, or should I turn back?"

The ship answered quietly, as though returning from a dream in another galaxy. "Traveling between decks must be limited."

"Should I turn around?"

"Proceed. Return another way."

I waited for a detailed explanation and was disappointed. The instructions from the wall screen above had been clear. Tons of residue was left behind and needed to be cleared out. Nothing in the academy had prepared me for janitorial duties of this magnitude. It wasn't hard to imagine the unpleasant nature of what I was about to face.

"Please don't be gross." My left foot pressed through the seal and couldn't be pulled back.

Great. This was a fantastic idea.

"I hope this restores your power flow," I said, then squirmed down the ladder and hoped I wasn't being eaten by a living starship. There had been a discussion about going to the wrong area and getting digested. That had been the farm, or the Hoyon crèche as I now knew it. As curious as I was, maybe I would leave that for another time when I was feeling brave. With luck, the armor upgrades would keep me alive if I made a mistake.

My body, then my head slipped through. On the other side was more of the same, though darker.

"Kayan, it's hard to see. That wasn't a problem before."

No answer.

For a ship linked to my mind and body, Kayan was difficult as hell right now.

"Maybe I'll let my eyes adjust."

Time passed. Boredom set in. The space around me felt smaller and smaller. Every United Earth pilot passed claustrophobia resistance tests. But I was human, and this was the opposite of fun. With no real options, I slowly worked my way down to a portal that opened at my approach.

Stepping into the passageway was at once a relief and a shock. I recognized the place. Now it was barely taller than I was and narrow enough to drag my fingers along both sides. Before, it had towered above me, and I had marveled at the lights pulsing in the textured walls.

That much remained, so I could see. Compared to the ladder shaft, this place was Vegas at night. Not only did I see pulsing veins of energy, I could differentiate colors, rhythms, and shapes. No starry night had been this wondrous.

"Kayan? Can you hear me now or are you sleeping?"

"My body requires rest, especially if we will be jumping often."

"I'll try to let you be. Why would we be jumping? Did Montow detect a Gavant?"

"No, but there is a derelict ship he wants to investigate between this planet and the edge of the heliosphere. In our experience, that always leads to trouble."

"Fair enough." I located tools in one of the walls and began scraping residue toward an airlock. The process was tedious and mind numbing, just what I needed after weeks of being overstimulated. Hours later I was still marveling at how much Kayan had contracted. She spoke occasionally, and explained there was an enormous amount of atmosphere generated and maintained for Hoyon.

Someday I wanted to see what a terrestrial version of Kayan looked like. For now, all I cared about was helping my ship recover and then figuring out if and when I could ever go home.

11

"STANDING ROOM ONLY." I strode onto the deck, clean from my shower and rested from a full, dreamless night of sleep. Scraping out corridors belowdecks improved my mood more than it should have. Kayan was practically glowing with health now. I didn't waste time pondering our neural connection. Both of us were alive and well. What else was there to say?

Grum looked around at the expansive bridge. "There is plenty of room."

I waved the comment away. Scratch barked half words, then retreated beneath rows of organic computer banks. His new favorite hiding place was hard to reach, even when I flopped on my belly and tried to pull the creature out—so I'd quit trying. He really liked squirming behind a panel at the front of the bridge. Someday, I hoped to learn what was back there. The ship offered zero help. In fact, it almost seemed she was conspiring with the little fur ball.

The workspace was tailored to our needs. All it would take for an entire crew to use it was Kayan activating additional pods and stations to go with them. A smile crossed my face as I activated organic touch screens and typed a mixture of English and Kayan symbols.

Don't overthink it, Noah. Just do the work. Occasionally, if I let my peripheral vision linger behind what I was reading, I noticed symbols I thought had been English when my eyes had passed over them.

The door spiraled open behind me. Wozim ducked through the entrance and slid his eyes around the room like he would kill anything ready to attack him. Seven feet tall, thick with muscle, and covered in tough, armor-like skin, the man was at least as intimidating as I remembered. The armor had been put away. I wasn't sure if that made him more or less shocking to observe. His tail dragged behind him like he'd forgotten about it. From time to time, I thought it moved of its own volition—like it was watching his back and was ready to go all stabby-stabby on someone. Had it spotted Scratch? The six-legged bundle of trouble was certainly watching it and keeping his distance.

"Wozim," Montow said.

The Tyton made a *what the fuck* gesture, hand wide open and fingers spread with his palm facing him. Montow nodded like this was the politest greeting in the galaxy.

There was no acknowledgement of me or Grum. The Walen seemed to be sweating with tension. I thought the young man both looked up to and feared the Tyton. The dude was intimidating.

His horns pointed at the view screens when he looked that direction. Kayan had three activated, still on power rationing but not quite as strict as before. The Tyton studied them carefully.

I waited for him to voice his opinion about the derelict ship.

And was disappointed.

Of course.

"You will grow accustomed to Wozim," Montow said. "This ghost ship hasn't lost atmosphere, and there are trace power readings. Someone could be alive inside. Odds are the crew abandoned the vessel after suffering more damage than they could repair. This thing isn't making it to port. Scrappers will eventually disassemble it where it is. Easier. Fewer questions."

Kayan orbited the vessel and recorded images for review. I spotted defunct engines and slipshod repairs to airlocks. "Did someone force their way onto the ship?"

"There was a battle. This vessel lost." Montow dedicated the third screen to scanning the system. "There are no ships close."

"Do the Gavant have stealth technology?"

All three of my companions stared at me in horror.

Montow recovered first. "If they have such a thing, we do not know about it."

"I'll go," Grum said.

"Wozim and Noah should conduct the search. They are best suited for exploring an unsecured warship that could lose atmosphere at any moment. There may be power, but again, it shouldn't be trusted." Montow pulled up maps and schematics of the derelict ship. "These are the standard designs for a Gavant vessel of that size and class."

"Where are the guns?" I asked.

"It was built for science, not combat." Wozim's voice caught me off guard. Deep and menacing, it sounded more powerful for being unexpected.

Montow answered my question, barely showing he was perturbed by the Tyton's interruption. "There were weapons on this thing, but whoever abandoned it, salvaged those and probably anything else they could. Some of that damage is from the crew taking what they could retrofit to a new ship or sell."

I nodded along and studied images of the ship, especially the airlocks.

"Will you go, Wozim? It is time you earned your passage." Montow's tone was firm, but nonconfrontational. With a guy like the Tyton, I understood why he strove for diplomacy.

Wozim grunted and left the bridge.

Which annoyed me. The guy wasn't that special. I faced Grum. "Looks like it's you and me, kid."

"I am not technically a juvenile."

"Figure of speech. What do you say, Montow? Can Grum and I handle this, or do you want to come?"

"My place is on our ship. And I am no longer as young as I once was."

I clapped my hands together. "Great. Let's do this. Grum, where is your extravehicular suit?"

"That is a word unknown to me." He worked on the translation until he understood. "Oh, yes. My outfit is not part of

Kayan as yours is. But it works. Montow built it and taught me to use it successfully."

I stole a glance at the captain and thought the man had concerns. "Everything good?"

Montow spread both hands. Some of his hair was showing gray today. "Perhaps this is a good time to practice. If you encounter resistance, return and I will send Wozim to handle it."

"Works for me. What about weapons? Is there an armory on this ship?"

"There is not," Kayan said. "Only Wozim bears that burden, and he is unlikely to share his sacred tools of destruction."

A funny feeling grew in my gut. The derelict Gavant science ship didn't appear to be a combat zone, but what could I really see from here? Acid slugs had terrorized me for days. What else could the galaxy have to offer in the way of things likely to render Noah Gantz dead?

"Let's gear up," I said to Grum.

"Yes of hell!"

"Close enough." I patted the Walen on the shoulder. "Stay close to me."

Grum nodded with far too much enthusiasm.

"I will assist with the pre-mission checks, then return to the bridge," Montow said.

MONTOW KNEW what he was doing. We went over every inch of Grum's space suit and compared notes. The design was Walen, but it was built by the captain and the ship. The end product was shaped like the picture in the design schematic. So that was good.

Following instructions.

Check.

Materials varied and there were a few creative workarounds that reminded me the Hellenger was a ship engineer, almost a surgeon in the case of Kayan, before he was a captain or a leader. What were the three tubes connected from the back of the helmet to Grum's backpack? I couldn't see a purpose. The air mixture came up through the bottom of the helmet. There was no need for anything to be transferred from his back.

Mystery pieces aside, it was masterfully done with nothing left out. The extra tubes wouldn't bother me. I leaned close to Montow. No need to upset the kid, but I had to ask someone. "What are these three thingies?"

"Snacks."

"Seriously?"

"As a catastrophic loss of atmosphere and gravity."

"That's pretty damn serious." A backpack full of tasty treats seemed pretty dang appealing right now. "Why don't I get snacks?"

"Ask Kayan. But finish your inspection first. Grum is getting impatient."

I went over the Walen suit a final time, then gave the captain a thumbs-up. "You do good work, sir."

Montow put away his tools as Grum moved around the room to test his gear. "My people train for one job in their lives. I was forced to perform in several vocations. Care for ships like Kayan requires a lifetime of commitment and a diverse set of skills."

I waited for more of the Hellenger's explanation.

"My decision to study living starships was not popular with my family. It is an academic career because there are so few of them. Years passed after my examinations, and no ship arrived in need of a crew. I traveled, hitchhiked you call it, across the planet of my birth, and then more and more systems in search of knowledge. In the end, I gave up on the pursuit and was assigned to a mono-rail system on Leesta 4. There was a terrible disaster on the same day I moved my family to the city." His face darkened. "Afterward, I had to board a Kayan to save someone who would become a friend but wasn't at the time."

"Was your family okay?"

"Yes. They did well afterward."

His answer was weird, off somehow. I wasn't sure what to make of it.

He changed the subject. "The young man I saved became a good friend. We learned that my Kayan education was indeed academic and inadequate. He also became frustrated that I wouldn't make him into an adventurer."

"You're talking about the Grum-ster."

"Yes."

Grum heard the last part and threw up his hands like he'd scored a goal or something. "What were you talking about? I wasn't listening."

"Nothing important." Montow waved the matter away with his normal brusqueness.

I saw the mannerism in a different light. "I'm sorry about your family, but I'm glad you were there for Grum."

He turned his soup can toward me and stared. For an instant, it seemed he would share even more. His change of heart was easy to read in his expression, even with the dark glasses. "Do your people do such things?"

"Oh, for sure." I floundered for a safe topic. "Walkabouts are totally a thing humans do. Usually disguised as a trip to Europe paid for by their parents and student loans. Always a lot of amazing stories afterward."

"Thanks, both of you," Grum said, then started walking back and forth to test out the suit. "This feels better than when I tried adjusting it myself."

Scratch sat watching, head cocked to one side, looking up at the Walen spacewalker. He seemed to be figuring out why the voice was familiar but the appearance was different.

Montow and I continued to talk as we watched the enthusiastic young man hop and skip. Scratch barked melodically and joined in.

"Mine is not a life any Hellenger parent wants for their children. Grum's story, well, you must ask him, but be prepared to hear the long version." He motioned toward me. "Put on your suit. I will correct your mistakes and explain them as I go."

I stepped into the clamshell armor and closed it. Each section was adjusted by the energy my movements generated. Extending my arms overhead caused other sections to fall into place and line up with my biometrics. Squatting completed the lower half of the tweaks. The extra layer of protection Wozim had delivered remained, and the software boost had the internal aspects of my gear optimized. Without waiting, I ran through internal systems checks and made certain Kayan could hear me.

Montow stared.

"What?"

"Your suit requires no adjustment. Your tool selection is adequate." He touched the collection of pry bars and cable spools clipped to the back of my armor. "I will be on the bridge to monitor the crossing." He left without another word. Not sure what just happened, I busied myself checking the codes Kayan shared in the HUD of the suit's helmet, then inventoried pry tools, cutting torches, and other levers I might need to get inside places the Gavant shipbuilders wanted to keep me out of. The visual display was grainy but fairly consistent today. We were still working at sharing images.

Crazy.

I was sharing headspace with a living starship. What could go wrong?

"What did you do to him?" Grum asked as he tried to scratch his nose inside of his bubble helmet. "Montow normally likes the pre-mission stuff, especially if it involves lots of tech."

"Not sure, but I think he assumed I would need a lot of help." Kayan arranged lights and colors inside my visor to point the way. A few months ago, I would have thought someone slipped acid in my beer. Now, visual chaos was my new normal. I stared right through it most of the time, like tinted sunglasses.

The ship's main airlock wasn't hard to locate. It was the same portal I'd used to go outside and observe her feeding routine.

The main deck was large and versatile. Day by day, I realized how much the ship expanded, contracted, and shifted elements around.

Grum stared. "Will that fit me?"

"It will adjust to your shape." I knew the statement was true when I spoke. Kayan was less and less chatty since the delivery of Hoyon. Part of me wondered if that was due to my increasing self-sufficiency. The idea of going solo was a new kind of lonely I wasn't ready for.

Grum waggled his hands at me.

"What is that?"

He did it again.

"Do you need to pee or something?"

He made a face that looked ridiculous inside his helmet. "You do this." He gave me a thumbs-up. "I make this face to mean the same thing."

I was learning so much. Wozim saluted with an FU gesture. Grum made an electrocuted gummy worm dance with his fingers to show he understood me. Montow's neck was the same diameter as his head, and he was rarely more expressive than a rock. I cataloged it all and wondered if nonverbal languages would be more complicated than written and spoken versions before we found safety.

"Let me go first, then just listen to Kayan and Montow. This small airlock is easy due to its size and design. Nothing could be simpler. Just put your back against it, wait for it to close around you, then wait for it to open to the void. Grab the hull right away and hook in with a safety line. No sense taking needless risks. We triple checked everything. It will be fine. Once outside, I will fly us across to the ghost ship. It's not far."

"Okay. Too bad we didn't get to see Wozim do this. He just wears his armor and jumps. The guy scares me, but that is what Tytons do, I guess."

"I've seen it."

"Really? He rarely puts it on. There was this one time when pirates tried to steal Kayan. Wozim had them all running back to their ship in terror—the ones who lived."

"How many did he kill?" I asked.

Grum did the waggly finger thing again, then shrugged as an afterthought.

"Great. Follow me." I cycled through the airlock nearly as easily as passing through an interior ship door. There was a slight delay as air pressure was checked. Outside I focused on my job. This wasn't a good time for stargazing. Grum might need help.

The airlock sealed, and if not for the ship instincts I shared with Kayan, it would be impossible to find. I made a mental note not to leave Grum out here by himself.

"Please look behind you, Noah," Kayan said.

I turned carefully and gazed across the twenty-meter gap between my ship and the abandoned Gavant vessel. Something was off about the scene.

"Wait, and you will see."

Sparks flicked on the surface of the Gavant hull, disappearing so quickly they seemed a part of my imagination. A moment later, electricity roped out like the arms of a glowing tapestry. It took me a while to understand what I was seeing.

There was oxygen venting near the ship, just enough to briefly support sparks. Beyond that, waves of electricity behaved differently from what I was accustomed to in atmosphere.

I could have watched the spectacle for hours. Before this mission, I had been a total adrenaline addict—all action, all the time. Now I wanted to soak in the mystery of this scene as long as possible.

Some of the twisting orange-and-blue field went past me and was absorbed by Kayan's exterior without apparent effect.

"Will that be a problem for us?"

"No. It looks more intense than it is. Grum's equipment should hold up well, but most of his suit is made of inorganic parts," Kayan said. "My castoffs and various materials forged or gathered by Montow were combined to make passenger protective gear. Your words, not mine."

"Uh, sure. PPG? I don't remember making that one up. Is Montow in this conversation?"

"No. Should he be?"

"I would like his input. He built Grum's suit and has more in common with us little bipeds than you do. No offense."

"None taken. You will know when I decide to pout."

"Can't wait."

Time passed before Montow and Grum were included in our chat.

"Are you having second thoughts about this mission?" Montow asked. "Wozim assures me that you could handle this alone. Grum could remain on board but ready as backup."

"Well if Wozim says." I let the statement hang and none of my friends reacted to my obvious sarcasm. "Is he here?"

"No. Wozim is meditating over his weapons," Kayan said.

"Seems useful." I shifted my attention between the airlock and the target craft. Hanging out in the void didn't cause as much stress as it used to, or as it should now. Respect for the ruthlessness of space was the first thing they had taught during advanced EVA training. "Grum, what do you think?"

I imagined him raising the thick plastic screen in the sleeve of his left arm. "The specs say my suit is insulated against electricity. Am I missing something?"

"We don't know what is causing the malfunction," I said. The last thing I wanted was to drag him into a dangerous situation without all the facts.

"That's to be expected, right? The ship was abandoned for a reason."

My eyes measured the gap between ships. "Why don't we land on the target and seal one of our larger airlocks to this airlock?" The question was for Kayan and I knew the answer. Risk versus reward. Why put the entire vessel in danger?

"Could be a trap," Montow said. "And that just isn't what Kayan does when we salvage."

"I am cautious," Kayan said. "History has not been kind to my people."

"Grum, it's your call. I'll go alone if you're having second thoughts."

The airlock began to cycle. I edged away from the opening

but kept my hold on Kayan's hull. A pause followed, then the exterior seal parted.

Grum lay against the hull, arms down at his sides. Kayan had turned him to face outward, which I hadn't expected. My advice had been to crawl, though that was much harder to do in low gravity than it seemed.

Low, not zero, gravity.

Kayan maintained the field outside of her hull. That was interesting and not something I remembered from my first space walk. I wondered if Montow knew of this feature, and I made a note to discuss it later. Right now, I wanted to focus on my partner for this mission. Losing friends in the void was bad form. Definitely to be avoided.

Grum reached forward, reminding me of a space corpse rising from the galactic grave. Light winged off his visor, which was reflective as a mirror now. He made his way to one side and clung to the ship like he was having second thoughts.

"You all right?" I asked.

"I think so. Everything is big out here." He reached behind his back and pulled one end of a safety cable free. "Can I use this, or will that cause problems if that electrical source is more powerful than it appears?"

"Kayan?"

"The risk is unknown, Noah. Take him across without the cable. I can fire a recovery line to you if necessary," the ship said.

"I haven't tested the maneuvering jets." My heart rate increased. The derelict ship appeared menacingly near but also too far away to reach without a miracle. It was like judging the gap between two buildings before jumping across. I'd never done that, but kids were kids, and I had made some leaps over creeks and crevasses that would have made my parents cringe. The obstacle course in basic training had been no joke. I could do this.

"All will be well." Kayan vibrated the controls inside the suit to get my attention. Situated like perfectly fitting gloves, each steering pad felt right. Confidence grew almost as quickly as my fear. "Screw it. Grab on, Grum. We're going for a ride."

I focused on the point Kayan thought best for landing. Faint grids appeared across the interior of my visor to help me aim and track my course. This wasn't the same as the living ship inserting images into my mental landscape, but regular manipulation of light and dark in the transparent material that sealed the front of my helmet.

Grum took hold of the tow line and waited.

"Here goes nothing." I jumped, sailed out two meters, and snapped back.

Grum held the cable with one hand and Kayan's exterior with the other. Whiplash was my reward for being part of this safety chain.

"Don't let go! Reel me in and we'll try again," I said.

"Sorry." Grum hooked his feet, then dragged me in hand over hand. "I forgot to release my grip."

Annoyed, I let him pull until we returned to our starting point. The controls felt as though they were born to me, so I could have made his life easier. It took a moment to understand why I was angry.

My safety wasn't an issue. Kayan would take care of me this near the ship. Grum was the dumbass who would get himself killed if he screwed up. Right now, I had two friends and would prefer they both remained alive.

"Take a second to gather yourself," I said in a much calmer and more reasonable voice than I felt. He complied, and I took my own advice. In with the good air, out with the bad. A yoga master I was not, but all pilots had ways of ratcheting down the excitement. Cool and calculating, that was the way to fly.

"Thank you," Grum said. "Should I detach the safety cable now?"

"Yes. I've got you. Don't worry about drifting away."

"Why doesn't Kayan give us all suits like that?" Grum said as he worked. "I've always wondered what is different about you. Me, Montow, and even Wozim are treated like passengers. You're the ship's most honored guest, almost like family or something. It's weird. Especially since you are the most recent arrival."

"I think it is the bond between rescuer and rescued." It wasn't my best theory, but it was a place to start. The feeling of attachment was real and that had to be enough right now.

Grum chuckled. "Like you and me then."

"I didn't save you. This wasn't a fatal mistake. We just look like idiots. And I might have peed a little."

That got a bigger laugh than expected, and I was pretty sure Grum and I were the best of friends again. Snapping at people wasn't my style. This space walk must be worrying me more than I was admitting.

"I'm ready," he said.

I physically checked every part of his suit and everything he was touching. "Yep. You're good to go. Hang on."

This time when I pushed off from Kayan's exterior, we sailed straight for the nearest hatch on the Gavant vessel. Grum made a melodic sound of awe as we experienced one of the harmless energy fields leaking from the dark ship. I paid attention to every detail. Who knew when I would experience something this fantastic again.

12

WE TOUCHED down next to the hatch. I spread one palm on the metal surface and magnetically locked us in place.

Grum found handholds and moved aside to give me room. "I can help with the pry tools if the codes don't work. But Kayan is pretty good with Gavant codes. It's true as the stars."

"Yeah. Let's hope so. I'd rather not break a sweat during the entire mission." Locating a control panel took time but wasn't difficult. I suspected counterboarding measures would be more proactive than locks on doors. This was United Earth thinking, of course. Our ships tried not to lock work crews outside during emergencies. And there was always an emergency.

"No power here," I muttered.

"Use one hand to provide the energy flow, and the other to enter the codes," Kayan said.

I could practically feel Montow listening and watching but

didn't ask for his advice. Our ship knew about other ships, even if they weren't the organic variety. Moments later, the circular keypad glowed with a faint light. I entered symbols I didn't understand. Trust the sentient, living starship, that was my motto.

"Well done, Noah. It should open soon. Take your time. We don't want to lose you or Grum," Kayan said.

"That is normally my line," Montow said, though he didn't sound bothered.

I let the ship and the captain talk. Working the code was easy, but prying open the hatch took all my strength and the longest pry tool I'd fastened to my back. Grum watched me heave against the bar for several minutes. All conversation died as I labored to move armor three feet thick on guide rails. The steel appeared to be high quality. I assumed it was layers of alloys bonded together for added strength.

United Earth ships weren't this tough. We didn't have warships, not like this monster. I said as much.

"That is only a science vessel," Montow said. "We talked about that. Why would you believe this is designed for conflict and destruction?"

"This hatch looks indestructible, and I can see there is a ballast layer with additional armor and sensors. We'll need to crawl for three or four meters to reach the actual airlock," I said, then handed Grum the bar for him to attach to my back.

"What exactly is your point?" Montow asked.

I didn't want to explain because that would lead to imagining a war between the Gavant and United Earth. We wouldn't stand a chance. No one on my home world thought anyone would be insane enough to fight in the void. Every preparation was for planetary defense or assault. "This science vessel is expecting to be attacked. Ship-to-ship combat is for lunatics. No one wins in the void."

"Agreed," Montow said.

"Good thing my people were on the other side of the galaxy." Saying it wasn't reassuring.

"Hmph. There is a saying that distance is not a defense in the Gavant realm."

Freaking great. "Follow me, Grum." I crawled into the tube, fully aware that the gravity here was missing. Was that because the ship was offline, or because the Gavant's gravity manipulators didn't compare to Kayan's?

I would either find out or I wouldn't. It was time to explore, not solve every mystery in the universe. First things first—that was the way to stay alive and learn from our discoveries.

The airlock at the end of the crawlway was small, but large enough for Grum and I to crowd inside. "Can you tell me what the Gavant protocol is for this?"

"It is designed for one engineer or soldier at a time," Montow said. "Boarding actions rarely focus on these narrow entrances for that reason. Of course, for some of their more ruthless assault teams, all of this is pointless. They cut into the ship where they want and leave their targets wrecked."

"Can't imagine that." And I couldn't. The idea of hanging out on the hull of this ship for five weeks with a cutting torch wasn't appealing. They surely had faster methods, but I didn't know them. Hopefully, I never would.

We manually cycled the airlock and tested the atmosphere once the seal was in place. The process was only comforting because it was more like UE technology than Kayan's organic systems and structure. I pointed to one side of the small receiving room, and then stood on the other. Grum did as he was told but didn't seem to understand my insistence.

"Don't group up. That makes us one target."

He looked around and nearly fell. "Are there still Gavant troopers here?" He swallowed hard inside his suit. The view of his face was almost comical. "I'm ready for them."

"Assume the worst and be prepared for anything," I said, then faced the door—without a weapon. That was something I needed to figure out. Kayan was either unwilling or unable to arm me. "My suit says there is minimal atmosphere and fair gravity here. Confirm?"

Grum worked his equipment, then started to take off his helmet.

I held up one hand to stop him. "Can you use local air and leave your helmet on?"

"Oh. Yes. That's smart. Quicker to go back on the bottle that way when everything goes wrong."

"Exactly." I pulled my flashlight and shone it into the only passageway available to us from here.

Grum tapped his helmet until two beams of light stabbed forward from each side of his large, bubble-shaped visor.

I cringed but said nothing. My helmet had a similar option,

but I didn't want Gavant troopers to shoot at the light mounted to my head. How to explain that tactical principal to Grum without freaking him out further? It probably wasn't possible.

"Do like this," I said simply. "Save the helmet light for later. I'll tell you when it is okay to use it."

Grum complied.

"Also, don't shine the light when you're behind me. That will turn me into a silhouette for anyone waiting for us."

He lowered his too-bright beam. "I can see pretty well from yours, at least for now." He shut his off and followed me.

"Exactly."

"You don't like being a silhouette?"

"No."

"What are we looking for?"

"People, then equipment. Crew members can help or hurt us and are the least predictable. Once we know the ship is abandoned and safe for us to traverse, we can search for Montow's list of parts," I said.

"This passageway is long."

He was right. I followed the slight curve and searched for doors, hatches, and intersections. One aspect was reassuring. The dimensions felt human, though I didn't know what a Gavant looked like.

"Have you seen a Gavant, Grum?"

Nothing.

I looked back.

"Oh. You didn't observe my nod. I did the upward thumb thing as well—all four of them. Yes. I have seen Gavant people.

They are sometimes taller than you, though not bigger if that makes sense. You remind me of them, except for the eyes and hair and shape of the head."

I laughed. "Exactly the same but totally different."

"Yes. You get it." Grum faced backward and used his light without explaining what he was looking for. I didn't mind. Checking our back trail wasn't wrong.

"Good work. Grum. We've got this," I said. "Doesn't look like anyone is home."

HOURS LATER, I regretted the statement. We found no evidence of life on the Gavant science ship, other than the barely survivable atmosphere. That felt intentional. Someone was here and wanted to stay alive as long as possible and was conserving resources.

Where had everyone gone? Whoever caused the drag marks probably knew. I counted dozens of blood trails where a live body had dragged a dead or dying body—mostly to the shuttle bays but a few unlucky souls had gone out one of the airlocks.

I compared the maps Montow and Kayan provided and found them reasonably accurate. We made updates and included notes on details that might seem important later.

Progress was slow, and as expected, the atmosphere was dangerously inconsistent. After the first level, we frequently resorted to bottled air. Three quarters of what I felt comfortable using on this mission was gone. Grum confirmed his remaining supply was slightly less but still sufficient to continue.

This felt like a scenario out of the Academy. What would a young commander do with an energetic and gung ho enlistee determined to soldier on despite the danger? The answer was, be diplomatic but firm. In training scenarios, this worked well. I knew from my enlisted time in Security Forces, and from my combat flights three years later, that reality generally screwed everything up. Individuals reacted unpredictably. Changing circumstances basically proved the universe was unfair as hell.

None of my instructors had anticipated I would be dealing with aliens on the far side of the galaxy. They probably could never appreciate how incredibly brave and loyal Grum was. An image of them staring dumbly at my friend, trying to figure out who or what he was, amused me but I kept the mental images to myself.

"We'll need to start transferring material soon," I said. "Head back to the airlock and contact Montow. Do not vary from the passageways we've already checked."

"What are you going to do?"

"Explore a bit further, and then I'll be right behind you. There is one thing I want you to accomplish more than anything else, and that is stay calm to conserve your oxygen."

He examined the plastic-covered screen attached to the left arm of his suit. Reading his expression was difficult with the bulbous helmet casting glare from my light, but I thought he was appropriately concerned for his situation.

"I don't have that much left, now that you call my attention to it," Grum said.

"Move slowly. Stay at the airlock. We can always make two trips. No need to be a hero," I said, then watched him go. It was a perfect opportunity to check my own VO2 use. So far, I was doing well. My peers back home would give me high marks for remaining cool and collected.

Honesty mattered, so I determined I would in fact only check the rest of this passageway, just as I had implied to Grum. I loaded the scenario in my favor, however, because this section of the ship seemed important. If I were the sole survivor, this was where I would shelter.

Controlling my breathing as I moved slowly, I cleared the final room, which appeared to be the bridge or some sort of control room. No station retained power, and there were no notes left by the crew or captain. Without downloading the computer, I doubted I would know what had happened here.

I reviewed video from my search thus far. There had only been two bodies, both extremely dead. One not dragged to a shuttle or an airlock had been Gavant. It was hard to evaluate his dimensions or features due to the way he had fallen, but the man's visor had been transparent and I had used my light. Definitely a dude, if I was any judge. Dealing with aliens gave me a headache. Assumptions were dangerous, but also natural.

His body had been stiff, from rigor mortis or exposure or some trick of their biology I didn't know. The power indicator on the side of his helmet was dark. Basically, he matched the description Grum had provided earlier—humanoid.

The other body had been a race my companion had called Altion. Again, the neck was slightly longer than it should be. There was a cast to his skin, an unreal blue sparkle around lavender eyes that stared at me accusingly.

Maybe the first condition was asphyxia but I didn't think so. There was a pattern to it that extended down the face like make-up or a metallic tattoo. Learning about them would be easier if I could find one alive.

Disappointed, I was making a half-ass attempt to check the rest of the closets near the bridge when I found the last body. Initially, I thought it might be one of the Altion according to the short stature and delicate physique. A little closer I saw a graceful, exotic face through the visor and thought it was woman. The other corpse had a masculine jaw and hard features. This one did not. I leaned close, aware I could have this all wrong.

"You barely look dead." My heart fell. "I wish I'd been here an hour earlier."

She raised her hand and I jumped back, launching myself with too much force in the weak gravity, and slammed the back of my helmet against the far wall.

I twisted to correct my course and managed to send myself into a corner like a billiard ball before throwing out my arms and legs akimbo in search of a surface to arrest my movement.

The moment my left palm touched the wall, it locked on with magnetic force, whipping the rest of my body in a tight circle. I put all four limbs against surfaces—two on the wall panel, one on the floor, and another on a chair. Stopping the madness was my priority, not looking cool.

Noah Gantz, human pretzel! Get your tickets now!

Heart beating madly, I looked toward the closet and saw only darkness. Was the person inside injured or hiding? Could this be a fanatic ready to die in combat? Most importantly, did this courageous maniac have a weapon, because I didn't.

"Did anyone see that?"

The sound of laughter filled my headphones. Apparently, Kayan, Montow, and Grum all had front row seats today. Of course they were watching when I spazzed out.

The captain regained his composure first. "We're here, Noah. Be careful. That figure, from what we saw for half a second, was wearing a Gavant uniform. Nonmilitary, but that doesn't always mean much with them. Could be a rebel, or a loyal officer sworn to fight to the bitter end. Oh, you can get down now. What are you, a Qurk?"

"I'm on my way," chuckled Grum.

I set my feet on the deck and cautiously approached. "Stay where you are. You don't have enough air for this if it goes bad."

"I am refilling now," Grum said, speaking far too quickly. "Kayan sent across an umbilical that I have plugged into my helmet."

"Great. But I still want you to stay where you are. Everyone, get off the radio and wait for me. I don't want to have to fight for airtime when I start screaming for help," I said.

The Altion was still on the floor when I reached the threshold. She held up her weight with one thin arm and reached forward with the other. Each motion mimed scooping air toward her helmet.

I visually scanned the small space and realized she had been hiding for a while. Maybe she had slept to conserve energy. My interest had startled both of us. A tank with a tube that seemed to belong to one of her helmet attachments lay near the door.

I picked it up and carefully offered it to her.

She fumbled the air tank, tried again, and finally attached it to her helmet. Relief took over her body language when she leaned against the wall to breathe deeply.

"Can you hear me? Can you understand me?"

Her helmet visor was transparent but still caught quite a bit of glare from my flashlight. I adjusted the direction of the beam but still couldn't see her expression well. That first impression of her, before I became a billard ball, stuck in my brain. The woman wasn't human, but neither was she strange, if that made sense.

"You talk like an idiot, but I know your words," she said. "Fortunately for you, I have a diplomacy rating and can translate obscure tongues in the field. Even when they speak moron."

"Fantastic. One intergalactic dumbass at your service. I'm going to get you help. How much air do you have?"

"Less after I talked to you. Your attack wasted too much."

"I wasn't attacking you. How am I going to do that with no weapons?"

She shook her head in disgust. A look of concentration grew in her expression. Her chest rose and fell more rhythmically.

"Noah! I did something wrong. The umbilical took my air

instead of giving it to me," Grum left his channel open for several seconds as he fumbled for a solution. The silence that followed felt ominous.

I heard both Montow and Kayan attempting to call the Walen, to no avail.

"What's going on? Can I fix it from here?" I asked.

Grum didn't answer, though his line was open. He gasped and begged. None of his words were understandable. I heard the distinct sound of his helmet clacking into things as he staggered into walls—then fell hard.

Kayan answered. "There is a simple valve he needs to reverse, but he won't listen. Oxygen deprivation is affecting him. You will have to go and do it yourself. Once there, you can fill a tank for the Altion. Tell her to remain where she is."

"Stay where you are. I've got another crisis but will bring back an air bottle."

Her eyes screamed at me, but she was smart enough not to waste her breath. I speed walked back to the airlock, aware that I didn't have an unlimited supply of oxygen either.

13

"You've got to admit I made good time," I muttered as I found Grum with one hand tangled in an important-looking bundle of wires and the other gripping the umbilical Kayan had sent across. "Okay, next time let's just bring that with us from the start."

"Good idea," Montow said.

Kayan subtly changed the lights in my visor. The ship had done this before. Now I realized it was a sign of embarrassment. The ship wasn't perfect. Anyone could make simple mistakes. I needed to stop relying on living technology and aliens. Assuming they were smarter and better than me because they were strange was going to get us all in trouble.

I found the switch and flipped it.

Grum started gasping, then sat up. He reached for the air supply, but I caught his hand.

"Stop. Listen. Breathe slowly and pay attention. I'm untangling these wires and don't have a lot of time."

He babbled in his untranslated language.

"Focus, Grum. I need you."

He stared like we'd never met. "I will be honored to help."

"You're a mechanic. Straighten out these wires and put the airlock in order. I need to fill a bottle and take it to the Altion."

He jumped to his feet. "The Altion! Did she have a weapon?"

"Only her tongue."

His eyes, though I thought it was impossible, went even wider than normal. "That sounds horrible. What does she do with it that is so dangerous?"

"Figure of speech. Get to work, Grum. I will be right back and will need your help."

"You have it now and always." He looked at the wires in his death grip. "Uhm, these are holding the airlock together."

I followed his gaze and saw a gap in the wall and darkness beyond. Grum had woven whatever he could find across the opening and tightened it down to keep this part of the ship together. This was why all the remaining atmosphere had leaked from the ship.

"How did that happen?"

He shrugged like a pro. His human body language was improving. "This is from before we arrived. I didn't understand how bad it was until I came back. Once I had the umbilical hooked up, I went to work and must have flipped the switch the wrong way. Got distracted, you know. I can't pull the walls together because of this tangle."

I watched his dexterous fingers twisting apart wires. He worked fast. There was music in the way he moved. The sight of his double opposing thumbs doing the impossible distracted me.

"That's amazing," I said.

"Taking me too long. There must be a faster way but I can't see it."

The solution appeared obvious. "Back up."

He released the section that was preventing him from pulling two parts of the wall together. It was attached to a hunk of equipment that had fallen or been knocked aside, and dragged other pieces out of place. Each time the gravity pulsed, it gave another tug to what was left of the structure.

I drew a small work knife, measured once, and cut through the middle of the knot. The offending glob of metal and parts fell away.

"Oh. That worked." Grum immediately reconnected cables and cords, then cranked them down in the middle to pull a section shut.

"Hold the ship together until we get back." I filled air tanks that had come with Kayan's lifeline.

"You say that like it will be easy."

"Counting on you." I pointed at him, then left in a hurry.

With a bottle of air for me and another for the survivor, I ran to the bridge, all the time wondering what I'd gotten myself into. Grum was going to follow me everywhere now. Hopefully I would earn that blind trust. The young man was holding the ship together, keeping us all alive a bit longer while I ran around like a chicken with my head cut off.

The bridge looked the same. I'd half expected it to be overrun with strange creatures and missing a wall. Why not just shoot a comet through here? Make this day complete.

The closet door was open. Darkness ruled its interior. I lit it up with my flashlight. The woman lazily shielded her eyes with one arm. I attached the bottle to her helmet. It took several tries. The universal connection wasn't perfectly universal.

Go figure.

Gravity fluttered, making the bottle heavy. I held it in place until she grabbed it with both hands. Retreat seemed like a good idea right then. I stepped back to the doorway and waited for the avalanche of thanks for saving her life.

"You stupid, mean, terrible person! What kind of man leaves a woman dying in a closet on a doomed starship?"

I slowly pointed one thumb at my chest. "This guy?"

"Yes! You! I was dying!"

"Hooray! You lived! Can we stop shouting! You're saved."

"Am I?" She glared daggers, or maybe laser beams, at me. Her chest rose and fell, probably from the sudden return of air but also from being really pissed off.

The woman was short, barely five feet tall and delicately thin. Even with the environment suit on, she was small. To be fair, the outfit wasn't bulky. Like most of the people I'd met in this corner of the galaxy, her neck was just a little longer than seemed right. An amazing blue powder seemed to tint her skin, especially around her eyes. The rest of her I couldn't see, but what did that matter?

Metallic silver patterns stretched away from her eye sockets like tattoos or paint. Right then, I realized she was the only female I'd seen on this side of the galaxy.

Random. Unsurprisingly, she was already mad at me. I had a way with women, and it was mostly to annoy them to the point of angry distraction.

"Is anyone else alive?" she finally asked.

I shook my head.

"What are you doing with your face?" She looked right and left as though searching for whatever had caught my attention.

I held up one hand, palm toward her. We needed to slow this down and establish some common ground.

She scrambled backward.

"Stop. This means stop where I'm from."

"Well, it means *now you die* here." Her breathy response seemed genuine.

I laughed nervously. "Good to know. Thanks." I shook my head. "This means *no*."

Her expression fell. "I'd hoped my companions lived through the discovery."

There were questions I wanted to ask, but waiting seemed the better policy, at least for a few minutes. Grum couldn't hold on forever. "Maybe some of them made it. There aren't many bodies. Just you and this other guy. A Gavant, I think."

"What the hell do you know of the Gavant, stranger? And

how do you speak even as well as you do? The inflection of your words has improved since we met."

I shrugged, then flinched in fear of what she might assume that meant. When she stared at me impassively, I continued. The Kayan suit hummed soothingly. It knew this language and mine. "My ship helps with language translation."

That got a reaction. The woman stared at me like I said I held a star in one hand and the keys to time travel in the other. "You are bonded with a Kayan."

"That's her name."

She narrowed her gaze, then attempted her own version of my negative head shake. "No, you idiot. A Kayan is a Kayan. Why would you think it had a name?"

"Well excuse me for being friendly." I struggled to catch up and felt stupid. This woman was going to be the death of me. I considered taking her air tank and shutting the closet door. Not seriously, of course. It was just one of those frustrated reactions to super difficult people.

She stood, stared at the floor for a second, then approached. "What is your name?"

"Major Noah Gantz, United Earth."

Her reaction was cautious. Instead of insulting me or asking questions, she just evaluated everything about the short statement and then shook my hand. "Solen Far, Science Officer to the Gavant ship *Holin's Reach*, which isn't much of a ship any longer, is it?"

"No, but we can cross back to Kayan," I said. "There is plenty of room." A new feeling came with the exchange. Maybe she'd been in a bad mood from oxygen deprivation and having the crap scared out of her. "Are you hungry?"

"I am, Major Noah Gantz. And you may be forgiven of a great deal if peace leads to food." She smiled.

I returned the gesture. "Funny that both our cultures have smiles and handshakes."

"Isn't it?" Her expression warmed, but also appeared worried. "I have used most of this bottle already. Something must be wrong with my suit."

"Turn around. Let me check you out."

She glared. "That means something different in our culture."

I blushed. "Well, I. Uh. Just let me see where you're leaking."

She crossed her arms. "Seriously."

"Do you like breathing air? I know I do." Kayan sent me a message as I inspected Solen's suit. "Looks like you were sitting on the leak."

She felt for the hole and went silent. There wasn't a snappy reply for that, apparently. Her bottle was already out and mine wasn't enough for the both of us.

I reviewed the message Kayan had placed in my visor HUD. The words faded in and out. Visual images were still hard for the ship to deliver at this range, even in the suit. We needed to work on operations away from the living starship. As soon as I had a chance, I would recommend a greater reliance on the visor tech and basic comms, rather than the mental bonding. Communicating with the advanced technology of the Kayan suit shouldn't be this hard. The holographic view screens on the bridge and elsewhere on the ship never flickered like this.

"There is an option. I can convert ambient gasses leaking from the Gavant vessel into something like oxygen," Kayan said. "You will breathe it better than she does due to our bond. But it will get you back to the airlock. Too long with this mixture will cause psychosis and possibly death."

"The ship has an idea," I said to Solen, and left out most of the details when I explained.

"The Kayan?"

"Yeah. I'm hooking our suits together. We don't have a lot of time, so you either come without arguing, or stay here."

"Not much of a choice."

"Nope."

"Let's go, Major Noah Gantz."

"Just call me Noah."

"That's a relief. Call me Solen. No need for Gavant formality."

I clipped her empty oxygen bottle to my leg, then connected our helmets by a tube running from the chest plate of my suit. "We can talk as we go. Be concise and keep moving. Are you a Gavant?"

Her horizontally long eyes unfocussed. Wide wasn't the right word, and neither did they slant upward or downward. To my Earth biased brain, it was as though she looked out from slots on a medieval helmet—but with dark pupils, spectacular irises, and crystal-white sclera. It also seemed like the metallic patterns around her delicate sockets glittered with internal light, just for a second.

She leaned on me and laughed. "Oh, yes. Your Kayan is

maximizing my biology's adaptive ability. Not sure what we're breathing, but I like it."

"Are you high?"

She chuckled and seemed ready to lose it. "I'm right next to you."

"Kayan, you got our new friend stoned."

"Apologies," the ship said.

Solen walked unsteadily. "You say the most fantastical things. Focus, sir. This is a highly dangerous situation!"

I suppressed the need to giggle. "Are you a Gavant or not?"

"Most Altions serve the Gavant Reach. They dominate many sectors of the galaxy. Your people will be no different if you are unlucky enough to encounter them on your home world," she said.

"That wasn't my question. Do you serve them? Should I lock you in a cell after we cross back to Kayan?"

"If you were going to do that, you shouldn't have warned me first." She walked beside me to keep the cable untangled and afford equal conversation. I liked that because she seemed like the sort of person people normally followed. The woman was a leader but was already treating me as an equal. Maybe that was intentional, but it seemed like her nature. "This was an uprising, though not planned. Many of my confederates were working on technology with the intent of holding back from our masters. That is how we may someday gain independence. The plot was discovered, and they began a purge. Gavant officers are famous for purges. I think they get an annual bonus or something."

"You're a resistance fighter? A rebel?"

She flinched. "Do not say that."

"Why not if it's true?"

"Not even… *rebels*… consider the term a compliment. And the punishment for being convicted as such is unspeakable." She stopped talking. This wasn't a topic that would make us friends.

The euphoric effect of Kayan's oxygen conversion tapered off. Either we were back on real air, or our bodies had adapted to the mixture. I watched where I was walking out of caution. There was no way I'd try driving in this condition.

"We're almost there. Grum is holding the airlock together, so we won't have time for long introductions," I said.

"Understood." She considered her next words carefully. "I've never seen anyone like you. Which means change is coming. And that always spawns sweeping violence and tragedy."

"No pressure."

She gave me a confused look.

"I'm saying there *is* pressure not to cause that."

"That makes more sense. My head is clearing. I hope your friend waits for us. Not likely, unless he is a Walen."

"Tell me what that means." I was curious.

"Walens are known for their aptitude for fixing things, their earnest work ethic, and loyalty. Most races use the word Walen to describe a valued friendship, no matter the race. You are Walen. Like that. It's a compliment."

"Interesting. So many things make sense now." We stepped through the final bulkhead. "Solen Far, meet Grum."

"Hello, Grum," Solen said with perfect civility. "I am Solen

Far, formerly the Science Officer of the Gavant Ship the *Holin's Reach.*"

No yelling or calling him names. Nice.

My friend eyed her carefully and said nothing, which seemed like a very un-Walen thing to do. He didn't shake her hand when she offered it. Instead, he retreated to his work and grimly continued.

"How are we looking?" I asked Grum.

"I should return last. Once you have her over there, Kayan can pull me back with the umbilical." He tied off several banks of wires. "We should bring the lifeline with us next time we board a ship." He addressed Solen. "Remain motionless, Gavant, while I mend your suit. Kayan cannot make up for what you are leaking."

She nodded and complied.

Attaching to a lifeline meant commitment, and that increased the risk of ambush. All things being equal, I wouldn't change a thing. Now wasn't the time for debate. "Solen, let's go across."

She nodded. "Of course."

The two of us cycled through the mangled airlock, then navigated the access tube single file. Her breathing was audible through our shared link. Neither of us talked until we were in the void.

"Your Walen friend is young," she said, sounding loud in my helmet. "I hope that he will forgive my association with the Gavant. There was no choice."

"We're all probationary."

"Explain." Her tone sounded guarded.

"We've only just met. Trust takes time." My willingness to believe people's best intentions hadn't always served me well, but at least I understood my propensity for giving everyone the benefit of the doubt. I wasn't an idiot. I mean, I probably wasn't.

Solen Far would likely disappoint me. Shit happened. I'd cross that bridge when we came to it.

She was quiet for a long time. "Thank you. I can work with that. Give me a chance, Noah, and I will reciprocate."

Tension killed the mood. Reaching Kayan was important. This was nothing to worry about, or that's what I told myself. What could go wrong? All I was doing was bringing a stranger wearing an enemy uniform onto our ship. Maybe I was foolhardy and reckless.

"Can you copy me, Noah?" Montow asked. "I mean, how copy?"

"Good copy."

"Ah, yes. Got it." Montow paused. "There has been a Gavant communiqué from a ship entering the system."

"What are the demands?" Solen asked.

"The standard list. Full acknowledgement of Gavant authority. Immediate compliance. We are instructed to wait at this location for inspection," he said.

Solen's tone burned through the comms. "Wait if you wish, but I will not."

The irrationality of her statement spoke volumes. I focused on getting us aboard Kayan. "We're at the airlock. Remain against it. Look at the stars, they're nice this time of day. Everything will be fine and dandy."

Solen laughed nervously.

It was kind of funny, given our location.

"Kayan will seal the airlock, then open it on the other side. Be ready because you will be back in full gravity much sooner than with a mechanical passage." I briefly checked her over as she assumed the position.

"Do your thing, Kayan," I said.

"Right away, Noah."

The ship closed over the Altion scientist. For a moment, I was alone on the comms with Montow. Solen continued inside without comms.

"My advice is to keep her under guard at all times." Montow didn't sound happy, not that his moods were easy to read. "Do not tell her of this conversation."

"Wouldn't dream of it. She's more fun when not screaming at me."

"I imagine that is true, Noah. Be careful. She may not seem like one of them, but she is."

I waited for my turn to enter the ship and thought about my life. What the hell was I going to do next? Short answer, wait for Grum, then learn all I could about the Altion scientist. Maybe she could help us deal with the Gavant hunters.

14

I LEFT Solen in the newly designated medical bay. That was something to know about Kayan. Rooms were general purpose, only becoming things like the bridge or galley when passengers needed them. The longer I was here, the more the place felt like home.

Dangerous. How hard would it be to have everything I wanted? The mental exercise occupied me as I considered what we'd just accomplished. A life was saved, but little else had been salvaged. All it took was the arrival of a Gavant warship and our day was ruined.

Kayan needed to refuel soon. I wasn't sure what Montow and Grum, or even Wozim, required. Who wasn't winning crewman of the month? This guy. Jokes aside, Pops would be embarrassed. My parents, less so. Sure they would want me to do the right thing and help out the only friends I had for about a trillion miles in any direction, but not with the same intensity as my grandfather. Life was about more than just getting by for Pops, it was about doing the right thing and being a good person.

Montow stepped into the passage. "I thought we could walk. The bridge has become a prison to me."

"Works for me, Captain. I was just thinking about you and Grum."

"Please don't. Such mental activities make it weird. Isn't that what you say?"

"More or less."

He removed his glasses and rubbed his never closing eyes. Then, after catching me staring at him, he put the huge shades back on. "The next person we allow on the ship must speak more sensibly."

"So like someone from Texas? Or maybe Kansas. You know, a place with that down home rural feel."

"I was thinking of an adept from the Wisdom. That's a rough translation to your language, by the way."

I relented with an understanding grimace. "You're probably right. That sounds like someplace we'd find a guru. Is it a planet?"

"No one knows." He seemed distracted and ready to move on with the conversation.

"Great. Not vague at all. At least Solen Far knows the name of where she wants to go."

Montow crossed his arms and canted his soup can head to one side. The effect was something like "really, then tell me," or "of course she does, the Altion sneak."

I soldiered onward. "She called it Milyn." I again watched the captain for his reaction, and got about what I expected—subvocal complaints and a lot of negative body language.

"What's the problem?" I asked. "She's sleeping. Kayan says she might do that for a while. There is no danger the scary scientist will catch us talking behind her back."

"Good. Because that is what I wish to do."

"This is getting weird."

"I owe the ship my life, as do you." He walked several steps before speaking again. "The Gavant captain will not take no for an answer. I have delayed with every possible excuse. She is one of them, no matter that her biology is Altion. We must surrender her, or everything we have worked for, including your rescue, will be for naught. They won't be kind to Kayan if they catch us."

I felt the truth of the last statement in my bones. "Apart from them putting the ship in a confinement system, we're just talking about our individual freedoms."

"No small thing."

How could I argue with that? We traversed a long, gently curving passageway that followed the length of Kayan's hull. Montow watched and waited. The man could be intense in a way that was hard to describe. Was he waiting for a specific response? Could this be a test?

Wozim emerged from his cabin ready to take on the galaxy. His tail, swear to God, looked at me with its spike—distracting me from my conversation with Montow. The spike looked hungry for my blood. Or maybe that was my imagination. Tytons scared the hell out of me.

"Kayan informed me of the pending crisis. Now is the time to fight." Wozim touched a small knife sheathed in his kilt—the only thing he wore. His bare feet padded the deck soundlessly despite his claws and the weight of his massive body.

"Are you going to put on your armor first?" I couldn't resist. The memory of him delivering my bundle stuck in my imagination. He'd looked like a tank on two legs with enough destructive power to take down an enemy fort. "You don't look ready for a major engagement."

Wozim pivoted toward me and took one step. I put my back to the wall before I realized what was happening. He'd moved so fast. Escape looked impossible, and I wasn't stoked about getting murdered. Today wasn't a good day to die.

"What did you say, human?"

"You're not wearing armor, and all you have is a knife." I pressed my hands forward, knowing I couldn't stop him but needing to take some kind of defensive posture.

Montow grabbed Wozim's huge bicep. "He is not the enemy, Wozim of Tyton VII."

Montow was big, but not a warrior like Wozim. And he was much older, like a person to respect rather than fight.

Wozim slowly turned to glare at the soup can head with sunglasses. His nostrils flared like they would shoot fire and his lips bared to show teeth like a shark. "You wish to fight Wozim?"

"No, friend. After all we've been through, you know I don't."

"Remove your hand."

A second passed, and Montow complied.

Wozim looked over his shoulder at me. "I am always ready

for the party, Noah Gantz of Earth. Kayan assures me you are as well."

I spread my hands, hoping the gesture meant the same thing in both our cultures. "I meant no offense."

Wozim snorted and walked off.

"I love that guy," I said when he was gone. "Really good energy. Vibes all day. Glad to know he feels violence is a celebration."

Montow stared after Wozim for a moment longer, then motioned that we should continue. "As fun as this has been, we should work our way back to the bridge and inform the Gavant captain that we will comply."

"Hold on. That wasn't decided. What happens if we turn Solen over to this Gavant guy?" Here my friends were fleeing across the galaxy, ready to face any danger not to be captured, and it was suddenly okay to give someone back to these jerks? The smell test was not getting passed here, not by a long shot.

"She will most likely be killed, even if she is loyal. The Gavant fear betrayal and take no chances. There was an uprising on that science ship. She was likely involved. By their reasoning, executing her post interrogation would make sense," Montow said. His tone was guarded. His expression harder to read than normal.

We reached the bridge while I was still formatting a strongly worded response to that bullshit. He went through the door and headed straight for his work pod.

"What if this captain asks for one of us?"

"Why would he?"

"Because you, Grum, Wozim, and even Kayan are fleeing from them, or did I get that part wrong?"

"But not you."

"What?"

"You're not fleeing from them, because they don't know you exist. Perhaps you will betray us."

I clenched my fists and paced, forcing my hands open to push back my hair and release my frustration.

"Kayan, show him proof," Montow said.

A screen glowed. Images of Gavant shock troopers jogging down a strange city street appeared. Every few paces, they stopped with chilling coordination. The front row took a knee and held forward shields while the others fired over their heads into shops and businesses.

Auxiliary troops followed behind. Some were Gavant, but many were Altion or other races resembling their Gavant cousins. They bound survivors, applied minimal first aid, and loaded them into prison cars.

The image ended. "The Altion cannot be trusted. They are not true fighters for the cause," Montow said. "You saw her kind enforcing the crack down. She isn't one of us."

"Rewind that and show me Solen Far. I didn't see her. Maybe I missed it because I am just a human." There was more I wanted to say but understood I couldn't take certain accusations back. Kayan's lack of participation in this argument bothered me. The ship was not a person. Remembering that could be difficult. Part of me wanted to agree with Montow, but mostly I trusted the woman even though her people were closely aligned to the Gavant fascists.

Montow mumbled Hellenger swear words under his breath as he reviewed numbers on another screen. "The Gavant warship is closing the distance faster than expected. It must be a new class. Never seen one move like this."

"Where is Grum?"

"Why?" Montow's voice remained low and gruff.

"He should have a vote."

"There is no need for that. A decision must be made. Consensus may not be possible. Survival is a prerequisite to all future decisions, right or wrong."

"We can't take this back. Once we betray Solen, it's forever."

"She is a stranger. Choose between her and Kayan. Our time is up," Montow said.

Energy readings flared on a screen I'd never seen activated. The numbers lacked a reference, but Kayan made it clear what I was looking at—a damage report. The Gavant ship was shooting at us.

"I deflected the damage." Kayan's voice sounded distant. "Future attacks will be worse."

Montow put all of his attention on me. My reflection showed in the dark lenses I'd asked Kayan to craft for him. "She will understand. Ask her, and she will confirm that she was amazed we did this much to help her."

Words came, but my mouth refused to cooperate. He wasn't wrong. Her expression, and the way she talked, had told me the truth, hadn't it? She wasn't in the same situation as Montow, Grum, Wozim, or Kayan.

Or me.

I couldn't just trust everyone I met. That's how people got killed in distant galaxies ruled by evil empires.

"Go tell her. She will need time to prepare," Montow said, and for the first time since the discussion began, there was compassion in his voice.

I left without a word, mind cloudy with misery and no brilliant plans materializing out of the ether. The passageway seemed too wide and longer than the ship. Guilt warped perception. I couldn't stop thinking of how she must have felt when I left her there with no air and no comms. Talk about suck.

You did what you had to. Who was saying that? My conscience? Yeah. Sure. Keep telling yourself that, Noah. She'll be really glad for this next bit of news. I had left her there, terrified, facing death in a closet after a taste of hope.

Not cool.

And now I was going to confirm all her assumptions about me and my friends.

Grum sat on a bench across from the woman. He handed her a bottle of water.

She drank it and glared at me sullenly. "Come to kill me?"

"Not really my style. But if you get on my nerves, who knows?"

Her laughter surprised me. It definitely wasn't my funniest joke. The woman wasn't amused, but bitter. Maybe Altion science officers had a sixth sense for betrayal. More likely that was the way things were done in this galaxy. Loyalty didn't seem to be a thing.

How the hell was I going to get home where people weren't crazy? That made *me* laugh, which confused everyone.

"You have to help me out, Solen," I finally said.

"Do I?"

"Yeah. Especially if you want to stay on this ship. There is a Gavant captain shooting at us for keeping you this long. Give me something, anything to bargain with."

She crossed her arms and leaned back.

"Great. Another mannerism that spans cultures. Apparently, attitude is the universal language," I said.

"They forced me to work for them, like they do everyone. Here is what happens. They seize your home world, kill everyone who resists or stands out. Imprison the rest. Decades pass and they give the next generation a chance to better their lives, to heal the wounds between civilizations. You take the opportunity to get out of the camps, off the prison planets, and promise to strike back some day. But that never happens because they're too strong."

What the hell could I say to that? Images of United Earth falling to the vastly superior strength of the Gavant fleet came easily to mind. Too many late-night movies provided the source material. I could see my parents and siblings getting separated and sent to camps. My world crumbled in my imagination.

The one element I couldn't picture was my place in the horror. Where was I?

On the other side of the galaxy, showing zero compassion for someone who needed it.

Solen Far leaned forward to rest her sharp elbows on her knees. "They will stop at nothing to kill me. And when I fall into their hands, it will be the death of your friends. Take me to Milyn, and I won't be your problem anymore."

"Water?" Grum asked, offering another bottle.

"Watch her. I'll be back." Leaving the room felt like my only option, despite my complete lack of a plan. Ideas wouldn't come. I could barely process what was happening, much less pull a solution out of thin air. Montow and the others wanted to find a safe planet called Ryyth. Her insistence of going to Milyn, wherever that was, wouldn't strengthen my case to help her. "Get Wozim in here to help you."

That caused her to sit up straight. "There is a Tyton on this ship?"

I left the room and stalked angrily around the outer passageway. This was wrong. Even if Solen hated us, she didn't deserve what the Gavant would do to her. Montow and the others were ready to do anything to escape their wrath. That was proof enough of their savagery.

Pops wouldn't have betrayed his worst enemy to a bully like that.

So screw these Gavant jack wagons.

15

"YOU'RE BACK," Montow said.

I had expected angry accusations. Instead, it seemed the captain of this ship was having his own crisis of conscience. Old and wise, he didn't appear ready to reverse himself despite the sour taste the decision left in his mouth.

"I talked to Solen."

"And she convinced you to help her."

I stepped into my work pod and faced the view screens, mostly as a stalling tactic. How should I word this? Could I convince the man? "Who do the hunters want more, a scientist or Kayan?"

"This is unknown."

"Probably because we haven't really talked to the woman yet." I was onto something. "If we could stall, see what she has that the Gavant want. Maybe that science ship was developing a secret weapon or a cure for a dangerous disease."

"Irrelevant. The ship is lost. They might salvage it with the help of the sole survivor. Kayan will always be hunted by our enemies. The safest thing is to put the Altion woman in a pod and leave her. Kayan can escape while they divert to reclaim their servant."

"Holy shit, that is ruthless. Do you want to get dumped in space? What if they go after us instead? Where does that leave Solen?"

Montow went pale and refused to look at me.

"Kayan, what do you think?"

"My opinion is irrelevant," the ship said. "Prepare for a message from the Gavant vessel."

Montow and I went silent.

The main screen flickered, then presented a towering figure.

"Why does he have the camera on the floor?" The words just popped out. *What a pretentious tool.*

Dramatic camera angle aside, the Gavant captain was obviously tall and lean. He stood with his feet slightly wider than shoulder width. Chest out, shoulders back, he projected strength by stretching the black uniform tight across his chest. Like an Altion, his neck was long. The difference was the thicker muscle and lack of metallic tattoos. The symbols marking the left side of his face were magenta and looked organized by a ruler or laser guide. On the right cheek was a single emblem, like a badge. His wrap-around eyes were little more than dark slits.

"I am Captain Ryg. Your compliance is required. Surrender

the traitor and open your ship. An inspection will follow. Illegal passengers will be transported to the appropriate jurisdiction for trial and confinement."

I spoke quietly and hoped only Kayan heard me. "Don't let them get close."

"The Kayan will be boarded one way or another. Choose peace. Avoid bloodshed. The high courts will consider your compliance during sentencing," Ryg said.

"He hasn't asked our names," Montow said. "Doesn't that feel rude?"

I stared. My roll-over-and-play-dead friend was talking shit. "I know, right? Kind of bullshit."

"Your identity is known. Wozim the murderer is with you, as is Grum Kalic 0192, the patent thief," Ryg said, then took a seat. This drew a new, more reasonable camera angle. He crossed one leg over the other, which accentuated his knee-high leather boots.

They looked like leather. With embroidered seams and soles.

"Grum's last name is Kalic?"

"No," Montow growled. "That is a label given by the Gavant to individuals they have judged subsentient. The number is a further insult, and all they really care about."

Ryg laced his fingers together and listened. The man seemed confident, unhurried, and amused. Around him, Gavant officers remained standing at attention. The guy had an ego.

"What's our play?" I asked.

Montow stared at Ryg. Near silence held the bridge. I wished

Kayan would talk to me, give me hints. What was it the ship had said, "My opinion is irrelevant?"

Did that mean Kayan couldn't interfere or fight back? I knew there were no weapons, but was the ship unable to resist Gavant authority in any way? That couldn't be all of it, because evading capture was an act of defiance.

Montow had made his stance known. Now he stared down the Gavant captain like they'd done this before. I needed information I wasn't going to get. Grum was busy watching Solen, and Wozim was just as unhelpful as always. At this point, I'd trade *him* to the Gavant for a shot at freedom.

"My ship can remain at relative rest for months if necessary," Ryg said. "The Kayan must feed. If my sensors officers advise me correctly, your ship is depleted." He checked something on the armrest of his massive chair. "Galaxy's balls, you delivered a Hoyon to a virgin world. That hasn't happened for a hundred years. Maybe this sector of the galaxy is on the mend. Very nice."

Montow lowered his "chin" and stared balefully at the man. I had my own death stare for Ryg. The guy was winding up for a big shot, a threat meant to have us pissing our pants and begging for mercy.

Yeah, that's gonna happen. Sure.

"It would be a shame to set back all that progress by blasting the Kayan who delivered the seed creature out of the void." He dropped his upper leg to the floor and leaned forward. "Make the right choice. I am out of patience."

Montow exhaled.

I knew I'd lost him. The old Hellenger had lasted longer than I'd expected. It was inconvenient, but like Pops always said, sometimes you had to just stir the pot all by yourself.

"Why not have it both ways?" I asked.

Ryg moved his attention to me like his gaze was a welding torch cutting open the scene. The bad boss pettiness vanished like this was a new person, a force of nature ready to crush me like it was nothing. Maybe that should have made me step back.

I locked my jaw and forced myself to think. This was the big league. There wasn't room for stupid mistakes or games. I was staring into the eyes of a man who tortured his enemies and absolutely would kill a Kayan to prove his point.

"Who the hell are you?"

"Noah Gantz." I omitted my rank. "Intergalactic traveler and man of mystery. But that's not important right now. The thing is, we got off to a rough start. Help us help you."

What the hell was I talking about? Suddenly, I felt like my Uncle Mike, used car salesmen of the year three times running in Fort Smith, Arkansas. A grin crept across my face, and I thought Pops would be starting to laugh. Mad Mike was exactly who I needed right now.

Captain Ryg crossed his arms and leaned back slightly. Was that the same as a human gesture of guarded curiosity? I hoped so. Because I was going for it. The bluff would be more effective if I was reading him right.

Montow was watching me now as well. He had no clue where this was going and didn't need to know I didn't either.

Momentum was the key, and attention. *All eyes on me, Ryg. You can't miss this deal of a lifetime.*

"Captain Montow and I have been talking about this for days. How can we get back in the good graces of our Gavant masters? I mean, not mine because I'm not from around here, but you see where I'm coming from. Nobody wants trouble. Don't start no SH and there won't be no IT."

Ryg furrowed his brow.

"Every day is a negotiation."

"Incorrect," Ryg snapped. "There is only obedience."

"Exactly! That's just what we were talking about. You see, we have all this cargo and these passengers to manage. Huge pain in the ass. We can't wait to unload them. And the Kayan. Don't get me started. So much damage. Sick as hell. You know how it is with living ships."

"No, I don't. They live or die in the confinement system and are no worry of mine."

"I know, right? But try telling them that."

"I'm no longer sick. What are you talking about, Noah?" Kayan asked.

I waved her question away and realized Ryg saw the gesture but didn't know what it was. His narrow eyes narrowed further.

"Anyway, what we need is about a week to put everything in order. Then you get everything you asked for—because it's all about obedience, am I right? My Pops always said that anything worth doing is worth doing well. Two weeks, and this entire mess will be cleaned up and ready for you to inventory. And that will take a while, because there is a lot of great stuff on this old ship."

"I'm not old," Kayan complained privately.

"You have three days," Ryg said, then killed the connection.

Silence held the bridge. Montow stared at me. Kayan also seemed concerned.

"What just happened?" Montow asked.

"I bought us three days." I checked Kayan's readings of the Gavant warship. It seemed to have slowed.

"That is unusual. Gavant procedure is to attack first and negotiate later," Montow's telescoping fingers flew over the split keyboards hanging from his wrists.

"He shot us." I stepped away from my emergency pod and paced. Movement helped me think.

"That was not an attack, that was a warning." He hummed for several seconds, which wasn't something I'd heard him do. "His ship is broadcasting repair traffic. If we moved close, Kayan could spy on them. I think we would see crews repairing battle damage. He hustled you."

"Ouch. You can't hustle the hustler. Whatever. Now seems like a good time to bug out."

"Maybe." Montow ceased his work. "He will not give us three days, that is for sure. Prepare the Altion woman for transfer. Her fate is not ours. Hard choices must be made."

"I'll talk to her."

"You are a good man, Noah Gantz. But she is not one of us. Avoid emotional attachments. There will be time for that later."

"When?" I asked.

Montow grumbled something but didn't answer.

I left him to his work. The passageway seemed different. I felt like every part of the ship was worried. "Kayan, I'm not surrendering her to the Gavant."

"I understand, Noah." A pause followed. "There will be immediate consequences."

16

GRUM STOOD outside Solen Far's room, his gangly arms crossed as he fidgeted with his double-thumbed hands.

"What's wrong?" I gripped his shoulder. Thankfully, that calmed him as I'd hoped. Physical contact wasn't a part of our shared, Kayan-translated language so far as I could tell. So the gesture had been a risk. All I'd done lately was make a mess of things. More actors on the stage meant more chaos. I needed to remember that when dealing with alien cultures, and tread carefully. Not everyone wanted to be my buddy or preserve human...sentient... life. That seemed like it should be a universal value, but was it?

"She pretends to be angry, and maybe she is." Grum looked at his feet, then at me. "But she is very sad, Noah. And afraid. I was like that before Montow saved me."

"I need to talk to her."

He shook his head in perfect imitation of my earlier body language. The Walen must have been practicing. What was I doing to learn his ways? Pops would cut me slack, but I still thought I should do better. "She was extremely clear that she wanted to be alone. Does shouting mean the same thing in your culture? When a person is that angry on Walen, we give them space."

I closed my eyes, rubbed my temples, wished I had coffee. There wasn't time for this. She needed to understand I was trying to help. Every relationship disaster from puberty to pre-FTL launch reared up. Famous last words. *You need to understand me. I'm trying to help.*

Now I had to understand the four people I shared this ship with or die.

"Are the Gavant coming?" Grum asked.

"Captain Ryg gave us three days, but Montow says he will board Kayan once his own repairs are done. The guy just came from a battle or something."

"Ryg is well known to the people of Walen." He looked at the door. "I wonder if she knows who is searching for her. This is bad news for us, and worse for her."

"Tell me about that. How do you mean?" The look in the Gavant captain's eyes was burned into my brain. I didn't want to stand in the same room with him, or even share a star system. Kayan's hunger warned of trouble. I'd never experienced it quite like this. The full body fatigue felt like long days in flight school with every minute a physical and mental test.

"Little is known about Ryg. He refuses to declare his patron. This is hard to explain, because most elite of the Gavant keep this part of their world secret." He shrank the aperture protecting his eyes and tipped his head side to side, just a millimeter each way, as though in deep concentration. This was Grum at his most earnest. He really wanted to get this explanation right. "When they become truly powerful, it seems it is with the assistance of someone higher than them. This is usually very public. That's why people speculate, you know, why they think it's a thing. Ryg has tripled his power and influence and become ten times as aggressive. But he refuses to declare the identity of his patron."

I mulled the information, avoided my gut reaction.

Grum looked up, clearly seeking approval.

This guy just couldn't stop being nice. "Okay, that's important. Let's start at the beginning and keep it simple. None of us want to get caught by Ryg."

Grum nodded and did his funny hand waggle. "Montow will understand. He's gotten us this far."

"That's the spirit." My friend seemed relieved, but I wasn't feeling it, not yet. We had few options.

Kayan could run, and probably escape, but not for long. Ryg's statement about fuel needs were on the mark. Sooner or later, the Gavant hunters would throw out a net too wide to escape and catch us while the ship was feeding. Then we might just learn the hard way who Ryg worked for.

"I really need to talk to Solen. Montow has his reasons, but so do I. It feels wrong to give anyone up to the Gavant hunters."

Grum's improved mood slipped a notch. "He's probably right. Running is one thing. Fighting the hunters is suicide. You and Montow will figure it out."

No pressure. I knocked on the door.

"What are you doing?"

"It's called knocking. Polite people do it."

"If you say so." He backed away from the door. "I'll wait outside."

No answer came, so I entered. None of the doors on this level were barred to me. Kayan opened them whenever I walked close enough, or my intent became clear.

Solen flew at me from the shadows. "You can't hurt me!"

I dropped into a fighting stance right as her body collided into mine. We hit the wall hard, but I caught both of her wrists. Her knee shot toward my groin. I twisted my hips to avoid impact and took a powerful shot to my thigh.

"Stop! I'm here to talk. Why are you attacking me?"

She shoved off my torso, relying on my greater weight as a base to propel herself to a safer distance. Nimble and surefooted, she landed in a fighting stance with both hands clenched into fists. Smart. The woman might beat me with surprise, but I had the size advantage in a protracted grappling match. "You have a funny way of announcing it."

I thought back to Grum's reaction. "Hold on, you're talking about the knock. What does that even mean here?"

She stood straighter and lowered her hands. "You've never heard of the execution knock?"

"For the love of Peter, Paul, and Mary." I massaged my right temple, then dropped my hand. "We really need an encyclopedia of nonverbal language. Knocking before you enter is literally the most polite way to enter a room in any culture."

And there I did it again. I wasn't in Kansas. My get out of jail free cards were running out.

"Not mine," she said. "Not for Walens or Gavants or even Hellengers. Your customs are as strange as your face and stumpy physique."

"Ouch. Now you made it ugly."

She shook her head and started to pace. At least that was something we had in common. Movement reduced stress. "Just tell me what you want? Frankly, I'm amazed I'm still alive. Sure, you toyed with my emotions and scared the hell out of me for no reason, but you did eventually bring me to your ship."

"A Gavant warship demanded your surrender, then fired a warning shot."

"Who is the captain?" she asked.

"Captain Ryg. I managed to stall, but Montow says he is only repairing his ship before attacking."

She stopped pacing and stared at me. Her wide eyes and rigid stance might not mean exactly what I assumed, but I was confident I had the general idea. She knew the name and didn't like it.

"You have a problem with Ryg?"

"Would you if he swore vengeance against your people? Ryg used to be a general before a failed mission to suppress an uprising on an Altion colony world. He'll do anything to regain power and have his vengeance." She turned away and muttered something I probably wasn't supposed to hear. "That, and other reasons. The son of a bilge sucker."

"I'm new around here, but there are a few things I figured out. All my friends, including the ship that rescued me, are running from Gavant hunters. This guy fits that description. We can't take you anywhere if we're killed or captured."

"So what do you want?" she asked. "And why can't you just take me to Milyn?"

"Come to the bridge, talk to Captain Montow. It's harder to condemn someone face-to-face." I was playing dirty pool, but this was life-or-death, and we were all in this together. It wasn't my place to explain everyone else wanted to go to Ryyth, where legend had it, people were free of the Gavant's influence.

Her resistance softened, or that was how I interpreted the new expression. "Montow? He must be a Hellenger, right? You do realize a ship like this doesn't have a captain, or any passenger hierarchy."

I moved toward the door until it opened, and I held up one hand to indicate she should go first. "Kayan is still helping me and the others communicate. I'm figuring out that a lot of the words we hear are less than perfect translations."

"You can say that again." She made an annoyed huff, but it almost sounded concerned. "Someone should've taught you the protocol for accepting passage with a Kayan. You're supposed to learn how to converse with other people on the vessel, for obvious reasons."

"I thought that was what we were doing."

She looked at Grum, then me. "It's better with some sort of organized curriculum. What were you planning to do, just randomly embarrass each other asking for clarification until you understand the nuance of each phrase?"

I looked at Grum from over her shoulder and tried to get him to go along with me. "Oh, no. We are very organized. Definitely learning each other's languages every day. It's like going to school."

"Yes, we are each other's teachers," Grum said. "We sit in a room and ask Kayan to abandon us. Shenanigans ensue."

"Leave me out of that," she said.

"You opened the topic." So many ideas for practical jokes flashed into existence. I hoped she stayed part of the crew for that reason alone.

Solen held up one hand and strode toward the bridge without needing to be given directions. "Fine, fine. I'll leave it to you then. Are we going to do this, or what?"

"You should let me do the talking, at least at first." I jogged to keep up with her and then found myself lengthening my stride despite her shorter stature. This Altion was a woman on a mission. Maybe my jokes could wait, even if we seriously needed a tension breaker.

MONTOW TURNED to stare when we entered. He removed his sunglasses and held them down at his side. The sudden return of his unblinking eyes reminded me I was far from home.

Like I needed a fifty-seventh hint.

No one looked, behaved, or thought like I did, including the ship. I'd made a lot of assumptions that had gotten me in trouble.

Now we were about to negotiate with a dangerous Gavant officer with a grudge. What could possibly go wrong? Who cared if he was on a vendetta to impress a shadowy figure in the Gavant power structure?

Grum moved to one side and found his emergency pod. He had it set up like a barstool with a tall back, a bit like a vertical lazy boy. Not a bad idea.

Wozim followed us in, stepping through the door just as it was closing. Solen jumped behind me and stared at the Tyton in alarm. "This just keeps getting better."

Wozim snarled at her.

I looked to Montow.

He shrugged perfectly. Someone else had been practicing my human mannerisms. "Natural-born enemies. The Tyton and Altion came into conflict over resources centuries ago."

"I love how everyone keeps me informed," I said, then looked to Wozim hoping he would be the first into this conversation when it started. "At least we're all here. Let's talk about our decision."

Wozim glowered menacingly but said nothing.

So much for that plan. I'd hoped he would support keeping

Solen from the Gavant hunter. The monstrous warrior seemed ready to throw down for any reason. He should be the quickest to resist Ryg's demands, even if his people didn't care for Solen's Altion heritage.

"I'm new on the ship, but it didn't take long to understand we are on the run from Gavant hunters," I said. "Ryg wants Solen Far. But you all know he won't stop there. He'll capture Kayan and everyone on board. Honestly, I probably have the best chance of surviving since he doesn't know me."

Montow laughed. "He does now. I don't think you'll be friends."

Kayan sounded a short melodic tone to get our attention. "Captain Ryg has attempted to force communication. I can resist, but it is uncomfortable. Their scientists have learned a great deal about our thought frequencies and can cause considerable pain."

"The ship is telling us we better talk to... *Ryg*," Solen said, struggling to say the Gavant captain's name.

Montow spread his hands in a gesture of surrender as though he agreed with her. "The Altion lives up to her people's firm grasp of the obvious."

"Can they read your thoughts? Listen to our comms?" I asked, feeling bad for extending Kayan's suffering but also worrying about a serious breach of operational security.

"No, Noah. They are only good at causing misery."

"Let's see what the man has to say." I only had to wait seconds but there was plenty of time to feel dread. Montow had warned he was just covering his need to make repairs. Apparently, his crew was fast and efficient.

Ryg's image appeared on the main screen. "And look at that, the usual suspects." The angle flattered him though it wasn't as severe as during our first encounter. He took in the scene, carefully measuring each of us. I thought he lingered on Wozim the longest but couldn't read his thoughts.

I glanced toward the warrior. He wore his space kilt and moon-shaped knife outfit. Probably slept in it. The armor I'd only seen once might have given our adversary pause, but maybe that was wishful thinking. Wozim was only one person, no matter how terrifying he was.

Ryg shifted his attention to Solen, and his eyes narrowed. He leaned forward, lowering his hand from his chin where he had been thoughtfully holding it. "Doctor Solen Far. You live." He gave a short laugh. "With a Tyton in the same room, my work is practically done. The Hellenger doesn't look pleased either. Pathetic."

"Don't forget me." I waved. "Noah Gantz. We spoke earlier. You gave us a week to get things in order."

His attention felt heavy and direct. I expected a crappy retort to my extension of the timeline, but he didn't flinch. If he saw something he didn't like in the Tyton and the Altion, his opinion on humans was complex and brooding. Unfair since I had to be the first Earthling he'd met.

I was a nice guy. Always trying to make a good first impression. What was his problem, other than the line of bullshit I'd fed him earlier?

"I have not forgotten you, Gantz." He regained his composure. Only then did I realize he'd lost it, even minutely. "Surrender the scientist. This is not a request."

"Let's say, for the sake of argument, that we go that route. Do the rest of us get amnesty, maybe even some kind of reward?" I asked.

Solen glared at me with laser beam intensity. On the other side of the bridge, Wozim seemed disgusted. He had no love for the Altion, but neither did he respect the idea of surrendering her to the enemy. I needed them to have a little faith.

Ryg said nothing. He was in full poker mode, unwilling to show his cards or even that he played the game.

"We've been reasonable," I said.

This annoyed Ryg, probably because it implied I was running the encounter.

I so wasn't. Desperately grabbing for any chance to save my friends wasn't the same as having a plan. That would come, I just wished it would come sooner.

"So far, I'm the only one proposing any solutions. You have to bring something to the table, Ryg."

He slammed one fist on his armrest as he stood. "Enough! Your time is up. Order the ship to admit my troopers. Pray, if you believe in the gods. And if you don't, then I suggest compliance and respect before you get on my bad side."

The connection died.

I glanced around the room. No one spoke. If my goal had been to create tension thick enough to cut with a knife, I'd earned an A+.

"I think that went better than expected." I sent a query to Kayan, then asked the same question of Montow. "Can we outrun Ryg's ship?"

Montow grumpily typed on his double keyboards. He stared at his work as though concentration could send me back to Earth and put Solen back where we found her. "If we act now," was all he said.

The ship agreed silently.

"Kayan, punch it. We're done with this system," I said.

Ryg chose that moment to reinitiate contact. Caught off guard, I fell back on old habits and gave him the finger. "See you later, loser."

Wozim imitated my gesture. "Zyzo!"

I laughed. "Yeah, Zyzo!"

"I swear by the stars I'm going to—"

This time, Kayan ended the link with much greater finality.

Silence held the room. Wozim faced me. His sharp, black teeth showed when he snarled. "We are brothers in profanity, nothing more."

"It's a start."

"Gods," Solen muttered, then her hands pushed forward defensively when Wozim whirled on her. "Touchy, touchy."

"Please secure yourselves in the pods," Kayan said. "This will be much rougher than usual."

Wozim grunted and stormed out. Because of course he did. The urge to shout *Zyzo* nearly overcame me, but I decided discretion was the better part of valor. I mean, the word was apparently so foul Kayan wouldn't translate it.

I backed into my pod, as did Montow. Grum hesitated and I realized he didn't think he belonged on the bridge. "Just grab one and close yourself in."

He waggled his hands and complied.

Kayan didn't bother to give a translation. The ship had more important work to handle. "Brace for incoming fire. Wozim should not have said that to Captain Ryg, and you should not have joined in."

"What does it mean—"

Dozens of missiles launched from the *Kon*. My attention diverted to waves of destruction heading our way. Kayan turned and accelerated as a third of the warheads raced to cut off her only line of escape. I cringed as red spotted my vision.

"Please close your eyes, Noah," Kayan said. "There is a reason I shut you and the others in life pods when accelerating."

I listened and said nothing. The ship didn't expect a response. Watching what happened next wasn't exactly what I did, because I wasn't viewing events through my senses. This was what it was like to be Kayan. Each missile attack was a single timeline. Pain lanced through my head as I realized the ship was processing everything simultaneously, something humans couldn't do. Our version of multi-tasking was actually flipping back and forth between thoughts.

It could feel like multi-tasking, but it wasn't. There had been a surprisingly large volume of psychology in our pre-FTL flight curriculum. I wondered if Tate Collins paid attention in those classes. A half dozen backups to the backup pilots had been in that room. I couldn't stop going back to those well-ordered desks, perfect uniforms, and physics I understood.

Nothing had been that orderly. My brain was seeking what it knew, then enforcing even more order on the memory. Comfort came in many forms, and it was hard to resist the lotus dream of lies. It didn't take much to recall coffee cups and stained napkins, scattered pencils and dog-eared textbooks.

Missiles crashed into Kayan's port side. The ship spun like a rifle bullet, then cut through layers of the galaxy I only vaguely understood existed. Knowing the rules that governed this between-space travel wasn't possible. Not for me. Not now.

Kayan sensed my participation and *frowned*. "See this? You are here."

All of my attention went to a top-down view of my pod. Beside it were others—Montow, Grum, Solen, and Wozim even though Wozim had gone to his room. Each coffin-like device was moving deeper into the ship, entering the vault, a place far inside the restricted areas of the living vessel.

"You are safest here," Kayan said. "I try to return the pods to their starting places when the event concludes."

"That's how we survive the jump?" I felt drugged and half-asleep.

"Do not worry so much about speed." The ship's voice sounded far away. I didn't hear explosions and suspected Ryg's missiles had been left behind. We no longer shared a star system with the Gavant officer. "Distance is all that matters when traveling."

Hunger ravaged my body. I groaned at the pain in my core.

Kayan told me to sleep or be consumed, but I couldn't stop marveling at how protected we were.

"No one has remained awake during travel," Kayan whispered.

"I'm a pilot. It's what I do."

Silence. Lights. Weightlessness. "Sleep, Noah Gantz. This was a long trip. Recovery will tax both of us."

17

Darkness gripped me completely. My lungs didn't work. I could only remember bits and pieces of what happened after Ryg opened fire on Kayan. Seconds passed. I expected to panic but felt fine. Maybe I was dead.

Not such a big deal. Standing in the dark was going to get boring. I struggled to care.

My pod cracked open. A razor-thin line of light blinded me. Eyes closed, I stumbled forward and collapsed as my bodily functions worked to catch up. The floor rushed up and punched me in the mouth about the time I reached forward to stop my fall. Too little, too late. Story of my life.

Agony wracked my body as I rolled onto my back. "Fucking Zyzo," I muttered.

"Noah, be nice."

"Sorry."

Sweat drenched my clothing. I peeled off my shirt, and only then looked around. My vision blurred. Dropping the shirt, I vigorously rubbed my face, then gazed at my environment. Nothing had changed in my small cabin. I hadn't spent much time here. The place was small and lonely.

"Kayan, how will my pod get back to the bridge?"

"Do you need to know how I move all of my internal organs during emergencies?"

"No." I went to the tiny wash area and splashed my face clean. "Maybe I should wake up first."

"Our version of coffee is waiting on the bridge, as is another pod. Why would I only have one?"

"I don't know?" The irony in my voice was probably missed by the living ship.

"The one you awoke in will be gone when you return to your room. We must have some secrets, don't you think?" Kayan asked.

"For sure."

"No one else has recovered," Kayan showed a diagram of each passenger with yellow lights marking their heads and hearts. "You should check on them."

"In their rooms?" I pulled on clean clothing and marveled at how tough yet soft it felt. In my rush, two legs went into the same hole. Before I could correct my mistake, the pants split apart and reformed in the correct configuration.

I leapt into the air.

"You are alarmed?" Kayan asked.

"Little bit."

"Where did you think I found clothing, coffee makers, and sleep masks?"

"Hey. Lots of people wear sleep masks."

"If you say so." A pause from the ship. "I use supplies purchased by the crew when possible, but some amenities are easy to replicate. Please let me know what else you need to feel comfortable."

"A six-pack of dark beer would be fantastic," I joked.

"Of course."

"Wait. What? Never mind. Show me the way to the rest of the crew."

Everything worked better today. My fatigue quickly melted away and I realized how high I had jumped when startled. Sleeping on this ship was like going to a spa for three days. How had I survived this long without Kayan? Damn, I felt good.

Wozim's quarters were the first I came to. I reached out to knock, thought twice, and opened the door then waited in the passageway. Remaining alive and in one piece was high on my list of priorities. At some point, I needed to discover how each culture *knocked*.

"Wozim, are you there?"

"Yes. You may enter. Why didn't you knock?"

"Seriously?"

"I am not afraid of the executioner's announcement. Death comes for us all."

I edged inside and saw him sitting cross-legged before a candle. On one side of the small cabin was a bedroll. On the other was a bundle of gear ready for transport. The door to the washroom was closed. His pod occupied most of the room and was more than twice his size, not something I'd noticed about mine. His could probably accommodate him in full armor, which I found interesting.

Not a speck of dust existed in the room. The sheets were neatly tucked around the bed roll. No drill sergeant would find fault with his housekeeping.

"Are you okay?" I asked.

"Yes. Go check on the others. Use the doorbell. They are not as…" he spoke several words that Kayan translated as stoic.

"Thanks."

"Don't mention it."

I made my retreat and felt pretty good. That was a serious conversation compared to earlier encounters. Maybe Wozim was all right.

There was no answer at Montow's door, so I entered and found the lights off. His pod stood in the corner. Careful examination revealed details I'd missed before. It was larger than mine, and there were patterns scrolling around the exterior, nothing like what I had seen on Wozim's version.

"Should I wake him up?" I asked.

Kayan answered after a distracted pause. "Better to check his vitals in the panel on the left, then leave him to find his own way to the land of the living."

"Sounds creepy when you say it like that." I searched for the panel.

Kayan created a softly glowing overlay in my vision to direct me to the right place. "No comment. Most races are preoccupied with the line between life and death."

"True. You're not?"

"I am a living ship, Noah."

"Right." I located the panel and read symbols that changed before my eyes as I understood them better. Montow was dreaming. Only his face was visible, and only when I knew where to look. A smile transformed his expression. I didn't want to wake him up. "Show me the way to Grum and Solen."

A map appeared in my vision. "Relax and the images will feel natural. Our communication is improving, even when you are not wearing a helmet with a convenient visor to support visual mediums."

The ship wasn't wrong. Kayan's constant support was growing on me. I would go into withdrawal if I ever did go home. "Thanks."

I hurried to Grum's pod and stopped when I saw his was located next to the main engine room. Much of the area had been converted into a shop with tools of Walen and Hellenger design. Patterns covered his life emergency pod like mosaics from ancient ruins, only with bright colors and images of Walens building a starship on some exotic world of forests, rocky canyons, and clouds that towered above everything.

His life signs were perfect, though he shifted when I approached. Before I could ask Kayan to let him sleep, the pod was opening.

I stepped back and waited. "You didn't have to wake up, buddy."

Grum staggered free of the parting front seals. "It is done. Why does it always feel so terrible when Kayan flies aggressively?"

"Must be one of the great mysteries of the galaxy." I didn't tell him I felt better than ever. "Take it slow. You should feel right as rain soon."

He waggled his double thumbs without meeting my gaze. All he seemed interested in was the floor and his feet. "Takes days. Why are you so loud?" He massaged his head and neck.

"Can I get you something to eat or drink? Would that help?"

He carefully shook his head. "Recovery will come. Where is Scratch? I never asked Kayan if there were pods for smaller creatures."

My heart raced. "Kayan, where is the dog?"

"Searching for the animal," the ship said on the public sound system. "The creature is a Qurk, Noah, not one of your canine species."

"Did you encapsulate the animal? I got the impression pod protection was needed to survive a jump." I was getting worried now.

"I believe the Qurk colonies relied on pod equivalents in my super structure and snuggled together in groups. Their nests held three to fifteen juveniles plus a parent. Perhaps these same family units shared what passed for pods in the under decks," Kayan said. "There was never a reason to pay much attention. Such creatures are survivors by nature. They find a way."

"So you can't find Scratch?"

"I fear the worst. This should not be so difficult. My internal awareness is very good for a member of my people," Kayan said. "But this small creature has confounded me. Unfortunately, he cannot shelter beside my control node during harsh acceleration, deceleration, or course changes."

"Control node?" I asked, immediately curious.

"Forget I mentioned it. Consider it a translation error."

"Okay, Kayan," I agreed but definitely wasn't going to forget it. The ship and the floppy six-legged animal had a secret clubhouse somewhere.

"I'll search," Grum said.

I stopped him. "Rest first. And eat something. You look like hell."

He gave me a quadruple thumbs-up and took a seat with one hand on a knee for support. I brought him a container of water before I left. On my way to Solen's cell, I searched where I could for Scratch. Rooms, passageways, closets, vents, and tubes—none held clues to the animal's fate.

18

I EXAMINED the contour of the door to Solen's cell. Nothing about it was different from mine, so maybe it was less of a detention facility than it was a passenger's cabin. The description worked for me. Much nicer.

No one guarded the prisoner. Kayan's evasive maneuvers had made that unnecessary, but we were back in regular space now with all the problems we had before the trip—except for Captain Ryg. We'd forced him to eat our space dust.

"That is the alert button—the doorbell I believe you would call it," Kayan said.

"Someday I need to give you a guided tour of my memories so you can actually learn English," I said, then pressed the raised section near the door. There was no light or the sound of a click to indicate anything had happened.

"That would be useful," Kayan said.

The door remained closed.

"Can you help me out with your sensors?" I asked.

"She is out of her pod but sitting stationary."

"Patch me through on the public address speaker for this room."

"Done."

"Solen, are you there? I came to check on you."

"Enter," she said. "I await civil discourse. Thanks for not using the executioner's knock."

The edges of the door spiraled away from the center. I stepped through. Dim light revealed the Altion woman sitting with her back to the entrance. She seemed to be packing but had evidently forgotten what she was doing and stopped in the middle of filling a backpack.

"Do you need help?" I asked.

She closed the pack and placed it near the wall. "No. Waking from a Kayan safety pod is difficult. Our people believe you should not do it more than twelve times in a person's life."

"Really? I feel fantastic afterward."

She glared at me like I was making a bad joke. Then crossed her thin arms. "You are strange."

"I'm a long way from home. I feel just a smidge out of place."

"I would like to clean up. Can you wait outside?"

"Sure." I headed for the door, but noticed she took the backpack into the wash area. That was odd, unless she had something valuable inside and was being paranoid. The pack was compliments of the ship. She hadn't brought it with her from the Gavant science vessel.

"Kayan, can you tell me if our guest smuggled something on board?"

"I have never tried to spy on a passenger in this manner. Is it necessary?"

"I don't want surprises. Montow and Wozim already want her gone. If she's sneaking contraband or weapons, it will hurt her in the end."

"Why don't you ask her?"

The ship had a point. "The more I know, the less chance she can lie. Maybe Montow is right. She could cause us a lot of problems we don't need."

"One moment," Kayan said. "Most items are undetectable to me if concealed. Electronics and what you call computers, however, are detectable. She has a device of unknown capabilities. Do you wish for me to decrypt it and look inside?"

"Only if you can do it safely, and not get caught. Something tells me she won't appreciate us snooping around in her secret data device."

Solen stepped through the door. Her horizontally wide but vertically narrow eyes squinted at me. Suspicion looked the same in both our cultures. "Is there a problem, Noah the United Earth man?"

"Just Noah. We're on the same side, remember? Us against the Gavant."

She stepped around me and was careful to keep the backpack on the shoulder farthest from where I stood. "We had that conversation?"

"More of an assumption. We're fleeing the Gavant. You're going to be blamed for a mutiny on one of their science vessels, even if you weren't an instigator. We have a lot in common."

"What is your actual point? Why are you watching me like that?"

"What's in the bag?" My next play would be threatening to get Wozim involved, even though I doubted he would play along. They were *natural-born enemies*, so the gambit should work.

She stalled for several long moments, then unslung the pack and handed it to me. "You'll just take it anyway. But don't get any ideas. The cube is encrypted. What gave me away?"

"Lucky guess." I pulled out a device that was small enough to conceal in a pocket, but not comfortably and not forever. "You brought this onto Kayan?" My indignant act could've been better, but it got the reaction I sought.

"There was no choice. The Gavant must not have it. I will destroy the data before surrendering a single line of code," she said.

"Is that the reason Ryg is after you?"

She looked ready to fight. "They're after everyone." Nothing I'd said or done had earned points with her, which was unfair as hell.

I negated her statement with a palm swipe. "Forget that. He's got a special case of angry for you. He barely mentioned Kayan or the rest of us. Right now, you're his focus. Why? I can't help you if you lie. What can I tell Montow and the others? I'll defend you, but not if you treat me like a mushroom."

She made a confused face, shook it off, and pressed on. "Why?"

"What do you mean, why?"

"You owe me nothing. I've not been nice. What is in this for you?"

That was a damn good question I hadn't asked myself. Or if I had, there hadn't been a satisfactory answer. "Ryg doesn't like my friends. He doesn't like you…" I spread both hands and shrugged.

"You're an idiot."

"I think you're one of the good guys. Pops always told me I was a good judge of character."

"Who is Pops?"

"Smartest man I ever knew."

She accepted the answer with a series of short, contemplative nods. "Maybe you are. Let me tell you a story, and see if your special instincts still approve of me."

I motioned that we should walk toward the bridge while she explained.

She fell in step. "Gavant worlds rarely have much population growth. Some, but not enough to staff their expansionist policies. Their colonies provide most support services because all of their young people serve in their military. That is where prestige is earned. The Altion were one of the first star systems to be conquered. We are more like them than any of the other races. You can almost be Gavant with Altion heritage."

"But not quite," I said.

She curled her lip. "No. It is never enough for them. But many of my people spend their lives earning their way into a higher class of servant. No Walen or Hellenger can rise as high as one of my people. Montow can be an astronavigator or an engineer, but never a recognized scientist. The Hellenger have been part of the Gavant Reach longer than most, but not half as long as the Altion. The Walen... are treated as little more than animals."

"Noah," barked a voice at our feet.

I scooped up Scratch. "There you are, buddy."

"Why are you holding that rat?" Solen asked.

"Not a rat. Trust me, I'm a vermin expert. This is a quality golden Qurk right here."

"A rat, like I said."

Scratch cocked his head. I put the animal down. We were near the bridge entrance. "So you're a hot shot scientist with a special data device."

She murdered me with her stare. "I was hoping you forgot." She motioned to Scratch. "Lot of good you are."

"Solen," the animal said.

I tried to remember using the woman's name and wasn't sure where the strange, six-legged creature had picked it up. Solen seemed unnerved as well. Mimicry was a Qurk thing, apparently.

"I'm glad we had this talk. Let's see what's shaking on the bridge." I led the way inside to find the bridge vacant.

"Nothing is out of place. I thought you said it was being shook." Solen toured the fresh pods and attached workstations. "Nothing is even a bit shaken."

"Figure of speech."

She raised one eyebrow and I realized that too was something she didn't quite understand. I dismissed the topic and focused on the data device she didn't wish to discuss. "The device. What is it? Why does Ryg want it so badly?"

"A real Kayan. I never thought I'd see one."

"The device." I wasn't letting her change the subject.

She locked her jaw and strode past me to examine the computer stations, one of which, I noticed, was the perfect height for her. "It would be easier to show you, but also dangerous. Are you sure this is a decision you wish to make alone? With knowledge comes consequences." She stepped back from Kayan's computer, then faced me.

I stalled. "Where is Montow?" What was her game? Was I missing something?

"Ntow," Scratch said.

Kayan answered on top of the animal's response. "I sent him to investigate an anomaly, which I now understand was the animal's pod. There are functions I need not think about, like your involuntary muscles. Scratch crawled into an insulation layer, which adapted to protect him outside my conscious intervention. Now I understand how his species survived what you call travel by FTL warp bubble," Kayan said. "Very logical. Scratch gets into places no one else does. Sometimes that's okay."

"Fascinating," Solen said. "I could build an academic career on what you just described, if every accredited Gavant university didn't have me on their watch list."

I stepped closer, then put my hand over Solen's, because she was trying to hide the device under the workstation. "Just tell me what it is, what it does, and why I shouldn't give you and the cube to Ryg. That is the easiest solution to all of this."

She pulled her hand free, retreated a step, and began wandering the bridge as she spoke. "I told you we have long been part of the Gavant Reach. Never has a year passed when we didn't resent our lack of freedom. Most of what they build should have been ours. Galaxy's stars, we built much of it for them."

"The cube."

"I haven't examined the contents, but I could, with time and the right equipment. That is why they chose me. My work for the Gavant was high-level, with corresponding security access—until the mutiny. Which wasn't supposed to happen. Migen was discovered, and we panicked. He would have died in silence for the cause, but how could anyone but his closest friends know that?"

I shut up and listened.

"I was hours away from destroying the cube, and the ship to keep this data out of the wrong hands," she said. "Not all of my people can be trusted. Some consider themselves more Gavant than Altion—probably because that means more status, and more status means more security.

"But you have no idea what it is." I wasn't convinced.

"I have some idea, but this isn't the time or place to talk about it," she said. "I'm not willing to speculate on something like this. When I've found what I need and have run tests, I might talk to you—if you're against the Gavant."

Montow stormed in with his hammer fists clenched and his shoulders pulled halfway up his soup can head. "Stop talking to her. She should be locked up. I went to her cell, and she was missing!"

"You weren't looking for Scratch?"

He cursed, then strode to his workstation and slipped on his split keyboards. His fingers flew across the letters and symbols until the main screen displayed a picture of Solen Far. "That is a Gavant Empire and associated systems-wide alert. Now we are all first-order fugitives!"

"You were already being pursued," Solen shot back.

"This is different. All Kayan ships have a bounty. Grum and I are essentially runaways. That does not compare to a true enemy of the Gavant!" Montow looked as big as Wozim right then, and twice as fierce.

Speaking of which… "What about the Tyton? Why are they after him?"

The questions let out much of Montow's steam. He didn't look at me when he answered. "They don't know who he really is. Better none of you learn the truth."

"I refuse to take all the blame," Solen said. "Take me to Milyn, and you'll never hear from me again. Win, win. Everyone is happy."

Scratch flattened himself on the floor and covered his eyes

with his two front paws. His weak sixth leg curled and twitched until I wondered if he was losing control of it, just like when he'd first crawled out of the Qurk nest.

"See, now you've upset the dog," I said.

"Rat." Solen drew away from us, fiddling with the bag straps.

"You must make peace with them, Noah. It is something I am not equipped to enforce," Kayan said in my ear.

I raised my hands toward each of them. "Let's take a breath and work this out. We're still heading away from the Gavant's sphere of influence, right?"

Montow growled. "Yes. That is our goal. Having every starship in the region after us won't make it easier."

"But it can be done. Once we're sure no one is following us, we can take our time to do things right. Figure out exactly what each of us needs. I'd like to go home someday. Just one example."

"Lucky you." Montow stormed out of the room, his legs taking longer, faster strides than normal.

Solen approached me coolly. "I'll see myself to my cell. Safer there. Between Captain Montow and the Tyton, I don't feel comfortable on these decks."

I watched her go, then sank into the *chair* of my new pod. Nothing about it revealed how Kayan moved them into the travel vault, or other rooms. That must be another reason she shut us inside. Safety first, right after secrecy.

"Noah, I can detect the cube, just to be clear," Kayan said. "Solen still has it. The ability to read its contents or manipulate its data is beyond my abilities."

"Could you crack the code, under the right circumstances?"

"Perhaps if we worked together," Kayan said.

"Tell me more." I took the scenic route to Solen's quarters as the ship explained how we needed to work together.

19

"REMEMBER, you must have it in your hands when you examine it," Kayan said. "I require all sensory information your human biology can provide, especially sight."

"You're the advanced biological life-form able to travel between worlds. I'll trust your judgment, though a little remote code hacking seems like it should be easy for you," I said, then stopped myself from knocking on Solen's door. "Almost did it again." The doorbell was easier to find now. Pressing the button-like panel felt natural.

A minute passed. Solen opened the door and stared at me. She looked refreshed, her uniform pressed and straightened. "What do you want?"

"We have to talk about the cube, and Ryg. Like it or not, we're in this together."

"Unless you turn me in," she said, then waved me inside.

"Then you would get a pass for about three seconds. Mark my words, Noah. He'll stab you in the back and twist the blade for as long as he can."

"Agreed. Montow may not say it, but he understands there is no bargaining with this guy. The moment we stop to turn you over, he'll rush us."

"So what do you want? What is your condition for all this honesty?" she asked.

"I need to verify you have the cube."

She took a step back and turned away. "What do you mean?"

I hated myself for realizing she'd given away where she kept it, and that I could take it from her if I had to.

Would I?

Maybe.

What a jerk.

"I need to know you are really keeping it from them, if it's that dangerous. You might be telling us that to keep you around, when in reality the cube doesn't exist, or you never had it to begin with."

She squared her shoulders proudly and raised her chin. "I have nothing to prove."

I waited. And then waited more. She was trying not to look at me but kept darting glances to see why I wasn't shouting.

She paced the width of the small room, turning sharply at each reversal. "You are the stranger here, and you understand less than nothing." Turn. "Why should Montow or anyone else listen to someone from another galaxy…" Turn. "…for all we know? I mean, who are you, and where did you come from, actually?"

I marked the movement of her hands. She touched the pocket too frequently, and I realized my earlier assumption had been wrong. She had expected a snatch and grab, and hidden it elsewhere, probably in the backpack or somewhere in the room. The last option was dangerous. She must have suspected that Kayan would help me find any hiding place that was part of the ship.

"I just need to confirm you have it, hold it in my hand. It never needs to leave your sight."

"You already saw it."

"Not the same. Stop being difficult. Makes you look guilty."

She flared her nostrils and narrowed her wrap-around eyes as she watched me with obvious suspicion. Was this another attempt to distract me from her true purpose, or just what it seemed—anger. Her features, her posture, everything about the woman was strange to me—not bad—but unique. The woman had my undivided attention, and she knew it.

"Fine." She went to the backpack, moved it, then popped a vent in the wall. Screening her movements with her body, she eventually turned and offered the cube.

"It was in the backpack," Kayan said. "In case you were wondering. Can you believe she was attempting to further deceive you?"

I signaled my complete incredulity and wondered if the ship caught my sarcasm. We shared thoughts, after a fashion, and there wasn't a movement I made on the ship Kayan couldn't observe. While that was disturbing, it was also convenient.

The device sat in the palm of Solen's silver-tattooed hand. "Go ahead. Hold it."

I plucked it up and examined it. She sat on a bench near the wall.

"Very good, Noah. Just a bit longer and I will have what I need."

Twisting it between my thumb and forefinger felt oddly satisfying. I was gazing at a piece of alien tech, after all. Not even Collins could say he'd done that. Who was the badass star traveler now?

The cube looked like metal. It had a texture that was possibly like braille, or just numbers, letters, and other symbols too small to differentiate from one another. "I hope you're not relying on me to read these."

Solen jumped up from the bench. "The ship sees through your eyes and feels through your hands! You snake. I would not have gone along with your scheme. Sneak! Return it immediately."

"What do you say, Kayan? Seen enough?"

"Asshole!" Solen forced the word between clenched teeth.

"Almost. I am sorry she is angry with you," Kayan said.

"Not your fault." I leaned away from the angry Altion woman. She was petite, but that didn't mean she wasn't terrifying. Her almost lavender skin grew flushed in places. The darker patches were mostly on her face. "I'll give it back. Just hold your horses."

The phrase stopped her in her tracks. "Excuse me?"

"How are we doing, Kayan?"

Solen rallied and shook a fist at me. "This ship is trying to look in my device!"

"Not at all," I lied in my best Monty Python voice. "No, no, no. I was just holding it for you."

"You are tampering with things you don't understand and want no part of." She lunged but was neither tall enough nor strong enough to seize the data cube by force.

I wasn't sure if I should laugh or feel like a jerk. "Come on, Kayan! Give me some help."

"Apologies, Noah. That was more taxing than expected. I have all that I can get without permanently depriving Solen Far of her property. It is hers. I confirmed that much. What is hidden within the hardware was stolen by her, from the Gavant science labs."

"Catch." I tossed back the cube.

She caught it with one hand, barely needing to look at the trajectory of the item. "Did you get what you were looking for?"

I shrugged. "Kayan, anything useful?"

"Possibly. You might be most interested in an intelligence report referencing Orth, though it might be properly spelled as Earth," Kayan said, careful to keep Solen out of our conversation. "Over half of the contents are inaccessible to me without dissembling each layer of its microcircuitry."

"Your connection to this ship is unique," Solen accused. "Do Montow and the others know how those have linked the two of you?" She motioned toward the visible parts of my arms. If she saw how much of my upper body, and parts of my legs were sheathed in Kayan material, she would really be freaking out.

"The topic hasn't come up." Waves of heat radiated through my shared body parts. "I didn't ask to be saved. Kayan found my ship damaged and asked for permission to … do stuff."

"Montow helped." Solen's words were not a question.

Kayan answered. "He is a skilled surgeon of my kind, and respectful enough to allow some privacy between a ship and its passengers."

"Have you heard of privacy?" I asked.

Solen surprised me with a softer expression. "I'm sorry for what happened to you. My interest is scientific. But I'm still very angry with you for trying to hack my data cube. Speaking of privacy."

I blushed. "Yeah. Uhm. Sorry."

"You were right, earlier. There is little choice but to trust each other. I have intel on the enemy, including worlds they plan to conquer, or destroy if they harbor life but don't meet their needs. The Gavant never leave a viable threat behind their lines, so to speak. If your home world is on their list of places to be destroyed, then you have my condolences."

"If they know about Earth, then they've been there. Which means they can go there again. And that means I can go home," I said, then waved away the obvious downside to this information. "Barring that annoying part where there might be nothing but an asteroid field there when I arrive."

Solen looked horrified. "How do you think they destroy a living planet?"

"Powerful death ray? Super galactic nukes?" I didn't know.

She shook her head in the unique, languid way she had done earlier. "Your people must be as bad as the Gavant to imagine destruction on that level. They have ways to end all life in a system without ruining the biospheres to lower life-forms and future use."

"I guess that's slightly better," I said. "I mean, as long as they don't kill the dolphins, right."

"Exactly."

"Wait, you have dolphins on Altion worlds?"

"Why wouldn't we?"

"Okay, I have a lot of questions." This conversation wasn't going as expected, but I did get hold of the cube as Kayan wanted, and it seemed Solen and I remained on speaking terms afterward.

Now if I could just convince Montow not to dump her in an escape pod for Captain Ryg and bug out.

20

"THE *KON* HAS ENTERED THE SYSTEM," Montow announced.

I shot to my feet. Since my meeting with Solen and experiencing many revelations I was still sorting out, I'd managed to adjust my pod to resemble a proper chair. Kayan had even been open to leaving the crew capsules on the bridge for short jumps between systems. I thought that would be more efficient than getting stuck in the vault every time we accelerated.

Kicking back and reading dull intelligence reports about Gavant ship movements, unfortunately, had a way of putting me to sleep. I shook away disturbing dreams of my rescue and focused on Montow's warning. "Just now?"

"Yes, Noah Gantz. Just now," he said.

I resisted a snarky comeback because he could have nailed me with several. Sometimes his mentor vibe was annoying. How could I be a jerk if he was being nice? I really needed someone to trash talk with before I got out of practice. Pilots back home were going to eat me alive if I ever made it to Earth.

"There is good news." Montow activated the main display screen where it floated before us. "Ryg must not know we're here because his warship entered the system far from us and is searching an asteroid belt in the other direction."

"Won't he scan the system?"

"That takes time, and Kayan is harder to detect than traditional ships—especially at this range. X-53-Alpha is a large system."

I reviewed reports and was only slightly put off by the glitchy translation. Words changed from symbols, to subtle variations of iconography, to English complete with my United Earth military jargon. A laugh escaped when I realized something else. The display wasn't in courier font, or any digital text. My less than perfect handwriting, complete with doodles, conveyed the information in luminescent script.

Nice.

Montow's attention slid my way. "You find the Gavant hunter amusing?"

"No. Hard to explain. I'm still getting used to Kayan's language processing."

He puzzled over the word for a second. "Ah. Yes. Translators are hilarious."

"I am evading Ryg's ship, but he will eventually pass near enough to guarantee detection. There is only one escape option in this system," Kayan said.

Data for a fifth of the star system populated the main screen, and also showed an estimate of what Ryg would currently see. The edges of the zones were too close for comfort. Following the outer rim of the heliosphere in the opposite direction from the Gavant warship revealed unidentified vessels.

"Who are they? And why are they crawling?" I asked.

Montow made a noise deep in his throat that sounded a lot like growling.

"Pirates," Kayan said.

"Really?"

"Could they be regular ship crews attempting to render aid?" Montow typed furiously on his hand boards. "Maybe there is another derelict ship out there?"

"Searching for distress echoes." Kayan displayed numbers and symbols. "There are warp bubble and sub light speed signal artifacts in this system. Thirty-nine are requests for protection against pirates and seem relevant to this situation."

I was curious about other transmissions but let it go. "Can we help them?"

"Kayan has no weapons," Montow said. "And self-preservation must remain our priority. Our altruism would draw attention and slow us down. We can help no one from a Gavant prison."

"Good point." I reviewed the system map from every angle and didn't like it. There was a lot we couldn't see, since Kayan had never been here before and there were no downloaded references from other travelers. All we had were stories about how sketchy this place was. Some of the reports I skimmed read like scandal magazines. "Can we at least get a better look?"

Montow dropped his "chin." Even with the sunglasses, I saw he had closed his eyes. It was either nap time, or he was just a smidge frustrated with me. "It is on the way."

"So what's the problem?"

"We have not known each other long, but I feel like you will do something reckless." He resumed working. "Like rescue an Altion spy and give her VIP treatment."

"Locking someone in their room doesn't make us a five-star hotel. Besides, anyone running from the Gavant must be half decent."

"Agreed," he said, completely missing the nuance of my statement. "Promise that when we pass near these ships, you will let Kayan and me handle everything. Traveling straight through this system will save us time and prevent Ryg from following. It is a notorious place with a great deal of trade and the raiding that goes with it."

"You want to keep our heads down and use the sketchy criminal element for cover," I said. "Like cutting through a bad neighborhood."

"Yes. That is correct."

"Are the Gavant afraid to travel this way? Doesn't seem likely."

Montow dipped his head side to side, just enough to notice. "Yes and no. They can't be bothered to police this sector. If they want something, they will take it. We must remain hidden for the duration."

"Tell me about these sketchy space thieves," I said.

"The pirates of X-53-Alpha are into every sort of criminal

activity. Resource haulers must pass this way unless they have the most modern starships, which they never do. Freighters on this route are usually old and cheaply constructed," Kayan explained. "The local organizations, however, are into every sort of illegal venture. Piracy, slaving, extortion, fraud, and even usury. Some are believed to indulge in cannibalism and sell questionable food products along those lines."

"Yuck." I reviewed the reports scrolling across my screen. "Sounds worse than the Gavant. Next thing you know they'll be playing their music too loud and ripping tags off mattresses."

Montow glared. "You think they don't do all these things and worse?"

I held up both hands, palms out. "My bad. I'll be in my chair minding my own business."

The captain huffed and began updating logs. I watched star maps change. Each blip glowed with an unheard story. Were they chasing down prey? Running for their lives? Starting over after defaulting on a bad debt to the space mob? I suspected most were boring tales of merchant marines creeping back and forth across this corner of the galaxy—but I still wanted to know.

Images came in range. Kayan displayed the ship sending the distress call. Other than the sub light speed comm message and the FTL emergency beacon, the ship was dark and quiet. Two dilapidated warships towed it toward the large, mountain-covered moon of a gas giant.

"There are others coasting without power," Kayan warned.

Montow tensed. "Alert Wozim, Grum, and Solen. That tactic always means trouble."

I reviewed the scan and saw what the ship had detected. Scattered around the towing operation were dark shapes. There were no power signals, and no comms, not even internal to the ship. Kayan wasn't always able to pick up that sort of thing but could usually determine there was ship chatter from this range.

"We're too close," Montow muttered. "Kayan, please proceed by momentum alone."

"Of course, captain." The ship cut forward thrust. None of us felt it, but the readings changed. "They were not likely to spot me even at half speed."

"Your entrance into the system didn't go unnoticed," Montow countered. "It's a good thing we arrived before Ryg's warship."

"We're passing the piracy incident. If it makes you feel better, Noah, there are no life signs. The villains are dragging an empty ship for resale or salvage."

Kayan's assurance made me feel worse, not better. There had been people on that freighter. I doubted anything good happened to them. The crew was either dead or on their way to a slave market. "What else is in this system besides heartache?"

"Lorin Solar," Montow said. "An infamous port orbiting the interior gas giant. Even the pirates fear doing business there."

"So we're going?"

Montow glowered at me from his pod. Sunglasses concealed his motives.

"You need supplies," Kayan said. "Unless what I synthesize is sufficient."

Montow's expression softened, but he turned back to his station to avoid close analysis. I leaned out to one side, trying to see what his face was hiding. For the first time, I regretted asking the ship to make him shades. He hunkered down and gave me nothing.

"Grum is on the way to the bridge," Kayan said.

"Get Wozim up here and we can vote." I was joking. The ship didn't get it, and neither did the captain.

"In here," Kayan said. "The command center is deep on the primary level for safety reasons. It also keeps the neural chains shorter for many of my critical systems."

"And allows you to store us in your vault during the more dangerous jumps," I guessed.

"Yes. That is also accurate." Kayan paused, seemingly to review recently gathered data. "There are Oort field derivatives stored in a warehouse on Lorin Solar."

"Seriously? What for?" I asked. "Do they sell to Kayans? Like some kind of farmer's market in space?"

"No. The fungi can be broken down into radioactive isotopes useful in several popular fuel formulas." Kayan displayed complicated documentation. "It is very concentrated and easy to store."

"You warned me those food sources are not ideal," Montow said.

"Correct. Consuming processed Oort material can be

dangerous. Some of my brethren have grown addicted to the spike, despite the crash that often follows."

I reviewed the data. "Can we do anything to minimize the hangover?"

"Yes. Feed normally within one standard week," Kayan said. "This seems easy but rarely is, especially since the worst problem with Oort derivatives is the false satiation effect. My kind are found drifting aimlessly in search of other Kayan or Hoyon entities. It never goes well."

"We should avoid the port," Montow said. "There are other dangers between us and Lorin Solar. Put it out of your head, Noah Gantz. Not worth it."

I saw his disappointment. Apparently, someone was tired of eating synthesized food. Or maybe he missed his people and needed a vacation from a Tyton, a Walen, an Altion, and me. What did he do for fun? Had I been a bad friend by letting him work nonstop?

"What about Grum and the others?" I asked. "Maybe they have something to say."

"Of course they do." Montow didn't look at me. "That doesn't make my decision wrong. Ask Kayan if you need a second opinion."

"The risk is not worth the reward," the ship said.

"Can we get close enough to see it?" I was curious and didn't agree. They probably knew best, but this was all new to me and the idea of visiting my first alien spaceport was intriguing. "Who knows, with better information, we might detect something useful. And you said the Gavant don't go there. Sounds like the perfect place to stock up on Twinkies and Coca-Cola."

"What is that?" Montow asked.

"Something humans call junk food," Kayan answered.

The Hellenger captain shuddered, and I wondered what the actual translation had been for him. He removed the glasses and wiped his eyes, then put them back on.

Grum entered. "Are we there yet?"

"That depends on where you thought we were going," Montow said.

"Oh, we're there," I said at the same time, then pointed at the Lorin Solar icon. The image showed a city covering a large portion of a moon orbiting a gas planet. Double asteroid rings tilted around it.

"I've never been to Lorin Solar," Grum said. "But I've read about it many times."

"Those were adventure stories." Montow pointed a thick, telescoping finger at the Walen. "Don't believe a word of it."

Grum shrugged. "We could get supplies, and stock up on Oort derivatives. Kayan kept that last batch for a long time before using them in an emergency. That's what you told me."

Montow muttered in his own language.

"It's settled," I said. "We'll get close enough for a look and see if there is anything worth our time. At the very least, the ship traffic might confuse Ryg's efforts to pursue us."

"I have set a course to pass the gas giant at a safe distance." Kayan displayed several markers from what she had scanned of the system. "All of these vessels are engaged in questionable activities." A pause followed. "This one is heading our way. I didn't detect the change of course at first because the captain was shadowing a convoy of freighters."

"Tell me more." I didn't like the image. It looked too much like a Gavant hunter, though battle-scarred.

"She is called the *White Knife*, a notorious pirate chieftain normally active in other star systems," Kayan said.

"Looks like Ryg's warship." I rotated the image. Spots were blank where there was no current data, but even what we could see at this distance was disturbing. There were a lot of missile ports and point defense weapons.

"I've heard of the *White Knife*. Talk is they took it by force, though that's scarcely believable," Montow said. "The Gavant would hunt them down for such an offense."

"Maybe they're too busy," I said. "I'm new in this part of the galaxy, but they seem like they're after a lot of people. How big is their fleet? They can't get us all."

Montow and Grum stared at me.

"Okay, point taken." I didn't disagree with Montow's theory. Playing the devil's advocate was habitual. Anything was possible. I was a stranded test pilot on the wrong side of the galaxy, after all. "Will it follow us to Lorin Solar? Maybe we can hide."

"That could work, but only for a short time," Kayan said. "Sooner or later, the captain of that infamous ship will guess where we are and merely wait for us to leave."

"The *White Knife* is a different breed of pirate ship," Montow said.

I understood his point, and not just because of the obvious

hardware. The captain had to know he was the top dog in the pack. Others probably did his bidding and hoped for his favor. We weren't dealing with just one pirate vessel, but a half-assed criminal armada.

Scans only showed the one aging warship, but I wasn't satisfied with what we could see. "Kayan, has the *White Knife* spent more time with any of these convoys than the others?"

"One moment." The ship computer went to work. Montow and Grum stared at me as we waited, probably wondering what I was thinking.

I suspected the *White Knife*'s confederates were in sheep's clothing.

"Solen Far is requesting admittance to the bridge," Kayan said. "She claims to have knowledge of this system."

Montow grumbled. Grum seemed excited for a visitor. I waited to see if Wozim would show up to make things awkward, but of course he didn't.

"Where is she?" I asked.

"I gave her the impression that she is confined to quarters," Montow said. "I don't know if Kayan actually locked the door."

"Her room was secured. Wozim saw to it. I denied his request to push her out of an airlock, and eventually compromised on stricter security until we trust Solen Far. She will need permission to leave, and an escort if you think it is appropriate."

For a moment, I wasn't sure who Kayan was speaking to but decided to wait and let Montow take the lead. He'd been here longer than me and I'd been making a lot of decisions and offering opinions without being asked—like I was the captain. It was an easy, comfortable assumption. Kayan was with me constantly and felt like my ship, though I knew none of us owned her.

"Send Noah," Montow said. "He has the most invested in the Altion. They have a rapport."

Grum and I laughed together.

The good-natured Walen spoke first. "Have you watched them interact? One of us should go to keep Noah from being stabbed in the throat."

Montow made a dismissive wave and returned to his work. "I will help the ship analyze our approach to Lorin Solar, since it seems you are determined we go there."

"Looks like it's you and me then, Grum." I unlatched from my safety pod and headed for the door, which spiraled open at my approach.

The Walen followed enthusiastically. "I've never seen anyone get stabbed before."

"Oh, yeah. You should definitely be there when it happens. Do you know anything about first aid?"

"First what?"

We traversed the hallway and passed through several bulkheads as I explained the basics. "Just try to stop the blood loss. If possible, keep her from stabbing me at all."

"Seems like smart thinking." Grum clapped his hands together and skipped to keep up.

I wanted to arrive before Montow or Kayan alerted Wozim.

As much as I complained privately about his lack of engagement, now wasn't when I wanted him to get involved.

"She should like you," Grum said. "What would have happened if you never found her? Not everyone would have gone back for an Altion working with Gavant soldiers."

"She said it was a science ship."

"Every Gavant is a soldier. They have, what would you call it, compulsory service. But they don't really have to be mandated. When you meet one of them, you'll understand. They all want to dominate their environment."

I pondered what he was saying and had a hard time believing there wasn't some variation. A lot of humans would fit his description of these ultimate Galactic bad guys, but that wasn't all of us.

The door opened when I approached, and Solen stepped out.

"No need for your death knock. I've been waiting. How long does it take to get here from the bridge?"

"We could go back. Grum was just telling me about your buddies back there on the Gavant ship."

She gave me a hateful look, then crossed her arms and retreated a step. The mannerism was basically what I expected. I reserved judgment, but also took the hint.

"The *Kon* followed us into the system, but we've stayed away from it."

"Good." Her voice was quiet. Gone was the bad attitude she'd hit me with when the door opened. This was a person ready to retreat if she only knew which way to go.

"We're heading for Lorin Solar. Could be supplies we need there." I wasn't sure what to expect, but hoped she would back up my decision.

"It's a dangerous option, but I see where your head's at." She started walking toward the bridge and we all fell in together. "We shouldn't stay there long, if at all."

"What do you mean?" She wasn't on my side, it seemed.

"I'm sure the other members of your crew tried to talk you out of it. That place is a den of thieves and murderers. The Gavant won't go there, but they have agents who will and can pay bounty hunters with deep roots in the darker corners of this galaxy," she said. "You want my advice, look before you leap."

I nodded. "Fair."

"But we'll never see Lorin Solar, not up close. The raiders in this system scare away Gavant patrols. What does that say about them?"

"You're officially off my list of motivational speakers."

21

THE WALK back to the bridge was tense. Grum no longer skipped or made jokes. He stayed on the opposite side of the passageway from Solen and waited for us to enter the bridge before following.

The first thing I noticed when we were inside was that Wozim had made one of his rare appearances. The second was that Scratch slept under my crash pod, but had one eye cracked to watch the Tyton. It wasn't much, but I thought the animal was faking dreamland to keep watch on the most dangerous person in the room.

"Nice of you to show up, Wozim." I made sure to keep myself between him and the Altion. "Are we going to have problems?"

He faced the central view screen and ignored me. Why would he do anything else?

I turned to Solen. "We *are* one big happy family."

Wozim showed his razor-sharp, jet-black teeth. He looked even bigger than the last time I'd seen him, probably because it was hard to really comprehend and remember his demonic physique. I didn't know how to describe him without monster references. His picture was probably beside the phrase evil menace in most dictionaries.

And here he was among us. Just standing there like a force of nature with no regard for our lives.

Solen stood her ground but didn't go too close to the brute. Montow observed the scene and didn't seem happy. This was my fault, so much of his displeasure was probably aimed at me. I would deal with that some other time. Right now, we needed to evade the *White Knife* in addition to the Gavant warship.

I went to my pod and adjusted the seat. Hands flying over the controls, I reviewed what had been done while I was away. "What was this planet we passed?"

"That is locally known as Lorin Solar," Montow said. "They're not big on originality. Each planet has the same name with a unique numerical identifier. X-53-Alpha is the Gavant designation for the system. Not popular here."

"Works for me. Less to memorize." Neither Wozim nor Solen appreciated my humor. Grum got it, so I gave him a fist bump which he seemed to think was the best thing that ever happened to him. The guy was fun to have around.

I reviewed summaries of three bubble-like cities on the planet's surface and counted twenty-seven platforms in orbit around the frozen rock. It wasn't large and reminded me of

Pluto, which was always a planet in my book. There were only so many times it could gain and lose that status. At some point, we needed to just make a decision.

Homesickness crept up on me like a ninja. I pushed aside comparisons to the Sol system. There would be time for those memories later, probably right after I discovered this place's equivalent of whiskey.

"We moved close enough to alert their flight control," Montow explained. "That will help screen pursuit. The *White Knife* or Ryg will have to do the same or give it a wide berth. It's not much, but every little bit helps."

I watched a pair of fighters shoot away from the most official-looking platform in orbit. Each ship sported flashy paint schemes that had faded and chipped over time. Radiation was hard on the most resilient colors, unless someone spent the money to have pigment infused into alloys, or calibrated shields to protect the aesthetics. These vessels had well-used guns and often-repaired hulls. I guessed they'd been purchased from military surplus, or stolen from junkyards.

A second and third pair launched and established orbits around Lorin Solar as the lead element confronted Kayan.

"LS 89 for unregistered Kayan vessel, follow the prescribed course and match our speed." The voice was both commanding and bored. "You don't want to make us match yours. We've got Spector 3000 missiles. Maybe you've heard of them."

I scrolled through screens, but quickly turned to Montow for answers. Kayan wasn't feeding me every detail at the moment. "Have we?"

"Yes. They accelerate twenty times faster than the fastest documented Kayan." Our Hellenger captain glowered at the screen that now showed the helmet and visor of the Lorin Solar guardian. "Not something to brag about, but enough to damage us."

"What would be an impressive missile speed?" I asked, also watching but not talking to the security pilot.

"The Gavant *Kon* has versions that move with a hundred times our best acceleration," Kayan said. "According to confirmed battle reports."

"Reduce speed and follow the course markers they're sending," Montow ordered.

Kayan complied instantly.

"Once the *White Knife* joins the queue, punch it and get out of here," Montow added. "They should not fire once they have other ships to deal with."

Out of the corner of my eye, I saw Wozim smile. Terrifying as that was, the image made me feel better. He did care! Maybe he would even do something if we were caught.

"Of course, Montow. I suspected this would be your suggestion and have primed all power sources for quick activation. Please secure yourselves," Kayan said.

"Not yet. If they see us strapping in, they'll be ready when it happens. We can't escape the *White Knife*, and the *Kon*, and Lorin Solar security patrols unless we surprise everyone." I took a seat but purposefully bumped the spiral doors open wider. Maintaining the careless, sloppy look was difficult because anyone who had been on a Kayan knew the pods closed dangerously fast.

Maybe LS 89 relaxed. It was hard to tell behind the helmet visor and bored posture. He was just another fighter jock.

"Respond," he said. "Or face immediate sanction. You don't want to wait for the next spaceport. Unless you're fat as a red dwarf on supplies."

Grum eased into his pod and activated a screen. "The *White Knife* has pulled into the orbit queue. The *Kon* is still at the system's edge searching asteroid fields."

"Good work, Grum." Montow typed furiously, an act that caused his hands to rise slightly. He almost appeared to be working at a human keyboard. Almost. "Solen, your expert advice would be appreciated, if you have any. That is why you were allowed on the bridge."

She smiled without really smiling.

A chill went up the back of my neck. I didn't want to be on her bad side.

"Check your projected course, because there is a merchant convoy near our best vector that is not really going anywhere." She stared into the captain's blocky sunglasses. "What do you think that means?"

I answered while he wrestled with stoicism. "*White Knife's* confederates are waiting for us to bolt." Kayan provided information almost faster than I typed. "We can use that."

"How?" Montow and Solen asked at the same time.

"The same way we were using the spaceport—by cutting it close. Kayan, plot a course that will take us past the *White Knife's* stealth armada. I want them to think we've fallen for it, and by the time we rocket past them, it will be too late for them to accelerate and overtake us. At the same time, our pursuers will need to avoid collisions."

Everyone worked on the idea. LS 89 had enough. "Respond immediately, and reestablish full comms with audio. You will be fired upon in ten seconds."

I held up both hands. "Slow down, buddy. We're trying to comply. This ship is hard to handle."

I am cooperating perfectly, Noah. Why would you lie? Kayan said privately.

"I'm doing what I have to do," I said for the security goon and the living starship.

"Ready," Montow said.

Solen nodded seriously. "Everything looks good."

"Match our speed immediately," LS 89 insisted. "And conform to these new coordinates. All crew and passengers will be detained for interviews."

"Punch it." I was stepping on Montow's toes. He was the captain and had more time invested in the ship.

None of that mattered now. This was a matter of raw survival.

I grabbed Scratch from the floor right before my safety pod spiraled closed. I assumed everyone else was safe. Two sensations overwhelmed my capacity for thought—colors and pressure. What I saw resembled every sci-fi movie and none at the same time. Kayan explained why this trip was different, but I couldn't handle the information for several seconds.

Now I understood why Kayan preferred passengers sedated and locked in a vault. Inertial dampeners were mostly theoretical where I was from, as were gravity generators and about every part of the living space voyager. Slowly, I realized Kayan was asking me questions.

"I don't feel keeping you awake while traveling at this speed is responsible, but suspect you want to be involved in our immediate fate," Kayan said. "Please be prepared for safety pod activation should the load become too great."

"Summarize." Thinking the words was an effort. My body tried to physically form the words, creating sounds best not recorded for posterity.

"We defeated the covert blockade," Kayan explained. "But there is a second element farther out that remains in our path. These three ships were able to calculate our course more accurately and are in position to attack. Should they score a hit at these speeds, we're done."

"Do what you have to." I forced the words out, then verbally abused the screen inside my pod. A little private ranting was just the thing to help endure this ordeal. No wonder Kayan normally rendered us unconscious by this point.

Why couldn't we catch a break? Every encounter was more screwed up than the one before it. This was like starting over in high school with acne and high-water jeans. Nothing got better as the days wore on.

The pressure eased. Kayan continued to accelerate, but at a more tolerable level. My pod remained closed, but suddenly I could think, speak, and work the keyboard. Montow was the first to use internal ship comms. Solen was the second.

"Kayan says there are three pirate vessels blocking our course," Montow summarized. "We were forced to slow before reaching sufficient velocity to pierce an FTL bubble. Pardon the crude and not entirely accurate description."

"Yep," Solen agreed. "Time is up and we need a new plan."

"Pirates have matched speed and are closing in from three sides. The *White Knife* is the next closest ship in pursuit," Grum said. "Wow, my head really hurts. Sorry. You probably didn't want to know. None of the disguised merchant ships will reach us soon."

I studied the tactical overlays. Three military-class corvettes tightened the noose around Kayan. They would land on the ship soon, and that probably meant boarding parties. All they needed was to keep us busy until the larger, more powerful pirate ship caught up and lowered the hammer.

"Can you break free of this trap with raw speed?" I asked.

"I cannot, Noah. These raiders are all engine," Kayan answered. "They have attached and are reversing thrusters to slow us further."

22

"IF WE'RE LUCKY, they just want to catch us," Solen said. "Sometimes these types focus on ransom, which means we could be set free for a price. They get paid, and their ships let go and fly away."

Wozim opened his pod. "They will board and kill any who are weak. Maintain consistent acceleration. Gravity favors the strong." Muscles bunched and relaxed from his shoulders to the middle of his thick upper back. I watched the images like a kid seeing a Godzilla movie for the first time.

"Stay in your pod," Montow said.

Solen exited at the same time I did. Scratch hopped to the floor and looked bored. Grum followed, and to my surprise, so did Montow. He appeared determined, if not happy. Wozim watched us gather but gave no opinion of our battle worthiness.

Lights flickered. Most of Kayan's bulkheads remained open

during normal operation. The sound of them banging shut throughout the ship was bone chilling. Wozim jogged away, nostrils flaring and vocal chords humming a battle dirge.

"He goes to his personal armory," Montow said. "We should follow and see if he will share, except for you, Noah. Don the armor Kayan fashioned and worry about weapons later."

"He won't," Grum said.

At the same time, I gave him thumbs-up and ran my own way.

Scratch loped after me barking near-words. "Fun!"

"Let's hope so," I muttered as I reached my living quarters.

Scratch gave me a curious head tilt that suggested the word didn't mean what I thought, or anything at all. The Qurk was an animal, a mimic at best, and still a puppy-kitten. Now wasn't the time to think he could talk, or that it understood what was happening beyond an instinctive level.

The Kayan suit stood against the back wall where I'd left it but was open and waiting for my arrival. The ship wasn't being overprotective or possessive. Not at all.

I focused on the positive. Each time I wore it, Kayan made adjustments or improvements. The armor had been strengthened during the Fyr crisis. I hoped that would pay off now. A thrill went through me.

To be fair, I wasn't a saint. How often had I behaved like I was the captain when Montow had far more invested in the ship's fate? What was I going to do when I found a way back to Earth? Abandon Kayan and the others?

Neither needed me taking over, just to abandon them.

No time for that now. *White Knife* pirates were landing assault corvettes on us.

Kayan sounded a ship-wide alert.

"We all know what's happening," I said as I leaned into armor waiting for me like an open clamshell. "Kill those alarms."

"Of course." The noise stopped. "You would call my reaction standard operating procedures."

"No worries. Give me details."

A flash of pain came with the ship's answer. "All three pirate corvettes are cutting through my hull and retrofitting their own airlocks. Wozim and the others have staged in a central location but will need to separate to block each boarding party."

"Where is the worst danger?"

Kayan didn't hesitate. "Wozim took the main deck. Only one of the corvette crews will emerge through their airlock, but it is the most likely location for the *White Knife* crew to reinforce them. When that happens, our chances for survival will decrease."

"Show me the way." I thought I knew but wanted to be sure. Making mistakes didn't interest me. Precombat nervousness faded the closer I came to the fight. There wouldn't be time for self-doubt when the shit hit the fan. Colors swelled at the edges of my vision to confirm each doorway I needed to traverse. We'd used the technique before. Day by day, I was getting better at communicating with Kayan. Words weren't always necessary.

I raced through the ship, and soon joined Wozim facing the primary breach point.

He wore his armor and helmet and appeared even more fearsome. For the first time since we'd met, he looked my way like he wanted something. "I brought you a weapon. Do not embarrass yourself." He pointed at a rectangle at his feet.

"Great! I was hoping for a box to fight with. This should teach them."

"You talk too much." He faced a square of sparks flowing through the wall. The raiders were using three laser saws to cut through Kayan's exterior.

"What is this thing?" I turned the long, heavy box over and over in my hands.

He muttered something Kayan couldn't, or wouldn't translate. I focused on the device, hoping it was a weapon and not a sick Tyton practical joke. Ha, ha! Look at the human dying with the useless cartridge box in his hands!

There was no trigger assembly or barrel. I ran my fingers around every edge, hoping for a way to open it and reveal a game-changing superweapon. This was dumb. Gone were the days when I could roll a saving throw versus stupidity and use that plus three intelligence stat I scored when generating my Dungeons and Dragons character sheet. This was a real fight, with real enemies, and pretend weapons I couldn't use.

"Piece of..." I hurled it down. On impact, the box sprang open. The parts of a beefed up Kayan welding torch and a nail gun scattered across the floor. A diabolically ingenious individual had put a lot of thought into this. This thing, if it worked, would be deadly.

Wozim had the grace to look embarrassed. "I asked Kayan

for everything needed. It seems there is some assembly required. Which makes sense. I thought my solution was a good way around the ship's inability to create weapons."

"Next time ask for a weapon that isn't from IKEA." I grabbed a bayonet that looked more like a tool than a weapon from the debris and rushed forward to meet the attackers smashing down a smoking section of wall.

"Kayan! Help me out here," I shouted as I looked for an opponent I might have a chance against. The ship sang words I didn't understand, and I realized it was the sound of pain. Having pirates cut you open couldn't be fun.

Wozim snapped his wrist to the right. A two-meter sword wider than a human palm extended. The Tyton charged forward with no loss of motion between movements. I followed on his left flank, hoping not to get killed by accident. The bayonet felt small, despite its heft and wicked point.

The first three pirates through the breach were Hellengers. None were as tall as my friend Montow. Lean, armored from head to toe, they wielded two-handed clubs crackling with electricity.

Wozim sliced the first weapon in half and continued the arc of the blade through the Hellenger raider. I expected to see the pirate cut in half, but the wound only opened his armor and the flesh beneath it. Wozim ran him over to get at the other two. Images at this stage of the fight were snapshots, appearing and disappearing too rapidly for my brain to fully process.

I side-stepped and watched the breach for more, then darted forward to scoop up the shock club. "This thing is heavy as hell." Squeezing the handle activated the pulse charge, but it stayed active when I let go. How long would that last? Didn't know and didn't have time to care. Action was everything. Consequences would come no matter what I did or didn't do.

The opening widened. Five pirates charged through, three with shock clubs and two with big shotguns. I gripped my new weapon with both hands and flung it at one of the gun-toting raiders aiming at Wozim's blind spot.

The club toppled through the air, sparking all the way and making a sound like the bass line in a dance mix. I'd been worried it would shut off. There wasn't time to loiter, but I saw the result of my attack through peripheral vision as I sought a new weapon. The business end struck my target in the side of his helmet, staggering the man.

Wozim turned and ran him through so fast I barely saw the kill.

Others rushed onto Kayan's main deck. I kicked a Gavant in the pelvis before he could crush my skull with his shock club. He stumbled.

Something was strange about his face. His Gavant magenta tattoos had been removed. I saw that much through his transparent visor. My foot only slowed him.

A Hellenger joined him and edged toward me. Words I didn't understand were spat at me.

More raiders climbed through the breach point. Wozim hewed in all directions. Razor sharp edges went through body armor like it was cheese. There was definitely more to the blade than met the eye. Blood slicked the floor. I didn't look at the damage too closely. More immediate problems had my attention.

"What are you?" snarled the Gavant.

I guessed at the reason for his missing tattoos. "Your worst nightmare, traitor." I lunged but didn't commit to the attack.

Both of my opponents froze like they recognized me, impossible with my visor mirrored. What had they recognized about me?

My words, or maybe my voice.

"Do I know you assholes?" I shifted to better screen Wozim's flank. He was fighting half a dozen pirates now. The least I could do was keep more from surrounding him.

"No, you don't. Your translations are strange," said the Gavant. "And I'm not a traitor, for your information. They put me out. You wouldn't understand. You don't know what it's like."

"I suppose you're going to tell me?" I scanned his armor, looking for and finding other weapons on his belt. One looked like a pistol that would be simple to use.

He sneered. "Too violent for the Gavant. Too merciless. Sometimes it's good to be a pirate."

I jumped forward and kicked him in the groin while he was talking. The strike wasn't perfect, but it was enough to drop him.

A glancing blow in that area could be as bad as a direct hit.

The Hellenger charged as his companion crumpled to the deck.

I ducked his first swing, hastily shoving away the electrified club as it narrowly missed. He drove his knee upward. I slipped to my left to avoid serious damage. His leg brushed the side of my helmet while my stance remained low. Something—probably his fist—punched the side of my helmet with surprising force.

This sucked like a car wreck. Getting knocked about wasn't a new experience. That didn't mean I liked it.

"You must convince Wozim to retreat," Montow said in my helmet. "We need your help on deck two. So many of them. Solen, help me!"

Dread fell on me like a hammer. Wozim needed help right here, right now. A pirate scurried up his back while two others held him at bay with spears. A fourth aimed one of the *shotguns*… and fired a weighted net that entangled half his body. At the same time, I heard the uncharacteristic sounds of panic from Montow and the others. Only Solen had it together, though there was plenty of tension when she barked orders at Grum and Montow.

So far as I could tell, no one was listening to anyone. We'd split up at the start of the engagement, failed to maintain comms, and had no plan. What the hell were we doing?

I aimed my ears toward Wozim, determined to be the change we needed.

"Don't let them hit me with another net, human! Pay attention. I have hailed you three times. You are no true warrior!" He heaved sideways, dragging the cluster of pirates across the floor as they tried to take him down. "How can we fight if there is no communication!"

"Coming from you, that's hilarious!" I ran up behind the second shotgun man. Everyone was focusing on taking down the Tyton. With no hesitation, and a shout of triumph I enjoyed too much, I kicked my opponent in the back of the legs and pulled back on his collar.

He fell in a heap. His net fired toward the ceiling.

"Thanks," Wozim grumbled as he flung pirates in three directions and lashed out with his tail. I turned away to avoid blood splashing across my visor and was surprised when nothing hit me.

Wozim had touched my helmet with the force of a kitten's paw.

"What the hell was that?" I hustled away from a new group pushing onto the ship. These men had white daggers painted across their chest plates.

"I was thanking you. A touch for honor. No more." He punched one of the original raiders halfway across the deck and faced a score of White Knives. "Now you must fall back."

"That's not how I roll, Wozim." Armed and armored men buried Wozim with their numbers and forced him to the ground. His tail harpooned one through a visor. He impaled two others with his sword.

But they had him. Even as I retreated from a new pair of net throwers, I saw two or three large men in battle armor pinning each of Wozim's limbs. Four of them wrestled the deadly tail.

I retreated into a passageway and searched for some way to help him. Once he was subdued, the rest of us didn't have a chance. I actually wondered if Gavant hunters arriving would help or hurt the situation. Maybe we could escape in the confusion.

Bad idea. I needed a miracle, not a deal with the devil.

"Are you there?" Solen asked.

The ringing in my ears covered her words, but I could understand most of what she said. My face hurt, which sucked because my helmet was still intact. How did I get a busted lip with the visor locked shut? I'd been battered in places I didn't remember. Such bullshit. Who said fighting pirates was fun?

"Yeah." My voice was different, like I'd seen the writing on the wall and was going through the motions needed to resist and survive. This wasn't me. My injuries must've been worse than I realized. If I knew what they were, maybe I could try some first aid.

"Wow, so humans have bad attitudes. Try trading places with us. We're on the run. That's where the suck is real. If you want to keep Kayan out of a confinement system, you better think of something brilliant." She paused. "You sound concussed."

"On my way. Don't surrender the ship." I hurried through the halls. Doors opened when I approached and closed the moment I was through. I worried about Montow in the molasses of my thoughts. Why hadn't he been the one to ask for help? The last I'd heard of him, he'd been asking Solen for assistance. That couldn't be good.

Smoke drifted from vents near the ceiling as I breathed through the mental haze clouding my thoughts. *Pay attention, Noah. Do the work. Worry about the pain later.*

Pops crossed his arms and watched me run the ball against bigger, older, stronger defensive linemen. Everything smelled like astro-turf and sweat. My first and last year of football had taught me one thing. I wasn't as big or tough as I thought, and the Gantz family never quit even when it was a good idea.

An acrid smell burned my nasal passages even through the helmet filters. So much for the memory of the high school gridiron. Doubts took a back seat to the here and now. "Kayan. Give me a damage report."

Numbers and symbols scrolled up the inside of the visor. I blinked twice to summon Kayan's translation boost. A new column appeared with an English version. My personal shorthand made it easier to understand, though my handwriting was getting worse as the situation intensified. The ship was in bad shape. I could see that easily. Everyone had their problems. No one was coming to save us.

"The raiders cut three airlocks as entry points," Kayan reported. "The wound damage will be hard to repair when their ships release. I believe they intend to remain affixed until I'm sold to the Gavant for a bounty. Help me, Noah. I am using too many resources to maintain life support for you and the others."

I rushed onto the bridge and saw too many raiders. White Knives had found their way here by other passageways, or had come through other breach points. Grum lay akimbo, his eyes staring at the ceiling and his wrench and hammer weapons still in his rigid hands. Three of the pirates dragged Solen away in nylon bonds that looked impossible to break. I couldn't reach them before they disappeared into their crude as hell airlock.

A dozen men of various non-human races lay unmoving. I didn't see as much blood here, but the wounds looked bad—

twisted necks and broken limbs. Most of their bodily fluids had been spilled inside their suits.

Montow knelt over Grum with a wound through his arm. He'd been shot, but I didn't know with what. My knowledge of local weapons and fighting tactics was negligible. Next time, I would be better prepared.

"Kayan, can you control the ventilation? The only answer I want is hell yes," I said, seconds before the pirates realized I was there.

"Hell to the yes, Noah. It is one of my essential functions."

"How much can you change the atmosphere? I'd like to see these mother truckers not breathing. Maybe that would send them back to their own ship." I made a note to school the ship on profanity and exclamations before its interpretation of my speech embarrassed someone.

"Most have functioning helmets, and the breathing apparatuses associated with ship boarding gear. Pirates are especially good at this sort of thing. They get a lot of practice, even if few of their prizes resist."

The pirates turned on me.

"Another one," said a tall Altion with scars crisscrossing his face.

His companion laughed. "What is it? So weird. Did someone step on that creature's head?"

"Just kill this one," said a third raider. "I'm ready to get back to port and spend our ill-gotten gains."

The group laughed and advanced in a wall of menace and jokes at my expense.

"Little help, Kayan." I backed up and looked for a door not blocked by my enemies.

"I can neutralize these organisms, but you must place anyone you wish to survive in pods."

"Tell me more." I measured the distance to my friends and planned the best way to drag them to safety pods. At the same time, I wondered if I really wanted fifty dead pirates stinking up the place when this was over.

23

Pops was gone. His appearance in my imagination felt so real I missed his absence. This would be easier with his help, or any member of my family. Mission control and a company of joint special operations commandos would also be awesome. The bridge and the adjoining passageways were crowded with *White Knife* goons.

I thought Kayan had altered the rooms and passages as much as possible to delay them. The safety pods could be moved into the vault during the acceleration to pre warp bubble speeds or other unsurvivable maneuvers, but I didn't know how it worked. There were no visible methods of transportation—no rails or elevators or speed tubes. Kayan had offered only vague assurances that everything would make sense if I remained onboard long enough—and had also suggested I probably didn't really want to know.

"Now, Kayan. I'm out of time."

"You sure as hell are," growled the leader of the boarding party. "Take off that armor and let us have a look. I'm thinking food processing for you."

"Okay, Noah. But please guard your mind. There are things no one should see."

"I'll risk it. Now, Kayan!"

The pirates charged—and stopped dead in their tracks as an energy field rippled from wall to wall. I felt gravity increase beyond comprehension and knew it must be an illusion, otherwise I'd be dead. My vision distorted to flattened fields of light and I couldn't breathe. Life before this moment had been a fleeting dream and my eternal everything was stuck to the floor of Kayan's main deck. Something like static burned through my vision and I forgot who I was. There was an image of Pops, but I didn't know what it meant or what he was trying to tell me.

Normal vision slowly returned, except that everything was a shade of red. The *White Knife* pirates didn't get up. I was standing because I had never actually fallen. There were advantages to remaining in Kayan armor. Being part of the living starship was paying huge dividends right about now.

"What did you do?" Drool ran from my face only to be whisked away by vacuums inside the helmet.

"I initiated, then immediately suspended an FTL acceleration sequence. Do not remove your helmet unless you want to sleep forever. There have been radical changes to my internal environment. You have fifteen minutes to get your friends into pods or the air mixture—and other forces—will kill them beyond any chance of resuscitation.

I reviewed the plan I had begun earlier. "Can I move the pods to my friends, instead of them to the pods? I know you shift us to the vault during major navigation events." Even before Kayan immobilized everyone on the ship, I'd had the idea of securing my friends in the crash pods to keep them safe.

"You can drag each device, or I can handle the transportation as though we were preparing for a radical course change."

"Do it. Then I can shove them inside before they asphyxiate."

The ceiling, walls, and floor spiraled open like space flowers in dozens of places. Vibrant colors, stunning textures, and pulsing veins of energy painted a picture I would never forget. Some of the process was too organic to stare at directly. About that, Kayan was right. Some things couldn't be unseen, so I looked away.

But most of it was miraculous. The ship really was alive, with its own cognition and will and ability to solve problems humans never dreamed of.

Pods from other parts of the ship emerged from each opening, then slid across the floor to stop next to Montow and Grum. Solen was nowhere to be seen. A smaller version of the Kayan FTL bypass creche grew near Scratch, who I hadn't realized was among the fallen. The other safety creches just waited for passengers who would never arrive.

"You must hurry, Noah." Kayan added prompts to my visor

HUD, and also to the visual medium we shared. With no time to resist the neural messaging, I saw words and images perfectly. I'd never been more in tune with the ship.

Montow was the first I pulled into a pod, then Grum. Scratch was the easiest to move. Once I'd dropped him into his kennel-sized device, I ran to find Wozim.

"Time is running out," Kayan said.

"What about me? Do I need to be inside, or will the suit protect me?" Solen was gone, taken by pirates for ransom or torture or whatever. There had to be a way to help her. I had no idea what it was.

Silence. Images from Kayan I didn't understand came and went before I received an answer. "You may remain as you are for a time, but I cannot recommend you disregard the pods altogether. The farther and faster I travel, the more dangerous it is for you, with or without the protection of the suit."

"Was Solen alive when they took her?"

"She was."

I kept moving. The Tyton warrior wasn't where I'd last seen him. His enemies had savaged him with shock clubs, blades, and cruel versions of electric whips. He was tangled in three nets and had been shot with projectiles I wasn't familiar with. Untangling him used the rest of the remaining time. Kayan stopped prompting me.

I wasn't sure what that meant. Did the ship no longer care because Wozim was beyond saving? Was I wasting my time, and did that even matter? Battlefield triage had been taught in the academy, but I hadn't practiced since my enlisted days in actual combat. Our method had been rude and crude. I scraped away blood and hesitated where some of it was coagulating. Hurrying now, I spread what I thought was clotting gel where he was still bleeding and tightened tourniquets on each of his limbs.

The order of treatment was wrong. I was treating whatever injuries I found as I came to them. He didn't have a pulse, but I was too busy to spend much time looking for one. After several minutes of the best medical care improvisation could provide, I shoved him into his pod and closed it.

"Are you well, Noah Gantz?" Kayan asked.

"I'll live."

"Good."

My head ached. Light pulsed in my vision in time with my beating heart. I forced myself toward the living pirates. There was one unused pod in the room.

I hesitated. "Is that one for me?"

"I can move another from the vault. Your hesitation suggests you wanted to place one of these murderers in this creche."

"You read my mind, Kayan. Almost." I smashed both of the raiders, a Hellenger and an Altion, into one pod and closed it. The first man's face was pressed into the second's armpit and their arms were everywhere.

Looking around, I didn't see my replacement creche.

"I sent it to the bridge, because I assume you will attempt to preserve the lives of all your enemies," Kayan said. "You should hope for Wozim's death, because he may kill you when he learns the extent of your mercy."

"I can't leave people to die. It's against the rules." I marched toward my destination through a haze of fatigue and self-doubt. Crazy ideas kept me company. I kept looking for Pops. He didn't repeat his appearance. Maybe he thought I was dead, or an idiot for getting myself killed to help merciless alien raiders who would not return the favor.

"It's your fault, Pops. Who do you think set the example."

He didn't respond. As a figment of my imagination, his specter was probably a product of my brain's depleted glycogen levels. Thinking was hard. Creative thought wasn't going to happen for about ten weeks. Assuming I woke up after this was done.

"Why is the floor sloping upward?" The thought took several minutes to become reality. I wasn't sure I'd spoken aloud. The situation seemed not only unfair, but unreasonable.

"Perhaps you should stand straighter and keep your eyes forward." Kayan adjusted the light to exactly the way I liked it and opened the next door before I arrived.

I watched my feet for a second and realized I was causing most of my own problems. My prior flirtations with staying alert hadn't gone this far. The air felt thick, almost like water. Particles floated around me. When I moved, they reacted as though the medium we shared had shifted. When the ship told me its internal atmosphere had changed, it wasn't kidding. Moving at speed inconceivable to humans and jumping across folds in time and space might be safer without air.

The safety pods made more sense. I pushed forward, wondering why I was bothering to save even one of the raiders. Surely, they were all dead.

"Kayan, check the life signs of our guests and mark any worth rescuing." I paused with one hand on the final bulkhead. Bodies lay everywhere. My friends looked safe in the oblong cases the ship used to protect us during jumps.

"There are thirteen you might save."

"What happened to everyone dies in fifteen minutes?"

"That was to motivate you, and I prefer a good margin of error." Kayan assigned each downed raider a number. "The lower the number, the sooner you should get them to safety."

"Okay." There were plenty of pods available, but I jammed two in each safety pod to save time. When it was done, I crawled to mine and closed the door without removing the armor. Sleep came immediately. No one dared invade my dreams.

"ARE YOU AWAKE?" Kayan asked.

I pretended I wasn't. Eyes closed, I daydreamed of a beach on Earth and a cold beer in each hand. The grit of Florida sand rubbed between my toes. Waves crashed in. Somewhere people were laughing and listening to Billy Joel sing about an uptown girl. I had one in mind and couldn't stop thinking about her. Alone, she looked at me from across the bonfire.

Yep. She was into me. Why else would she ignore the jacked and tan fighter pilots trying to pick her up? Jimmy Buffett broke into Margaritaville, and I knew that was where I wanted to be.

If wishes were fishes, beggars would eat.

Thanks, Pops. Very helpful.

That was a long way from this living starship, and I knew it.

"Noah."

"Yeah, I'm up. Can I rest just a while longer?"

"It has been seven hours and the captain of the *White Knife* has gathered additional ships. If you sleep now, you may not wake up." Kayan stood up my pod despite all my efforts to keep it reclined. "They have Solen Far, and your attachment to the woman has become my attachment."

"It's not like that." This wasn't a romantic beach scene at the start of the best years of my life. I was an intergalactic traveler facing the unknown, and Altions, as aesthetically pleasing as they were, weren't my type.

"What is it like?" Kayan asked with complete alien starship innocence.

"Never mind. How are the others?"

Kayan paused for a few seconds to gather updates. "Your friends need substantially more time to recover. Leave them where they are."

I reviewed recent events and woke myself up the best I could without coffee or a shower. The armor was starting to chafe, despite its perfect fit and disturbingly comfortable interior. "What are my options? Can I negotiate? Flee? Kick their asses with weapons you didn't tell me about until we really needed them?"

"I would have given you a weapon if I had any."

My armor was intact. The ship was free of invaders. The *White Knife* loomed in the center of the view screen. I opened the pod and initiated communications with the battered military frigate. It looked like a menacing dagger had been painted across the nose of the vessel, but time, solar radiation, and impact with space dust had erased all but a hint of the image.

"Unidentified vessel, this is Noah Gantz of the starship Kayan," I said, making up the address as I went. Using my rank seemed like a good way to involve the United Earth Government in events with unforeseen consequences, so I didn't. They'd trained me as a test pilot, not an intergalactic ambassador. Discretion had to be the better part of valor when it came to representing my people.

"*White Knife*," said a shrunken Tyton wearing a formal coat of black fabric. The ivory dagger I'd seen his raiders marked with was perfectly embroidered across one breast. Ropes of silver hung from his shoulders. One of his metallic black teeth gleamed like an ebony pearl. "The name of the ship. You know it. Don't be a fool. That leads to being dead. I am Hoggs, champion of the free lanes."

I gathered my wits and shoved my reaction to his name deep. This Tyton was a scrawny husk of a warrior compared to Wozim but was still packed with muscle. His height was harder to determine, but he seemed much taller than I was if his Altion pilots and bridge officers were a reliable reference.

"My bad."

He snarled.

"I have your raiders prisoner—"

"All of them?" He leaned forward, challenging my statement.

"The ones who didn't get themselves killed." I could feel him sacrificing his shock troops. This guy didn't give a shit. My job was to change his outlook. It was time to channel Uncle Mike again and do some fast talking. "Only the strong survive, am I right? These men are the best you have. Things can be replaced, but good people are priceless. Release my ship and I'll return them unharmed."

"You could never hold my warriors prisoner."

"I locked them in safety pods. You probably don't know much about Kayan—"

"I'm familiar with the living ships. Nearly died on one. We didn't hit it off. You might say I'm owed compensation for my treatment, which I will collect by turning this weakling child ship in for the bounty," Hoggs growled. His words had a rhythmic, artificial effect.

"What is with this guy?"

"He is using a cheap language translator, which is overloaded by your unusual communication style," Kayan explained. "I can smooth it out but didn't see the need."

"Leave it." Solen had warned me I needed to work on my language chops. So far, everyone I'd encountered had some technology for handling the problem. "Do you know anything about his background?"

"No, but it is possible he was transported on a Kayan. The Gavant rose to power when they developed an imitation of our star drives. Before the development of that technology, the only way to travel beyond a solar system was to catch a ride, so to speak. All transportation, regardless of who was going where, was handled by my kind."

Hogg banged one fist against the armrest of his chair. "Stop talking to your ship and face me."

I held up one palm for him to chill and continued my conversation with Kayan. Too late, I remembered the gesture could mean *now you die*, which explained why he snarled as I spoke. "When did that change, and how long were your people the only way to the stars?"

"Our services were cherished for thousands of years before the Gavant, then other sentient races, developed their own technology." Kayan displayed a picture of one of her kind on screen beside the one displaying Hoggs. It was five times as large as Kayan and glowed from rivers of light cascading around its form. "That is how I should have developed, but constant flight from Gavant hunters stunted my development."

"I'm really sorry." Suddenly, this powerful living starship seemed like a lost and lonely child who needed my help.

"Don't be, Noah. There is no need for sympathy. Our meeting was fortuitous. Now we should deal with Tyton Hoggs."

"How?"

"I was hoping you knew."

Great. My best idea so far had been to stall and bargain for our freedom with the lives of pirate flunkies Hoggs had sent to steal my ship or die in the attempt. That would be like waiting for pigs to fly. "Thank you for your patience, Captain Hoggs. I was just checking to see what else we can offer."

"Who else is the ship transporting? You don't matter. There is no bounty for… whatever in the black void you are. But I know there is someone valuable on that stinking abomination of a ship. Otherwise the *Kon* would not be searching the system. Hand over the prisoners, and I will consider letting the Kayan go. Hate those things. Maybe it will get itself killed during an escape attempt from this system."

"Listen, Hoggs. I can't help you if you're going to snarl and yell."

He screamed something. His tail thrashed behind him. The Tyton was standing without a safety pod or whatever the equivalent was on a nonliving starship. "Don't press me, *stranger*. I have the Altion scientist. Anger me, and I will destroy the hated Kayan and settle for the smaller reward she'll bring."

My blood ran cold. He was serious. Her fate would be torture and death, and she had the cube. Gut instinct came naturally to pilots, and was honed through rigorous training and application in the most perilous situations. "Kayan, is the data cube still on board."

"No. Solen Far was carrying it when she was captured."

"New deal," I said, striving to convey confidence I didn't feel. "Return the Altion and I'll send back your crew alive. Mess with me, and I start spacing them. One every five minutes until you come to your senses."

The sound of a Tyton belly laughing was not something I wanted to ever hear again. Kayan shuddered at the noise. In that moment, I realized that Tytons and Kayans were natural enemies, which made me wonder about Wozim and his relationship with this vessel. Maybe his people were natural allies with her's.

24

"CAPTAIN HOGGS HAS ENDED THE COMMUNICATION," Kayan said.

I stared at my reflection in the blank holo-screen hovering about the center of the bridge. All of it was a projection—a powerful illusion I had accepted with relative ease. I just stared at the spot after the images vanished. Kayan must have thought I didn't realize my opponent had hung up on me. To be fair, that was the reason for my stunned state.

My limited options had vanished, if they'd existed in the first place. I had missed an important tactical reality just like I'd missed the truth of the Kayan's view screens.

"He hasn't sent additional boarding parties." My voice was low, barely audible.

"Correct," Kayan confirmed.

"He can't send more raiders, because he doesn't have any," I explained. "Which means a counteroffensive is possible. I need to wake up Wozim."

"He was the last you put into stasis, and the least recovered."

I hustled to his pod on the main deck. It was strange to see my friends stored in random locations. Life on this side of the galaxy wasn't like anything I'd imagined. How hard would it be to adjust after learning so much? Could I go home?

I tapped on Wozim's pod.

"Are you sure this is the best course of action?" Kayan asked.

"Yep. One hundred percent."

"Your biometrics suggest otherwise. Elevated heart rate. Dilated pupils. Tension in several major muscle groups."

"That's part of being human. I've got the luxury of ignoring all that crap." I stepped back as the hatch spiraled open. For one second, Wozim was wrapped in a clear layer similar to cellophane. This pulled away from him like it was alive. I shuddered, but reminded myself Kayan was taking care of us. We're creatures from a horror movie, just passengers trying to get by.

"You live," Wozim said as he stepped out.

"Surprise, surprise. Listen up, because we don't have much time. You're going to love this plan."

"Doubtful."

"Hoggs sent his best people, maybe all of them, to storm Kayan and capture us," I said as I retreated a step to watch him stretch. The sight almost stole my ability to speak. As warrior races went, the Tyton were unequaled and Wozim had to be a top specimen. It was like watching a lion lumber out of the shade and prepare to make a kill—muscles rolling easily after each stretch, his eyes alert and dangerous. Everything about him radiated strength and menace. "Our ships are still connected by airlocks. Hoggs is making demands but taking no action to enforce his will. He's bluffing. Now is our chance to execute a counter-raid."

Wozim held my gaze. "Hoggs is a Tyton name."

"I was surprised when I saw him. The dude scares me, but he's smaller and less nourished than you."

Wozim grunted.

"What do you say? Are you in?"

"You propose a battle to crush our enemies. Of course I am *in*." He adjusted his armor and checked his sword. Each time he extended and retracted it was faster. "Lead the way, Noah the Human."

"Just Noah."

He didn't respond, probably because he didn't give a damn. I checked my gear and picked up one of the firearms a *White Knife* raider had dropped. It looked more deadly than the cutting torch/nail gun mash up Woz had asked the ship to make me. I turned the pirate's weapon over several times, hoping to figure out how it operated. It seemed to be missing some pieces, like a trigger.

Wozim took it, then placed the stock against his shoulder while pointing the barrel at the far wall. "This is the activation zone. Pull your finger across this field and it will fire. Do I need to explain the business end?"

"Got it. Thanks."

He grunted, then continued. "It will not fire unless the stock is pressed firmly into your shoulder, and your support hand grips it like so."

I paid attention, no joking around.

"This model needs to be reloaded after one thousand pellets have been fired. You will see, hear, and feel indicators that there are less than one hundred remaining."

"Feel?"

He shook it to imitate a vibration. "Tiny shaking, your word is, vibrator."

"No, it's not. Haptic feedback. That's what you're looking for."

"Yes. Fine. A haptic feedback vibrator. It will also heat up. Be very careful if a weapon like this becomes difficult to hold," he said. "The micim, what you call a magazine, contains a power cell, ammunition pellets, and a heat sink. Good design." He returned the weapon.

I hefted it and ran through the functions he described but didn't fire it.

"You did not awaken the others," he said.

"They'll try to talk us out of this."

He studied me for a long moment. "I have misjudged you. When do we begin."

"Now," I said.

"Not now," Kayan interrupted. "Hoggs has broken contact and accelerated toward the asteroid belt between our position and the outer edge of the heliosphere. Something convinced him to cash in the bounty on Solen Far. He will also receive a smaller reward for information concerning our whereabouts and condition."

"Can you catch him?"

"Yes, but you must help me shake off the pirate corvettes stuck to the crude airlocks they fashioned through my exterior."

Tyton's expression darkened. "You expelled them easily last time."

"That was one vessel, and care was taken not to create new damage. They were fixed in place using an ancient technique known as welding. My biology responded poorly and has grown over some of the worst wounds.

"Can you jump with the ships still attached?"

"Possibly," Kayan said.

The Tyton rubbed the back of his thick neck. "Not worth the risk."

I had an idea neither of them would like. It wasn't my favorite either. Several factors needed to be considered, the most pressing being time. Once Hoggs reached Ryg, our only option would be to flee.

"It is honorable that you wish to rescue Solen Far," the Tyton said. "Though she is an Altion, she fought well. That is more important than historical feuds."

I almost mentioned the data cube but felt like a jerk. Sure, I wanted to help Solen and would do whatever I could to free her from the Gavant hunters, regardless of the data cube. But it did matter. Earth's coordinates were on that device, and that meant my home was in danger. This was no longer a personal choice. It was my duty to protect United Earth.

"You have more to say," Kayan guessed.

"We might be able to use those corvettes."

"They could be towed in place of the observation modules you and Grum are fond of," the ship said. A long pause followed. "I believe I can operate effectively, but separating them from my hull later will be painful and require additional resources during my recovery."

Wozim stared at me like he thought this was my decision. Kayan said nothing. I wished Montow was here to take charge even if he made the wrong choice. The only option I saw was to cause pain to a living starship who had saved my life and risk the rest of the crew's lives.

"The Academy didn't prepare me for this," I said with an ironic laugh.

"Is that a school for warriors?"

"Yes?"

"Why would that be a question?" Wozim asked. "The inflection of your words lacks decisiveness."

"I think our definitions might never be exactly the same. UE officers must do more than fight."

He bared a good portion of his teeth. "You insult me. A small portion of my jiikiij revolves around violence."

"That word didn't translate," I said.

"Kayan does not know it, and neither will you. Make the decision, human."

He was right. There wasn't time for second-guessing myself. "Kayan, catch the *White Knife*. Leave the corvettes where they are for now. I'll do whatever it takes to fix you when it is over. You have my word."

"Please return to your pods. Leave your armor outside," Kayan said. "I will need to fly aggressively."

———

THIS TIME, I dreamed of parking Kayan in the largest garage I could find on Earth, a vacant football stadium outside of Kansas City. The details were hazy like in all dreams. Waking up confused everything. Only images of the ship parked on the fifty-yard line remained clear.

No one bothered us, which was another dream fallacy. If I returned to Earth with Kayan, government officials would swarm us. When the public found out… chaos. Chilling with a few intergalactic friends to help with repairs would not be in the cards.

"We are closing on the *White Knife*. Docking will be easier since we decided to leave the pirate corvettes attached. You might call it poetic justice," Kayan said.

I exited my protective cocoon and noticed the translucent layers sliding off my body. Now that I'd seen it, unseeing it was impossible. How much else was strange about the starship if I knew what to look for?

"That was a much easier jump, even for a short trip across the Katter system," I said, looking for Wozim. The warrior had that *up and at 'em before anyone else* vibe. His pod was next to mine.

Kayan had moved it while we slept, but he was still enclosed in the mechanical cocoon-like device.

"We are both adapting," Kayan said. "I have learned much from you."

"You're giving me too much credit. What have I actually done differently from the other passengers?"

"Everything."

I let the issue drop, because I didn't see it. Kayan's compliments were nice, however. Why ruin them with ingratitude? "Can you wake up Wozim?"

"He is once again attempting to revive himself. While it is possible in theory, he has never succeeded. Few do without a direct link to the host ship."

"What about Montow and Grum? Are they okay?"

"Scans of their physiology and brain waves suggest they are healing well and could be safely revived." The ship displayed diagrams of the Hellenger and the Walen with yellow dots near heart, head, and other critical areas of their anatomy. "Do you need them now?"

The answer was *probably*, but I told the ship to let them sleep.She didn't ask about my ulterior motivation, though Wozim had guessed correctly. Montow would argue for preservation of the ship above all else and would be horrified we'd left three pirate vessels attached to Kayan's hull.

I inspected each site as Wozim roused himself and performed several half-naked Tyton rituals. Some things just weren't meant for me to see. The first two of the crude airlocks looked unchanged. The third connected to the main deck and looked like the twisted landscape of a nightmare.

Kayan had grown around the connection points. Using view screens and other technology unique to the ship, I examined the exterior portion and observed it was even worse. Guilt cooked me from the inside. Now I was too embarrassed to wake up Montow or even Grum. Maybe I could rescue Solen, then leave before I had to face their judgment.

"I'm sorry, Kayan."

"For what, Noah?" The ship sounded fine with the situation and gave no indication of blaming me for the disfigurement.

"Putting you through all this."

Kayan didn't answer immediately. "There is always something to endure. Space travel is not easy, even for my kind. We evolved for it, so it should be natural and effortless. The reality is that the void between worlds is a harsh, unforgiving place. My discomfort is minimal. I do not experience pain in the same manner as other sentient beings. You will make it right, Noah. I have faith in your intentions and your abilities."

"How could you?"

The question confused Kayan. "Establishing a neural link has never been possible—not with Gavants, Altions, Hellengers, or any of the races I know. I learned good and bad things about you, and what you perceive to be the reality of your people and your universe. I know you well."

"I barely understand anything about you," I said. "Why do you think we have this connection?

"Can you see me shrugging?"

293

"No."

The ship rolled a peculiar combination of sound and neural signals through me that I realized was Kayan laughter. I suppressed a chuckle as I spoke. "You are incomprehensible."

"That is understandable. I have seven million times the neural mass you possess."

"Ouch. Are you saying I'm dumb?" I joked.

"Knowing everything about me would cause significant overload in your cerebral cortex. We should stick with the high points."

"I'm in your hands, Kayan."

"What hands?"

"Nice, the living starship made a dad joke."

Wozim approached in his armor. This time he had two swords partially expanded across his back and held a box-like gun at port arms. The weapon could have been an artillery piece back home, or a Barrett M82, a weapon best operated from a prone position due to the extraordinary recoil. That huge gun could punch through concrete walls and some armored vehicles. This was something else, but I didn't want to be on the receiving end of its wrath.

"I am ready to test your theory, Noah of the Earth United."

"United Earth," I said. "Maybe don't spread that around. I don't want the Gavant sneaking up on my people before they are ready."

He narrowed his gaze. "Wise. You are a true warrior."

"I try."

Surprisingly, he laughed. The sound was slightly terrifying, but I could get used to it.

"Please ready yourselves," Kayan said. "I have begun the docking sequence despite the *White Knife*'s attempts to twist free."

"We should discuss tactics," Wozim said.

"Agreed. What do you think, dynamic entry, then flow the rooms with designated breach points and crossover?" I asked. "I was security forces before I got my act together and went to OCS for officer training and flight school. It's been a while, but you know it's like riding a bicycle."

His eyes seemed to dissect me, and the meaning of my words before he replied. "Stay close to me, but do not get caught in the back swing of my sword, and do not cross the barrel of my kikik, which is our word for rifle."

"Okay, I can do that."

"Prevent anyone from attacking my back, and call out if you cannot."

"What about that thing?" I nodded toward the blade tipped scorpion tail.

"Do you want it?"

"What?" Holy shit it was looking at me again.

"It has a name, Ufri. To be honest, I doubt you have the mass to carry it as a battle passenger, but you are welcome. It offsets my balance at inopportune moments."

Ufri the alien scorpion tail lifted to eye level and tilted side to side. There was no visible eye, but it was definitely examining me.

"It's alive?"

"Yes. We are symbionts, though not good ones. I cannot command the creature or restrain it when there is anger in the air," Wozim said.

"Hello, Ufri. I'm Noah Gantz." Who the hell knew why I introduced myself.

It quivered for several seconds.

"Interesting," Wozim said. "Ufri is either laughing or quivering with rage."

"Yeah. Great. Very nice. I'll just stay out of your way, and Ufri's way."

The symbiotic death tail dipped, almost like a polite bow.

I wondered if I had hit my head during the test flight and was medically sedated in a psych ward.

"You would love wearing the tail," Wozim said as he strode into the airlock, rifle ready. "Think of the respect you will get from your top warriors back home."

I couldn't help but laugh. Maybe that was just what I needed before storming a pirate starship.

25

"RUN!" Wozim rushed forward, ignoring closed doorways and barely glancing into those that were open.

The layout of the ship was strangely refreshing. I'd grown accustomed to Kayan's organic, changeable floor plan without realizing how much I missed more familiar places. This was another alien starship, but it seemed to follow mundane design logic. I didn't love hurrying past doors, but Wozim was leading this charge. My job was to watch his back.

"Stairs," he grunted before bursting through an open bulkhead. He swept his weapon left, then right, then back to center—all of it on the go. Huge and monstrous as he was, these movements were familiar. He could have been a Navy SEAL or a Green Beret, maybe a SWAT operator.

We reached the first turn of the stairs before he slowed. His chest rose and fell, just enough that I saw it. He was blocking most of my view. Ufri snaked up Wozim's back and looked in the direction we were going. The Tyton snarled when he felt it near the side of his helmet but made no move to push it away or guide its movements.

"I am so not in Kansas anymore."

"I heard that but do not understand what it means," Wozim said, then took a position on the landing outside a closed door. "This leads to the bridge. I have captured many warships of this class. Be ready for anything."

"Trust me, it can't get any weirder." The Tyton had incredible hearing. His ability to multi-task was impressive. I was learning a lot about my fellow passenger, but only because we were heading into a fight. Was there more to the warrior than combat effectiveness? I didn't know.

"We can't rely on Kayan to open doors here," Wozim said. "Stand back and give Ufri some room. He turned slightly, but kept his weapon aimed forward.

Ufri raised higher, examined the door, and then began stabbing it fast as a cobra attack—one, two, three, five, nine times. Hinges fell away and the door slowly toppled inward.

"Fuck me that was terrifying."

"My thoughts approximately," Wozim said.

His variation on the common phrase started a belly laugh I couldn't reel in before we were forced to move. Standing around after a breach was a mistake. Wozim charged down the passageway and set Ufri on the door to the bridge. This took longer, but the symbiont was unstoppable when it came to opening doors.

"Surrender, you faithless coward!" Wozim roared the moment he was inside.

I saw the direction he was pointing his shoulder cannon, but not the target. Pushing further into the room gave me a better view, and I witnessed Hoggs standing with his arms crossed over his chest.

"Show me your hands!" I shouted as I aimed my own weapon.

"That is the traditional position of surrender," Wozim said. "Can't you see how his arms and hands are positioned for the funeral pyre?"

"I'd rather see what is in his hands."

Hoggs dropped into a shooting stance and opened fire with two pistols. Pulses of purple light scorched the air as they passed. I shot him twice in the chest and once in the head, something I'd been trained to do but never pulled off during my Air Force Security days.

His body wavered as his hands fell and the weapons tumbled onto the deck. The pirate Tyton was dead on his feet but refused to fall. Wozim stowed his rifle on his back with his swords, marched forward, and kicked him backward. The pirate's body hit the control panels, then tumbled to the ground where it lay unmoving.

Wozim faced me. "Your instincts were that of a warrior. He had no honor."

"I know, right? And look where that got him."

Wozim didn't laugh.

I felt sick. Shooting an alien pirate boss didn't feel that much different than shooting a human on Earth. I'd never liked it, and I didn't like it now. But what was I going to do, ask the walking killing machine and his death tail symbiont to talk through my feelings?

I missed Kayan, though I didn't know what the ship could do for me. One thing I had learned in both ground combat, and later when I engaged enemies in fighter jets, was that keeping busy helped. It didn't remove guilt, but it partitioned it from everything else.

"I will stand with the body while you find Solen Far," Wozim said. "Ufri says you strike well."

"It talks to you?"

"Yes. The conversations are one-sided."

"Good to know." I slung my rifle and searched the *White Knife*'s version of computer screens. The keyboards made little sense. Numbers and letters ran diagonal and looked random. "This is screwed up."

Wozim stepped to a terminal, ripped the seat out of his way, and bent forward to type and read. A map appeared on the main screen. "That is the location of the brig. I have changed the code to 1-2-3 Win. If I let her out remotely, she might wander around the ship, and we don't have time to look for her."

"On my way." I jogged from the bridge and began my search. The *White Knife* was far smaller than Kayan. I almost felt claustrophobic in the comparably low ceilings of the narrow passages. The brig was two levels down. No pirates materialized to stop me.

It was pretty cool to be right. Hoggs had sent his entire crew to capture Kayan, which probably said something about how much a living starship was worth to the Gavant hunters. He'd really wanted the prize.

Until he realized Solen held something more valuable.

"Boog!" Shouted a stocky Gavant man pointing a net shotgun at me.

I hoped it was for shooting nets. Just because I'd seen one used for the less lethal projectiles didn't mean all large bore firearms did the same thing. For all I knew, it was sending a slug, or a grenade, in my direction.

I was already moving toward the cover of an intersection. These and other thoughts came and went in a flash. Aiming on the move, I fired as soon as there was a target—which happened pretty damn quickly. The rifle kicked hard, unbalancing me as I sidestepped.

Blood fountained from his wound. He pulled the trigger and blasted a huge hole in the wall behind where I had been walking. The thunderous report of the weapon was muted by my sealed Kayan helmet.

My next shot failed to fire because I wasn't holding the stolen rifle correctly.

He blasted my position three times, pushing me farther back. My field of view diminished, giving him the upper hand. Despite my military training and experience, I knew he had the advantage. This was a familiar environment. He knew the layout.

And he understood what our weapons did.

"Boog! Just kell-kell und Boog!"

"Boog yourself!"

Silence.

His shotgun clattered into view. Blood streaked one side of it. "Translation allowance?"

I puzzled out his odd phrasing and grasped at the fringes of understanding. My immersion in multiple languages had been running in my subconscious. I felt like I should know what he was saying and wished I'd put more directed study into translation skills as Solen suggested.

"Uhm, we both Boog? Stop?"

He edged into view holding his bloody left arm. The wound was high, damaging both the bicep and the anterior shoulder muscles. Sad misery showed on his face. He'd removed his helmet.

I pointed my weapon at his feet, then advanced. This made him nervous, but he remained submissive. "You surrender."

"Yes."

"You lock yourself in a cell." I chopped the words to mimic his pronunciation.

"Yes, but help."

I pointed at a medical pack on his belt, just out of reach of his good arm. "Do not move." With one hand, I freed the pack and handed it over. At the same time, I kept my weapon as far from his hands as possible. This could go wrong in so many ways, but I had to try.

Neither of us improved our language skills much, but we did get him patched up and locked in a holding cell.

"Thank you for the wound. I retain honor. No death sentence for Hoggs."

"I can pretty much guarantee that, buddy. Good luck." I closed the view screen and left him there to ponder the error of his ways. Three doors down was Solen Far.

I stopped at the door, gathered my wits, and punched in 1-2-3 Win.

The door slid open.

Solen stood ready to fight empty handed.

"Good to see you too. How about a ride?"

She relaxed. "That would be greatly appreciated. Can you take me to Milyn? Then you never have to rescue me again?"

"Not up to me but I'll put in a good word for you."

"Gee. Thanks. I'm practically there already." She walked past me and headed for the airlock like she was perfectly familiar with Gavant ship layouts.

Because, according to Montow, she was one of them.

She stopped to examine the fallen slug gun and spattered blood. "Problems?"

"Nothing I couldn't handle."

"So you're a tough guy?" she asked.

"How did you pick up my language so quickly?"

She narrowed her already narrow eyes. "I can show you. There are tricks. With the foundation Kayan has probably layered into your subconscious, it should be easier for you than almost anyone."

"I recently learned my limitations."

She nodded. "Better now than when there is a ship full of these assholes. How did you convince Montow it was worth the risk, and please tell me you didn't take advantage of the Walen? Grum would do anything you told him, including get himself killed."

"They're back on the ship." I drew her toward the airlock and advised Wozim we had what we came for and were leaving.

"I will meet you there," he answered.

Solen watched me but said nothing. She was worried about the Tyton, that was evident in her guarded movements. The number of times she looked over her shoulder or otherwise checked her environment increased. She talked less and didn't move like someone ready to run for it—not with us, anyway.

Wozim met us at the airlock dragging four large packs. "There are two for you to carry the rest of the way. These contain items Montow will find useful, and weapons for the two of you."

"Me?" Solen said, pointing at herself.

"Yes. You also are a warrior. Once proven, your honor can never be in doubt," he said.

Solen blushed lavender around her metallic tattoos. "You're a battle lord."

Wozim grunted and hefted the largest pair of bundles. He entered the airlock without looking back.

"What did I miss, Solen?"

"There are never more than ten Tyton battle lords. I doubt your people have an equivalent rank."

I shouldered my back and hopped until it swung into a good spot on my back. The armor made it easier, but I was also feeling the youthful strength that had been returning day by day since I awakened. "What does that mean for us?"

Solen heaved her own load into place. "I don't know. It could be good, or it could be very bad."

"How could it be bad? Don't hold out. Give it to me straight."

She paused in the threshold. "Whatever forced him to hide on a Kayan could come for us, and that will probably be the other nine battle lords."

"Fantastic." I led the way with a lot on my mind. Wozim remained his usual stoic self. Solen stood on the other side of me and kept her own secrets. Nothing could ever be easy.

"I disabled the *White Knife*," Wozim said. "They will not follow us. The *Kon* will come, learn what they can, and pursue us. Kayan should hide sooner rather than later."

"She needs fuel." I didn't have to ask. I just knew. That wasn't everything on my mind. We needed a better plan to escape cleanly. My ideas could definitely use refinement, however. Now wasn't the time to pitch a half-assed idea.

"Then right after that. Speed and decisiveness will remove us from harm's way while we recover." Wozim strode into Kayan's passageways the moment our side of the airlock opened.

Solen grabbed my arm to stop me. "Thank you, Noah."

"Anytime. You would do the same for me."

For some reason, she laughed.

26

KAYAN LOITERED near the Oort field while the Gavant *Kon* methodically searched every planet, debris field, and anomaly in the X-53-Alpha system. Locals called it Katter while non Gavant visitors just called it that system with Lorin Solar and lots of chances to get rich quick. I only thought of it as that place I really wanted to leave before we were caught.

Captain Ryg's patience bothered me. He seemed completely confident we couldn't escape his detection in this system. It felt like time was running out despite the lack of urgency of my companions.

"They do not see us," Kayan said. "I will consume the resources I need as quickly as possible. Your concern is warranted, Noah."

"Should I stand by to assist? Could there be Clieg like that first time?"

"No. Help the others search for the best way to Ryyth, unless you have succumbed to Solen's demand we travel to Milyn instead."

"Let's not get carried away," I said.

"The persistence of the *Kon* has ruined Montow's plans, and he is days, maybe weeks, away from a full recovery. We cannot use many of the spaceports he knows from previous travels. There will be Gavant hunters alerted in those regions," Kayan said. "This Oort field is small and remote. There should be no contamination. I believe it has been lost from the Gavant records, or was never on file. We are safe, for a short while."

"Hours or days?" I asked and plotted a way to send Ryg on a wild goose chase.

"Days, and then we must continue the journey. With luck, Captain Ryg will believe us gone by then." Kayan shut down all the workstations on the bridge, which was a clue. I wasn't needed here. "You might also choose to help Grum. He has one of the pirate vessels cast loose but struggles with the second."

"Sounds like a plan." I headed for the door. "Let me know if you need me."

Wozim met me at the first intersection. He grunted as he strode by. I grunted back.

That was an improvement. Sort of. We weren't quite a band of brothers yet. Shared combat experience should have made us close, but he was back to his old ways. At least the man was consistent.

There was work to do. Kayan had shifted her exterior to help us as much as possible. All three of the pirate ships, and the airlocks their crews had fashioned, were away from the bridge and the main deck. That didn't mean they were near each other. I jogged half the distance, and it still took a few minutes to arrive. Grum's good-natured complaining echoed into the passageway.

"By the sprites," he cursed. "One thing after another. Heroes don't burn their fingers re-wiring circuits, do they? Black holes and comet backwash. This is fucking through my day."

I stifled a chuckle. The guy didn't have a handle on human profanity. A good friend would discourage him. For all I knew, his previous outbursts were shocking and foul, though they sounded Saturday-morning-cartoon safe to my military-trained ears. That last part... could transform into something embarrassing.

He peeked through the doorway and busted me.

"Noah? I didn't realize you were there."

"No worries. How are you doing?"

He stood and wiped his hands on a shop towel. "These half-butt pirates had no respect for safety regulations or maintenance routines. Next time we run into *White Knife* followers, it might be smart to just stall until the clowns blow themselves up."

"There aren't going to be anymore *WK* crews," I said.

He shrugged. "They'll follow some other criminal. Maybe become mercenaries. That's the only way they can work for the Gavant, since most of them are wanted. Montow says that sort of private contracting happens. How is he?"

"Still recovering. I didn't realize how many muscles, ligaments, and bones were damaged when he was shot." I shuddered to think how close he'd come to dying. The stoic Hellenger did a lot more for Kayan than I'd realized before he was put out of commission.

"I could use his help." He cleaned up some tools, then paused, clearly working up his courage to ask a question. "Could you teach me how to be a hero? Or at least fight. Montow was showing me some things, but he's more of a manager than a warrior."

"Can he fight?"

Grum nodded vigorously. "Oh yes, very much. And he *is* brave and heroic. You probably don't see it, but he fought to defend Kayan one time. I was stuck fixing things while he fended off pirates. Amazing story."

"And you're the one who's going to tell it."

He shook his head and held up both palms. "Oh, no. Not mine to tell." Another pause. "I want to be a hero. It is possible for my people, but rare."

"You can be anything you set your mind to." The empty promise tumbled from my lips before I thought about it. How many times had I been told that growing up? How many times had it been proved, if not a lie, then seriously conditional?

"Really? That is not something my people say. Duty. Hard work. Friendship. Those are the Walen ways."

"Sounds pretty good to me, buddy. Where I'm from, that would make you special. Not all heroes wear capes."

"What do fashion statements have to do with anything? Wozim is a Tyton battle lord. Montow captains one of the last free Kayans. Soren is a scientist and a spy," he said.

I wasn't convinced on the last part, but he wasn't totally wrong either.

"Look at me, the mechanic. I could be more, but I need help."

"Trust me, your gig is just as important as anything they do. Seriously." This was not in my job description. At the same time, I felt immense responsibility for leading the Walen into adventures and other mischief. He was so earnest, and I was a mess. If not for Kayan and the others, I'd be floating in a ruined FTL ship on the wrong side of the galaxy.

There would be a hero's funeral back on Earth.

"Are you okay?" Grum asked.

"Yeah. I'm okay."

"Will you teach me to fight and stuff?"

"Sure, Grum. I'll need your help no matter what happens next."

This brightened his expression. "Fan-fucking taster!"

I laughed. "Let's dial back the United Earth profanity for now. Even though I love your word salad."

"Okay, sure. Can I use sure? You like that word."

"Uh, yes. Absolutely. It's not a swear word, but thanks for calling me out. I totally won't have a complex about it now."

He hurried back to his work. "Thanks, Noah Gantz."

"Anytime, buddy."

Scratch padded through the doorway and sat looking at me.

"What?"

"I already fed him," Grum called from under a section of the pirate airlock.

"Noah!" barked Scratch.

I played with the animal until my brilliant ideas coalesced. "Grum, wrap that up. I need help with something."

He leaned out to get a better look at me. "Like what?"

"We're going to convince our *White Knife* prisoners we're heading the opposite direction we actually are."

"That's an excellent idea! Where do you think of this stuff?"

I blushed and hoped he didn't know the significance of my embarrassment. "Movies and stuff." The plan felt too simple, and too direct. But I thought it could buy us time.

"Should I be watching movies? Will that help me be more heroic?"

"I'll make a list, though I'm not sure where we can get them." I helped him clean and organize his work area, then went in search of Montow, if he was awake, and the others.

SOLEN CROSSED HER ARMS. "Ryg might believe our destination is Jangu if we let that information slip."

"You don't want to head for Milyn?" I expected this part to be a problem and wished Montow was awake to put the brakes on her single-minded goal. The truth was we couldn't even start the next leg of the journey to Ryyth. I'd started considering compromises once the star charts made it clear how sidetracked we were. Now she was throwing curve balls at me.

She surprised me. "Not until we can actually make it without a Gavant hunter hot on our trail. Call me selfish, but I'd rather destroy the cube than hand it and the assets on Milyn over to Ryg. He's the worst of them, an officer trying for promotion. He'll do anything to seize glory. Capturing a spy, a Kayan, and Tyton battle lord would earn him medals. Gavant love those."

"How do we get them to believe us?" Grum asked.

Wozim wasn't here for the strategy session.

"They need to work for it, or they'll know it's a scam," I said.

"We're waiting," Solen said.

"I set them free, say it is a tradition of my people. They won't know any better. Wozim comes in and shouts me down—says we should kill them in combat or something a Tyton would say. When he storms out, Solen gets in a second argument in the passageway that the soon-to-be-released pirates overhear."

Solen started pacing. Grum nearly bounced on his toes with enthusiasm for the idea.

"You are devious," she said. "I'm almost afraid to meet another human."

"Timing matters, and they have to hear what you're saying. Would they know your language, or Wozim's?"

"They will definitely understand Altion. I'll handle that part. Maybe I shout at him in my language and he complains that he doesn't understand," she said.

"Now look who is devious."

She flourished a bow. "Let's get Wozim on board and do this. They should be long gone before we leave the Oort field. Better that way. Less chance they watch us depart and gain clues to our real destination."

"Perfect," I said. "We can practice the script on the way."

Solen came up with a complete version of what she would say, and explained how she thought Wozim's part would play out. Grum made several excellent suggestions and Scratch bobbed along beside us grunting Noah.

Wozim answered before I could drop the death knock on him. He listened to the plan, then immediately agreed. "This is a good tactic. We must set them up for a crushing blow, not waste our lives on heroic deaths."

"Exactly." Not saying *yeah* was hard. Thanks, Grum for making me self-conscious. It was like when you bought a blue Camaro with your enlistment bonus, then saw copies of the car everywhere.

Grum and Solen went to double and triple check the corvette we would put them on. Weapons had been removed, or jettisoned if we weren't able to use them. Wozim claimed Montow could break them down for useful parts if nothing else. There were some devices, however, none of us wanted to touch. Poorly maintained particle accelerators from long outdated, and thus unserviced designs, were simply too dangerous to move, much less store inside Kayan's hull.

Every clue about where we'd been or where we were going was removed, though there was little the Gavant could have repurposed. With stakes this high, we wanted to be sure. It was one of the few things we all agreed on. I thought we were making progress. Someday we might even be a team.

"Noah!" barked Scratch.

"That's right. You and me against the galaxy, buddy. Just a boy and his dog on a living starship in constant peril." I herded the animal out of the way and pointed. He seemed to obey. I wasn't sure which of us was spouting more nonsense. The floppy, six-legged creature was growing on me.

"Try to look fierce." Scratch tipped his head sideways, confused and uninterested in the game. I bared my teeth. He imitated my jokingly fierce expression and I nearly jumped out of my skin. "Yeah, do that when the prisoners start acting brave."

Wozim regarded the animal for several moments. It seemed like he would give advice, what kind, I didn't know. The Tyton warrior was unreadable when it came to Scratch. Was he a dog person? A cat guy? Or did he think he could turn the creature into a hunting and killing machine in the service of galactic honor and justice.

Who knew?

He loomed behind me when I removed each of the pirate prisoners from their double-booked pods and lined them up against a wall. Every last one of them glared at me with raw hatred. Their attitudes cooled when they noticed my Tyton friend and his bloodthirsty tail spike.

"We're not afraid to die," the leader said.

Wozim snarled. Ufri the symbiotic battle tail raised high and swayed side to side as though choosing a target.

I leaned toward the de facto pirate boss. "You assholes are on really thin ice. I don't know if I can hold him back. Give me a break and zip it."

Mouths shut and remained that way. Eyes avoided looking at the Tyton. When I said move, they moved. We headed for the first crude airlock. Every one of them searched for landmarks that weren't there and hunched their shoulders. Kayan's ability to expand or contract passageways and rooms, and to shift the exterior hull like it was clothing—or armor—made life here interesting. I was used to it, as was the crew. The *White Knife* raiders were overwhelmed. Each face had the look of wanting to be anywhere but here.

Wozim's feet thumped the deck behind us. The prisoners attempted to rush forward, but I shouted them back. A few threats and warnings did the trick. They couldn't know my warrior friend didn't normally make a sound when he walked the decks. This was a show, and he was giving an award-winning performance.

Each heavy footfall was like a hammer striking steel, and it put me in a fiercely grim mood. "Never send to know for whom the bell tolls; it tolls for thee."

The leader's voice squeaked. "What does that mean?"

I locked eyes with the man. "It means you're on borrowed time, and I'm barely interested in holding my friend back."

"We're doing everything you say. Don't kill us. We were only following orders. I never wanted to be a pirate. Just keep him away from us. No one relies on a Tyton for mercy. No one."

I said nothing for the rest of the march.

Grum stepped out of the way as I took them into the stripped pirate ship. We continued inside.

"Why haven't you killed us?" asked the leader. His voice sounded like dry paper rubbing together.

"My people have certain traditions. You cross me once, I give

you a second chance—within reason. We meet again, and it's—"
I dragged one finger across my throat.

They stared without a hint of comprehension.

"Off with your head."

"Ah. That makes sense. The finger is supposed to be some kind of head remover." Several of the soon to be free pirates nodded and chattered. Nervous laughter broke out in half of them.

All that work, and I killed the mood with a single gesture. Freaking strong work, Gantz old buddy.

"Silence." Wozim pushed by me. "What is that Gavant chattering? Be still or be dead."

A man in the back wept.

Wozim stomped toward him. The others dove out of his way, parting like the Red Sea to let him through. "You will feed the ozzo pits with your guts! Say one more thing. Give me a reason to do this right. This mercy is a farce. You should all be slain immediately."

I tried to signal Wozim. His act was going from convincing to melodramatic. "Dial it back," I mouthed, knowing I had started it with my crazy quotes and tough guy act.

Wozim narrowed his gaze. Now I was the one about to be murdered. Note to self, be careful with recruiting Tyton actors. Their improv skills are terrifying. Our victims seemed convinced, even more so because his menacing presence threatened me as well.

I motioned them away from Wozim. "Get over here and

listen to me. This is your last chance. I'm not dying for you jerks."

Wozim stormed out of the room to confront Solen just outside the doorway. I began a boring, step by step instruction of the navigational route they *had* to follow.

"You didn't kill them?" Solen asked in a stage whisper. "What kind of Tyton are you! If you want a thing done right, you have to do it yourself."

"Stop, Altion. They are mine to slaughter, not yours."

"Unhand me, brute!"

I worried the pirates would notice they were shouting in the most common of all Gavant languages, and in a dialect pirates preferred. We needed some acting classes.

"Just do it before we start for Jangu," Solen hissed. "Our friends there can't protect us if Gavant hunters show up with warships."

I clapped my hands loudly. "All right, that's it. Get on this piece of junk and follow the course I explained. And remember, next time we meet…" This time the finger across the throat gesture had a more sobering effect. They hurried into the ship and disembarked as soon as I left the airlock and Kayan released them.

Wozim, Solen, and Grum gathered around me. "What do you think?" she asked.

"None of us should quit our day jobs."

My friends stared at me with zero comprehension.

"What's a day job?" Grum asked.

"Never mind. We either fooled them or we didn't." I headed for the bridge. "How is the re-fueling going, Kayan?"

"Very well, thank you, though there is less here than I'd hoped. We will leave within the hour. Do not come to the bridge. Get some rest, all of you."

"Rest is for warriors when they are not killing." Wozim headed for his cabin. The rest of us stared.

"Quote of the day," I said.

Both Solen and Grum burst out laughing.

27

I JOGGED around the air base watching fighter jets take off two at a time. They were only practicing, but to me, here on the ground, it felt like they were flying directly into battle. My training had been intense. I had the highest security clearance of anyone at my rank. The squad I led was tight, both on and off duty. All in all, this was a good life. Hard enough to challenge me, but not overwhelming. I got to shoot guns, drive fast during scenarios, and daydream of the day we sprang into action to defend the base.

"Did you apply?" Sergeant Terry Fortune asked. He was my second-in-command but destined for his own soon. Too many sergeants in a squad made it feel like a Special Forces unit. We weren't far from that, though saying it aloud would draw endless shit talking from the rest of the armed forces. We didn't do high-altitude, low-opening parachute insertions behind enemy lines or scuba dive from submarines. Nothing in our mandate required us to train freedom fighters in third world countries threatened by communism, or terrorists, or out-of-control drug cartels.

But we were the last line of defense for the top-secret weapons of war and bases few people knew existed. The jets were impressive, cutting-edge weapons of war that always stacked the deck in our favor. But there was a space program being developed underground. None of my team had seen it, but we all knew it was a long-term investment by the new United Earth government. If things went seriously wrong, our assignment was to rescue hostages, take back critical infrastructure, or fight to the last man in defense of the facility.

Serious business even if no one made movies about us. All that crap where guards are easily taken out by heroes or villains —not even close to reality.

"I sent it."

Fortune smiled. "Good man. You'll get in. You have top percentile ASVAB scores and advanced pilot certifications. How many of these ground pounders can fly airplanes and helicopters except in movies and shit?"

I picked up the pace, hoping my friend would talk less.

"You should have gone into the officer corps and flight school from the beginning," he said.

"But then I would have missed all this." I swept one hand to encompass the tarmac and desert mountains in the distance. "What is it going to be today, one hundred and eighteen?"

"Something like that." Fortune held the pace for a time. "I'm really glad for you, buddy. Promise me that in a year, I'll be watching you take off."

Another sortie of F-50A jets blasted skyward.

"Fine. But only because you asked nicely."

"Don't make me laugh. Going into oxygen debt already."

"We have arrived in the next system, Noah. You may exit the jump pod."

The memory slid away as I awoke. There wasn't much I wanted less than to be running across asphalt that was already a hundred degrees at eight am. We should have run, then lifted weights. Terry always prioritized getting jacked over optimizing cardiovascular efficiency. He was married last time I checked, so that might have changed.

"Thanks, Kayan. I'm awake." Climbing out took longer than normal. The last few days had been a mad compilation of dodging Gavant hunters, jumping system after system after system, and constantly feeding the ship. My Kayan wristwatch claimed two days had passed since I hit the rack.

"How long did I sleep?"

"You already have the answer, Noah." Kayan sounded relaxed, which was good. We deserved a little downtime.

Grum met me in the passageway. "Noah, I am ready to begin."

"Excellent!" I patted him on the shoulder and headed for the galley.

He followed. "Is this the first heroic test?"

"You promised to train him," Kayan provided privately.

There was no need to thank the ship. I'd mostly broken the

habit of talking aloud when others could only hear my half of the conversation. I waved for Grum to walk beside me. "First rule of fight training is not to start on an empty stomach."

"That is the opposite of what Wozim, Montow, and now Solen have told me when asked for advice."

"Well, I'm hungry. Let's see what isn't Kayan-made today."

"The meals I compile are perfect."

"Of course they are, Kayan. Thank you."

Grum dutifully agreed. "Very excellent. Much better than the ration paste back home. This warrior breakfast ritual is intriguing. I can't wait to feel the power."

This made me laugh more than I should have, but the Walen joined in and took it for what it was—a great start to a day full of potential.

I led the way to the kitchen and rummaged through industrial-sized refrigerators and pantries that, while mostly empty, still contained a lot of variety. The *White Knife* pirates had lived large before meeting us. Now they were hopefully convincing Ryg and the other Gavant hunters to head for Jangu. Solen assured us the locals of that system could handle the attention. They would stall, then allow searches until Ryg and the others realized they'd been tricked.

Hopefully, he would never catch up to us to exact his vengeance. He didn't seem like the type of man who endured humiliation well.

Scrambled eggs, hash browns, pancakes, and bacon—Grum was amazed. None of it looked like the morning grub back home, but it was essentially the same. I was working with rough equivalents.

"This is what humans eat every day?" Grum shoveled food into his mouth.

"More or less. Not if you're vegan."

"Don't know or care what that is. Sprites! This is life-changing."

I removed my apron and sat down for my first helping. Grum was already spooning over seconds. My culinary pride turned to caution. "Slow down, buddy. Food tastes better if you chew it first."

"Does it?" he said while mashing eggs and hash browns with his teeth.

"If I'm lying, I'm dying. It also prevents choking. Enjoy it. Take your time."

He complied immediately. "This is better. Thanks. Are we going to have breakfast every morning before we start training."

"Hopefully," I joked.

"What will we do first?"

I thought about it as I worked through a few bites. This wasn't my military occupational specialty, though I'd been on the receiving end of combat training often enough, both as a soldier and a pilot. "Let's start with some conditioning, and then evaluation. There's no use doing a bunch of drills if I don't know your current skill level."

"Wozim says I have no skill outside a mechanic's workshop."

We finished breakfast, ran three miles, and did some calisthenics and stretching. The skills assessment confirmed

Wozim was mostly correct. So far, Grum had managed to survive with enthusiasm and hard work.

"The first lesson is that the hands kill," I said once we were on the training mat Kayan made for us. Too late I realized Wozim was watching us with crossed arms.

Whatever. He had his chance to teach this class. Grum deserved the best instruction I could provide.

"KAYAN, let me get there before you open his pod," I said. Grum and I had trained and talked until lunch. He went to check his machines, and I took a shower and changed clothing. Putting on the soft and durable jumpsuit the ship fabricated for me was like going to a spa—or so I imagined. Feeling refreshed, I strode straight to the medical bay where Kayan had placed Montow's pod.

Healing this way wasn't new. They had kept me asleep for weeks after rescuing me from the damaged United Earth prototype vessel. I checked the monitor and saw his arm and other peripheral damage was freshly healed. Kayan had saved his life, not for the first time.

On the way, I noticed the door to the training room was open. Grum was probably in there practicing basic stance changes and strikes, or maybe how to break his fall. His old method was to just suffer in silence when he hit the deck. The first time he managed a smooth roll had opened his eyes. There were easier ways to fight. "Stop being your own enemy" should probably have been the first rule I taught him. His willingness to endure suffering wasn't like anything I'd seen—and my life on Earth had been full of stubborn, self-destructive people.

Grum was like the combination of a Boy Scout and a stunt double—equally comfortable with helping little old ladies across the street or falling down a flight of stairs, only to get up and do it again if required. My duty as a friend was to show a better way.

I ducked inside. "Hey, buddy, way to practice!"

Wozim turned slowly. Grum was nowhere in sight. "You talk nonsense."

I held up both hands. "Sorry. Thought you were someone else."

"What would I be doing with my time if not this?"

That irritated me. "Relaxing. Reading a book. Having a normal conversation with a friend. Anything but being a dick all the time."

"Those are *your* hobbies, and they do nothing to advance me toward my goal."

I stepped fully into the threshold. "What is that exactly, your goal?"

He returned to performing an admittedly beautiful kata. His movements enthralled my imagination, despite how frustrating everything he did was. Seven or eight feet tall, packed with lean muscle, the man was truly alien. What had Solen called him? A battle lord?

I hoped I never ran into the other nine in a dark alley.

Grum, as it turned out, was working in his shop. He had

three piles of salvage disassembled and was measuring and cataloging each piece by hand, then entering it into Kayan's computers. The ship spoke a different language to the Walen when he performed this type of work. I decided to leave them alone.

Montow was sitting on a bench in his room, head hanging halfway to his chest, and his shoulders slumped when I arrived. Kayan flashed me a message saying the captain had initiated his own revival, something that was possible but not easy or pleasant.

"Can I come in?"

"Yes. You are welcome," Montow said.

"I thought you would be mad."

"For which thing? The fact you left me out of major decisions, or kept me sedated to speed my healing?" He worked his fingers through several patterns, an instinctive warm-up of some sort, then stood. The Hellenger was a lot bigger than me, something that had been easy to forget with him encapsulated and out of sight.

"We gambled and won," I said. "That isn't your style."

"It is not." He buttoned his shirt and put on a jacket that barely went to his waist.

"You look ten years younger," I said.

"Two weeks in a Kayan life pod can do that for a person. Gavant oligarchs keep them in confinement systems for a reason, or didn't you know?" He asked.

I thought through what he was saying. "They're held in captivity for spa treatments?"

"No."

"They're being kept in captivity, like prizes," I offered.

"Essentially. But also to limit star travel. This is less important with so many races mastering their own ways to jump long distances in an instant, but still part of their doctrine. The Gavant rose to power when they gained control over the most capable Kayans."

I waited while he finished dressing, slipped on the sunglasses, and stepped into the living area. "My head is killing me."

"Can Kayan help?" I knew the answer was no when I asked.

He shook his head slowly.

We faced each other just outside of his room. Looking up at him, I realized he was controlling his anger. This wasn't over and I hadn't gotten off easy. The man was... disappointed.

"Your arrival changed Kayan. This is not something you can truly appreciate. For that, I will always be grateful. When you make decisions that endanger the ship, and to a lesser extent, all of us who are passengers, I will hold you accountable."

"That's fair," I said, and meant it. "We need each other. Kayan said your plan to reach Ryyth will have to change with the increased Gavant activity. Solen really wants to head to Milyn instead and believes there will be a lot of bounties out on us now, and on the ship."

"She is correct about the hunters, and her choice of destinations has some minor merit." Montow stopped when he saw the open door to the training room. "Wozim should not be provoked. You worked with him and possibly gained a measure of respect with the Tyton. Do not press your luck."

"Noted." We resumed our walk, checking in on Grum and then Solen, who didn't answer her door. Every time I reached out, she was hunkered over the data cube attempting to recover more data. She either sucked at code hacking or was lying her ass off.

"You made the correct decision to assist the Altion woman," Montow said. "I was selfish, and afraid of the consequences. At the end of the day, we are all in the same quandary. She will be useful when we go to Milyn."

"That's what she wants."

"As much as I resent the delay it will cause, we don't have a choice." Montow rubbed his head. It didn't look like he got much relief from the pain behind his eyes. "Milyn is our best chance to remain free of Ryg in the short term."

"Tell me about the pods and system jumping. Each time I figure it out—"

"You learn you haven't," he finished.

"Pretty much." I reviewed everything we'd done differently while Montow was in a Kayan coma. "I was able to remain conscious during some maneuvers the ship normally protects us from."

"Were you in your pod?" Montow stopped outside the door to the bridge.

"I was."

He tilted his head side to side a fraction just like Grum, which made me conceal a smile. I wasn't the only one cribbing mannerisms off the rest of the crew. "You have a good heart, Noah. That is why Kayan was drawn to you. Fleeing from the

Gavant hunters is a tireless and unforgiving business. Everyone we encounter has an ulterior motive or ten, and we have been betrayed many times. Don't ever do that."

Heat rose in my face. For one second, I felt irrational guilt. It didn't take long to realize the source. I desperately wanted to go home and would leap at the chance. Odds were, that would leave the rest of the crew, and Kayan, high and dry.

There had to be a better way. I was determined to find it. "Let's call a meeting, and this time everyone attends."

"I was hoping you would say that, Noah Gantz of United Earth. Our next move should require a perfect consensus."

We entered and put out the call. Grum and Solen came within minutes. Wozim took longer, and seemed uninterested in us or what we were about to discuss when he arrived. I almost thought he'd arrived at random, rather than by invitation.

"How are you feeling, Captain?" Solen asked.

He flinched, and I realized her manner probably felt like that of a Gavant officer to the Hellenger.

She dialed back her formality by lifting one hand casually and leaning against the chair of the other open pod.

He released a cleansing breath and nodded before answering. "Kayan has greatly improved my health. Thank you, all of you for persevering."

"You want to go to Milyn?" Wozim asked. He looked from Montow to Solen.

Montow shared a glance with the Altion science officer and answered. "That is the only viable option. We must agree that is our course, however."

"There will be fighting no matter where we travel," Wozim said. "You have my consent to select our destination. The Earth soldier can fight beside me."

"Pilot," I corrected. When had I explained my enlistment-to-officer-candidate-school-journey? Never, not to Wozim the Tyton.

Now they had me talking like that.

"Pilot. Soldier. Both fight when needed." He left.

Solen, Grum, and Montow watched him. I fought down the urge to shout something to start an argument, anything to get a reaction from the monster.

"Let it go," Montow said.

I nodded.

"Does anyone disagree with the decision?" he continued.

"I'm behind it one hundred percent," Solen said.

Grum gave us a quadruple thumbs-up.

"What about you, Kayan?" I asked.

"No one has requested my opinion before now." The ship didn't sound upset, but Montow wilted with shame. "Montow has always put my interests above his own, and I trust you, Noah. Grum would not harm me, and Solen's desires are clear to us all. She wishes to take the data cube and disappear among her collaborators."

My eyes snapped to her. If she thought she was ditching me, she had another thing coming.

"Wozim's story is tragic," Kayan continued. "Give him a break."

"Sounds like something you would say." Solen pointed at me.

"But I understand. You won't see me getting too close to the Tyton. Staying alive is one of my favorite pastimes."

Montow waited, then spoke to Kayan. "Solen has the coordinates to Milyn. She won't give them to any of us."

"I can get us there," the ship said.

"Then let's do it." I watched Solen. The data cube she carried was the key to me going home. Keeping track of her, no matter where we went, was now my highest priority.

28

KAYAN REVIVED me before the others but didn't explain why. Sensor readings showed communication buoys at the edges of the heliosphere of the Milyn system. Apparently, that was a sign of stability among civilized regions of the galaxy. The ship located another small Oort field and quietly refueled while I wondered why the rest of the crew were asleep.

Scratch plopped down his butt near me and swiped at me with three paws.

"Good morning, Scratch-meister." I leaned over and rubbed behind his ears until he adjusted his stance to avoid getting pushed over. "There's a good boy! You hungry? Stick with me, we'll fix that."

Pops had talked about the value of solitude and the companionship of animals. He said the first required patience and self-acceptance, while the second was always a gift. I'd been five years old asking him why he liked to read when everyone was outside enjoying the barbecue. His chocolate lab, Duke, had a face full of gray whiskers, and wagged his tail without getting up. I knew why the animal liked Pops.

The man had always been a titan in my world, especially then. Never did he shrink from conversation or confrontation. Holiday meals at the Gantz house often involved lively debates.

No one bothered him when he disappeared to read. My mother had said he could be benevolently intimidating, whatever that meant. In very rare instances, he wore his USAF bomber jacket, something he valued more than his general tabs. He'd been both a fighter and a test pilot. Tough memories came when he pulled on the leather and retreated into solitude.

I'd never left him alone when he did that.

"I'm all peopled out." Pops motioned to another chair in the den. I'd sat with one of his books, unable to understand a single word. He read long after I fell asleep. Don't ask me how I know. Later, I suspected he manufactured the scene to provide an escape for me, not him. Three of my third cousins were twice my age and rough as hell. Pops had always offered sanctuary at these events. I wondered if he had a book for me now.

The veteran of three wars was strong and hale last time I saw him, but I suddenly felt a powerful need to return to Earth immediately. Pops, Grandma, extended family, and dozens of close friends would have attended my funeral. Strangers would have paid their respects as well, just like at the public service for Lieutenant Colonel Tate Collins after the first FTL test failed. Public was a relative term in this case. Professional associates and close family would be more accurate. The failure had been kept as quiet as possible—which meant the internet was rife with speculation and conspiracy theories.

Kayan moved away from the sparse field of radioactive nutrients.

"Is everything okay?" I asked, then picked up Scratch. "You're getting heavy, dude."

"Yes. We are fine," Kayan said. "Ryg has not yet located us. Should he arrive in this system, he will rightly assume this field is not worth a Kayan's time and pass it by."

"Are you still hungry?"

Scratch barked.

"Not you, super mutt." I shifted him to my other arm, then put him down. "The question was for the ship."

"I consumed what I could. Taking more would destroy the regenerative ability of this field, and deprive future ships from its bounty. You have another question?"

"Why did you wake me up before the others?" I checked power levels and thought the ship was putting on a good face. If that Oort field had satisfied Kayan's hunger, then I was a professional ice skater.

"You awoke on your own, Noah." The ship changed course to head in-system, but at an easy pace. "I thought you knew you could do that at will."

"How?"

"I wish that living starships like me could shrug. It seems a useful expression, because I can't explain the process." Kayan displayed the vitals of the crew. Each was sleeping naturally, which was different from the state the ship placed them in during faster-than-light travel or maneuvers that should crush us. "It is far easier for you due to our bond."

The weird thing about this conversation was that I understood what the living starship meant. Waking myself up from space jump sedation *felt* possible. Kayan claimed I had already done it. Unfortunately, there were no buttons to push or magic words to say.

"Perhaps we should practice and experiment. I am new to this, Noah. We can learn together."

"Tell me more about the jumps you make," I said. "You're not moving faster than light."

"Of course not. I am slipping or twisting through bends in the fabric of this galaxy. This does require extraordinary quantities of momentum, which comes from speed, but we do not in fact turn into energy. Would you like to see the math in numbers and formulas more familiar to you?"

"I'll need to spend some time on it."

Calculations flowed onto my work screen. Some of the structure and order of operations were familiar. There had been a lot of math and theoretical physics during the three years of training for this mission. I made notes and found myself intrigued by what Kayan revealed.

"The ship that brought you here operates on far different theorems. Someday, I might understand them." The ship cycled through systems checks, including the passenger safety pods. Each crèche had been placed on the bridge during the seven back-to-back interstellar jumps it took to reach Milyn system. It appeared Solen would be revived first. Scratch curled up near her door, but not until after casting me a judgmental glance I assumed was due to the scarcity of Qurk treats for him.

We should all have food first thing. I hurried to the galley and started making omelets from raw materials the ship provided. "How long do I have?"

"For what, Noah, making your fellow passengers breakfast?"

"You got it in one." I started hash browns and bacon, marveling all the while at the ultra-modern kitchen. "This never gets old."

"The cooking facilities?"

"You made parts of this ship just for me."

"None of the others knew how to cook or had a desire to learn."

"Insanity. Am I the only person who gets bored?"

Kayan paused. "You do require a significant amount of stimulation."

"Not a bad thing," I said with mock defensiveness. Thirty minutes later I was wheeling a modified food cart out of the galley. Scratch trotted beside me, occasionally offering enthusiastic but nonsensical advice and begging for choice bits. The dog reminded me of ship protocols. "I forgot to ask, is there a rule about eating on the bridge?"

"It has never come up, though I suspect Montow won't be as excited as you are hoping," Kayan warned.

I resisted the urge to drink my glass of simulated orange juice while still en route. A memory of my parents sending me off to boot camp came back with forceful clarity. A tingle went up my back. At the time, I hadn't appreciated their barely contained nervousness. It hadn't been concern for my welfare, though there was probably a ration of that. More likely, it was my personality that worried them.

"Keep a grip on that impulsiveness, Noah," my father said, as my mother gave me the last hug she ever would.

They hadn't been wrong. Leaping before I looked was a thing. Smiling, unrepentant, I wheeled the best food in the galaxy into the room just as Solen was climbing out of her pod. Who had instilled my thirst for adventure? My parents, and they loved me for it despite their worry. As it turned out, I hadn't been the one in danger but that was another story for another time.

Solen looked at me like she was seeing an alien—which of course she was. One pushing a cart loaded with enough breakfast food, orange juice, and coffee to feed a squadron of hungry star travelers.

I missed my parents even more than Pops, but there was nothing to be done. No attempt at the Gantz family breakfast could bring them back. It would make them smile a lot, if they were in a place they could see us.

"You are the strangest creature I've encountered in this galaxy," Solen said as she rubbed sleep from her mysterious Altion eyes. Her skin had a healthy sheen. It wasn't long before she'd dropped her pod down from vertical and sat on the edge with the cart in easy reach. "Montow's waking up." She pointed with a piece of surprisingly realistic bacon.

"Wish me luck," I said. Solen laughed.

The pod opened to reveal shadows. That wasn't unusual, and

I'd already witnessed the lethargy of the Hellenger's previous dismounts. The last time I'd thought he would prefer to sleep in, as it were. His appearance now was different. Stress creased all faces the same, regardless of pan-galactic biology and culture differences. The man was worried.

"Did you sleep at all?" I asked.

"Sleep!" barked Scratch.

The best part about the safety pod protocol was the regenerative side effects. Montow should have been fresh and feisty after a few moments to shake off the transition.

"Of course I did, but this system is full of unseen danger," Montow said.

Solen gestured with a different half-eaten piece of bacon. "He's not wrong."

I brought the captain a tray of food, then made a second trip for coffee and orange juice. "You need to fuel the machine, boss. Never make decisions on an empty stomach."

He explored the eggs with a fork. "That seems like very random advice." Before long he was focused on the meal. "This is very acceptable. I will make the next post-jump breakfast."

"Fantastic." I dug into my own food and kept an eye on Grum, who I already knew would be a fan of the meal when he awoke. Wozim's giant pod was also quiet. "I love starting new traditions."

Solen stiffened, but relaxed once we established this was our thing, not something dreamed up by the Gavant. Apparently, they did that sort of dog and pony show a lot—holidays, parades, special announcements and so on. The idea of a government powerful enough to rule hundreds of star systems started to sink in. Would United Earth be better under the same circumstances?

I would do my duty to make sure it was. That had to be the difference. The Gavant people must have given up on democracy, if they'd ever had a version of it here.

"Did I miss pancakes?" Grum said, catching me by surprise.

"Hold on, we have a carb emergency!" I pushed aside my plate and hustled to the food cart. The Walen's eyes lit up when I uncovered the tray. "Hold your horses. I'm bringing it all at once. Can't have you filling up on one thing."

"Yeah, that seems best." He swaggered over to help me, and I realized he was the best at imitating human mannerisms despite his scrawny Walen physiology. "Horses must be a big problem on your homeworld."

"You have no idea," I said, then faced Wozim's crèche as it opened.

He emerged alert and ready for anything, but without wasted motion—or words.

"Good morning, sunshine."

"Good morning, near-warriors."

"Ouch," Solen said, then rolled her eyes when her back was turned to the Tyton.

"Food?" I asked.

Wozim loomed over the selection. "This will provide macronutrients and calories. Excellent choice. You may prepare all my meals in the future."

I stared. So did the others.

Wozim chuckled, then served himself a meal big enough for the entire offensive line of an American football team.

I laughed with the others. "Wozim's got jokes."

"My humor defeats all lesser jests," he said, then cut his bacon with a knife and fork. The almost delicate attention to this task surprised me.

"Glad to have you, Wozim."

"I reciprocate your emotions." He plopped bite after perfectly sliced bite into his mouth.

"Woz!" Scratch barked.

The Tyton snuck several morsels of food to the animal when he thought no one was looking.

None of us worried much during the meal. I drew it out as long as possible. Time was of the essence, but we did have a solar system to cross, and that didn't happen with a snap of the fingers. Even Montow relaxed. Eventually, we turned cleaning up into a team effort and laughed at Scratch's antics as we stowed everything in the galley.

"MILYN DEFENSE SQUADRON ONE FOR KAYAN vessel, please alter course. I sent you required navigation points, please confirm," said a man with no image broadcasted.

"This is Montow, Kayan friend and captain. We are altering course per your instructions." The Hellenger maintained a cool professionalism I respected. He had our image projectors off as well. Fair was fair. Only he was talking to them, which allowed the rest of us to discuss our decisions.

"Everything is in order," Solen said. "That is standard operating procedure. The nav points change on a randomized schedule with verification codes generated at the same time. To the rest of the galaxy, Milyn is a rich commercial port with a small security force to maintain Gavant regulations and tax collection."

I watched ships lining up to approach the planet and felt homesick. Milyn was as blue as earth. Brilliant white clouds protected much of the planet. Oceans, continents, and the lights of thriving cities on the dark side of the sphere reminded me of home.

The land masses were different. Radio chatter was hard to parse even with Kayan's help. I tried to work the conversions solo. Both Kayan and Solen had coached me to use hardware the ship had implanted in my neural network along with other connections to the ship. If I ever returned home, I'd be a boss on the multi-lingual scene, especially if I put in some study time.

"Your approach vector looks good," MDS 1 said. "You've been randomly selected for inspection. Stand by for a boarding party. If you've defiled the Kayan with weapons, put them away. MDS 1, out."

"Should we be worried?" I asked.

"No. We weren't randomly selected," Solen said. "The Rights of Sovereign Planets Movement wouldn't pass on the chance to inspect a Kayan. Years ago, an ambitious Gavant counterterrorist team used one to attempt an infiltration of the

ROSPM. It almost worked. Plus, living starships are rare since the confinement began."

"How great must our compliance be?" Wozim asked.

Everyone looked to Montow, including Solen. Kayan assured me the Hellenger had more experience with this sort of thing than almost anyone. The ship must have given the same talk to Solen Far, because she seemed ready to listen to the man.

He took his time to answer, but seemed firm when he did. "We will allow them to separate us but remain within sight. Grum, go with Noah and show him how to set up the main deck. Make sure there are no blood stains from our previous misadventures."

The Walen moved immediately to the door, nervous but ready.

I followed but looked to the captain. "You're sure about this?"

He gave me a thumbs-up. It wasn't the exact gesture I was looking for, but I assumed it meant yes.

"What about ROSPMs? They seemed pretty specific about that point," I said.

Wozim stood and dusted off his hands, his meticulously neat dining habits on full display. "I will see to placing them in a vault. It is a violation but never challenged. Not even the Gavant would dare violate that section of a Kayan vessel. The ROSPM have never harmed a living starship."

"Good enough." I followed Grum and listened to the rest of the meeting in one ear. Kayan kept the connection crystal clear, and I almost felt like I was still in the room.

"The real danger, Solen Far, is you and the item you carry," Montow said. "What do you propose as a course of action?"

"I'll retain the device and face the consequences. If these people are who I think they are, I'm known to them and won't be molested without being taken to their base."

I surveyed the main deck, and the largest airlock on the ship. Seven passageways opened to this area. We'd faced tough fighting against pirates, and I'd witnessed significant expansion and contraction of the room during my time aboard. There were limits to this area as it was associated with the vault deep within Kayan's center of mass. Tertiary sections, like the observation pods and their connecting tubes, were easy for Kayan to shift as needed. It was even possible to tow small craft close to the ship's belly, as it were.

"Last time Montow had me close all the doors and police the area for debris," Grum said.

"Was that a problem?" I'd rarely seen disorder beyond the subdeck problems with Qurks and Fyr slugs overbreeding during the Hoyon transport.

"There were other passengers who didn't respect Montow's rules, or Kayan's welfare," Grum said.

"What happened to them?"

"Wozim encouraged them to leave at the first port we reached."

"So he is useful." I knew the Tyton was, of course. The giant warrior had helped me rescue Solen and the data cube. And he was warming up to the team—I hoped. I hurried to do my job. Montow and the others arrived and changed the lighting so there were five places to stand with good illumination, plus the zone near the entrance.

Montow gathered us into a circle. "They may search the ship but should return to the general area we have defined for them. Interviews will be conducted in these cones of light to maximize the ship's ability to monitor each of us. If the Milyn Defense Forces turn out not to be ROSPM agents, we should still be okay."

"The MDF will respect due process if we are in violation of their laws, or the Gavant's," Solen said. "Like all franchise worlds, they must make reasonable efforts to enforce their master's regulations. Avoid calling attention to yourself, and do not argue no matter what they say."

Lights flashed above the main airlock.

"The Milyn vessel has docked. There are twenty-one soldiers, including their squad leaders and officers, preparing to board. Each wears MDF uniforms and insignia," Kayan said.

"Is that normal?" I asked.

"Yes. Follow my lead or Montow's advice. This is a necessary part of contacting people who can help us."

29

MDF TROOPERS ENTERED BY SQUADS, one right, one left, and the third down the middle to hold the center. Getting surrounded sucked. Wozim tracked their movements with his eyes but seemed unconcerned. Big surprise there.

Solen did a careful 360-degree turn to see exactly which passageways the troopers were now barring us from reaching. Grum imitated the Tyton and the Altion, but I could see he was nervous. He spent too much time checking on his friends when he should be focused on our visitors.

I stood with Montow to face the officer in charge.

"I am Lieutenant David Rochs," said a middle-aged Altion barely taller than Solen. The rank was a translation. A more literal interpretation was something like soldier boss II. I filed the distinction for future linguistics study and continued to think in terms I understood.

"Which of you is the captain of this Kayan?" he asked.

Montow answered. "Me."

"Log."

Montow handed over a tablet Kayan hadn't fabricated, which probably meant there was a chance it wouldn't be returned. The Hellenger waited as stoically as Wozim minus the black teeth and eyes glowing with muted hellfire. The sunglasses helped conceal his intentions, I thought.

Rochs read carefully. He swiped to new displays, then back once or twice.

"Problem?" I asked.

He looked at me with the enthusiasm of a preacher who had just spotted a muddy hog in church. "What brings this Kayan to our world?"

"Food and fuel. None of us want trouble," Montow said before I could put my foot in my mouth.

Rochs returned the tablet. "Your crew will be quartered on our secure base." He returned his attention to me. "Our conversation will continue. Please come with me."

"Just like that?" I didn't like this development for about ten reasons.

"Go with them, Noah," Montow said. "I will inform the others."

"Kayan, help me out," I murmured.

Rochs, who had been turning to issue orders to his subordinates, snapped his attention my way. "Did you just speak directly to the Kayan without us hearing her response?"

The ship sent me a private warning. "I will help you, Noah. For now, be careful. This was expected."

"Is there a problem with talking to a Kayan?" I asked Rochs.

All eyes were on us. He moved nearer. "I have three encounters under my belt, and I scored high marks on all training related to living starships. To say a private neural link is unusual is an understatement."

"Lucky me. Don't hate the players," I said.

His nonreaction was intimidating as hell. MDF guards surrounded me. My journey to their base began immediately. Each of my friends were put on separate shuttles and flown to the base.

The ride was short but still gave me too much time to think. "This is happening too fast," I whispered.

"Be careful when we talk," Kayan said. "I will stay in touch for as long as possible. Rochs suspects this will cause me discomfort. His goal is to put me off balance. The man is a liar. This is not the first time he has witnessed a neural link between my kind and another species. Otherwise, he would not have reacted so abruptly."

"Thanks. I'm out of my depth." I watched Kayan grow smaller on the view screen. It was the best view I'd had of the starship. My chest ached with loss. Energy flowed through me, almost like the flight or fight response. What could I, what should I, do with it?

Lieutenant David Rochs sat on a bench across from me, then cocked one leg over the other as he stretched his arms out to both sides to support his backward lean. "You are very interesting. Not an Altion or a Gavant. Definitely not a Hellenger or a Walen. A Boakmin, maybe?"

This dude was fishing for free information. That wasn't going to happen with his attitude. "I'm just trying to get by. Don't want any trouble."

"Avoidance is often the best policy in that regard. Who wants bad things to happen? Not me." Something beeped on the collar of his body armor. He touched one ear, then excused himself. "I need to take a call. Don't go anywhere."

"Ha, ha. You're hilarious." The guy wasn't listening to me now. I surveyed my environment and learned very little from this section of the shuttle. Guards watched me but didn't seem afraid. Boredom was the order of the day. That could be an act, but I didn't think so in this case. Their boss might be fascinated by my strangeness, but they didn't seem to care.

The shuttle landed. Guards switched out with other guards. Rochs showed up to point down the ramp, and I was taken into the spaceport. Once clear of the exit, we stopped. Four MDF troopers and a team leader stayed with me. Montow, Solen, and Grum each emerged with a similar security escort. Wozim had two squads and Lt. Rochs around him.

"At least they're afraid of the right person," I said as I took in all the other activities around the landing zone. This place was like the Star Wars cantina in daylight. Humanoids of every shape and size went about their business.

One of my guards laughed, and it sounded friendly. "The Tyton is badass. Hell's pastries, I wouldn't be surprised if he is a battle lord."

I turned toward the voice and saw just another helmet visor. She looked and sounded female, but I reserved that judgment for later. You just couldn't jump to conclusions when it came to aliens. Not that it mattered.

"Can we talk?" I asked.

"I don't know, can we?"

"Seemed like your boss gave your team orders not to." I had questions and suspected this might be my only chance to get some straight talk. "Are we going to be queued up like this for a while, because that'll be boring."

She removed her helmet, and I nearly fell over at the sight of her crystal face. The contours were human, in the most exotic sense, but there the similarity stopped. Her skin was like cool blue diamonds over quicksilver and her eyes were as vibrant as Earth from space. The crown of her head was ruby red, and she kept her gloves on like she was embarrassed to show her hands. "I'm a Gleam, because I know you're wondering. What I can't figure out is what you are. Not a Boakmin or a Slim, but close."

"Ever met a human?" I asked.

"Nope."

"Well now you have."

She laughed. "All right. That's diamonds. Your language is easy on my translator, even if you look like funky Friday at the cinema."

The other guards watched us but didn't seem to care.

"Are all of you Gleams?"

The three with their helmets down grunted and muttered, almost like they didn't want my translation software, or the

353

Gleam's to decipher their opinions. None of them liked me, but I didn't think they appreciated being stuck with the sparkling-faced, blue-eyed chatterbox either.

She shook my hand, which caught me off guard—again. How could she be so weird and familiar at the same time?

"Call me Leana. Family name is Brightness, but you don't really have the context to appreciate that much."

"Noah Gantz." I left out where I was from. Fair was fair. She had done the same thing. "You don't seem like you belong with this group."

"Part time gig." She stepped away from the other three who were talking trash on someone or gossiping like professional soldiers stuck on a bullshit job. "Used to be an MDF regular, but they have a lot of rules. And my supervisor didn't appreciate my interpretation of resource allocation."

"Not enough going to him?" I asked, sensing where this was going.

"Her, but that was exactly the problem. I never steal or defraud. You wouldn't believe how many resources are available if you know who to ask and how to ask them," she said. "Look me up if you need supplies for your ship. Kayan's are awesome. Better watch out. Here comes the boss man."

Rochs strode our direction. My guards put on their game faces and stood at attention. Leana put on her helmet and snapped into position like a pro.

"Take this man to an interview room in section five, level two. The guards are waiting and will relieve you of responsibility for this individual," Rochs ordered.

"Right away, boss," Leana said. "Let's go boys. This assignment isn't going to end in a paycheck all by itself." She pulled me ahead of them by one arm, then settled into a comfortable stride.

"Thanks," I said, not sure why.

"These dudes are boring and hate Gleams. Probably Walens or Boakmins under those visors. You know how *they* are."

"I haven't met an asshole Walen." I watched the crowd as we moved out of the spaceport and into the station proper.

"You haven't stolen anything from them and then sent an invoice for payment of services," she said. "Long story. Big misunderstanding. You're right. They are nearly as friendly as my people, under the right circumstances."

"That's enough talking," said one of the other guards. "We'll take it from here, Leana." His gravelly voice resonated with menace.

"Chill out, tough guy. I'll walk him the rest of the way and make sure you get paid, with a bonus."

All three guards loomed above us, staring down with unreadable visors. They were obviously a group. Leana was the outsider. Half a minute passed as they silently considered her proposal.

The leader finally answered. "You better not pull a fast one. I know you can get us a bonus, but none of us trust you."

She spread her hands and looked away. "Fine. Stay poor. I know all the forms and how to get them through the system is all I'm saying. If you want to put forth more effort for less pay, good for you. Very admirable. I bet Rochs will offer the lot of you a full-time position."

The leader poked her in the breastplate with one gauntleted finger. "Don't make me regret this. Full pay, and whatever bonus you can get. We'll be at the Stardust if something comes up." He looked me over. "You got no credit with us. Run off on the Gleam, and we'll run you down like a three-legged Qurk."

"I'm shaking in my boots."

He cursed at me, then left with his friends.

"Why did you do that, Leana?"

She motioned for me to start walking beside her. "Those guys are boring. Definitely Boakmins. Besides, I want to know all about the Kayan and your other adventures."

"You're part of the E4 mafia," I said.

"What is that?"

"Where I'm from, there are certain enlisted soldiers who specialize in supply issues." I gave her a chin thrust. "That's you. A real hustler."

"Hmmm. My translation aid is flip-flopping on that term." She held up her hands like a scale measuring two similar weights. "Good or bad?"

"I mean it in the best possible way."

She laughed out loud. "I like you, Noah Gantz the human. And I really want to hear all your stories, but we've arrived, and I need to see about getting the three jerk faces their money."

Ahead of us was a passageway guarded by regular MDF soldiers. Solen was being led into a room with several official-looking men and women. My blood pressure increased. All my attention went to a pair of armed men marching toward me.

"Let me share a secret, Noah."

"Make it quick."

"Rochs paid me to do the transport instead of his regulars. The three morons joined at the last minute and screwed up my mission. He wanted to know how you talk directly to the Kayan."

"What are you going to tell him?"

"I'll make some shit up and get paid."

"Why are you telling me this?"

She hesitated. "I'm not sure. See you around, human."

"Hey, Leana. Can you check on one thing for me, just in case."

She waited.

"See if there are any food sources for a Kayan that don't require traveling to the edge of this system."

"I'll do what I can."

The MDF regulars put me in a cell and stepped out immediately. I surveyed my environment and talked to Kayan without words. It was the hardest form of communication we shared, mostly because I didn't practice enough. Why would I? Until now, there had been no one spying on me.

One wall was reflective glass, and I assumed there were cameras and microphones. There was one table and three chairs, straight out of an old-style cop drama—places for one suspect and two interrogators.

Kayan analyzed what I was seeing and agreed with my

assessment. *The MDF is not the ROSPM, though they are closely associated.*

Good to know, I thought. *What about the Gleam who brought me here?*

Kayan hesitated as though to watch and listen using my senses for a moment. *She is not like most Gleams. There is a sect of their species known for mischief. Perhaps Leana is one of them.*

I liked the Gleam woman immediately and hoped she wasn't looking for a chance to betray me for money. Instinct suggested I needed someone like her. Milyn was familiar to Solen, but I was a stranger with a lot to lose. It might be good to have a guide.

The door opened. Lieutenant Rochs strode in and dropped a battered computer on the table. "You are on the run from Captain Maxtin Kilis Ryg, the most notorious Gavant hunter in all twelve regions of their empire. Why, for the love of all that is sacred would you lead him here?"

"We didn't lead anyone anywhere. In fact, we sent Ryg on a wild goose chase," I said.

"I'm sorry, a what?"

"He came after Kayan, we dropped clues to some pirates about a false destination knowing they would run to him with the information."

"Clever, if it works."

"Did it?"

His reaction suggested he lacked proof to say my plan had failed. So far, none of the enemy had come after us in this system. I maintained a confident expression, while inwardly I worried that someone like Ryg wouldn't be fooled for long, if at all. My good intentions wouldn't buy a lot of points with Rochs, or anyone else.

"Solen Far has friends here, but you knew that when you came," he said.

I kept my mouth shut.

He smiled and leaned back. "You have restraint. That's good. Solen says you're different, though I can't see how. Other than poorly balanced features and a native language that strains my translation gear, I don't see much of interest.

"Right back at you," I said. "Are we done? Because I need to get back to my ship."

"Why?"

"It needs fuel. Gavant warships have been destroying Oort fields wherever they find them. It isn't easy to travel on a Kayan."

He leaned his elbows on the table and lowered his voice. "You could surrender it to the confinement system. Even Ryg would give you a full pardon, and maybe a reward. Ever thought about that?"

"Not once."

"Because you are so honorable."

"Something like that." I waited until he was about to speak, then interrupted him. "I'm not a criminal. Getting treated like one pisses me off."

"That is understandable. Unfortunately, all of this is necessary." He stood to leave. "My scan is complete. You may move about this section as you please, but do not leave. The cafeteria is open day and night, and there are several wholesome entertainment options available to you free of charge. Do not attempt to contact your crew or your ship. And no gambling or consorting with strange women in ponds."

"Dang, because that is what I normally do when I'm in port." The Monty Python reference jumped out like a rainbow in a storm. Had it been random, or was there another human around here somewhere dumping movie quotes into the local lexicon? Was that good or bad? Did I dare risk finding out until I knew more?

"Follow the rules. Stay in approved areas." His inflection lacked human nuance.

Maybe I hadn't heard him correctly or had mistranslated something. Either way, it was time to push back just a little. "What gives you the right to detain me when I've done nothing wrong?"

He looked confused. "What a strange question. Good day, squire."

I watched him leave and struggled with his answer. This was not the world I was accustomed to. Once again, I reminded myself to doubt everything and base conclusions on first-hand experience as much as possible.

Test one, check the door. It opened. There were no guards outside, so I strolled the way I'd been brought in. There was a large processing room near exit doors large enough to fly a ship through. It seemed like I could just walk out like a patron at a shopping mall.

Three guards in heavy armor changed my mind when I tried. They effortlessly predicted my path and moved to block me. Negotiation didn't seem like much of an option, so I waved and headed back to explore the rest of the section.

Kayan, can you read me?

Barely, Noah. I am conserving energy at the moment. Please tell me there are nutrient vendors sufficient for my needs, the ship thought.

I'm working on it. They're keeping me confined to the MDF-secured area of the station. I'm not sure where Montow and the others are.

Kayan responded slowly. *None of them are able to communicate at this time. Your best option is to find Solen, as this was her destination of choice. She must know her way around, and have contacts.*

Thanks. I'll do that. Take care of yourself, Kayan. And call me if you need me.

Yes, Noah.

We need to work on my translation hardware when I get back.

I will prepare an update, the ship promised, then ended the link.

I wandered aimlessly, eventually arriving at the galley. A hundred people were spread out over dining space sufficient for five hundred. The twenty-four-hour food service was running on a skeleton crew from the look of things, but it was open. I perused the buffet.

"I suggest the pies," Leana said as she snuck up behind me. "Right there. What would you call them in your language?"

I moved closer to an abomination of a pizza and informed the Gleam of my assessment.

"What's wrong with it?"

"Well, that looks like ham and pineapple for starters."

"And that's wrong?" She grabbed a slice and took a bite. "This is one of my favorite things on this entire space station."

"No eating in the line!" shouted a food prepper.

"Sorry, I didn't know!"

"You lie like a Gleam gone bad," the large-bellied Hellenger said.

"Come on," she said to me. "Pick something that reminds you of home and let's get a table. There are also rules against talking while in line. Lots of rules here. Not so bad as in the Gavant proper, but pretty strict. My theory is they're trying to avoid attention, so they mimic their galactic overlords."

I picked four different entrees, none of which were quite what I expected. "Aren't the Gavant your overlords as well?"

She snorted and waved away my comment. "Please. I don't do overlords. The Gleam have never recognized any government other than our own. We just play along to avoid a purge. Gavants, and some of the others if we're being honest, love their purges. Don't you know?"

"I'm not surprised."

Leana picked a table and put down her tray without any interest in the small bowl of eggs she'd selected. The whites of the eggs had been fried into the patterns of stars. She dropped into her chair, leaned forward, and interlocked her gloved fingers. "Tell me everything about your meeting with Rochs. Is he as big a prick as everyone says?"

I stalled by arranging my plates and silverware, then slid the tray onto another table. Familiarity overwhelmed me. Plates were round. Forks were basically forks. Glasses of milk were… I took a sip… not milk.

Leana laughed. "What is that face?"

"This wasn't what I thought it was. Still getting used to life in a new galaxy."

She perked up even more. One thing about this woman was her positive energy. "You really are a traveler. Do you think you're from an entirely different galaxy, or really far away in this one?"

"Got a picture," I half joked.

She tapped a band on her wrist and projected an image between us. My heart jumped. For a moment I thought I was looking at the Milky Way and wasn't that far from home. Her projection showed a *you are here* dot that was right between the Perseus arm and the Scutum-Centaurus arm. So close.

Only it wasn't.

She sensed my disappointment and mellowed. "Bad news?"

"It looks so much like my galaxy it's uncanny."

"Could it be an alternate universe? There are some popular religions that claim such places exist." She turned the image to see all sides, and then zoomed out. Nothing looked remotely familiar. Years of star gazing and daydreaming of exploration hadn't revealed anything like this.

"I doubt it. At first glance, your galaxy and mine are alike, but the colors are wrong and it seems thicker."

"Very scientific. Humans must be a lot like Gleams."

Easy laughter felt good. She matched me and it was like going home, except instead of a fellow UE test pilot or family member, I was staring at a woman with liquid mercury under her diamond skin. The pale blue came and went. I tried not to stare or wonder why she was hiding her hands.

"What are you doing here, Noah?"

"Are you on a secret mission to gather information for Rochs?"

She waved my comment away. "Nah. I made up a bunch of stuff. Specific enough to get paid but vague enough it can't be checked."

"Sounds scrupulous."

She waited a second for her translator, then about shot "milk" across the table at me when she guffawed. "You are a cheeky hypocrite, aren't you?"

"Slow down, Gleam. This is about you inventing my backstory for fun and profit without letting me in on the charade. What if he pulls me in for another interview and decides you lied. He could have you arrested or whatever they do in this galaxy."

She drew a serious breath, then let it out. "It might be time for me to move on. Sadly, not everyone appreciates my creativity. I never actually lie to these assholes—I just let them tell the story and nod along. Maybe embellish here and there. They believe what they want anyway. Why shouldn't I get paid, especially after they turned my ancestors into financial slaves and teach our children what benevolent saviors they are. Pulled us up out of our primal and destructive ways."

"I'm curious. What did you tell Rochs about me?" I knew better than to trust her, but I recognized a kindred spirit in some ways. Lying wasn't a thing my parents, or Pops, tolerated—ever. Had I told some creative stories to motivate people or slip clear of trouble? Absolutely. Where was the line?

She pushed aside her barely touched food, leaned back in her chair, and spread her hands to begin the presentation. "You joined the crew after running away from an arranged marriage. Your people are big on that. Worse, there was a family expectation for poor Noah to become a doctor."

"Really?"

She leaned forward. "Sadly, you can't stand the sight of blood or the weight of commitment. Catching a ride on the Kayan seemed like the perfect solution, until your fellow travelers couldn't decide on a destination and the ship ran low on fuel."

"Great story."

"Is it true?" she asked.

"Little late for that." I wanted to tell her my real backstory but resisted the impulse. Trusting people too easily had gotten me in trouble more than a few times. Pops had given me the advice to trust but verify. The phrase sounded great but was hard to execute.

"Someday you will tell me all about it, from start to finish with funny side stories to keep your journey interesting." She lifted her upturned palm to where the galaxy projection had been. "Maybe we'll learn why our homes are exactly the same but completely different."

Neither of us laughed this time.

"I need to get back to my ship and gather my crew," I said. "We can't leave Solen behind. I promised not to abandon her."

"Is she running from an arranged marriage?"

"No idea. Can you help me?"

She didn't answer. Her response, when it came, was serious. I thought I could trust the mischief-maker with certain things. The Gleam was easier to talk to than anyone on the ship, including Kayan.

"Be patient, Noah. I'll do what I can."

30

Rochs summoned me a few hours later. My escort of four guards didn't speak because they were MDF regulars and not mercenaries hired to steal my life's story. I wondered about Leana's three confederates and decided they hadn't known why they were hired, and had been window dressing—a red herring, basically.

They put me in the same interrogation room. I didn't have enough investigative or interrogation experience to know if that was good, bad, or meaningless. It might have been an attempt to limit what I learned of their facility, except that I'd been given the run of this section so long as I didn't leave.

There were inaccessible passageways and rooms, of course. Sealed bulkheads and guard stations protected these. None of the helmeted troopers expressed humor, or the willingness to chat. Good for them. I hoped they were getting paid to stay that focused.

I waited half an hour for Rochs, who entered just as he had the first time, full of disapproval. He dropped his battered computer on the table and sat with one leg on the edge.

"We have nothing on you."

"That's because I'm an upstanding citizen who obeys the law."

"Hmm. Citizen of where?"

I cycled through Leana's fabricated tale and couldn't remember if she'd invented anything that specific. Telling them I was from United Earth didn't seem like a great idea. Could you ever be too cautious when being held without probable cause by a previously unknown alien government?

"We have no laws against travelers. You should register before leaving. Your next stop will go smoother. Strangers make people nervous," he said.

"How do I register?"

He pulled a card from a slot in the much-maligned laptop and slid it toward me. "Fill this out, or tell one of my agents your information and they will enter it for you. The Gavant Register of Homeworlds is public record, though anyone submitting an inquiry must state why they are running the background check." He paused and remained half sitting on the table between us. "Which brings us to your current dilemma. You don't exist."

I tried a version of the truth. "I don't know how I got here, and my ship was destroyed. The Kayan saved me."

"Now that is interesting."

Silence held the room as he stared straight into my face. I gave the hard look back to him with interest. This had been one of my best events in junior high school. Don't blink buddy, I dare you.

"So you're not running from an arranged marriage?"

"I'd rather not talk about that. Really embarrassing. Can I leave?"

"You are different, Noah Gantz. I will have your papers processed once you complete that form and find an escort from this section of the base."

I sat straighter. "You're not taking me back to my ship?"

"You can find your own way. Perhaps that Gleam will take you, for ten times the price it should cost. Don't trust the red-marked ones."

"Why not?"

"They're known as mischief-makers. Red crowns, or red hands." A too-satisfied smile barely touched his lips. "The thing is, she has both, and that makes her a regular menace. Watch out for Leana-seven-hax-tro. Oh, wait. She didn't tell you her full name. Big surprise. Hax-tro was her hereditary military rank before she won her freedom in a card game. Complete the form. Get registered. You'll thank me later."

I sat thinking about what he said for a long time, then started entering information. How could I be truthful without betraying too much to the Gavant, or countless others I didn't know?

My name was out there, so I used that. United Earth became Colorado. The Sol system became Nunya-business and the Milky Way became Hollywood.

I was tired and needed to get back to Kayan. The ship hadn't reached out to me for a while, and the link seemed weak. This place was cramping my style.

I STROLLED through the hall with a complimentary bottle of water and a paper-like pamphlet explaining my rights as a registered traveler in the Gavant Reach. Most of the people here were Gavant, or Altion, but I saw a few Walens and Hellengers. No Tytons showed themselves. I didn't know if that was because they were rare, or just not a fan of Milyn.

Something was wrong at the exit. The wide, shopping-mall-like mezzanine beyond the final guard post was completely empty. A sole bot sped across the gleaming white floor like it had been forgotten. If machines could panic, this little dude was freaking the hell out. That made me worry about Scratch, but there was nothing I could do from here. Kayan would look after the animal.

A hilarious image of the puppy-kitten exploring the galaxy with his trusty living starship and no one else threatened to make me laugh. I searched this side of the complex and witnessed a much different scene. There were more people inside the blast wall than ever, and it was being closed.

I grabbed a passing Walen by the arm, hoping he would be as helpful as Grum. "What's going on?"

He squinted. "Sorry, lord gentleman kushtec, my translator is not a fucker."

"Uh, no worries. I'm listening. Take your time. What has happened?"

"Piss trees are in the attic of the Gavant."

"Okay, while I find that intriguing, I don't understand."

He clenched his fists in frustration and stared at his feet. When he came back up, there was nothing but resolve on his face. Walens really did try hard. "A Gavant hunter has been sighted. In this system. Not like a regular fucking patrol, jerk face."

Where exactly was his translator drawing my language template? I needed to ask Kayan or Montow for a better explanation of the tech. Maybe some of it was an error on my end of the process.

"Captain Maxtin Kilis Ryg leads a notorious sponge force. Full of noodles. Rumors claim he is in a special rage. Ready for a dance off to the death."

"Dude, this is the most fun I've had in years."

He smiled wide and his eyes brightened. "Thank you, whatever you are. May I find my family and shelter them? The Gavant marked my line for asteroid processing jobs, and we decided to take our chances with the Rights of Sovereign Planets Movement."

"Sure. Sorry to bother you. Stay safe."

"Thank you, short-neck thick-head." He hurried away before I could respond to his questionable description of humans.

Three loud chimes sounded over a public address system. Everyone stopped where they were and looked toward a screen on the wall opposing the now closing blast doors.

"Galaxy's fortune on you, good people. All who have elected to shelter here must attend a general assembly in thirty minutes. Make your arrangements. Should you choose to leave, speak not of this section or what we do here."

The man's image disappeared and was replaced by lists of departing flights and other travel information. I stopped another Walen. Why not? They were the most helpful race I'd met. "Excuse me, who was that man?"

"General Pon Keppel of the ROSPM, but never say that beyond these walls," the Walen woman said.

"Does he really expect to keep any of this a secret?"

"Of course." She went on her way.

I was careful not to slow her down in case she was off to protect her own family. *Kayan, can you read me?*

Not well, Noah. There are many changes being made to local security algorithms.

Ryg has been spotted in this system and everyone is freaking out, I thought.

That is true, but there is more. A Gavant armada has arrived. Ironically, it is the only thing slowing him down. I believe he was called in to make a report and will need permission to pursue us further. Unfortunately for us, that will likely mean he will be given additional resources to achieve our apprehension.

A massive MDF trooper, at least the size of a Tyton, pointed at me. "You there. Get moving. No standing in the center of the trafficway."

"Yes, sir. Moving now."

He watched me. My response had drawn more attention

than intended. I wondered what his translator had provided him. His open-faced helmet showed he was another race I hadn't encountered, definitely not a Tyton. There was a catlike structure to his face.

Groups of people left after what appeared to be a rigorous separation interview. How could the ROSPM keep this place a secret? Or had they? Maybe the Gavant allowed its existence for their own reasons.

"Are you Noah Gantz from Hollywood?" asked an Altion guard with a Hellenger backup. "Don't lie, because Solen Far sent us, and if I take back your picture and she says you ditched us, there will be heavens to Betsy."

"I really need to tune my translator output," I muttered.

He seized my sleeve.

I knocked it loose with an outward forearm chop—short and only as powerful as needed. His grip popped free as I took a ready stance. "Hands off. I'm coming. Where is Solen?"

"In General Keppel's ready room. Follow me. Chuck will follow the both of us, just to keep you honest."

I made no comment. The prisoner-not-prisoner treatment was getting old. Solen was with her people. We owed each other nothing. It was time to get the hell out of Dodge. I stared through the exit and wondered if I could make it to the spaceport on my own. The trip here had been confusing, but there were only so many launch pads. Kayan would guide me when possible.

Kayan, can we refuel and get out of here? I focused on the message as we walked. My guards took my silence for compliance.

There is not enough for me here. Or more accurately, I cannot obtain what is here. Find Montow, or Solen. Maybe they can broker a transfer of resources to get us to the next system. Kayan's voice faded in my mind.

Seek out a Gleam named Leana-seven-hax-tro. She may have a connection. We needed someone with ties to the local black market.

Yes, I see her listed in the exonerated of guilt lists. Many times. The woman does not appear trustworthy, but I am already tracing her access into many things I need to refuel and refit.

Good luck, Kayan. You're fading.

As are you. Keep your head swiveling.

My attempts to reestablish contact failed, and that worried me. I addressed my escort. "How much farther?"

"We arrive when we arrive, Colorado," the senior guard said.

I fumbled through his statement and realized that the semi-truthful information I'd put in the Gavant register was already uploaded. Colorado, to this guy, was synonymous with United Earth. He didn't know what that was, and he had never heard of humans. That worked for me. So far, I wasn't impressed with this crew.

We hurried up a set of wide, switchback stairs. My escorts kept me to one side as more important traffic passed us.

"That's General Keppel, so behave," said guard number two.

I counted eleven men and women in the entourage, five of them bodyguards. The very important people talked energetically until Keppel spotted me and stopped. He held up a hand for his soldiers and they immediately formed a perimeter. Only one of his companions remained inside this wall of security and I assumed he was either a close friend, direct subordinate, or a trusted assistant.

"You're new."

I wasn't sure how to answer. Had this man really picked me out of hundreds, maybe thousands of individuals now seeking asylum from the Gavant hunter armada? Of course he had, because I was the only human in the place. Easy.

"Yes, sir."

He had no problems with the translation. "You're almost a Boakmin, but not quite. Tell me your origin, and be quick. I'm a busy man."

"I'm from a planet called Earth. You probably haven't heard of it."

He glanced at his wrist then back to me. "That isn't what you put on your register. Rochs entered it personally, and he's normally very thorough."

The general had gotten all of that from a half-second peek at his watch. This told me two things: his gear was the best in the room, and he was smart as hell. "I'm not sure who to trust. Everything in the register is true but lacks context."

He seemed neither pleased nor disappointed with my explanation when he gave orders to my escort. "I'm on my way to an important meeting. Fill in with my guards and stay close enough for a handoff. If I tire of his glatka-crap, you will remove him immediately."

"Yes, General Keppel."

He motioned for me to walk beside him and his companion, who said nothing but watched me carefully. Keppel was an

Altion. His advisor was a tall, lean Gavant with a dour face. The markings around his eyes were pale, almost like they had been intentionally bleached to reduce his resemblance to a Gavant officer.

"Is there a problem? I'm just a traveler."

Keppel looked me over again as we reached the top of the stairs and strode down a wide passageway. "You bear a striking resemblance to a high-ranking commander in the Gavant fleet— someone above Captain Ryg."

He pointed at the leader of his security element. "I need a private room right now."

Two of the general's personal guards jogged ahead and evicted a group of officers from a conference room. They swept it with electronic hand scanners, then saluted Keppel who guided me inside. I wasn't sure, but I thought he might shove me forward if I moved too slow. The weird part was this didn't bother me. He was that important. If I screwed around, I deserved what happened. The sensation was powerful and unique, something that had occurred twice in my lifetime.

"Damien, you stay. Everyone else, wait outside," Keppel said. His assistant, Damien, entered and said nothing. He was one cool character who seemed to have the complete trust of the general.

"I don't want to cause trouble." This about to go someplace unexpected.

He closed the door then took his time returning to the table. "Let's cut to the chase. I am extremely familiar with every race under the Gavant's thrall. Many races, species, variants—whatever you like to call them—resemble one another."

"I look like the Boakmin and the Slim," I said, trying to take back part of this conversation. "I get it."

"Yes and no. Physical appearance isn't everything. The way you stand, the speed of your movements, which of these you favor… and your language. My translation aids are the best available. I hear you as no one else but a Kayan does," Keppel said.

Damien leaned toward him and whispered.

Keppel nodded. "You came on a Kayan sought by Captain Ryg." He paused and transformed. I didn't know if he was about to take me under his wing or push me from an airlock. "That changes things. Damien tells me you brought Solen Far, saved her life in fact. That earns you a chance with us."

I needed to jump ahead and seize the initiative. "Tell me about this Gavant asshole. My resemblance caught your attention and put a lot of other meetings on hold, I think."

"Send two of my men to bring Solen Far," Keppel said.

Damien stepped out, gave orders, then returned.

Keppel waited. "Tatum Collins Three. Does that name sound familiar?"

"I thought you had the best language translating hardware available." This was dangerous, but I didn't have a lot of options. The fact that my blood just turned to frozen sludge and my mind was doing summersaults didn't help.

"What do you mean?" Keppel asked.

"His name is Lieutenant Colonel Tate Collins III—the third, not three."

"You know him." He wasn't asking a question.

I interpreted it as one to stall for time. "Not personally. He went missing almost a year ago. If we're being completely honest—"

"We are, unless you want to walk the galaxy without a space suit," Damien said.

"Uh, right. He's a real douche bag."

Keppel frowned. "You have pushed my translation ability against a wall. That doesn't happen often. What does that phrase mean?"

"He's not cool."

Damien went pale.

Keppel nodded knowingly. "The temperature reference sounds like something he would say. Before Damien was pulled from deep cover, Collins declared he wasn't cool, then promised to torture him under the ice shards of Ulonade 5."

"Do you send a lot of people on dangerous assignments like that?" I asked.

"No, but it is necessary. Until now, we have recovered them all. Only one man remains in their prisons, but we will get to that." Keppel paced the room to clear his head.

A pair of MDF guards knocked and announced they had Solen Far.

"Send her in," Keppel ordered.

She entered cautiously, dividing her attention equally

between me and the general. After a few seconds, she merely nodded to the important man. He returned the gesture.

"You've got really important friends, Solen. Who knew?" I pushed my chair back from the table as a test. How much could I move before they called in the guards? Could I pace? Go to the door? Leave?

"We were talking about Collins," Keppel provided.

Solen nodded. "They're both human. I suspected as much but haven't spoken to the Gavant puppet master face-to-face. This one is shorter, I think."

"Bingo," I said. "Not all of us can be six foot five. Both of us are big for pilots. Thanks for noticing." Anger surged up at the entire situation. I controlled it with effort.

"What did you want me to do? Ask if you worked for the incarnation of evil?" Her face flushed lavender across her cheekbones.

Right then, I wondered if I was on the wrong side. Collins had always been a prick but not evil. The man was prideful, ambitious, and unfairly gifted. That didn't mean he could have started an empire in less than a year. "How long has this Collins character been working for the Gavant."

"Three years or more," Damien said.

I shook my head. "He's been dead less than a year."

Keppel actually laughed. "Now that will take some explanation. Are you suggesting the man is a zombie? What an interesting concept."

"We didn't recover his body." My brain was processing too

much information, and my tongue was getting loose. I'd dug myself into a hole and needed to simultaneously talk myself out of it and shut my mouth. "Unless his name and human appearance are coincidences, there has been a misalignment of time and space." I laughed nervously at science beyond my grasp.

Keppel and his assistant went deadly quiet. The air in the room seemed charged with potential violence. One wrong move, a single misspoken word, and I was cashiered from life. Finito. Finished. Done and dusted. Fucking dead.

My fingers drummed on the table. The sound drew my attention but not that of my interrogators. There was a point in every showdown where the balance tipped. Dogfights had their own type of chaos where nothing made sense until that one opportunity presented itself.

I'd successfully identified and seized that advantage four times in my fighter pilot career, which resulted in four kills. Once, during my last aerial combat incident, my eyes had seen the shot and the maneuvering it would take to set it up. My hands had gone to the controls, but my brain refused to seize the initiative, and I'd been shot down.

Ancient history.

No one blamed me or called me a failure. An eighty percent win ratio wasn't bad if you survived to tell the story. Yet, Command had never put me in another fight.

Bored and seeking redemption, I had become a test pilot.

"Speak your mind, Noah Gantz from Colorado. I have led many great men and women and can see when they are standing at the precipice overlooking a bold decision," Keppel said.

"There is only one way to confirm this Tate Collins is the same person I know." Conviction seeped into my bones. "I've got to meet him."

"Then what?" Damien asked.

"Bring him over to our team, or remove him from the game."

Keppel leaned back in his chair and analyzed me down to my DNA, or that's what his stare looked like it was doing. In a weird way, his skepticism was comforting. I didn't mention that I hadn't decided if I was on the right team.

Solen kept her eyes on me but spoke to General Keppel. "I told you he would say that."

31

WAITING for Keppel's answer was killing me. Seconds felt like years. He was hard to read. I would never play poker with this guy. At the same time, he didn't appear to hide his thoughts. His aura of command was just that effortless. Damien and Solen waited on opposite sides of the room. Their positions would make it easy to see if I switched my attention back and forth between them. Liars searched for the easiest person to sway in situations like these, especially if they were panicking.

I had a couple of things going for me—the truth, and experience with high-stress situations. It was like Pops always said, panic was for the weak. What was the worst that could happen? They weren't going to eat me.

Keppel eventually leaned forward and made a pointing gesture that seemed very human. This guy had already processed much of my body language and gained fluency just like he had in United Earth English. I doubted he even needed translation assistance at this point.

"You have huge balls, human. I'll grant you that." He paused. "I'm obligated to make one serious offer before we proceed. It's more than just custom, but law. Otherwise you will be risking your life on a false premise."

"What is that?" I asked.

"That you can't go home without help, but I can send you there."

"Great. Tell me more." Something was off, but I couldn't put my finger on it. When an offer was too good to be true, it was probably a trap.

"We retained access to older technology that was dropped by the Gavant and other space-fluent civilizations. Before the jump technology was perfected, there were only two ways to travel significant distances, by Kayan or what was called High Energy Consumption Voyaging."

I listened and thought of the desert where I'd begun this odyssey.

"Launch pads were built on moons or small planets. Each travel event destroyed the facility and its host body."

"Sounds wasteful," I said.

He nodded. "It was. Very. But that isn't the worst part. Small communities of fanatics always protested these harsh blast offs. One of the reasons the technology fell out of favor was that to execute a HECV, you have to accept the protestors will die. They were given every opportunity to vacate prior to launch, but never did. It was an ugly business."

"If you think I am going to trade one life for a trip home, you've lost your ever-loving mind and I am on the wrong side of this rebellion." Blood pounded in my temples even though I understood the offer was bullshit. My hands needed to grab him.

He smiled, then faced Damien and Solen. "I knew he would pass."

Damien nodded slowly. "You are a better judge of character than I."

Solen muttered something under her breath and relaxed.

My breathing gradually slowed. "You guys are real assholes."

Keppel stood. "It is a simple but necessary test. We can't let just anyone into our sanctum. Come. We need to relocate and start the real conversation."

I followed the Altion leader and his Gavant assistant. The offer to send me home had never been real. That didn't reduce the effect it had on my emotions. Distances didn't even compute. The galaxy Leana had shown me was unrecognizable despite years spent looking to the stars. I was a test pilot and an astronaut, not an astronomer, but still.

"Are you well?" Damien asked.

Solen fell in beside me and intervened. "He's fine. This is a lot to take in. Imagine if the roles were reversed."

Damien's expression soured. "I would rather not."

Four guards resembling the seven-foot-tall cat-faced man I'd encountered earlier stopped us from entering a heavily armored bulkhead. Keppel submitted to a security scan and passed through in seconds. Damien went next and was scrutinized more carefully. Solen told the guards she would go last.

I stepped onto an X painted between a pair of sensor panels and raised my arms to match the diagram. "So, how long have you gentlemen been with the TSA?"

My joke fell flat. I followed instructions and emerged inside. When Solen caught up to me, she explained the guards weren't allowed to engage in banter. "Maviks are fun once you get to know them, but that takes a lot of work."

"Those men were Maviks?" I asked as we rejoined Keppel and Damien.

She nodded. "Extremely fierce when provoked, but hilarious if you can catch them off duty."

"There are three more checkpoints. No time for idle talk," Keppel said. A new contingent of bodyguards fell in behind us, though I couldn't see how anyone would threaten the general here. "Listen carefully, because this is the plan we will follow."

"I'm all ears."

Keppel smiled, shook his head, and continued. "You must betray me. Damien will compile verifiable, but out-of-date intelligence reports the Gavant will believe. We'll adjust our new efforts accordingly, since we will know that they know more. You make a run for it in a small but very fast ship we have wired for surveillance. We've used this tactic successfully. They didn't suspect a thing."

"Do you have a problem with people fleeing your side? Wouldn't that mean you're as bad as the Gavant to some people?" I had other concerns. Namely that a tactic used too often became ineffective.

"We are, depending on who you ask. But we are not the

Gavant. Trust me, Noah. You are on the right side. Our cause is freedom and equality. The Gavant promise security and prosperity in exchange for personal, and even global freedoms. Bending this entire sector of the galaxy to their will is the only acceptable outcome for them," Keppel said. "Only fools deny the truth."

Our discussion paused as we passed through the next two fortified guard posts. I tried again to contact Kayan. The signal was weak.

There are a lot of MDF soldiers in the spaceport, and warships are preventing me from leaving, the ship said. *Not that I would abandon you or the others.*

"Thanks, Kayan. I'm looking for the rest of the crew and trying to get back."

"No talking during the security screening," the guard station supervisor said.

I complied but listened in case Kayan had more to say. The ship was better at using our neural network without sound. Distractions made it harder, especially when everything around me was new. Other than general assurances, the ship was done transmitting.

Keppel stood among his badass bodyguards and scrutinized my every move. Damien did the same. I looked back when the security team finally waved me through and saw Solen getting the full treatment, just like me.

She was clearly a trusted operative for General Keppel. It didn't seem like that was common knowledge. Guards turned out her pockets, scanned her twice, and made her repeat the body scan. When it was over, one of them brought Keppel the data cube.

I knew better than to stare at it, though it was hard to resist the impulse. The device appeared insignificant but was the key to going home.

Solen held out her hand when she joined us.

"Wait until we're in private," Damien said, "And show some respect."

"My apologies," Solen said, though her gaze never wavered. By human standards, she didn't look contrite. Both Keppel and Damien seemed satisfied, however, and walked ahead of us to consult with officers reporting in.

Solen walked beside me.

"Do you know where Montow and the others are now?" I asked when it was just the two of us.

"They are being treated well, according to my source. And don't ask who that is," she said. "What do you think of this plan?"

"That depends on this ship he wants me to use. My gut tells me to use Kayan." I surveyed the meticulously clean passageway without spotting cameras I suspected were watching. There were no windows this deep into the station and none of the personnel acted like civilians, not even those lacking uniforms. "Is this the ROSPM headquarters? How do they hide from the Gavant hunters? This place doesn't seem difficult to find."

"This base orbiting Milyn, and the supporting nations on the planet's surface, are just strong enough to prevent direct confrontation. That day will come, and everyone knows it," she said. "Basically, it would be a public-relations nightmare to assault a member world in good standing, and they like to think they know where our greatest strength is concentrated."

"The big raid is coming quicker than expected, or is the arrival of an armada commonplace?"

She stopped to consider her answer, because Keppel and his entourage had ceased walking to review something on a portable computer. It looked like video of Gavant warships.

"Times are changing, Noah Gantz. Are you willing to risk Kayan's freedom? Propose the change if you dare. Fleeing in an at-large living starship will guarantee aggressive pursuit by our galactic overlords." She jutted her chin a millimeter toward the general. "He's coming. Have your proposal ready if you're gonna do it."

The ROSPM leader strode toward me, but what struck me was the appearance of the scene behind him. Men and women, soldiers and support staff, walked or jogged or marched deeper into the complex. The passageway was wide and about fifteen or twenty feet high. For three seconds, all I could see was them disappearing into the Eisenhower Tunnel back home.

I thought of Pops and hoped he was proud of me. For all he knew, I was dead, which meant he'd lost his son, daughter-in-law, and grandson. It was hard to imagine him without a half grin on his face as he sized me up. Right now, I wanted nothing more than to tell him I was alive and coming home.

"Walk with me, Noah," Keppel said, then he directed everyone else, including Damien and the guards, to give us room.

"I need your honest assessment. You will be taking the greatest risk. And you must be able to handle General Tate Collins."

"Which part are you worried about?" I asked the question for a reason. My gut told me to figure out what he thought was wrong with the plan before I explained my own reservations.

"Loyalty."

I waited. Had he expected me to get defensive?

"Solen Far believes you will do the right thing, and Damien is correct. I am a good judge of character," he continued. "But correct me if I am wrong. Both you and Collins are far from home. What would I do in a similar situation? That is what I ask myself."

"What is on the data cube?"

He crossed his arms and held my gaze. "You tell me. I assume the Kayan decrypted it behind Solen's back."

"Partially."

Relieved, he exhaled, then started over. "This isn't our only base. The cube contains everything the Gavant know about us, and other information that is less useful."

"I think it has the coordinates to my home."

"Do you think Collins would take you there?" Keppel asked. "Wouldn't he have already gone if he was going?"

"I've asked myself that question a few times."

"What is wrong with our plan, Noah?"

"I should use Kayan. The ship is more versatile, and it offers added incentive for the Gavant to pursue us. Collins likes to win big. He'll get greedy and go after us himself. Then I can make the identification and sway him to the cause."

"And if you can't?"

"Then we escape for real." I looked back at the others. "There should also be a backup plan. While I'm negotiating, you should have other assets attempting to recover the Gavant copy of the data cube."

"I never said there was one."

I laughed. "Nope. But that's your real aim. If I succeed, great, but that is not what you're after. You not only want what Solen has, you want to be sure no one else does either."

"I should recruit you into our espionage unit." He paused. Nervousness showed—barely—for the first time. The man was playing a dangerous game and wanted it to be over. He sighed in resignation. "Your ignorance of the infiltration team would have provided an extra layer of security, but there is no way to put the knowledge back into the void. My best people will steal back the information. All they need is to get close. Do your job, and don't worry about the rest."

"I'm using Kayan. If things look sketchy, we bail."

"I suppose you will. That would be my response, so I can't blame you." His mood lightened like someone had just taken the weight of the galaxy off his shoulders. "Come. I'll introduce you to the support team."

"They aren't really a support team."

"You're killing me, Noah Gantz. Just play along and allow them to do their jobs."

"They stay out of my way, I'll stay out of theirs."

32

"INTERGALACTIC SPY MISSIONS require a lot of sitting and waiting," I complained.

"Tell me about it." Solen had been leaning her elbows on her knees for a while. The forward posture was the attitude of an experienced operator resigned to a test of bureaucratic endurance. "Damien is probably individually reviewing the mission with each of the infiltration specialists. The guy is nothing if not detail oriented."

I went to the door as Montow, Grum, and Wozim were brought in. All three looked tired but otherwise unharmed. They spoke little and kept their distance from the guards when they could.

"Good to see you three," I said. "Did they split you up?"

Montow answered. "Yes. This is the first time we have been

in a group. I've been through this before, but Grum and Wozim haven't."

"You all right, Grum?" I asked.

"They didn't kill me and the food wasn't bad," he said with a smile. "These rebel types don't have much use for Walens. Too passive and helpful for their tastes."

"What about you?" I asked Wozim.

"They asked questions, and I answered when they weren't foolish. As usual, the ROSPM interrogators are morons," said the Tyton.

"I thought this was your first time?" I noticed that Montow was also curious to hear the answer.

"It is not, but why would I talk about these things?"

"Good point. Never stop being you," I said.

Solen waited for our reunion to conclude but seemed impatient. She alternated her attention between us and the infiltration team assembling through another door. I got the feeling she knew some of them, or at least recognized their faces. My first time in the combat pilot training school had been like this. Everyone had been a superstar and as intimidating as hell.

When I thought they were all here, more entered. There were pilots, commandos, and spies dressed as Gavant officers and technicians.

"Kayan, are you seeing this?" I asked. My friends remained quiet, aware that I talked directly to the ship but still not quite accepting the full implications of that relationship.

Yes. I am cataloging faces into my recognition software, Kayan thought.

"You practically read my mind. I can't learn all these people and remember them in time for the mission." My nerves were strung tight. Complexity without appropriate preparation and practice led to failures. I spent months going over every move I made prior to my FTL bubble test launch. This operation felt rushed.

Until I realized everyone in the room except for my crew had likely been planning for this for months or even years. They all knew each other and were exchanging banter and funny stories not for us outsiders. What felt spontaneous and reckless to me was actually the accumulation of thousands of hours of preparation.

"Elite soldiers and super spies," Solen said.

"Go over there and hang out with your friends," I said, testing a theory.

She gave me an *eat shit* look. "I'm an outsider like you."

"Why?" Montow asked.

Wozim answered. "Her role is compartmentalized, kept from the others in every way. Those people are accustomed to a very high security clearance level. It bothers them not to know what she is about."

"That sums it up," Solen agreed. "Nothing but jealousy."

"Makes sense." I gathered my people in for our own private conference. "That's the longest speech I've heard from you, Woz."

He chose not to reply.

"You clearly have information we don't," Montow said. "Share it, and let's get back to the ship and get out of here.

This armada won't turn away from the ROSPM base this time."

"Agreed." I organized my thoughts. "General Keppel recognized me, because I share some features with a man named Tate Collins."

None of my crew knew the name. They waited for more.

"He's from Earth, just like me. According to Keppel's information, he's become a high-ranking leader in the Gavant military." I paused. This was harder than I assumed it would be. "I need to find out if he knows a way to get home."

Montow rubbed his short beard thoughtfully. "Understandable."

Grum seemed a bit sad, but supportive. Wozim just stared at me with his stoic monster face. I wondered briefly what Scratch would think, and reminded myself he was just an animal that wouldn't miss me when I was gone. Someone else on the crew would become his best friend. Maybe he'd be *a little* sad.

"Keppel wants me to attempt a positive identification on Collins, then convince him to switch sides. At the same time, his infiltration team will seek and secure critical information and take it back to the ROSPM for analysis," I said.

Everyone stared. Wozim spoke. "This special infiltration team are not assassins?"

My stomach seemed to fall out of my body. I didn't have an answer. Had I been duped into becoming an accessory for murder? And who would be the target, Collins?

"If you want your old Earth friend to live, I suggest you

convert him quickly. The man is more powerful than his rank suggests. He rules from the shadows," Solen said.

"Gavant do not allow outsiders to have real power in their organizations," Wozim argued. "Even Tyton battle lords are given insignificant roles that are disguised as great honors."

"Doesn't matter." Solen remained firm. "This launch has gone too far to stop. If you want out, you better plan something good. Like it or not, you are part of the ROSPM now. Those kill teams can just as easily wipe us out as attack Collins and the other Gavant VIPs. They are practically herding us into this mission."

As though on cue, Keppel called the meeting to order. "Everyone gather around the central planning table. We have a lot to cover in a very short time. I'd like you all to welcome Noah Gantz and his crew to the mission. They will be providing a distraction with a Kayan starship. Please note subsection A, part five of the allowances for augmented distractions in the master plan for this operation.

All eyes were suddenly on us despite the directive to check the mission plan. Not everyone seemed to be a fan, but they guarded their thoughts and said nothing.

"We will have three support vessels shadowing the Kayan in full stealth mode. You must not be detected until it is time to retrieve data unlawfully stolen from us."

I listened carefully and asked Kayan to take notes whenever possible. For most of the meeting, the starship was able to listen and observe, so I considered that a win. With luck, we would have time to scrutinize every aspect of the mission. It wouldn't be long before the Gavant came after us, but I intended to use all of it. In the meantime, Kayan grew more uneasy about talk of stealth ships.

They're on our side, I thought.

Still dangerous, Noah. I don't like it.

KEPPEL APPROACHED us once everyone was dismissed to their ships. "I'll take you to the flight deck just to speed things up. We can move much faster with my security clearance."

"Thanks," I said. The good vibes surrounding this guy had definitely expired. My gut said to be wary. "That's super generous. You're a real pal."

He frowned. "Have I done something wrong?"

I weighed the decision of confronting him right here. It would be better if he didn't suspect I was onto him and his assassination backup plan. The Altion was an excellent leader, truly impressive from what I had personally witnessed. Hopefully, we were wrong about his ulterior motives.

"I understand operational security." Hundreds of prior mission briefings flashed in my head. Compartmentalization served a purpose. This felt different somehow. "But there need to be a few assurances. Are your infiltration teams going to interfere with what I've been assigned to do?"

"Say what you mean."

I spread my hands and shrugged. "I don't know. Is a sniper

going to take Collins out while I'm in the middle of negotiating with him?"

"Is that how they do things where you're from?"

"Sometimes."

My honesty took him by surprise. He drew back half a step, then rallied. "I should have included you in planning the contingency options. If Collins refutes your arguments, you will need all the help you can get to stay alive. Think of my people as a quick reaction force. Losing agents is never part of my plan. Everyone comes home, every time."

Yeah, okay. Sure. I seriously doubted this man or his organization had a perfect track record.

A scene grew in my imagination. I visualized a surprised and relieved Lieutenant Colonel Tate Collins greeting me with open arms, then excitedly sharing everything he'd learned since his arrival. My cautious self pushed back because it remembered the disconnected timeline. The Gavant Collins had first drawn notice three years ago. The United Earth version had been missing and presumed dead less than a year.

There was also the fact that Collins wasn't a people person. The chances of him acting like this were unlikely. He wasn't a bad guy, but he was stiff and awkward around groups, especially during informal situations. A social butterfly, he was not. His reputation as a demanding leader who expected the best and got it from his people was well known, however.

I understood enough of the FTL bubble technology to suspect there were a lot of dangerous side effects from traveling so far so fast. This could be, probably was, the Collins I knew. I had to be ready for that reality when I met him. We could figure out the details of the extra-galactic jump later.

The imaginary scenario was interrupted by ROSPM tactical teams bursting into the scene, guns blazing. *Great. This was going to be so much fun.*

"Who gives them the order to engage with lethal force?" I asked.

"I do, or Damien."

"I want control of that option."

His face showed anger for the first time.

"How about a compromise," Solen interrupted.

Every member of my crew was watching the exchange.

Keppel crossed his arms. "Please, enlighten us on the changes we should make to a plan that was years in the making."

"Give the QRF assault authority to Wozim. He'll use it most responsibly," Solen said.

To my surprise, Keppel slowly nodded agreement. "That is a good compromise. You are proving your worth again and again, Solen."

"You want the cult of the warrior guy to make that decision?" I shot a look to Wozim. "No offense."

"None taken." Wozim's tail slashed lazily across the deck.

"Tytons never shy from battle, but an equally important part of their code is to not engage in unnecessary hostilities," Solen explained. "That way, when they fight, they're able to fully commit without self-doubt or guilt. That's the idea, anyway."

I held Wozim's intense gaze. "Is that accurate?"

"I will not order Keppel's assassins to kill this Collins person unless it is necessary," Wozim said.

"Montow, Grum, are you guys cool with this?" I asked.

"I trust Wozim," Grum said. "He is one of the ten Tyton battle lords."

Montow took a moment longer to answer. He rubbed the back of his soup can head, then removed the sunglasses and cleaned them on his shirt. His unblinking eyes added severity to his words. "Wozim is the right choice. My concern is that we engage in this endeavor knowing there is a possibility events could blow up in our faces."

"Kayan, what do you think?" I asked. This drew a lot of attention, especially from Keppel and Damien.

"You can talk to your ship this far into the station?" Keppel asked. "Our security tech advisors need to update their assessments."

I held up a hand for him to wait and realized a second too late that I had effectively shushed the most powerful man outside of the Gavant organization. Kayan answered quickly, and I stuck to my guns. Nonverbal gestures were going to get me in a bind, but now wasn't the time to beat myself up. They'd probably do that for me if I wasn't careful.

We are speaking privately, Kayan began. *I have an idea that could be useful but would endanger anyone unfamiliar with my flight protocols. We used something similar with the* White Knife *pirates. This would be a simple variation.*

I mentally asked Kayan to explain.

In the event of boarders, I could accelerate fast enough to kill most creatures, sentient or beast, on board. You would need to get the crew into life pods very quickly, the ship said. *With gravity generators suspended and inertial dampeners disengaged, any unwelcome guest would not live to inconvenience me, or my passengers.*

You're savage, Kayan. And I mean that in a good way.

There are many risks. This is not guaranteed to work, but it is something I came up with and you should know about.

"Well?" Keppel asked.

Kayan spoke through the public address speakers, which Damien seemed annoyed about because my ship was taking control of comms inside a ROSPM facility without asking permission. Even on a micro level, that was a serious breach of security for most installations. "I will not submit to Gavant restriction."

"No one is asking you to surrender or live in a confinement system," Damien said.

"You misunderstand," Kayan said. "I will self-destruct if I cannot escape."

Keppel and Damien scoffed at the idea, but the general spoke for them both. "Your kind are incapable of anything approaching self-harm. You can't use our weapons to hurt others. How likely is it you could blow yourself up? I appreciate the sentiment, and can assure you, we will not allow the Gavant to take you for their experiments."

Kayan spoke just to me. *That was what I was attempting to learn. They know what the Gavant are using us for—experimentation, most likely related to star travel. I wished to learn the truth of this suspicion, without becoming a victim to find out.*

I thought the ship was spot on but wasn't sure now was the time to push for answers. "Thanks, General. I appreciate that, and so does Kayan. For the record, there is no way in hell I'm allowing Ryg or Collins or anyone else to steal the ship."

"Then it's agreed. Let's get down to details." Keppel summoned everyone to the table and began an exhausting planning session.

MONTOW WORKED with Kayan to arrange the bridge into the needed configuration. His version of what it should look like was closer to what I envisioned of a starship, which was influenced by real military vessels and popular movies. There was no shame in my appreciation of cinema. The changes weren't difficult. Kayan moved pods and workstations easily and often, every time we were sedated for a jump, in fact.

"How is that?" Kayan asked.

I gave the large holo-viewscreen at the front of the stadium-style seating a thumbs-up. "Very nice. I'm putting you in for the Living Starship of the Year award."

"Taking manual control," Montow said, then pushed forward on a sturdy steering yoke. Smaller screens showed the Milyn spaceport slipping away.

I checked radar and other scans, then marked ships along the trafficway. Flight control was still doing their job, so that was nice. Was it suspicious that we left in such an orderly fashion?

Maybe. This was us making a run for it, or that was what it was intended to look like.

"Gantz for Keppel, is this channel secure?"

"Guaranteed." His confident reply came without hesitation. "I maintain a dozen private lines for one-to-one comms. No one is listening, not even my own people."

I suspected Damien and other high-ranking members of the ROSPM were in the command room but didn't think that was a problem. "We're ready for the challenge."

"Stand by," he said.

A minute later, flight control hailed our ship. "Kayan vessel, you are executing an unscheduled and unapproved departure. Please return to your assigned docking station."

"Negative, flight control. We have authorization to depart. Who do you think you are, the Gavant?" Montow said.

"Kayan vessel, you must return as directed. There are other ships using available approach and departure vectors. Let's calm down and not have a wreck."

"Returning to the assigned docking station now. Sorry about that, flight control." Montow said, then did the opposite. We sped away from Milyn and the Milyn Orbital Station at several times the prescribed speed.

"Gavant forward scouts seem to have noticed our violation," Grum said. "I'm picking up increased comms traffic between them and the Gavant main force."

"So far, so good," I murmured as I checked the navigation screens. My heart beat faster. Excitement made colors brighter and sounds deeper.

No one spoke for several minutes. Kayan was the first to confirm Gavant squadrons of void fighters were racing to intercept us, followed by Ryg's heavy cruiser, the *Kon*.

Wozim left for the main deck to prepare defenses. He wore his heaviest armor and carried an impressive selection of weapons secured to his back, waist, and thighs.

"Grum and I will be there in a hot minute." I slipped out of my pod and closed it. My next movement was to adjust the Kayan suit. It wasn't time to seal the flexible helmet, but it was close.

"Good," the Tyton said.

Montow held up one finger. "You should see this first."

"Yes," Kayan agreed. "This is not something I have witnessed."

I walked slowly toward the screen. The *Kon* was accelerating past the much faster void fighters. For this in-system distance, the smaller ships normally had a decisive speed advantage.

Until now.

"Why hasn't Ryg come after us with that level of tech before now?" I asked.

"Some Gavant captains are more devious than others," Montow said. "Consider this a boon. We've learned his capabilities when we were wanting to be caught. Be thankful."

I closed my helmet and jogged to the main deck with Grum close behind.

33

Wozim strode on my left, Grum on my right as we checked every possible entry point. Solen was elsewhere checking surveillance equipment and passages we hoped to hide from our enemies. We might need them to flee through the ship when this went bad. Because it probably would. "Kayan has been shifting internal mass and hardening potential breach points after the pirate attack."

"The Gavant will do less damage than the *White Knife* brutes," Wozim said. "They desire Kayans intact when they capture them."

"Why do you think that is, Woz?" I asked, hoping to see if his theory matched up with what Kayan and I had learned.

"My people have long suspected the Gavant wish to retrofit a living starship for war," Wozim said. "Others believe they are conducting deconstruction experiments to discover a new version of faster than light bypassing."

"What does that mean?" Grum asked, though his expression suggested he knew the answer. As a Walen, his thinking went easily to issues of mechanics and engineering. He understood the brutal implications of that phrase. "They can't possibly believe that would work with a living creature. Kayan isn't a machine." He shifted his gangly shoulders and arms to adjust the fit of his armor.

"Stop doing that," Wozim said. "Your armor is fitted properly. I checked it."

"Doesn't feel like it."

"Moving around changes nothing," the Tyton insisted.

"You'll forget all about that soon." My armor was supremely comfortable. I tried to empathize with the young Walen. "We don't have much time left. Remember, we need to put up a good fight without getting killed. Flee deeper into the ship. Allow Ryg and his goons to catch me. After that, I will need to get them to take me directly to Collins."

"The Gavant *Righteous* is close behind the *Kon*," Kayan said to the three of us. "Securing a video interview to Collins on his ship should not be difficult and would have several advantages when it comes time to escape for real."

"Can you outrun the *Kon*'s new top speed?" I asked.

"There will be a cost." Kayan neither elaborated nor provided text in my helmet HUD. Not this time, which meant the result of such a race would be bad for us. "The *Righteous* has numerous small ships that will also be difficult to evade."

"Fantastic."

"It is not fantastic," Wozim said.

Grum winked and nudged the Tyton. "That's human sarcasm."

"He should study with a master and learn to use the technique correctly." Wozim grunted and met with Solen about the hiding places she'd scouted.

That seemed like a weird match up, but the Tyton was full of surprises. I got the feeling he intended the hiding places for anyone on Kayan's crew but him.

I hurried past the rest of the possible breach points and returned to the barriers we'd constructed near the main passageway leading deeper into the ship, and eventually the bridge.

"Prepare yourselves," Kayan said. "The *Kon* has latched onto my exterior and detected the primary airlock. That will mean less damage this time."

"Hashtag winning." Fear would come, but right now I felt pretty good.

Solen and Grum turned as one to stare.

"Your prebattle ritual is lame," Wozim growled.

"I don't see *you* giving an inspirational speech." My pirate rifle felt light with the Kayan suit to augment my strength and speed. We were ready to rock and roll, even if the show would be short.

Wozim stood to look over the stacked crates filled with something like iron filings. The material was the foundation for much of the ship's self-maintenance and construction projects.

Kayan and the crew claimed it made superior sandbags, or sandboxes in this case.

The Tyton flexed his neck, shoulders, and upper body until it seemed his muscles would burst from his armor. I took a ready position near Grum and Solen slipped into the shadows as agreed.

Wozim spread his feet into a fighting stance and roared at the first Gavant soldiers to rush aboard. One tripped and fell. The others lost momentum. I tried not to laugh, because we were still pretty screwed.

The Tyton took a breath, then shouted. "Go back to your ship, Gavant liars! No true battle lord will ever fight on your side. Do not think I will grant mercy to honorless thugs, no matter their uniforms."

"What was that about?" I asked Kayan.

"Wozim's relation to the Gavant is complicated. We should discuss it another time."

I tracked enemy movement even as I agreed. "Copy that." Things were happening fast.

A second and third squad rushed forward and lowered shields too heavy to carry for long. I heard powered wrenches connecting them to support braces. Their barricade was already better than ours, and now allowed the rest of their troops to flow through the entrance, then veer off to each side to secure doorways Kayan attempted to keep closed.

Ryg strode into view.

I wanted to shoot him. Wozim put one hand on my arm,

stopping me from taking the shot. Kayan gave an update at the same time. The ROSPM stealth ships were in place and ready to deploy reinforcements.

"There are a lot more troops than we planned for," I said. Kayan shared my update with the infiltration team/quick reaction force. "Wish me luck. I think these negotiations will be one-sided."

"Understood," Montow said. "Don't take this the wrong way, but the sooner they take you to the *Righteous,* the better. Kayan will sustain less damage if this ends quickly. Do not be stubborn."

Our plan was unraveling, even if I was the only one to see it. Maybe I was a pessimist, but the show of force by Ryg didn't bode well. Keppel and the others had assumed he would send a fast-moving tactical team, not an occupation army. Looking back, I couldn't see how the ROSPM leader could have missed this move.

With this many Gavant soldiers marching onto Kayan's main deck, and their well-planned, well-equipped teams, I thought we were about to get a visit from someone really important. Instead of dragging me to an interrogation room, they were taking the entire ship right now. This wasn't just Keppel's fault.

"We should have seen this coming," I muttered. "Getting caught is one thing. This is on another level."

"Seen what? Another level? Do you have something to say, Gantz?" Keppel asked on what he probably thought was a secured line. At this point, I wasn't assuming anything was under our full control, except my neural link with Kayan. Next time, if there was one, I was going to take a more active part in the planning process, no matter how long they had been preparing. I opened my mouth to answer but was interrupted.

"We have another problem," Montow warned. "Those void fighters they sent first weren't for us. And the *Righteous* just deployed two additional squadrons to sweep areas where our friends must be concealed. Keppel, get your people out of here if you can. We're burned."

"Stealth works until it fails," Wozim said.

"So no reinforcements, and no covert infiltration." I tracked Ryg and his bodyguards staging near the main entrance. "This is all on us. What could go wrong?"

Wozim looked at me strangely, then spoke with his back to the Gavant boarding teams. "It has always been up to us, Noah." He smiled. "Everything that can go wrong for us, can go wrong for the other side."

"Thanks, Woz. That's really helpful." I raised both hands and stepped into view. "Let's talk, Ryg. We got off to a bad start. What do you say this time we really listen to each other. Empathize and all that new age stuff. Help me help you."

Ryg stepped away from his officers and motioned for his guards to hang back. "It's too late for that, human. My patron has arrived. The two of you are about to have a very interesting conversation." He swept one hand around at Kayan's interior. "This is a fantastic ship. Much better than older variations. So young and full of potential. I bet it adjusts well to the new demands General Collins will put on it."

Gavant guards snapped to attention as a tall, fit man in a Gavant officer's uniform strode through the junction between the *Kon* and Kayan. An image in my HUD informed me the *Righteous* was docked to the other side of Ryg's ship, granting Collins access to all three vessels.

Scratch wiggled free of a ventilation shaft and ran to my side. I wasn't sure what good the animal could do, but at least I knew where the six-legged furball was. He yowled at the Gavant entourage approaching us.

Collins looked older than I remembered. Gray streaked through the sides of his hair. Like me, he'd remained clean shaven. Some habits were hard to break with pilots. His eyes were bright, his posture tall, and his manner full of energy.

"Are you wearing a cape?" I asked.

Collins stopped, which caused the cape to flourish briefly. "Major Noah Gantz, you will salute your superior officer, or have you forgotten the United Earth military code of conduct?"

I delivered a perfect salute, which he didn't return.

So that was how it was going to be. *Jerk.*

"You understand the limitations of my position?" He indicated the Gavant troops with his eyes and hit me with a shitty smile. "I'm more than a general here. Would it really be appropriate to return the salute of some criminal they've never seen before? I think not."

"Let's try again," I said.

He crossed his arms, which accented the shoulders of his heavy cloak. "Oh, wonderful. You're all about second chances today. Didn't you attempt this approach with Captain Ryg only moments ago?"

I had to try, despite every signal this was a fool's errand. It was time to invoke the most sacred traditions of our profession. "I don't know. Maybe we could grab a beer at Rocket Corner. You know, the dive bar in Houston. Once we get home and make our reports to the UE Space Exploration director." A sinking feeling in my gut ruined most of what I'd planned to say. The bar had been a fixture of astronauts for more than a decade before he disappeared. Looking at his humorless face, I wondered if he'd ever been.

My friends had gotten me in a lot of trouble there. We'd all become amateur pool hustlers and darts experts. Smart phones and social media apps weren't allowed in the joint. Brothers and sisters had been bonding and baring their souls there for generations. That was where we needed to be for this conversation—someplace away from the ego fest holding Collins up.

His expression darkened. "I always hated that dive. Wasn't the same for me. You were popular. Fun. Everyone's hero before you even did anything. I'm an actual combat ace, you know— five confirmed kills. You have four."

"Does it matter?" I hadn't been comfortable with the whole ace thing. There were times I wondered if I hadn't let the fifth one go. Enemy pilots could survive being shot down, but it wasn't common in modern dogfighting. Going for the throat never came easy for me. That was a good way for someone to get hurt. What was the quote about "give me a good sword and let me never have to use it?" That was me. The training and toys were more fun than drawing blood.

I forced myself to focus.

"Yes, Gantz. It does matter. You came after me. Your rank is lower. I was more accomplished before I left the Milky Way and I definitely am your superior in every way now," he said. "You are on the right track, however. Returning to Earth is something we must do. Might as well take the trip together. You will earn your passage, and my trust, in time."

"Holding rank in any organization outside of United Earth is against the rules, Collins, and you know it," I said.

He stepped into my personal space and looked down into my eyes. The guy was a few inches taller. Right now, this felt like staring up at Stonehenge, or into the eyes of a Greek god. Tension gripped the room. No one moved or spoke.

I hoped my friends, and Kayan, could escape when this went bad.

"You haven't seen a fraction of this galaxy, Gantz. Trillions of lives will be lost if someone doesn't restore order. Tell me, with the small amount of this place you have witnessed, do our old *world* views measure up? The rules are different, and the stakes are higher. You must think on a galactic level, and you must work with me or not at all."

"Fine. I retire. Someone bring me my flip flops and cargo shorts."

He didn't crack a smile, though something in his expression twitched. *This guy really doesn't like me.*

"You're not even the reason I'm here, Gantz." He abruptly strolled around the room. "Bet that surprises you."

"I'm starting not to give a shit, Collins." Okay, maybe it wouldn't be that hard to draw this dude's blood.

"You will address him as General Tatum Collins of the Second Tier," said a dangerous looking Gavant bodyguard.

I did what any responsible person would do in a life and death stuck in a hostile galaxy, I ignored him like he was my seventh-grade math teacher assigning homework.

"I cannot command your Kayan... yet," Collins said. "So please ask her to display her best view of Milyn Station and the planet. It is past time for the ROSPM to learn their place."

"Gantz for Keppel, how copy?" I glared at Collins who had stopped to watch me with an asinine expression of false concern. "Kayan, make this connection no matter what. We need to warn them."

Of course, Kayan said privately. *The Gavant ships are not interfering with our comms.*

"Great." I repeated the hail but all that came back was shouting and confusion in the ROSPM command center.

Collins smiled and resumed his tour. "Warning them now is pointless."

"Kayan, show video."

Holographic images projected into the center of the room. Warships, Milyn Station, and the planet Milyn were slightly transparent when shown without a proper backdrop. Enemy weapons and explosions were too bright. The effect remained

416

startling despite the mediocre presentation. ROSPM agents were getting blown apart or captured.

Montow let out a long, pained breath. Grum looked like someone had killed his dog—which made me search for Scratch and find him standing by my left leg. Solen and Wozim seemed angry, but dangerously calm. Maybe they had been through worse.

Collins stopped in front of me. "Like I said earlier, I'm not actually here for you. That was a ruse to force your hand."

34

HAIR ROSE on the back of my neck. This wasn't the man I'd followed through the UE test pilot ranks. His face was the same. I expected him to sound like the man from media briefings and lectures, and maybe the basic characteristics of his voice were the same.

But this was not Tate Collins, or if it was, none of us had seen the man for what he was. I felt helpless to stop him as he spoke to Solen Far. She looked small and fierce, like a cornered animal about to fight free of a trap.

"You have something that belongs to the Gavant," he said.

"You're a dancing fool if you think I would bring it on a mission like this," she snapped. "Your overlords should fire you."

He flinched, then set his jaw and stared daggers into her.

My ability to intervene was limited.

Noah, Kayan whispered in my head. *There are more Gavant ships on the way. The odds are stacking against us.*

I focused on communication through our neural link. Holding the connection was hard with so much going on.

Collins laughed at Solen, which angered her. Dark lavender spots grew on her cheeks and her eyes narrowed until they seemed to disappear. If anyone was about to make a rash decision, it was her.

"I always knew you were a traitor," she said, her words strong but not shouted.

Collins twisted the metaphorical knife. "Yours was a copy of a copy. Did you realize that when you stole the information?" He spread his hands like a preacher. "Everything you learned about us, is out of date. My agent at Milyn confirmed this at the highest level." His hands clenched into fists as pure malice grew in his eyes. "And everything we learned about your weak friends in the ROSPM has proved perfectly accurate. Look at the fall of Milyn!"

"Listen to yourself, Collins." I moved forward, causing his bodyguards to aim weapons at me. "You don't have to give up anything. The UE will understand the circumstances, and they'll want you to be the liaison between our society and this new one. Think it through. How much more can you get with diplomacy than aggression? Everyone can win."

"You would like to think that," he said. "I've learned different. Life is a zero-sum game. You win or you lose." He spread his arms to indicate the army of Gavant soldiers. "Looks like I picked the winning team, and you weren't picked at all.

Neither of you have a chance. Unless you come with me right now and kneel before the Gavant."

This asshole was going to be the death of me. Sorry, Pops. I can't let this go. "Never was a kneeler, but you do you." Then, using my absolute best effort to communicate with Kayan by pure mental link, I asked the ship to warn our crew that they would need to get into pods very soon. Anger masked doubt. Could this trick work twice? Why not? The basic concept had stood the test with the White Knives.

Collins lunged forward with the speed of a striking cobra and backhanded me. I should have seen it coming. When you poke the bear, you get mauled. And lose your brain lock with your living starship friend. Kayan got the message, I thought. It would have been nice to confirm some of the details of our secret plan to escape this disaster.

He stepped back and massaged his hand. "Thank you for delivering the spy, and thank you for the Kayan. Perhaps you should think long and hard about who put you in this situation. In my experience, the ROSPM tends to eat itself."

"What do you say?" Wozim demanded.

I held back a hand to calm the Tyton battle lord. This wasn't a good time to lose our strongest fighter. "Let me handle this, Woz."

He snarled and flexed his fists as he paced along the line of Gavant troopers. If anyone was ready for a fight, it was Wozim.

"It's quite all right," Collins said. "I'm happy to answer his questions. Perhaps I should have been clear from the beginning." He dropped his chin as he composed his thoughts, then nodded several times, and finally met my gaze. I didn't like the nasty smile touching the edge of his expression. "Please inform General Keppel that his place among the Gavant leadership has been granted. He will still need to bring Damien's head, of course."

Solen screamed and flew across the deck to attack him. Wozim snatched her out of the air and carried her back kicking and screaming. "Kayan is trying to soothe you, Solen Far. Stop kicking me and read your HUD."

Collins looked at the Tyton suspiciously.

I jumped forward, literally waving my hands to distract the sociopath. "Just let us stay on the ship until you put it in the confinement system. But don't lock us in the pods. Those things are a nightmare."

"You think this ship will be confined like the other, older versions? That would be a waste, but you wouldn't know about advancing technology. What do you think I could do with UE FTL bubble tech, Gavant space jump science, and a young and vital Kayan? That has always been your problem, Gantz. Too busy making friends and thinking small."

I didn't like any of that but had a lot of chess pieces to move in a short period of time. Collins could rant all he wanted, as long as he didn't detect Kayan powering up for a jump.

As much as I wanted to beat some sense into the man, I didn't want to murder him, or anyone else. This was war and there were going to be consequences. I grasped for ideas to take prisoners instead of kill.

Thoughts of Keppel distracted me. Everything about the

Altion leader had impressed me. He seemed smart, honorable, and concerned for his people.

And yet he had sent everything Collins wanted straight to him. His undetectable stealth teams had been immediately apprehended and no one was coming to rescue us. He'd kept Solen Far from the rest of the ROSPM and fed her information only to put her in the hands of the enemy. Of course the Gavant would reward him.

Damien had been a double agent, a deep cover operative pulled from his assignment when the Gavant learned of his duplicity. Keppel had shared the fact to earn my trust. He'd done a lot of things to put me, Solen, and Kayan right where we were now.

You are too far from the nearest pod, Kayan said. *Everyone we like has been notified by HUD, though they don't seem to understand the importance of my request. Montow replied that it won't do much good to escape if we bring our enemies with us. You might also wish to know I lured Scratch into a safe place, a version of the pods his kind have been using to travel with me for years. Easy to locate now that I understand the creatures and their needs."*

Don't ask. Tell them. I turned away from Collins in case I was moving my lips. Thinking to Kayan without speaking was harder than it should be right now. Each time I grabbed hold of the trick, it slipped away. Stress, fear, or whatever was killing my vibe. *Ask them what they think will happen to anyone unprotected when you accelerate to near light speed, and then open your version of a warp bubble.*

They seem to be getting the message now, Noah. Now get yourself into a pod, or convince that void sucking Collins to put you in one. I saw what you started to do earlier. Very clever. Please don't put me in the pod, you big, bad Gavant jerk. Is that a human trick?

I listened to Kayan, but realized I needed something from Collins, and the idea of murdering these Gavant soldiers, even though they wouldn't hesitate to slaughter me and my friends, was still repugnant. I'd been in combat. What the hell was wrong with me? How was I so concerned about my enemies?

Pops refused to materialize and give me advice. There wasn't time to discuss it with my friends or even Kayan.

I needed information and saw one way to get it.

"Collins, I need to talk to you in private."

He sensed something about my tone and stepped almost nose to nose again. "Talk, Gantz. This is as close as you will come to getting me alone. I know your reputation. And I'm not fighting you one-on-one. Why do you think I brought an army."

"I fucking hate you," I said.

"Of course."

"I ordered Kayan to jump. Anyone who doesn't get in a pod, is going to die badly."

"What the hell are you saying?" Collins widened his eyes involuntarily, or so it seemed. Surprise and worry were written there for me to see. "This is crazy even for you!"

"You've never traveled in a Kayan." I smiled. "The inertial dampeners have limits."

He whirled to issue orders. "All personal, requisition a Kayan safety pod immediately and get inside. Do it now! They are scattered throughout the ship and can be moved."

"Maybe you ought to be nicer to Kayan," I said, backing

toward a pod as it arose out of the floor. Kayan didn't like to do this so overtly, but I'd not relocated closer to one.

"You evil son of a bitch!" Collins shouted.

"Turnabout is fair play. You play stupid games, you win stupid prizes."

"The ships are still connected," he argued, desperation blatantly evident now.

"We've got that covered." I reached out to Kayan privately. *We do, don't we?*

There will be damage to my exterior, and to theirs. If their captains know what's good for them, they will release me. I am also dumping the remaining pirate salvage.

Ryg sprinted back to his ship with a portion of his soldiers close behind. A few of Collins's personal army hesitated when they saw this but quickly started running passageway to passageway, searching for pods.

"Let them find safety", I said aloud. "We can handle them later. They can't get out of the pods until you allow their freedom, right?"

"You might have asked that question first," Kayan said. "But you are correct. Once the jump pods seal, they belong to me."

A shiver went up my spine. That didn't sound like the Kayan I had come to know and love.

Solen stared at me as her pod sealed around her. Wozim, Montow, and even Grum gave me the darkest looks imaginable. Apparently, saving the men and women who had been intent on enslaving and/or murdering us was an unpopular decision.

I wasn't sure, but it seemed like the screams of a lot of

Gavant troopers ended when Kayan accelerated away from the *Kon* and the *Righteous*.

"Collins ordered a platoon to remain outside the pods in case this was a trick to confine them in the crèches without actually making a jump." Kayan sounded sad in a uniquely Kayan way, like she was disappointed with the cruelty of other life-forms. Her voice resonated inside my creche. "Intentional cruelty confounds me. He did not need to do that."

"Not your fault," I said.

35

I FORCED myself back and found Kayan waiting in my head.

"You're awake," the ship said. "I told you it was possible. Do you want me to rouse the others—our friends?"

"No." I climbed free of the protective shell and massaged my face before donning the Kayan helmet. Stretching my arms above my head felt normal, as did walking easily until I was fully awake. "How many Gavant died? You said a platoon, but I'm betting their T/E is different from ours."

"Thirty-five Gavant soldiers, including two of Collins's most trusted officers attempted to withstand the acceleration, and then warp bubble penetration."

I found them easily but was surprised they were smashed against every wall and ceiling. "Why aren't they all on the same end of the room?"

"I attempted to save them by pressurizing each room they

occupied. You may remember the effect, though you were not supposed to, from your earlier experience on the ship," Kayan said. "It was effective for several minutes, until the acceleration was too great no matter where they were located. After that, there were course corrections. The bodies are not located where they died."

"Shouldn't there be a lot more blood?" I asked grimly. This wasn't a question I wanted to ask. The words just came out. What was done was done, and these were the consequences.

"I advise against opening their armor or helmets," Kayan said.

"Noted." I started dragging them to one room and asked the ship to keep it cold enough to prevent decomposition.

"It would be better to eject them into the void."

"Agreed, but I think I will give Collins a chance to do a funeral, if Gavants follow the custom."

"They have farewell ceremonies," Kayan said. "May I suggest you ask for help?"

"The crew isn't keen on me right now."

"Wake them up and make amends. You know this will be necessary eventually, and time may not be our friend. The Gavant hunters will redouble their effort to find us and rescue their leader. Our next encounter will go much differently. I don't want to be turned into an experiment."

"You're right. Start with Montow," I said.

"There is good news." Kayan displayed lines of text in my HUD. "Collins possessed a copy of the data cube, or perhaps the original. There is indeed an enormous amount of information regarding the ROSPM, and Keppel definitely gave us up. But there are other facts you may find interesting."

"Like what?" I had my suspicions and wasn't sure how I felt about confirming them.

"The very complex, and ambitious, route to Earth is thoroughly documented, as well as promises of unending wealth and power to be found there," Kayan said.

I thought about what that meant as Montow climbed out of his pod. He smacked his lips and rubbed his unblinking eyes. The sight made me cringe, but didn't hurt him, apparently. Probably felt good.

He took the water bottle I offered him, drank it all, then slipped it into a bin Kayan managed. The vessel would be whisked away, refilled, and refrigerated until one of the crew needed it.

"We take so much for granted," I said.

Montow rubbed the back of his neck with one hand, then slipped on his heavy sunglasses with the other. "The water bottles?"

"Everything."

He tipped his head right then left like Grum often did when agreeing. Weirdly enough, the gesture felt right now even though I'd also seen it as a negative response. Someday I would need to catalog all of the things I'd grown accustomed to since joining Kayan and the others.

"Let's get our people out first," Montow suggested.

"You're in my brain."

He grimaced. "Yuck. That sounds repulsive."

We laughed as we headed to free Grum, Solen, and finally Wozim.

"I'd like to get the Tyton first, but this is different. He becomes irritable when enemies are close at hand but unavailable for combat," Montow said.

"You mean he won't kill helpless prisoners even if he wants to," I said.

"Something like that." He served water and nutrition packets to Solen and Grum while I faced the Tyton's pod.

It was larger than the others, bigger even than what was required for him wearing armor. I wondered about that and asked Kayan but got no answer.

The crèche spiraled open. Wozim stepped out ready for action.

Of course he did.

"Where are the Gavant?" he asked.

"Still locked up."

He grunted.

I waved everyone into a circle. "Let's talk. There are some decisions we should vote on."

Wozim made another rude noise.

"Can we not go back to cave-man-grunty-guy? I'd like to get your input on our new plan of attack. We were making such good progress. Use your words, Woz-man."

"Attack is always good," he said.

"It's a start." I faced the others. "We could have killed all the Gavant officers and soldiers, including Collins."

Wozim flared his nostrils as he glowered menacingly. "Without honor."

"Would have been a waste of intel," Solen said almost on top of his statement. "You made the right call. It just caught the rest of us off guard. Worse, there are consequences to taking Gavant officers hostage."

"Enlighten me," I said.

Grum answered. "They will show no mercy until Collins and the other leaders are returned to them. The—what would you call them—noncommissioned officers and line soldiers matter less. They won't pay ransom or negotiate for them."

"Can we leave them on a planet?"

No one appreciated my humane plan, which surprised me. When they were done bitching and moaning, I held up one hand. "Okay, you don't want to risk a detour to save a few lives. I get it."

"Enemy lives," Wozim said.

"What happened to honor and whatever?" These people were making me tired. "We can't hold them prisoner forever, can we? How much food and oxygen can you produce, Kayan?"

"Enough."

"Great. Very scientific," I said, fully aware I was the last person who needed exhaustive details when the ship already handled day-to-day stuff.

"Other Kayans have delivered entire Altion colonies to far flung worlds. And you must have forgotten my transport of the Hoyon. That creature used more nutrients and power than a hundred of your kind—and by that I mean any life-form of comparable size that is not Kayan. We have sufficient resources to keep the prisoners alive. You see only differences among your small, fragile races but you are very similar."

"We all look the same to you," I joked.

"Two legs, two arms, small brains and bad jokes—you could all be human, or Gavant, or Altion."

"What about Walen?" Grum asked.

"Apologies. Leaving you out of the description was rude. I am merely a living starship prone to the occasional mistake. Forgiveness is requested."

"None of you compare to my people, so don't appropriate our name for your hodgepodge of sentient life-forms," Wozim said.

"Kayan wouldn't dream of it." I steered the conversation back to immediate concerns. "I want to wake up Collins and grill him for information."

Every one of my companions made horrified faces. Kayan didn't intervene with a translation, which made the moment awkward. I mimed frying an egg and flipping it. They flinched backward at the image.

"What kind of man are you?" Wozim asked.

"Relax. That is a figure of speech."

"Yes, but where did it originate?"

"Okay, that's a good point. Disturbing, but good. For now, let's agree that grilling someone for information means asking questions and getting answers, nothing more."

"That is dangerous," Wozim said.

Montow, Grum, and Solen agreed.

"Kayan, what is the most humane way to get rid of all these prisoners when we're done?" I asked.

"I sluff off a portion of my biomass as time passes. It would be simple to construct life pods out of this material, then drop them along transportation routes known for regular Gavant patrols. They would remain unconscious to minimize oxygen and nutrient use, and to prevent mental degradation," Kayan said. "Or we could take them to a planet and revoke their travel pass, as you might say."

"Great. We have options and a plan. I will see what I can get from Collins." I looked straight at Solen. "He has a cube, possibly the original."

"He will have the full translation algorithms as well. If we can get that, it could save the ROSPM." She visually checked with the others, lingering on Wozim. "I respect you, Tyton, though our people will always remain at odds. Back my play, and I will back yours."

Wozim growled, then nodded his assent.

"Then it's agreed. We remove Collins, and only Collins, from his safety creche and make plans to unload the others as soon as possible," I said.

Montow stood from where he'd been sitting. "It is a good plan. I will be at my terminal searching for Oort fields. Kayan is hungry."

"I am," the ship said.

My friends discussed details and ways to stretch the resources Kayan held in storage. When the ship truly began to starve, we would all suffer. That wasn't what filled my gut with dread.

Something was horribly wrong. I knew, because Kayan dropped out of the increasingly animated discussion.

My crew followed me to the detention pods for Collins and his bodyguards.

They talked. I half listened. This was the right course of action. Collins was here. I wouldn't get another chance to turn him to our cause, or at least find out what the hell went wrong with him. The guy should know better.

I worried that no one had really known the man back home. At the end of the day, who really knows anyone. Dark thoughts of friends lost… family lost… filled me with second thoughts and worry. "We should move him to an isolated location."

"Yes. That. Would be. Ideal." Kayan's voice sounded distant. "There is something wrong with his bodyguards. They were alive when you put them in there, correct? I mean they were not machines. The crèche is made for biological entities, not robots."

Everyone stared at the six pods near Collins.

"Let's ask him," I said and waited for Kayan to release the man from the protective cocoon. The door spiraled open to show him sleeping like the dead. Montow and Grum pulled him out and checked his vitals. He submitted at first but pushed them away the moment he had his wits about him.

"You're an idiot, Gantz." His words were like a growl.

I advanced, determined to get answers. From the corners of my eyes, I saw Wozim, and then Solen, draw weapons.

"Maybe I am, and maybe I'm not. But at least I don't use robots as bodyguards." It was a pretty lame attempt to trick information from him quickly, but there was a pressure building in my head and chest I didn't like.

He laughed darkly. "Their suits are mechanized. When I couldn't teach my elite guard the trick of awakening from a Kayan pod, I found *another method.*"

"What the hell are you talking about?" I demanded. "Don't get crazy on me."

"Machines must be held elsewhere on a ship like this. Life-forms in machines are controllable by a Kayan. Good thing my followers know how to die when ordered." His eyes hated me. "Now only the mechanized armor remains."

"I really don't like you right now." The words were hard to push out. I bent at the waist as pain wracked my body. Spots of color glowed in my vision. Kayan was trying to use our neural link, but everything was scrambled with never before experienced pain.

"Activate and attack." Collins tapped a panel on the arm of his armor. Six lights turned green. He marched forward, only stopping because Wozim blocked his advance.

"I don't feel so great." My words came out in parallel to Kayan rasping the same message. Every member of the crew collapsed from the ship's agonized cry.

36

"Get up, human."

I rolled onto my back and saw Wozim extending one hand to pull me to my feet. Red lights filled the room, simultaneously casting the Tyton in shadow. His silhouette was something out of a noir comic. His armor seemed to suck away my vision like a black hole. Ufri, the symbiotic tail swayed through the air with urgency.

"Dude," I said as he pulled me up. "What is wrong with your gear?"

"The blackout feature is not something I use lightly. Do not look at me directly. It can break the minds of weaklings," he said. "Now talk to the ship. Find out what is happening?"

I staggered forward three steps before my neural link with the ship synchronized. For the first time since being rescued, I felt cut off and alone. Terror burned through my insides. "Kayan. Talk to us."

The ship didn't answer.

"Where is Collins?" I demanded.

"He took his death machines and went to take control of the bridge," Wozim said.

I searched for Montow and saw him sitting on the floor with his head between his hands. "Can they take control of Kayan from the bridge?"

Confusion and doubt warred on Montow's face. "We don't know how they control the Kayans they force into the confinement system. This could be something worse. Collins may have just gathered data on how Kayan penetrates the warp fields. He'll want that from the bridge because it is something he couldn't get without being onboard during a jump."

Solen joined us. She looked equally stunned, but also pissed off. Her slender, powder-blue face was covered with purple splotches. The metallic identity patterns around her eyes reflected the red emergency lights—and the determination in her eyes. She grabbed Montow by the back of his shirt and hauled him to his feet. He came when she pulled, allowing her to manhandle the much larger Hellenger.

I was already running beside the Tyton. Grum followed. At the first door, I heard Scratch sprinting to catch up. When excited, five of his legs worked better than the sixth, giving him a ridiculous gait. Enthusiasm handled the rest.

"Noah!"

A trail of dark fluid marked the center of the passageway.

Large boot prints showed the passage of Collins and his six unnaturally powered bodyguards.

"Kayan, talk to me."

"The intruders are inside the bridge and attempting to close the door behind them. Please hurry, Noah. I cannot resist the collar much longer. Do not let them take me."

I dashed ahead of Wozim, which seemed to surprise the Tyton. As large as he was, the battle lord still thought he was faster than anyone on the ship. Freaking crazy ass warrior races, always competitive.

There was no air in my lungs for banter. Half of the improvements Kayan had made to my physique since rebuilding me were negated by the agony rippling through the ship. This was more than the life pods getting torn open by the mechanized armor under Collins's control. The ship was in mortal danger.

My mind abruptly refocused when I charged onto the bridge and ran into the first bodyguard. His visor was down, but clear. Dead, horrified eyes stared past me while the armor encasing the soldier's body stomped forward. The limp Gavant body was taking a ride.

"Distracting," I complained as I dove away from glowing pulses of energy zipping toward me. The Gavant armor moved with conviction. The macabre cargo did nothing but horrify me. I'd figured out that Collins was an egomaniac, but this took him to a new level of psycho. What he would do to win was now clear.

Wozim arrived a half second later and blasted the Gavant golem with his own energy gun. Purple light slammed into it, knocking it sideways. I had my own problems—other Gavants rushed us—but I saw just enough to understand the first of them wasn't down, only staggered.

It turned on Wozim and blasted away. The light sucking Tyton armor had an effect. Most of the blue-white bolts went wide.

Solen dove and rolled to avoid dying. Montow tackled Grum to the ground and held him there. Wozim rushed between us and the advancing enemy. All six of the mechanical monsters aimed and fired. Every shot scored a hit, forcing the Tyton backward.

He grunted in pain and his return fire missed.

"Woz!" It didn't look like his spooky black hole armor was working. What had he said, it destroyed the minds of weak men?

Well, these were dead men, and the machines weren't affected, apparently.

"Collins. You win. Let's talk!" I held my spare parts rifle down at my side and slightly back.

The attack paused long enough for Wozim to glare at me like I was the bad guy. At least he got a chance to recover his balance. I assumed he would thank me later.

"If you can convince the Tyton to surrender, the lords of the Gavant Reach will make you governor of a star system." Collins laughed. "Until then, lay down your weapon and stay out of the way. Trust me, Earth man, it's the best you can do for your home."

"We're both from Earth, asshole."

"Gantz, you just never learn. None of this is about merit or even seniority. Your scores were higher than mine in almost every category. Did you know that?" He didn't wait for me to answer. "How does that make you feel? Angry? Righteous? Sad?"

"Woz, are you ready to teach these dudes a lesson?" I asked.

"Yes."

Collins flicked away our conversation as his six death-bots tightened their line to protect him behind it. "Why do you think I got the first flight over you, Gantz?"

"Because you kiss a lot of ass and know people."

"You're half right."

"That isn't something to brag about."

"Stop being a child. My political connections in the UE are stronger than you imagine. Some of us understand how to penetrate an organization and grab the controls."

"What are you, a parasite?" I shifted for a better angle, though there was no great way to get around the wall of steel. "How will they feel when their golden boy shows up alive and betrays humanity to the Gavant asswipes?"

He sneered.

My comment had struck harder than I'd hoped. This guy's ego was out of control. Calling him names and poking holes in his plan was fun. I was probably going to hell for messing with him like this. He would definitely kill me in about five seconds to test the theory.

So why not double down? Why not seize the initiative?

"Listen, I have news from home. Everyone thinks you're dead. They sent me to test the FTL warp bubble with improved technology."

"And you lost the ship. How disappointing," he said. "My bet is that your Kayan learned a lot during that process and has all the information I need to get there. Once I crush the ROSPM, my true ascendancy will begin and for the first time, a non-Gavant governor will be named. But that's not the good part. I'll be the only Gavant representative in the Milky Way with no one to resist me."

"That's super. Very nice. I'll mark you down as an intergalactic villain for the history books!"

"I am bringing peace!"

"Looks like it."

Collins fought down his rage, which made his death-bots shift nervously. They weren't as independent as he wanted us to believe. If he went down, they went down.

I caught Wozim's eye, then the attention of the others. We all saw it.

"Noah," Kayan whispered. "His reinforcements are almost here. You must hurry. "

"Order the ship to surrender and cooperate or it will be permanently damaged," Collins said with perfect timing.

I froze and could feel my friends hesitating. There had never been any doubt we would resist, but could we afford to lose when Kayan would pay the price for however long a living starship lived?

Noah, breathed the ship.

Kayan needed help. I could hear it in her voice.

What the hell was I going to do? How could I get us out of this mess? The impulsive spirit my parents and Pops had worried about was rearing its ugly head. Throwing myself into an unwinnable fight was one thing. None of my friends had signed up to follow me. This wasn't the UE military.

Collins raised his chin slightly. "I have all the time in the world. Don't rush on my account."

"That's because you're stalling."

"True. But not because I must. My bodyguards don't fear the Tyton, and they can't be killed. Make your move, Gantz. I'll talk to your grandfather when I get to Earth—since your parents died so unexpectedly."

I sprinted forward, then jumped as high as I could, asking Kayan to reduce the gravity as I moved. Sounds, numbers, and colors flashed through my senses, and I understood that I'd caught even the ship off guard. Gravity lightened, but not much.

All my post-rescue strength surged. The Kayan suit responded to my will, infusing my legs with power. As ninja leaps went, this was one for the record books. I clipped the center death-bot in the head with my knees. He grabbed for me and missed while the others opened fire.

Wozim came at them next but seemed like he was a mile behind me. What he said was a mystery. I was too focused for banter or second thoughts. The powerful feeling only came to me during my toughest dogfights, or in test flights on the bleeding edge of UE technology.

I swung the alien rifle around to my shoulder, aimed, and fired all in one movement. A blast of energy punched into Collin's armor. The sight of his uniform sizzling away around the hole indicated how distorted my time sense was. Move fast, feel slow.

Pops had said that without ever explaining. I knew now. This was what having the initiative meant. I felt more than saw Solen, Montow, and Grum begin to move. To my incredible surprise, Scratch was ahead of me. The animal had darted between mechanical feet and started lashing out with his tail like he thought he was Ufri on a rampage.

My rifle discharged a second and third shot as Collins stumbled backward toward cover.

A Gavant energy bolt crashed into the back of my armor. I turned involuntarily, just far enough to see the defensive line breaking apart. Most of them were coming after me, of course, but that didn't mean there was any kind of order now.

Congratulations, Gantz. You started your first space brawl.

The deck rushed upward with the return of normal time flow. I hit hard and rolled like a ninja, or a kindergartener learning to tumble in PE. Impacts slammed into my back, then the side of one leg, then both shins before I clambered to my feet and took a final insult in the face shield.

That one hurt. Stars filled my vision as I was hurled backward to land on my back. I hit and immediately searched for Collins, who was racing toward a control station with a metal spike. There wasn't time to be sure, but it looked like it was covered with circuitry.

I aimed and fired, striking the shoulder connected to the hand Collins was using to hold the wound to his chest plate. He staggered, but in a display of unexpected toughness, turned his back to me to absorb further damage as he continued to work. His unencumbered right hand rose high into the air, and plunged the spike down into Kayan.

Lights flickered and the ship trembled. Gravity went crazy. It didn't disappear but changed in multiple bands. My left foot was tugged toward a wall that seemed to be the floor while my right leg, starting with the knee, was yanked upward like the ceiling was the correct place to be. I spun out of control and suspected I had it easy compared to everyone else.

An image of Scratch cartwheeling past me stuck out in time. Solen with her face pressed into Grum's armpit was another. Wozim fought three opponents as they flashed away from each other. Maybe he could have just let them go and found them later, but that wasn't the Tyton way. His sword sliced off a hand. His rifle blasted another in the groin for all it mattered with the death-bots. Ufri harpooned one so savagely his body—organic and mechanical—fell in two pieces.

"Kayan!" I screamed.

What had been dim disco lighting now felt like living on the sun. Everything was so bright I couldn't make out details. For one second, I thought Solen had been burned into a skeleton, but I realized she was fighting off a death-bot attempting to choke her.

Montow rushed to her aid. Moments later, they broke free and went to help Grum who was on the floor beneath two adversaries.

Wozim knelt in the center of the room with a rifle bayonet

lodged in his chest. His hands were open and his weapons lay on the deck.

No time.

Kayan was in worse trouble.

Power currents raced through the ship, taking control of systems large and small. The ship resisted when it could but burnt out its circuits when necessary to slow Collins's control spike.

Gravity back, I charged across the room and tackled the former test pilot like I could take his head off. Any referee would throw a flag on this hit—maybe all the flags. He never saw me coming and my nice-guy gene had burned out, apparently.

My target bent backward like a contortionist. If I wasn't in his way, his head and heels would have touched near the small of his back. No one would walk right after a hit like that. Was his armor protecting his spine?

It didn't freaking feel like it.

We landed on the deck, and I flattened him out the other way without trying. At this point, momentum handled everything. Kayan again altered the gravity, making it nearly impossible to stand up. When I looked down, Collins was struggling to breathe under the weight of his own body and armor.

"Sucks to be you."

He hissed at me through his helmet comms, because without assistance, the guy wouldn't be able to do more than squeak. "Hold on to your friends, unless their suits are rated for the void."

He thumbed what looked like a grenade but quickly proved to be far worse. Heat shot out from both ends of the device, then drew a circle around him. My brain was still wrestling with the image when I understood it was boring straight through the ship.

Collins, the crazy asshole, was leaving.

"No you don't!" I lunged across the wall of flame, ignoring the strange, inverse effect of what he was doing. The heat didn't rise upward but cut into the deck. By the time I made my grab, he'd fallen several feet.

"Kayan, he can't go all the way through. Won't that damage the vault and the engines?" I hoped the ship could hear and respond.

Pain rocked my world. Again, I was sharing Kayan's worst moments. For some reason, damage to materials inside, like the pods and the deck, was worse than suffering exterior damage.

Which of course made sense. The ship was made to withstand asteroid strikes and solar radiation.

"I must expel him." Kayan's voice rasped like that of a dying man. "And shield you from the agony before it kills you."

I watched Collins fall another foot, then get grabbed by a life pod and whisked sideways between decks. A death bot stomped toward me. Annoyed, frustrated, and wounded, I faced him. The smell of blood and fried circuits filled the inside of my helmet.

Wozim pushed himself to his feet. Then, holding his side with one hand, picked up his sword and engaged the remaining bots. Montow and the others tried to help him but were quickly shot down or smashed aside.

My own problem barely looked damaged. None of our hits

had broken the macabre giant and the mirrored visor looked determined. Its hands reached to tear me apart. I didn't need to see the horror inside to understand my destruction was all it wanted.

I glanced into the side of my pirate rifle of alien parts to be sure it was charged and loaded, then quickly aimed and fired. He did the same. I shuffled sideways as I pulled the trigger and nearly fell into the escape hole Collins had burned through the deck.

My first round hit the death-bot in the face shield and rocked his head back. His initial attack missed, so I had that going for me. I poured shot after shot into him and kept moving. Kayan tried to give me updates on Collins. The safety pod had only partially contained his burn device, resulting in a horribly damaged safety pod basically pushing him toward an exterior layer of the hull.

My opponent kept coming. I kicked him in the pelvis to keep him back and fired again.

He blasted me in my chest plate, but I barely felt it this time.

Feeling feisty, I executed a spinning back kick, caught him just below where the rib cage would be inside, and forced him back several steps.

Wozim spun away from a recent victory with a roar and set Ufri on my enemy. The tail spiked the machine several times in the back. Half coagulated blood and sparks came from his chest when Ufri delivered a killing strike that stabbed completely through him. The mechanized armor finally fell to its knees and stopped moving.

"Gavant reinforcements have arrived. They are pulling their ship alongside to rescue Collins," Kayan said.

Out of breath, I searched for Collins's escape route. "Kayan, send me another pod."

"Where do you go now?" Wozim asked.

I dropped into the smoking hole and was caught by a fast-moving creche. The ship raced me after my adversary at a speed that threatened to make me pass out. When I arrived, there was a Gavant ship opening up and a team pulling the badly wounded general inside.

A pair of Maviks pushed off in armored space suits to block me. I wondered if they knew what had become of Collins's other guards. Might not be great for him to let the word get out on that horror show.

Solen joined me in her own pod. "Not worth it, Noah! Let him go. We've got a lot of other problems to deal with right now."

"Screw that. He's gonna pay for this."

She grabbed my arm.

Kayan moaned in the back of my head. The sounds seemed meaningless. What happened if the ship died, or blew up, or was too weak to escape?

"Collins learned what he wanted of Kayan's star drive, but now we know how they catch and restrain Kayans. He left the spike," Solen said. "Come back. All we can do is damage control right now. Take the win we can get. Don't throw this away to feed your damn ego."

I let the Altion woman tug me deeper into the ship as the

Maviks retreated and closed their airlock. Before long, I couldn't see the enemy vessel as it fell away from our vector.

"What about the others? Wozim looked hurt," I said.

Solen's voice caught in her throat. "Everyone is wounded. Even that stupid animal." She was hiding her own damage. Something was broken or sprained in almost every one of her limbs and there were blood smears on her armor.

I led the way back, though the trip was easier. Kayan didn't talk, but I sensed our enemies had fled with some of what they came for. Had we won? Not really. But we weren't dead yet.

The deck was a mess. Montow held Grum's head in his lap. Wozim was stapling his own abdomen together with his armor lying in a mangled heap next to him. Ufri had detached from his back and was curled around Scratch protectively.

"Okay, that's weird," I said.

Solen stared with wide eyes. "Agreed."

"Kayan, can you talk to me now?"

"Yes, Noah. Be careful how you remove the spike." The ship projected instructions on the inside of my visor.

I read carefully, aware my brain was sluggish after a huge adrenaline dump. Temporary badassery came with a price. Every check I'd written was coming due at the same time. All I wanted was to sleep.

37

I HOBBLED SLOWLY toward the main airlock. The deck had been cleared of bodies and large debris, and Kayan had performed the magical cleaning process that removed not only blood, but any variation of dust or other daily detritus. Wozim and Grum stood guard over the Gavant survivors. Montow and Solen had tied them to benches, which were being slid into a disposable life-shuttle.

"You can't push us into the void," the Gavant officer said.

"Just be glad you met a better fate than Collins's elite bodyguards," Solen said before I could respond.

The man stared at me with unconcealed hatred in his eyes. "What did you do to them?"

"Collins killed them in their suits, then used them as battle-bots to defeat the pod restrictions." I let the words sink in for a second, then gave them the gritty details. "Let me tell you, looking at a dead face inside the visor of a machine trying to kill you is no fun."

This wasn't the first post-traumatic event I'd dealt with. Defending Warp Tech Laboratories, Inc had been worse in most ways, and I'd been fighting people who looked and talked like me, even those who didn't speak my language. That had been Earth. Now I was so far away from home nothing seemed real. Death looked the same, and seeing those bodies inside their relentless war machines had awakened a new level of dread.

Collins must have ordered the visors to translucency. Or maybe the pilots had left them on that setting. I couldn't blame every evil on the traitor.

That was what he was. The man had given up the world he was born on, and his humanity. I needed to make sure neither were lost to what was coming. The United Earth military could not stand for long against a portion of the Gavant Reach. We needed allies, and a plan.

Every one of the Gavants we pulled from the pods went silent and still. My trip down memory lane had done nothing for them, but I thought their heads were full of their own speculation. If I was reading their body language correctly, the horror of what Collins had done was sinking in. They could be next in line for that special *honor*.

"You're lying," said the officer.

That pissed me off. My self-control wavered. This guy and all the blind morons like him were going to keep Collins, and probably a of other Gavant Reach overlords, in power. Why couldn't they see what was right in front of them?

I reined myself in. They hadn't been there. Why would they believe some stranger with a short neck from across the galaxy?

"Ask Collins. He'll tell you. The guy didn't seem remorseful or embarrassed," I said.

Solen joined in. "Remember who you're working for, is all we're saying. Now, get ready for a few weeks on rations. No eating each other. Cannibalism is against directive three-ninety-two, in case you forgot. The rescue beacon is active and will broadcast at maximum range as soon as we're clear of the area. We've dropped you along the Olsiin Trade Route. You won't have to wait long."

"I recommend a gentle pastime, however," Montow said. "Maybe read a book or learn to play rock, paper, scissors."

"Never heard of it," the Gavant said.

"Ah, well, maybe Collins can teach you. It's a human game, apparently." Montow motioned for Grum to close the door to the shuttle. "Safe travels."

"And to you," said the Gavant by rote.

I watched my friends seal the airlock and cycle the shuttle through. Before long, the only remaining threats to the ship were floating away.

Solen pulled me aside. "A lot happened back there."

I nodded.

"Do you trust me?"

"Should I? Seems like no one is who they say they are. Did you know Keppel had gone to the other side?" I asked.

Her face tightened with anger and possible embarrassment.

"No. I suspected Damien, and still do if I'm being honest. Double agents are tricky."

"Says the double agent."

"That's fair."

"We need supplies, and we need to disappear." I thought of Leana Brightness on Milyn and hoped she'd made it free of the attack. Instinct told me she could help us get what we needed. Kayan started searching travel logs and other data points for her whereabouts, but I didn't share that with my fellow passengers, especially not Solen. "We're stuck with each other for a while."

"You want to find your home world. I want to see the end of the Gavant Reach. We should be allies. Let's agree to trust but verify," she said.

"Sounds like a plan." Scratch slammed into my legs, so I picked him up. "Man, this little monster is getting heavy."

Solen made no comment.

"Montow, what do you say we head to the bridge and get the hell out of this system before Collins sends another freak show after us?"

"I say let's do it." The Hellenger gathered up Grum and Solen and headed for the door.

To my surprise, Wozim followed.

He grabbed his symbiotic tail and reattached it, while at the same time taking Scratch from me and dropping the animal on his huge shoulder to talk to Ufri. "They bonded, apparently."

"I see that. Good for them."

"No. It will end badly."

"Okay, mister positive."

"That is not who I am," he said.

"Clearly."

"Now you attempt humor. Didn't I inform you that my jokes are superior to all others?"

"Prove it, big guy."

A very different light twinkled in the Tyton's eyes.

That was when I learned dad jokes were universal, though his versions seemed to be a lot more violent than most.

"Noah," Kayan interrupted.

"What's up? Can you share it with the group?"

A pause followed.

"Kayan?"

Everyone stopped to watch me and listen for the ship's voice.

"There is another of my kind entering this system, but it has weapons."

Amazon won't always tell you about the next release. To stay updated on this series, be sure to sign up for our spam-free email list at jnchaney.com.

Noah and the rest will return in FORSAKEN CROWN, available on Amazon.

GLOSSARY

ORGANIZATIONS

Gavant Reach

The GR began as a terrestrial empire on a planet now lost and presumed destroyed by frequent wars. The Gavant took ten thousand years to begin their journey into the stars, often relying on complicated and deep-rooted trade and transport agreements with the Kayan—living starships. Once they, and a few other races, developed their own version of system jumping, the Kayans became unnecessary.

The Gavant, however, weren't satisfied and soon established a monopoly on star travel, which led to confining Kayan starships to one system. No outsider has seen them in this new habitat and returned to tell the story. The Gavant run their Reach like an empire, and keep their figurehead hidden and protected.

Rights of Sovereign Planets Movement (ROSPM)

The ROSPM began as a political movement seeking reform and granting rights of citizens. While there are official embassies and officers with token votes in the Reach, most associate them with paramilitary revolutionaries building a secret army to confront their galactic overlords.

PEOPLE

Brightness, Leana

Leana's family name translates as Brightness but its actual spelling is not known outside blood relations. Gleams hide that information from their Gavant masters and are thus given computer generated names instead. Her name is Leana-seven-hax-tro in the Gavant system.

She has cool blue skin under a veneer of diamond-like Gleam exterior. More notably, she has a red crown and at least one red hand.

Collins, Tate

Lieutenant Colonel Tate Collins piloted the first United Earth attempt at faster-than-light warp bubble technology. He received a private funeral for co-workers, certain VIPs, and family. During his days as a test pilot, he was the man everyone wanted to be, the type of person voted most likely to star in his own movie. He is taller than most pilots, including Noah Gantz.

Far, Solen

Solen Far is an Altion scientist in the servant of the Gavant Reach. She may be sympathetic toward the Rights of Sovereign Planets Movement. She is short even for an Altion, graceful, and consistently scores high on Gavant service evaluations. Stronger and faster than she appears, the woman is not someone to be crossed lightly as she does not forget grudges. She has the white hair that is commonplace, metallic silver identity marker tattoos around her eyes, and every other trait common to her people.

(Pronounced Sol-len Far)

Gantz, Noah

Major Noah Gantz is a human who was selected to test the second United Earth faster than light warp bubble technology. He is a Major in the UE Exploration Fleet.

At six feet, one inch, he is one hundred and eighty-five pounds and extremely fit. Brown hair, no tattoos, he follows easy rules and has a reputation for pushing the boundaries where it is more exciting. His first attempt at college was a struggle which resulted in two enlisted tours in the Air Force before applying for officer candidate's school, finishing his degree, and becoming a fighter pilot. He is a combat veteran in both military occupational specialties, having defended a top secret base that was briefly overrun and engaged in numerous combat sorties.

Grum

Grum Son of Gramm is a Walen mechanic serving on Kayan, a living starship.

Grum has two brothers: Androw and Borsiin.

As a Walen, he is eager to please, loyal, and hardworking. He dreams of adventure and wants to be a great warrior, something rarely achieved by more than a few Walens.

Like many humanoid races in this galaxy, Walens have long necks, though not freakishly so when compared to humans. Unlike some others, they have no hair and very trusting eyes.

His most distinctive Walen features are the double

thumbed hands of extreme dexterity, especially for mechanical tasks. He is shorter than Noah Gantz and a bit gangly. When he puts his mind to it, Grum is surprisingly agile.

Kayan

Kayan is a living starship who rescued Noah Gantz when his ship arrived badly damaged. Kayan also picks up passengers in a wide variety of places, and for reasons only it understands. Kayan is also the word commonly used for this type of ship and not its *family* name.

Kayan vessels are extremely large, especially at full maturity, which this one is not. They must occasionally transport a Hoyon to a planet ready for new life. Hoyons are related to Kayans, but cannot travel in the void without assistance.

There are parts of a Kayan not accessible to passengers. The vault is at the ship's core, and passengers technically do enter there, but only in life pods or safety pods controlled by the ship. Passengers are not conscious during these extreme safety measures. During most other travel between the stars, a Kayan must shelter passengers in pods or kill them due to lack of inertial dampeners and other technology.

Exterior skin can be smooth as a porpoise, tough as steel, or rough and extra durable. Special radiation-resistant qualities protect the exterior of the ship and it is tough enough to withstand asteroid strikes and other unintentional or intentional impacts.

Kayans feed primarily on Oort fungi, a radioactive extraterrestrial organism normally growing in fields near the limits of a star's heliosphere. Gavant patrols destroy these fields when they can, and when they find them.

(Pronounced Kay-yan)

Keppel, Pon (General)

Pon Keppel is an Altion general of the Milyn Defense Force, but also of the ROSPM. He serves both on Milyn Station orbiting the planet of Milyn.

(Pronounced Pon Kep-el)

Montow

Montow is a Hellenger captain aboard a living starship currently known as Kayan. He is five feet and ten inches tall with the distinctive Hellenger physiology. His friend and fellow adventurer, Noah Gantz, affectionately calls him Soup Can, or Soup. Montow has grown a short, cropped beard and hair to appear more human, and wears shades over his unblinking Hellenger eyes.

At one hundred and seventeen, he is past middle age for his people though still fit and powerful.

Montow is the captain of Kayan, and has been aboard longer than other members of the crew except Grum, who he brought aboard for medical attention.

(Pronounced Mon-tow)

Ryg, Maxtin Kilis

Maxtin Kilis Ryg is a Gavant warship captain of which little is known.

Scratch

Scratch is a six-legged Qurk puppy-kitten who was left behind by his litter mates because two of his legs didn't work well when born. He mostly has control of all his limbs now, including his tail which will grow to be quite dangerous.

Ux, Damien

Commander Damien Ux is a high level ROSPM double

agent currently loyal to the ROSPM, and in exile from the Gavant.

Wozim

Wozim of Tyton VII is a Tyton battle lord on the run for unknown reasons. He is nearly eight feet tall and a wall of muscle, even for one of his race. He has horns like a bull and a symbiotic battle tail named Ufri.

(Pronounced Woz-zeem)

PLACES

Katter System

Katter 9 is a planet that reminds Noah of Pluto. It has three bubble-like cities and twenty-seven orbital platforms). The Gavant designation is X-53-Alpha.

Milyn System

The planet of Milyn, and its orbital trade and transport station exist in this system. Milyn Station is a massive city in space. The Gavant designation is X-11-Alpha.

RACES

Altion

The Altion have the longest association with the Gavant Reach and have assimilated more completely into their society. They are generally short, petite, and extremely graceful. Unlike their Gavant cousins, they have long hair that cannot be cut without harming the Altion in question. Hair styles generally conceal the true length of an individual's hair. This is normal white, but can be jet black or vivid red in some instances. In the latter cases, this usually causes there to be less of a metallic patterning around the thin eye sockets that reach horizontally across much of their head.

Altion can rise higher in Gavant culture than any race but Gavant. Many others such as the Hellenger, Walen, and Tyton understand this. Resentment against them is common. Most still see them as better than the Gavant rulers, though they are not easily trusted in matters of government.

Gavant

Lords of the Reach. Every citizen holds state-sanctioned authority over other members of the Reach including the Altion, Hellenger, Walen, and even Tytons, though few assert any kind of demand on a Tyton without a military contingent to back them up.

Gavant are tall humanoids (taller than their Altion cousins and also taller than humans). They have long necks, eyes that are horizontally wide and vertically narrow or short. Most Gavant grow magenta tattoos around their eyes (as the Altion grow metallic versions of the same markings) to accentuate this effect. It often appears as though their eyes continue onto the side of their heads, as though they can always see an enemy coming for them. Their tattoos are status symbols, and can be painfully removed when sent into exile or otherwise punished.

Gavant lack the metallic or vibrant color to their skin and are normally ashy gray with haunting eyes and sharp facial features.

The Gavant do not allow merit to elevate non-Gavant into their own ranks, but ruthlessly enforce such standards on their own. Gavant officers who fail tend to disappear after one or two major incidents of disgrace.

Gleam

Gleams are one of the more unusual races in the Gavant Reach, a region of space where the Gavant have forced many societies to coexist under their law. Gleams are known as fun and vivacious, and are the most sociable with humans despite radical differences in appearance.

Gleams appear to have fluid gemstones for skin, usually something resembling diamonds over cool blue. Some have purple or sea green hues. Red crowns or red hands are the mark of mischief-makers, and since they are already spirited, this can lead to significant frustration on alien worlds. A Gleam with both red hands and a red crown are so rare as to be almost mythical, and shunned for the implications this generates.

Hellenger

The Hellenger are an old race in the Gavant Reach, second only to the Altion in their time of subservience. Generally stocky, slightly shorter than humans, they are physically strong and emotionally stubborn. Other races often notice their neck being the same width as their head and their otherwise flat features.

Hellenger males and females are hard to tell apart and their society makes little distinction in public. Some speculate their true social order is a mystery, because they have been serving the Gavant, and following their laws, for so long.

Hellengers cannot close their eyes and enjoy rubbing them. Some will learn, however, that shielding them with helmets or eyewear brings significant comfort in many social situations and can have technological benefits as well.

Major Noah Gantz fondly addresses his Hellenger friend, Montow, as "Soup Can" due to the distinctive cranial and spinal junction. By all reports, they are the best of friends despite a growing repertoire of *trash talking*. For a Hellenger, this is a significant development as they are normally wise and serious at all times.

Maviks

Maviks are large, strong, and agile humanoids with cat-like facial features. They prefer to operate in small groups, though there are certain sects that hunt alone, so to speak. They can engage in banter, but often rely on silence and intimidation to earn high wages as guards. Their bodies are covered with short, tight fur of almost any color but are normally black with vibrant yellow eyes.

Tyton

Tytons are the most-feared race in the Gavant Reach, though their subjugation has a long and complicated history. Few Gavants will describe one as subservient to their face. Leaders, both civilian and military, have long attempted to form bonds with the ten Tyton battle lords —a secret order of legendary military prowess. Their existence is well known, and some believe they understand their martial ways, but there is far more about them that has never been discovered.

Tytons are far taller than humans, and always muscular. They have a thick, durable hide that provides natural armor but also have manufactured gear that is stronger and more advanced depending on rank within their society. No one understands the rules of hierarchy. Males and females are almost never seen together.

All warriors have dangerous horns, and usually maintain a symbiotic relationship with battle tails—fierce organisms even they don't particularly understand. Contrary to popular belief, most Tytons are not warlike and have only nubs for horns and no tail symbionts. Nonwarriors keep to themselves and rarely leave their homeworld even with an escort.

Walens

Walens are thin, awkward humanoids with hearts of gold. Calling someone a Walen is to imply they are a true and loyal friend. Many sentient races take advantage of their good nature.

They have four fingers and two thumbs on each hand and are excellent mechanics. Their dexterity is legendary when it comes to tools or games. Many dream of adventure but few pursue it. There is a very select order of Walen warriors who are without rivals, though no one knows how to join this order of heroes.

Like many races associated with Gavant space, they have necks that are slightly longer than humans. None have hair. They are known for their trusting eyes that close from all directions at once like a camera lens.

SHIPS

- Gavant *Holin's Reach*
- Gavant *Kon* - heavy cruiser
- Gavant *Righteous* - battleship and flagship of General Tatum Collins
- *White Knife* - medium cruiser and flag ship of Tyton Hogg's White Knives
- *Kayan* - living starship

CONNECT WITH J.N. CHANEY

Don't miss out on these exclusive perks:

- Instant access to free short stories from series like *The Messenger*, *Starcaster*, and more.
- Receive email updates for new releases and other news.
- Get notified when we run special deals on books and audiobooks.

So, what are you waiting for? Enter your email address at the link below to stay in the loop.

https://www.jnchaney.com/homeworld-lost-subscribe

CONNECT WITH SCOTT MOON

Want to know when the next story or book is published? Sign up for my newsletter:
https://www.subscribepage.com/Fromthemoon

Thanks,
Scott Moon

---

facebook.com/groups/ScottMoonGroup
twitter.com/scottmoonwriter
instagram.com/scottmoonwriter

ABOUT THE AUTHORS

J. N. Chaney is a USA Today Bestselling author and has a Master's of Fine Arts in Creative Writing. He fancies himself quite the Super Mario Bros. fan. When he isn't writing or gaming, you can find him online at **jnchaney.com**.

He migrates often, but was last seen in Las Vegas, NV. Any sightings should be reported, as they are rare.

Scott Moon has been writing fantasy, science fiction, and urban fantasy since he was a kid. When not reading, writing, or spending time with his awesome family, he enjoys playing the guitar or learning Brazilian Jiu-Jitsu. He loves dogs and plans to have a ranch full of them when he makes it big. One will be a Rottweiler named Frodo. He is also a co-host of the popular Keystroke Medium show. You can find him online at **scottmoonwriter.com**

Made in United States
Troutdale, OR
07/13/2023

11180966R00270